THE LADY
IN THE PARK

THE LADY IN THE PARK

David Reynolds

MUSWELL
PRESS

First published by Muswell Press in 2025
Copyright © David Reynolds 2025

Typeset in Bembo by M Rules
Printed by CPI Group (UK) Ltd, Croydon CR0 4YY

A CIP record for this book
is available from the British Library

ISBN: 9781068684463
eISBN: 9781068684449

Our authorised representative in the EU for product safety is
Easy Access System Europe, Mustamäe tee 50, 10621 Tallinn, Estonia
gpsr.requests@easproject.com

Muswell Press, London N6 5HQ
www.muswell-press.co.uk

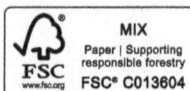

MIX
Paper | Supporting
responsible forestry
FSC® C013604
FSC
www.fsc.org

For

*Arthur Broome, Christopher Scott
and Thomas R. Barnes*

1

I was looking out through Laura's white louvred shutters. Crisp brown leaves filled the gutter and the plane trees had shed patches of bark. A white mini that I didn't recognise was parked behind Laura's dirty black BMW. As I turned away, something moved out there: a young girl walking quickly from left to right on the other side of the street. She looked familiar, though I couldn't think why. Then she crossed the road and stopped in front of Laura's fence. She looked straight at me, but she didn't seem to see me; I was hidden behind the louvres and my back was to the light. Next thing, she was pushing at the gate, flipping the doorknocker and, without waiting, rattling the letter box.

Dan glanced up at me. He was watching a Lego movie. Dan is my grandson – he's six; I've been looking after him, off and on, since he was a baby. He looked back at the screen. He was used to urgent knocks at the door; used to men standing there holding brown cardboard boxes – things his mum had ordered.

I opened the door. And knew I had met her before: a girl

from round the corner called ... Ruby, maybe. She was out of breath. There was sweat on her lip and her forehead.

She spoke quietly, almost whispered, 'Can you help me, Mr Domino? I don't know who to ask.' Then she was in tears – almost. 'Please!'

I led her in, sat her at the table and she began to talk, in jerks, between big gulps of air. Her mum had been found about an hour ago on one of the ping-pong tables in the park. 'She was unconscious,' she said, and gave me a stare: the kind of stare that, for an instant, made me think that she thought it was my fault. She looked down and dabbed at her eye with her knuckle. 'They took her in an ambulance. Muriel told me when I got home after football. Muriel's looking after the kids. Could you ... could you come with me to the hospital? I don't know who else to ask.' She was crying now and wiping her eyes on her sleeve, her voice a high-pitched whine. 'I'm sorry to bother you. I don't know what to do.'

I guessed Ruby – that *was* her name – was fourteen or fifteen. I'd seen her sometimes in the park when I was there with Dan. She was slight with a long, alert face, freckles on her nose and brown hair loosely tied back. I'd seen her kicking a football with a group of boys: anything between two- and five-a-side on the tarmac pitch with the miniature goals; sometimes she was the only girl, sometimes there were one or two others. She was kind to, protective of, smaller children like Dan. I'd noticed that.

She wanted me to take her, drive her, to the hospital. And go in with her and find out what was going on with her mum. And I said I would, of course.

'Thanks, Mr Domino,' she said. 'That's so kind. Cool.' She leaned forward on the chair with her hands between her knees and smiled a hopeful smile.

2

Only thing was: I'd have to take Dan. I was minding him that evening. I often did that, and sometimes – not that day – I collected him from school.

'Who is Muriel?' I asked.

'Our neighbour. Next door. She's really nice, and her husband, Joe; he works on the barrier at the station.'

I got my jacket, car keys, Dan's coat. It was just after 6 pm. Dan's dinner was in the oven, fish fingers and chips, and I had green beans in a pan, ready to be simmered on the hob. I turned the oven off. Laura, my daughter, Dan's mum, wouldn't be back till midnight. Laura is a jazz singer: 606 Club that night, a wedding somewhere on the Saturday, the Vortex the next week, and on it went – gigs all over the place: Brighton, Bristol, Manchester.

I put Dan in his seat in the back of Laura's Beamer. I'd no idea when we'd get home. It could be hours. It wasn't ideal. Dan had school in the morning and he should have had a proper meal instead of the cold hot-cross bun that he was chewing on. But he was enjoying this; I could tell. He knows about me being a detective, and what detectives do – and he takes an interest, sometimes. 'What you been detecting today, Grandpa?' he'll say. And if it isn't too grisly, I tell him.

I looked in the rearview mirror. He was smiling to himself. He likes a drama – and we've had a few, he and I. You could say we're best mates. When he was three, he told Laura that I was his best friend. I loved that.

Ruby was beside me, sitting forward in the seat, staring ahead. I thought about her mum, whom I didn't know at all well. She was a playground acquaintance – one of many I've stood beside at the swings – chatty sometimes; distracted, a bit tense, at others. And that didn't surprise me; I knew, somehow, that she had five other children, all younger than Ruby, and a reputation for wildness.

3

We were moving slowly in a line of traffic on Peckham Road and I was thinking for the first time about whether what I was doing was right. Should I be involved with this girl? Should I even be alone with her in a car (apart from Dan) for instance?

But she hadn't made this up. How could she? Why would she? What would be the point? Silly! Silly thinking. Don't be a wuss. I was doing the right thing. Of course! It would have been cruel to say no.

'Why did you come to *me*, Ruby?'

She looked towards me and then away. 'People say you're a good person – and you used to be a policeman.'

Why had I asked? I'd expected her to say something like that. 'You trust policemen, then?'

She was still looking away from me. She shrugged. 'Mostly.'

'They're mostly good. They want to help people: policemen and policewomen. But they have a hard job, and it's getting harder all the time. Budget cuts.' I almost said 'silly rules', but that wasn't the time and Ruby wasn't the audience.

She pulled out a phone in a rainbow-striped case. 'I'm phoning my brother, to tell him what's happening.' She tapped with her thumb. 'Luke ...? Everything all right ...? Muriel there ...? Listen. I'm with Mr Domino; he's driving me to the hospital ... OK ... Shit! I don't know. I'd forgotten that. There's a cake, isn't there ...? Yeah. Decide tomorrow ... Let them stay up, unless they wanna go to bed ... OK ... Call you later.'

She looked across at me. 'It's my little brother's birthday tomorrow. I'd completely forgotten.' She was welling up.

'Well ... Right now, your mum's the important thing.'

'Can't do his,' – her voice cracked – 'birthday without Mum.'

4

'Maybe leave it till she's better.'

She sat back and drew her knees up to her chin.

I drove past King's College Hospital, turned right at the top of the hill and parked under a streetlight beside Ruskin Park. As we got out into the cold, the moon was over the trees sliding out from behind clouds. I pointed so that Dan saw it, and he watched as thin clouds drifted in front of it. Then I zipped up his coat and he took my hand.

★ ★ ★

As we approached the reception desk, I realised that I didn't know Ruby's mother's full name. 'Caroline Swann, double *n*,' Ruby said.

Caroline was on the fifth floor, in intensive care. A policewoman in uniform and a man wearing a baseball cap and a denim jacket – almost certainly CID – were standing beside a hand-sanitiser with their backs to us. I squirted gel into my palms, rubbed them together and watched as Dan reached up and did the same. 'Well done, Dan. Good stuff.' He looked up at me with a grin.

'Jim! What you doing here?' The plainclothes policeman was smiling at me with raised eyebrows.

'Charlie! Well . . . what are *you* doing here? It's good to see you.' A while ago Charlie Ritchie had been my sergeant. 'This is Ruby. Her mum's in here. We've come to visit her . . . if we're allowed. And this is Dan, my grandson. I'm looking after him tonight.'

'Hello Ruby. Hello Dan.' Charlie leaned forward and smiled. 'I'm a police officer.' He pushed his cap back. 'What's your mum's name, Ruby?'

'Caroline Swann.'

'Your mum is why we're here, too.' Charlie smiled. 'This is PC Das.'

Unlike Charlie, the policewoman had taken off her hat and she was holding it in front of her; her hair was glossy and cut in a bob. She too smiled at Ruby. 'Your mum's asleep. We want to talk to her when she wakes up, find out what happened – you know.'

Ruby stared and spoke quietly. 'Yes.'

We found a nurse who fetched a doctor whose badge read, 'Dr Patricia King, Intensive Care'. She asked who we were, and how old Ruby was – fifteen, it turned out – and led us into a small room. Ruby and I sat in little stuffed armchairs. Dan stood straight and still beside me. I put an arm round his shoulder. He knew this was important.

Dr King was firm but friendly, a nice-looking woman with hair in short, perfect cornrows; she sat on an upright chair and looked at Ruby. 'Your mother has had a serious blow to her head, and it's caused a fracture – a break.'

I heard Ruby draw a breath, and I put my hand on her arm.

'Try not to worry,' the doctor said. 'We're doing a scan to see what we need to do.' She glanced at me and then back at Ruby. 'We hope she'll be OK, but we aren't sure when she'll wake up; it may take time.' She was talking to Ruby as if she were an adult.

'Can I wait?' Ruby asked.

'You can. But she probably won't wake up for a while.' Dr King coughed. 'I mean . . . you might be here all night. It could be better to go home – and we'll contact you when your mum can see you.'

Ruby looked at me. 'That sounds best,' I said. 'And your brothers and sisters would like you to be with them, wouldn't they?'

We took the lift down. I got a cup of tea for Ruby from a machine. Then, from another machine, a Lion bar for her, and mango juice, a ham sandwich and a Kit Kat for Dan – I knew he was hungry. I told them I was going back up to talk to the policeman who was a friend of mine. Ruby pulled out her phone and tapped in her passcode. When I told Dan that he must stay sitting next to her, he stuck out his lip and suddenly looked tired.

'I won't be long,' I said.

I took the lift back up and found Charlie and PC Das. Everyone – *almost* everyone – at the station had been on my side. They knew, those who'd been there three years before, that my suspension had been a nonsense. Anyone who knew anything about me knew that. I'd done the right thing; it was just that the right thing was against the rules.

Charlie was more than happy to talk. He told me that Caroline Swann had been found just after six by a boy who had gone back to the park to collect his football; the boy had seen her lying on the ping-pong table, lit up by the moon.

'And that was lucky,' PC Das said. 'The moon shining – so he saw her. She could have lain there all night and died of hypothermia. She was wearing jeans, T-shirt, sweatshirt and anorak. The anorak was unzipped – wouldn't have kept her warm, not all night. She'd have frozen.'

'Is that suspicious, the unzipped anorak?' I asked.

'No,' Charlie said. 'No signs of assault apart from the blow to the head. She only lived round the corner. She could have slung on the anorak, walked the short distance to the park and not bothered to do it up.'

'And you don't know why she was there?'

'We don't know, Jim.' Charlie shrugged. 'We're hoping she'll tell us. The blood on the table was still damp when the paramedics arrived, which suggests the knock was administered less than an hour before the kid found her. So she was hit between about quarter past five and six, either there, in the park, or somewhere else and was then brought there in the dark – probably already unconscious.'

PC Das told me that the park was closed, lit with flood-lights and being searched. Of course, it would be. And the streets were full of police knocking on doors, trying to find witnesses.

'Jim, you can tell the girl, the daughter—'

'Ruby, isn't it?' PC Das said. 'And, by the way,' – she smiled and held out her hand – 'my name's Sunita.'

'Oh! Hi Sunita.' I took her hand, which was small and slight. 'I'm Jim. Jim Domino.'

'I know who *you* are.' She was smiling.

'Jim,' Charlie said, 'Please tell Ruby that PC Sunita Das and Sergeant Charlie Ritchie and the rest of us at Southwark are doing everything we can to find out what happened.'

2

It was cold and dark as we walked uphill to the car; the moon had disappeared. Danny had no gloves – my fault. Ruby nodded and shivered as I told her what Charlie Ritchie and Sunita Das had said.

By the time we got back to hers, it was after eight, Dan's bedtime. Ruby reached into the letterbox and pulled out a piece of string with a key tied to it. We went in and found so many kids on a long, squashy sofa that I had to count them: seven – all huddled around a tired-looking woman whom I recognised: another acquaintance from the park, Muriel. She knew my name, called me Mr Domino, and seemed pleased that I was there.

A small boy with curly blond hair was staring at Dan, and Dan was looking back at him with an odd smile. I squatted beside Dan. 'Do you know him?'

Dan whispered. 'He's in Wool, in Year One. He's called Jake.'

Dan is in Felt, also in Year One; for some reason the classes are named after types of cloth, and Year One is actually the second year of primary school.

A man came into the room carrying a tray covered with steaming mugs. 'Meet my husband, Joe,' Muriel said. 'This is Mr Domino, Joe.'

Joe grinned. 'Hello Mr Domino,' he said. 'OK. Hot chocolate, kids.' Children stretched out their hands. Joe put the tray on a low table and began to pass out mugs. 'You want a hot chocolate, Ruby? You, Mr Domino? And what about you?' He looked at Dan.

'This is Dan, my grandson,' I said.

'Dan, you look like you'd love a hot chocolate.'

Dan nodded and said, 'Yes . . . please.'

Ruby wanted a chocolate and so did I.

A tall, thickset boy – Luke, I presumed – was having a muttered chat with Ruby in the doorway. The children didn't all have the same father; I knew that. And two of them were obviously Muriel's and Joe's.

The telly was on – *Bake Off*; Noel Fielding, his head sideways and grinning above a row of tarts. I sat down on an upright chair beside a table covered in kids' drawings, crayons and felt tips, and lifted Dan onto my knee. I looked around. It was a large, cosy room: soft, beige carpet; bookshelves crammed with books for kids and grown-ups; a couple of small armchairs as well as the huge sofa; paintings and prints, including a Dufy I recognised and a poster for last year's Paul Nash show at Dulwich Picture Gallery – I'd seen that with Laura and Dan. On the back wall was a long pin board covered in photos, kids' paintings and drawings, certificates with gold stars from school.

Dan was wriggling on my lap. He'd got hold of a piece of paper and he was reaching for a pencil. I looked over at Ruby. 'All right if he does a drawing? He loves drawing.'

'Course he can.' She came over. 'Here, Dan. Here's some felt tips.' She picked up a jar and put it in front of him.

A girl, perhaps ten or eleven years old and, from the look of her, a full sister to Luke, was staring at me hard. 'Is Mum all right?' she said. 'When's she coming home?'

I answered as best I could. 'Your mum's resting, sleeping at the hospital. She could be home tomorrow.'

'Are you going to stay with us, Mr Domino?'

I hadn't thought that far ahead. 'I don't know. I've got to sort this one.' I gave Dan a hug. He had drawn a brown road and was adding a red house.

'We can't ask Mr Domino to stay, Ella!' Ruby looked shocked.

'No. You don't worry, Mr Domino.' Muriel looked up at me from the sofa. 'You've been very kind with Ruby already. Me and Joe will look after these. It's OK.'

Ruby and Luke came back into the room. Joe brought our chocolate, and I took some sips; just right – hot and sweet. Ruby took two long, grateful gulps and wrapped her hands around the mug, as if she were cold.

A small boy, perhaps three years old, was nestled up to Muriel and looking up at me. 'Is my mum going to die?'

I tried to smile. I wasn't expecting that. 'She's just sleeping at the hospital.' Muriel hugged the boy tighter.

'She got hit on the head, Sammy,' Ruby said. She bent over Sammy and smiled. 'But she'll get better – maybe later tonight, or tomorrow.' She took Sammy from Muriel, stood up and hugged him tight. Then she held him away from her and looked into his eyes. 'I talked to a really nice doctor who's looking after our mum. She'll be all right.'

Dan was rubbing his eyes, leaning against me, drinking chocolate; he'd drawn more houses, some people and trees. Ruby took Sammy and another little one upstairs to bed, and Joe took his children to their home next door. Muriel said she would stay, and that I should get Dan home. She was right; today was Tuesday and he had school tomorrow. I put my number into Muriel's phone and told her to phone if she needed me. Dan finished his chocolate and picked up his picture. I put a bunch of mugs in the sink in the kitchen.

★ ★ ★

Dan had been pretty quiet through all this, not speaking unless he was spoken to. As soon as we were in the car, he said, 'Grandpa – is Ruby's mum Jake's mum?'

'Yes. All those children – except the two who are Muriel's and Joe's – are Ruby's mum's. She's called Caroline.'

'Is Caroline going to die?'

I told him I hoped not, but that I didn't know for sure. I always try to tell the truth – particularly to kids. The world's confusing enough for them anyway. But I do lie about Father Christmas and the tooth fairy.

About three minutes later I parked outside Laura's. Dan scrambled out of the car, looked up at me and said, 'What happens when you die?'

'Well,' – I was unlocking the front door – 'some people think you go on living in another place, and other people think you just aren't there any more.'

'What do you think, Grandpa?'

'I think you aren't there, but you *are* there in people's heads because they remember you. The things you did and the things you said and when you made them laugh.'

Dan didn't say anything. He just yawned. Then he opened the drawer where Laura keeps the biscuits and pulled out a flapjack stuffed with raisins. He tore it open and munched away. Then he grabbed a banana and ate half of it. Then I took him up to bed.

'Why did somebody hit Jake's mum?' He was looking up at me, eyelids drooping, his head on the pillow.

12

'I don't know, Dan, but the police will find out – and then they'll probably tell us.'

He turned on his side. I pulled his duvet up around his shoulders and sat on the floor next to him.

'Do you want a story?'

I picked up *Tim and Ginger*, Edward Ardizzone. He likes it and I like it, but he was asleep before I'd finished the first page.

Downstairs, I flipped the lid off a Peroni and gawped at the telly – people surviving in the rubble of Mariupol – while Danny's uneaten fish fingers, chips and beans were warming.

I fetched another Peroni, sat in an armchair to watch the news and ate Danny's dinner. I nodded off soon after Sarah Smith reported on the US mid-term elections.

I came to during *Newsnight* – Victoria Derbyshire talking about creepy Gavin Williamson's resignation. And James Naughtie talking to ordinary people somewhere in Ohio. Interesting – but my brain strayed over to Caroline Swann. I knew very little about her. An apparently single mother of six who, judging by her kids and her front room with its soft carpet, books and pictures, was an educated type who had a source of money – enough to feed and clothe them all and keep them in a decent-sized house. Did she have a job? Six kids! Did any of the fathers give her financial support?

Why had someone hit her? And why that hard? Were they trying to kill her? Random crazy attacks were rare – though a cyclist was killed in Richmond Park not long ago by a schizophrenic who had just come out of hospital. Mistaken identity unlikely. Someone wanted to hurt Caroline – or kill her. To punish her? Or warn her off? Or shut her up – perhaps permanently? What could she have done, or be planning to do? Did she know something? Or did someone hate her? Resent her for some reason?

They're still talking about Gavin Williamson and the ministerial code. Mute it. Put on some music. Miles – or the Barr Brothers? Miles helps me think. *Milestones*. Light off. Just the dim table light.

Charlie said he's working with Dave Lightfoot. Both smart coppers. They'll find out. Soon, probably; there's usually something – something obvious. When she wakes up, Caroline might tell them what it is.

★ ★ ★

Midnight. *Gogglebox*: much giggling from Jenny and Lee. Upstairs to check on Danny. More Miles. *Round About Midnight*. Tea and thinking. Could be a jealous man – father of one of those kids.

★ ★ ★

'Dad? You all right, Dad?' Laura's hand on my shoulder. Quarter past one.

'Fine. Fine.' I sat up. The all-night news was on the telly, muted. I stood up and stretched.

'Dan all right?'

'He's good. Asleep.'

'Thanks Dad. You're a wonder!'

'How was it?'

'Great! Love working with Jason; such a cool pianist. And it was packed – unusual for a Thursday. *Three* encores.' She yawned. 'I should go to bed. But . . . never sleep well after a gig. Brain keeps going over it – I've told you before – the good bits and the mistakes. But Dan'll be up early, so . . .' She shrugged.

'Well he might not, actually.' I began to tell her about Ruby and Caroline Swann.

She gazed at me, shaking her head and frowning. And she went into the kitchen, picked up the bottle of Famous Grouse, waved it at me with her eyebrows raised and poured two glasses. 'So Danny spent the evening at King's College Hospital.' She filled a jug with water and put it on the little kitchen table.

'Yes.' I sat down at the table. 'And then he had hot chocolate at the Swanns'. He was fantastic, polite to everyone all the time. Amazing.'

She was shaking her head again. 'I was wondering why you were still up.'

'Yeah. And Danny was just great! He met policemen and women, nurses, doctors ...' She sat down across from me, and I noticed her mascara – not too thick – and the brownish eye shadow; she had to look good, singing in a spotlight – and she did. 'And he met Ruby Swann's brothers and sisters and their neighbours, Joe who works at the station and Muriel who's a nurse, and their kids.'

'So *what* happened? She was hit on the head and left on one of the ping-pong tables in Warwick Gardens?'

'Yes. And lucky to be found in the dark by a kid who'd gone back to find his football.'

'Jesus!' Laura took a gulp, swilled the whisky around in her mouth, swallowed and grimaced. 'I know her.'

'OK. I wondered. One of her kids is in Danny's year.'

'Yeah. Not well. Can't say I'm a friend. I've talked to her in the park, in the playground. Nice woman. Quite a character – bit weird, sort of hippy in a good way.'

'Well – six kids, these days.'

'She adores kids ... actually likes being pregnant! One of those.' She swallowed some more whisky. 'But ... bloody hell!' She breathed a long breath out. 'Attacked in the park! What's going on?' She looked up at me. 'Frightening, Dad!'

15

'I know. There'll be a reason for it. Unlikely to be a random nutter.'

'But there *are* nutters around here.'

'I know. But they don't tend to be violent.'

'Are you going to look into it? Do some detective work?' She smiled.

'No. I can't butt in. Don't want to. They'll work it out. A couple of my mates are on to it. Remember Charlie Ritchie?'

She screwed up her face. 'Not sure.'

There was a cry, more of a shout, from upstairs. Laura stood up. 'I'll go.'

I stayed where I was with my hand round the whisky glass. I could hear Dan crying and Laura speaking softly, soothing.

She came down after about fifteen minutes. 'Poor lamb. He was quite upset, and I can see where it came from.' Dan had dreamed that Jake – Caroline's son, the one he knows – had fallen out of a tree in Warwick Gardens and knocked himself out. Dan had been the only person there and hadn't been able to wake him up, hadn't known what to do.

'I'm sorry. I shouldn't have taken him to the hospital.'

'No. Not your fault. You had to help Ruby.'

'I could have sent her in a taxi – or got someone to mind Danny. Chris, maybe.'

'No, not Chris. He has enough trouble looking after his own children.' She looked at me and raised her eyebrows. 'Another wee drop?'

'Sure,' I said, 'a little one.' And she poured us each a quarter-inch.

'When it comes down to it, Dad, *I* should be here. Or that jerk I married should be . . . But,' – she laughed – 'thank God he isn't.'

I sipped my whisky and dribbled a little water into it from the jug.

'You know I could get a more regular babysitter – now that Juliana won't do evenings.' She swilled whisky round her mouth and eventually swallowed it. 'Bloody annoying that she got a boyfriend.'

'Not surprising!' I grinned. 'She's a looker with a good brain and a sweet nature.'

'Yes. I know you fancy her,' Laura laughed.

'I do not!' I clammed up then and tried to smile; I didn't want to dig myself into a hole. Juliana was a smiling, if sometimes moody, childminder from Brazil who shared daytime duties with me. Until a man intervened, she had done some nights as well. 'Do you want to – get another babysitter?'

'No.' She shook her head. 'He loves being with you, but ...'

'I love being with him.' I took another sip. 'Well, most of the time, anyway.' I laughed. 'But Chris is there in an emergency – like we are for him. And Charlotte might have been there.'

'Probably not. She's done a lot of nights lately. She's very dedicated.' She looked at me. 'A hospital doctor and a jazz singer. Quite a contrast, your daughters – except that they both work nights.'

'Yes. Amazing how well you get on.' I was looking back at her. 'You do, don't you?'

'You don't need to ask that, Dad. You know the answer.'

'I know. Silly question.'

We went to bed soon after that. I lay on the bed in the spare room and stared up at the familiar white paper sphere. I liked staying over at Laura's. I was here so often that I had my own drawer in the little white chest: pants, socks, washbag, a book of poems by Lorca and a large box of Rennies.

I stood up, fetched the book and lay down again. Opening the book randomly near its middle, I read: When the moon rises/ the bells hang silent/ and impenetrable footpaths/appear. Caroline Swann had been saved by a boy who forgot his football, and by the moon.

3

I left Laura's at about nine, heading for my place; I had work to do. Laura was out, taking Danny to school.

As I reached the end of the street, I saw Mrs Mumford on the further pavement. Laura calls her that: Mrs Mumford; it describes her better than her first name, which is Pauline. A talkative woman, she tells new acquaintances her name and then says with a high-pitched laugh, 'but I don't have any sons,' and her chins heave as she adds, 'just a daughter.'

She waved at me and came across the road. 'Jim, have you seen? Warwick Gardens is closed. Police all round – and a tent. Is it called an incident tent? What's happened? Do you know?'

'No. No. I didn't know about that.'

'Well, it's bound to be something to do with drugs.' She stared into my eyes. 'Don't you think? Dealers from different gangs.' She waved her arms. 'It's getting worse round here, when it should be getting better. Remember last month: the stabbing outside the station.'

'Yes. Yes, I remember that. Terrible.'

'Well, I won't keep you. You must be busy. You must

have plenty of work.' She laughed again. 'With all the divorces, finding the co-respondents.' She giggled, and poked me in the shoulder.

'Not these days, Mrs Mumford,' I smiled. 'Pilfering from warehouses is all the rage now ...'

She pulled a face and turned away.

'And drug-dealing,' I muttered as I walked on. Could the attack on Caroline Swann be connected to the gangs? Only if someone had made a mistake, a big mistake, surely. The cliché: mistaken identity. Highly unlikely.

My phone rang: a number I didn't recognise. 'It's Charlie, Jim – Charlie Ritchie. You all right?'

'Yes. You?'

'Fine. Jim, I'd like to talk – about Mrs Swann. Anything you might've picked up – from Ruby or wherever. Can we meet for a quick chat?'

'What's happened? Has she woken up?'

'Not yet. I'm not there, but they're keeping me informed; they'll call me when she comes round. Listen. Can we meet sometime today? You know the girl, Ruby. Maybe you could give me some background.'

'Sure. I don't know much, but ... OK. Anything to help.'

I said I'd see him at the station at two o'clock – and walked on. The park was as Mrs Mumford had said: wrapped in scene-of-crime tape with a couple of uniformed on the gate and a square white tent hiding the ping-pong table. A line of police were crawling slowly uphill on hands and knees raking the grass with their fingers. A couple of plainclothes stood talking in the doorway of the tent: Dave Lightfoot and a woman I didn't recognise.

I thought about the Swanns. How were Ruby and those kids getting on? Would they have gone to school? Did they need help? They were less than fifty yards from here. I walked that way and found myself thinking about Lightfoot: a DI who wears jeans and T-shirts, a little overweight but fit, a hard man who could turn soft. Lightfoot had a degree. I smiled. Criminology from Cambridge. It annoyed me – though I knew it shouldn't.

Ruby came to the door and asked me in. She looked tired. She smiled, but it didn't last. 'Mum hasn't woken up yet. They're going to phone when she does.' She turned and led me into the living room. 'Luke and the littl'uns are here; we took Ella and Jake to school.'

'Did you get any sleep?'

'A bit.' She shrugged, and spoke quietly. 'He woke up a lot.' She nodded towards Sammy who was at the table, kneeling on a chair fiddling with a jigsaw. 'Not happy. Wanting Mum.'

Luke was sitting between Sammy and the small girl whose name I didn't know. He looked up and I raised my hand. 'Just dropped by to see if I could help with anything.'

Luke looked up – so young, and so responsible. 'We're all right. Aren't we, Rube?'

'Yeah, we're OK. But thanks, Mr Domino. Do you want a cup of tea?'

'No. Thanks. Is anyone coming to help out? You've got Muriel, next door ...'

'Yeah. Our gran is coming.'

'Oh good.'

Ruby seemed to frown.

'Well, I hope it's good.'

'She's all right.' Luke said it, and he seemed to mean it.

'Your mum's mum?'

'Yeah. So she's gran to all of us.' Ruby smiled now. 'And we're going to get a visit from your dad, aren't we.' She was looking at the two little ones. The girl, pale face and blonde hair, glanced back at her, bit her lower lip and looked away. Might it be that she didn't want to see her father? At the same time, Luke gave Ruby a quick stare, eyebrows raised.

'Is *your* dad around?' I asked Ruby.

'No. He's in Canada, Montreal. He's a singer, poet.' She smiled broadly. 'He phones me and I see him now and again. He's lovely. I've been over there.'

'What about your dad, Luke? Is he . . .'

'He died. Nearly six years ago – just after Jake was born.' He looked down at the table. 'Had a brain tumour. He kept going into hospital – the one where Mum is. Then one time he just died.'

'I'm sorry.' Luke had turned away, had an arm round Sammy's shoulder. 'So Ella's your sister and Jake's your brother. There's three of you had the same dad.'

'Yeah, but Ruby's my sister too – and so's Lily, aren't you.' He looked at the little girl, who glanced up at me with a little grin. 'And this bloke's my brother.' He pulled Sammy close to him so their cheeks touched.

'We have different dads, but Mum loves all of us.' Ruby's face crumpled and tears came. 'I just . . . hope she's going to be all right.'

'She will, Rube. She will.' Luke got up, came over and hugged her. 'It'll be all right, Rube. Don't worry.'

'Will it?' She wiped her face. 'Will it be all right?' She was looking at me.

'It should be. I hope so.' They both seemed so young. And yet they were the elder ones, with four younger than them. I didn't want to make false promises – just in case. 'Maybe she'll wake up soon.'

'God, I hope so.' Sammy had begun to cry. Ruby rushed over and picked him up.

It was awkward. Nothing more I could say, or do. 'I'd

better get going.' I was talking to Luke. 'I've got stuff to do and I've got Danny again this evening. When's your gran arriving?'

'Sometime after lunch.' Luke wandered back towards the table. 'She comes from Woking on a train – it takes a while.'

'Look, phone or text me any time if you need help.'

'Thanks, Mr Domino.' Ruby seemed better. 'Say good-bye, Sammy.' She lifted the little guy's arm and he opened his hand and shut it again.

'Text me if you need help getting to the hospital. And stop calling me Mr Domino. Call me Jim.'

I headed for the door.

'Bye, Jim.' They both said it.

'And thanks,' Ruby said.

'Yes. Thanks.' Luke raised a hand.

'And by the way, if you want to, come round to Laura's . . . text first to check, but I'm there with Danny most evenings this week – and probably next.'

I walked back past Warwick Gardens. The fingertip search was five feet further up the hill – and there was no sign of DI Lightfoot. I kept walking until I saw Mrs Mumford, some way ahead, chatting to a young woman with a dog. I crossed the road and kept my head down.

Back home, I returned a call from Kylie, one of my team – in fact, a major part of it now – along, of course, with Clayton. Kylie is a friend of Laura's from when they were at art school. She's been with me off and on since I started the agency, three years ago now.

'How's it going?'

'I've nailed it, boss.' She was whispering. 'There's three of 'em. Also a driver. I'll call you later.'

She was in an Oxford Street store, dressed, coiffed, perfumed, made-up – and trained to sell cosmetics. The

23

security chief had hired us. Pilfering by staff was rampant in cosmetics and jewellery. The driver was a surprise. Could three shop assistants be nicking enough stuff to need a driver to whisk it away? More likely Kylie had somehow identified a delivery driver operating a separate scam – maybe the old one where someone signs for more items than have been handed over.

I slid Jimmy Cliff, *The Harder They Come*, into the CD player, emptied my dirty-clothes basket into the washing machine, turned up the sound and did my usual work-out. My wonderful, now old, sound system with its NAD amp and AR speakers is great for everything from Bach to reggae. I warmed down during 'Pressure Drop' and lay down on my old Moroccan rug through 'Sitting in Limbo'.

Then, shaved and showered, I headed for my old work-place, the nick on Peckham High Street.

4

Charlie Ritchie collected me from the Enquiry Desk. 'Thanks Jim. Appreciate you giving up your time.' We climbed the familiar stairs, still painted brown and yellow and still those cracks in the concrete steps. He sat me down beside his desk in the ops room and went off to fetch coffee. I could see Lightfoot sideways-on, lounging on a sofa in a glass-sided, carpeted corner office, a bit smaller than the one I used to have – well, he's only an Inspector. Charlie came back carrying a china mug and a cardboard cup for me. The mug showed a picture of a panda sitting in a clump of bamboo.

'Any news of Mrs Swann?' I asked.

He shook his head. 'No. She's still out, but the medics say they aren't worried. There are brainwaves and her breathing is settled.'

He sat back in his chair and looked straight at me with a little smile. And I recalled that this was a good man, tough and totally straight, who was happy to remain a sergeant. 'It's good to see you, Jim.' He glanced across the desks, most of them empty, to the glassed-in office in the corner. And his smile developed into a wince. 'Why don't you come back? You were only suspended. We need good people. That crap was long ago; it's forgotten.'

'Thanks for the thought.' I raised my hands. 'But—'

'You know Avril is the Super now?'

'Yes, I heard that. Good for her.' Ten years ago Avril Miskiewicz had been assigned to me as a rooky DC; she made it to DS in less than two years. Tough, tall and out-spoken, she took no shit from men or women.

'You know she backed you more than anyone when the crapula hit the fan. Almost got suspended herself.' He chuckled. 'She'd *love* to have you back.'

'Yeah? I suppose she would; it must be fun to have your old boss working for you.'

From chuckling, Charlie moved on to beaming like someone's uncle, and I was remembering a moment of unforgettable cringe. I'd taken my section for a drink to celebrate something – probably nicking somebody; as a joke, I addressed Avril, then about twenty-three years old, as Miss Mischievous. She leaned into my face, made a cha-rade of yawning, and muttered, 'We're not at school, DCI Domino.'

I noticed that Lightfoot was standing up with a phone in his hand. 'But, no thanks ... Nothing against the force, but I like my life now – mostly. My own business, plenty of work, the freedom to say no, freedom to do other things – like take a day off, go for long walks, look after my grandkids.'

I looked across the room. A young policeman wearing a black sweatshirt was lolling in his chair, legs stretched out, idly looking at a computer screen while filing his nails. I looked back at Charlie and raised my eyebrows. He was smiling: dimples in his cheeks and wrinkles radiating from his eyes. He reached into the wastepaper bin beside him and came up with an envelope, turned it over, scribbled a few words and pushed it along the desk. He had written, 'DC Haydon. Plays ukulele.'

'Really?' I said aloud.

'Yes. That's a requirement.' He rubbed his fingernails. Then pulled back the paper and scribbled some more: 'Probably a gig tonight.'

'Oh.' I drank a little coffee and looked back at him. 'You seem happy, Charlie. Content.'

'You know me. I'm not like you or Avril or,' he tilted his head about an inch in the direction of Lightfoot, 'him – Dave. I'm a number two, or three – however you want to count it. I enjoy my job. I know what I'm doing. I've got plenty of work. DCs, recruits – most of them – look up to me. And I sleep at night. I couldn't be number one.' He shook his head, then rolled his chair closer to his desk and put his elbows on it. 'Anyway, enough. I wanted to ask you what you know about the Swanns. Like: how well do you know the girl, Ruby?'

'Not well. We've chatted in the park ... you know, standing next to each other, pushing kids on swings, beside the slide, running about chasing them, all that. I know a lot of people who go to that playground, because I take Laura's Danny there – and sometimes my other grandkids: Charlotte's kids ... you know, my other daughter.'

'Any idea why Ruby turned to you last night?'

'I asked her that. She said she knew I used to be a policeman. So I asked if she trusted policemen and she said she did – *mostly*.'

Charlie smirked, rolled his chair back and looked at his feet which were stretched under the desk. Then he looked at me, not unsympathetically – yet I felt awkward. I seemed to have to explain why a teenage girl had sought me out at my daughter's house.

'She was upset – which isn't surprising. She gets home and is told that her mum's in hospital after being hit on the head in the park. She didn't know who to go to for help, she said, and she wanted to go to the hospital to see Mum. I don't think she'd have gone there by herself. To me, it was a no-brainer. And I dropped in there this morning to see if they were OK.'

'Does *everyone* know you're an ex-cop?'

'Well, the parents of kids. You know, I collect Danny from school. Playground gossip. Stuff gets around.'

Charlie seemed satisfied. 'So what do you know about Mrs Swann?'

'I barely know her. I see her in the school playground. and then there's a nodding mateyness by the swings in Warwick Gardens, but I've never talked to her – not properly. I told you I probably couldn't help you much.' I picked up the coffee cup and took a sip. 'But you've had a bit of time. What do *you* know about her?'

He drew a breath and frowned. 'She seems quite isolated. None of the neighbours seems to know her well – which seems odd for a woman with that many children. But I got onto her sister who lives in France – Toulouse – and visits two or three times a year; she says the children have friends, and she looks after them well. She works for a charity part-time; sourcing food for foodbanks. She's political, belongs to Extinction Rebellion, committed to the Green Party.' He rolled his chair backwards and forwards and tapped his desk. 'The sister seems to admire her, but she worries about her: the politics, direct action, afraid she might glue herself to something and get in trouble.' Charlie rolled his eyes and went on. 'There's some family money, and Ruby's dad pays regularly and is generous apparently.'

'He has a good relationship with Ruby. She told me.' I swallowed some coffee. 'Shame he's on the wrong side of the Atlantic. You probably know that the kids have three different fathers, and one of them's dead.'

'Yes. One dead. One in Canada. And the other has a restraining order on him and lives two miles away, in Nunhead. Know anything about him?'

'No. Why the restraining order?'

'Violence towards Mrs Swann.' He picked up a file, flicked through and pulled out an A4 sheet. 'He lived there for three, four years. Then he began using drugs in the house, and around the children. She objected – and he got violent. She got the order in March this year. He moved out, but he comes back, upsetting the kids. Neighbours have called us,' – he turned the paper over – 'twice. The last time was in September – three months ago. We could have booked him, but we seem to have let it go.'

'Well, look. Ruby and brother Luke, the next eldest, are expecting him to turn up.' I put the cardboard cup down on the desk. 'In fact, Luke looked worried when Ruby told me that – and so did one of the younger kids, one of *his* kids. They need protection—'

'Yeah? We wondered. A uniform is going there – should be there by now. And Sunita Das is due there as well. Meanwhile, we're looking for him.' He pulled a photograph from the file. 'This is him.' He held it up in both hands. 'Ever seen him?'

A thin-faced man with strong features, long blonde hair, blue eyes, white T-shirt, leather jacket with the collar turned up. He looked a bit like Tom Petty. 'Looks sort of familiar. I might have seen him in the Warwick Gardens playground.'

'Gary Jackson. Born in Glasgow. Age thirty-nine. Carpenter and part-time musician. In a band called, wait for it . . . the Rude Things.'

I shrugged. 'OK.'

Charlie leaned back and smoothed the hair at the side of his head with both hands. And I realised – he'd done that a few times – why he'd kept his baseball cap on in the hospital when Sunita Das had been holding her police hat. Charlie Ritchie had gone bald – pretty much. He just had a rim of hair, like a cartoon monk.

'One more thing.' He pulled out a photograph. 'Do you recognise this bloke?'

It took only a glance: a bearded guy in a long coat sitting on the pavement in front of a shop window holding out a cardboard cup. 'Yes. Called Tony, I think. Often stands outside the Victoria shouting at people. Occasionally gets close to people. He frightened my grandson one time. Shouted some nonsense in his face. But I wouldn't think he's up for hitting anyone – not hard, anyway. Lives in sheltered housing somewhere, I would guess.'

'That's right. We've been there. Odd thing is he hasn't been seen since yesterday lunchtime. Didn't sleep in his bed last night. Which is unusual, the supervisor says. But you've never seen him do anything violent, or holding any kind of weapon – say a brick or a lump of wood?'

'No. Definitely not.' I swallowed the last of the coffee. 'So you haven't found a weapon, but you think she was hit with a brick or a piece of wood?'

'Or maybe a piece of metal. There's a curiosity. The medics say there's an indentation made by something the shape of a large hammer, like a sledgehammer. But they say it can't be a sledgehammer because that would have crushed her skull completely, and it didn't; it just made a shallow dent.'

'Strange. So the shape, but not the weight, of a sledge hammer?'

'Yes. I was wondering about a weight – some kind of not-too-heavy exercise weight, but I don't know.' He smoothed his remaining hair again. 'Well, thanks Jim.' I started to stand up, and so did he. 'Of course, what we want is for Mrs Swann to wake up and tell us who did it. Will you stay in touch with Ruby and the rest of them?'

'Yeah. I'll drop in, keep an eye out.' We were walking towards the stairs. 'Their gran is coming, Caroline's mum, and you lot are there, so I'll leave it a day or two. And you watch out for the Rude Thing.'

He chuckled. 'It's good to talk to you, Jim. Been too long.'

'Well, it's good to see the place again. I didn't expect to feel so comfortable. I'll see myself out.'

'Thanks.' He shook my hand, turned and walked back to his desk.

5

I spent the night at Vic's place in the World's End. I hadn't
been hot on lawyers until I met Vic – three years ago
now. She hired me to find a missing witness in a case where
a woman was on trial for the murder of her violent, bullying
husband; she'd stabbed him sixteen times with a kitchen
knife. I found the witness, a retired social worker who
would have preferred a quiet life and, as a result, Vic's client
was found not guilty of murder, on grounds of diminished
responsibility. After spending more than a year on remand,
she was set free amid much publicity.

We had a quiet evening in: coq au vin, a bottle of Rioja
with liquorice accents, *The Repair Shop* on in the background. And I told Vic about last night – about Ruby and
Caroline Swann and Danny. And then about my visit to the
cop shop and my chat with Charlie Ritchie.

She gave me a look. 'You don't want your old job back?'

'No ... I liked that job. I *could* like it again. But I've got
other stuff going on now.'

We were sitting on the sofa, the news muted on TV. 'You
used to say you loved that job.'

'OK, I did love it. That doesn't mean I want to do it again.'

'And you like the private-eye stuff.'

'Yeah.' I took a big mouthful of wine, swilled it a little. 'I'm my own boss. No one to answer to. Problems to solve.'

'You wouldn't want to answer to Avril whatsername?'

'Miskiewicz. Well.' – I thought about it – and Vic waited. 'Answering to her would be a bit weird. But . . . she's good at her job and she respects me; I taught her a lot, helped her get where she is.'

Vic took my hand and squeezed it. 'Look, I don't care whether you're a policeman or a private eye. Not my business, anyway. You've been great at both, and you've got your own business now. I just—'

'Yeah. Plenty of work. Too much. I might have to take on someone else.'

'I was going to say, I just want you to be happy.'

'Well, I am. Apart from anything else, I can take time off when I like. I can spend time with Danny . . . go fishing, go for walks.'

'When did you last go fishing?'

'About . . . well . . .' It was a good question. I hadn't been fishing for over a year.

'I know Danny's important.'

'Of course.'

'It's all right,' she said, and I realised I'd answered too fast, too abruptly, as if I were on the defensive. 'I understand.' She let go of my hand. 'Danny is lovely *and* important.'

'Yes, he is.' I picked up her hand and felt its warmth. 'In effect, he doesn't have a father. That drip, that selfish, sanctimonious creep, doesn't want to know.'

'I know.' She sighed. 'And it's wonderful that you're there for him – and for Laura.' She squeezed my hand again.

I stretched out my legs, leaned sideways against Vic and pulled her towards me. 'I know Laura might, probably will, find another man – a stepdad – though there's not much sign of it. But I hope she does – in time, when she's ready. And then . . .'

She was stroking the back of my hand and my wrist. It felt good. 'Then what?'

I swallowed some wine. 'I suppose . . . I'll see Danny and Laura and the new man, like I see Charlotte and Lola and Leo and their dad.'

★ ★ ★

For most of the night I seemed to be half-awake, thoughts and dreams moving and merging. Images, notions, repeating, revolving inside my head. Danny running towards me, arms out, on the pavement in the shade of the plane trees. Charlie Ritchie grinning like a hopeful child. 'She'd love to have you back. I just know it.' Laura with a man, a shock-headed pianist in a white shirt. Avril Miskiewicz, older, behind a desk, facing me, smiling. Danny's little fingers in mine . . .

And Stark, of course, staring at me in the back of the squad car and, at last, telling me what he had done – and eventually where she was. And Stark staring in court. And that was OK – not unusual. OK, because I was awake and remembering. Not like the dream where he doesn't speak, tormenting me with silence so that I don't know what I *have* to know: whether Jessica is alive or dead. And no dreams of Jessica now – just a memory: the fixed gaze, the bruised forehead, the blood in her hair, earth on her skin and the orange ants.

My knee in the crook of Vic's knee, my hand on her thigh – wriggle toes, relax toes, and on up, eyelids, eyes – and nothing, warmth, weariness, sleep.

In the morning Vic left before me. I stood by the door and promised to lock up when I left. As I kissed her goodbye, she squeezed my bum and said, 'Nice cock. What was your name, again?' I went out soon afterwards, aiming for Oxford Circus where I was to meet Kylie in a Caffè Nero.

On my way to the bus stop in New King's Road, I passed the 606 Club where Laura often performed, and remembered how Vic and I had seen her there once – when Danny had a sleepover at his Aunt Charlotte's. We had sat at a table at the back, away from the drums, and Laura had dedicated a song to us: the Gershwins' 'How Long Has This Been Going On?' We would have liked to get to more of Laura's gigs. Trouble was that when Laura was at the 606 or anywhere else, I was usually with Danny in Peckham.

★ ★ ★

Kylie was sitting at a table by the window with a laptop in front of her. 'Hey boss! How you doing?' She shut the laptop and tapped its lid. 'I'm ready – all set to wake up the stiffs.'

Kylie frequently talked about stiffs, and I used to think that she meant all men in suits and ties – but it was subtler than that. Some, not many, men – and women – in suits were OK. 'Stiffs,' she told me once, 'are boring people who can't unbend and have fun; most of them are white.'

I'd told her that to people like me, who were fans of Raymond Chandler and Philip Marlowe, stiffs were corpses.

'Same thing, Jim,' she'd said. 'Stiffs *are* corpses – in a metaphorical kind of way.'

In twenty minutes we were due to meet the stiffs to show them what had been going on in their flagship store. I gulped a cappuccino as she ran me through evidence proving that three shopworkers had nicked seventy thousand pounds' worth of cosmetics and jewellery in three months. As well as dates and times, quantities and values, there were photographs that she had taken with a lapel camera. Kylie would present this on PowerPoint and hand out dossiers marked 'Confidential'.

'Whaddya think, boss? Is this enough? Gimme another week, I can get a lot more.' She stared at me without blinking. 'Also, there's the other scam, with a delivery driver and someone on goods inwards. I'd need more time for that.'

'It's enough – plenty. Well done. We can look at the other thing with John McCormick. Maybe he can lever you in as a van driver.' She pulled a face, but I could tell that she fancied that. McCormick, a quiet, strangely neat former cop, was head of security; my long acquaintance with him had got us the gig.

* * *

We waited at a long, light-wood table, laden with clumps of bottled water and baskets of biscuits, in a thickly carpeted boardroom where the door shut itself noiselessly and wouldn't be hurried. A huge screen was fixed to the wall at the end of the room away from the window. Kylie switched it on and pressed some keys on her laptop. A double-one, black pips on cream, the logo of the Domino Agency, appeared on the big screen.

'Magic,' I said.

'It's wireless, Jim,' she grinned. She grabbed a Kit Kat and was mid-munch when the suits showed up: three directors, led by a woman with steel-grey hair combed in a perfect bob, followed by McCormick and a young woman carrying a notebook.

McCormick introduced us and we all sat down babbling

nervously while a young man in immaculate jeans handed out coffee and tea. Then Kylie got started – and was soon dazzling her audience. Grey bob's mouth opened and stayed that way for the full twenty minutes as eyes swivelled between Kylie and the screen. Questions were asked. Kylie answered them.

Grey bob – or, as her card revealed, Anne Weatherill, Managing Director – was outraged, as were her henchmen. McCormick said nothing and seemed embarrassed; he had hired us – but perhaps a little late.

'What do we do now?' Anne said.

It wasn't hard to persuade them to take no immediate action against the women. 'Call in the police,' I said. 'They'll track the women and find their fence. You'll be doing yourselves and the rest of the retail trade a huge favour.'

One of the suits – a young bloke with expensively tousled hair – asked whether Kylie or I could follow the women and find the fence.

'Usually,' I told him, 'we do the work the police haven't time for, like shop-floor pilfering. But they love catching the Mr Bigs. And there probably won't be just one Mr Big; there'll be a Mr Bigger and a Mr Biggest. Layers of fences that they can wrap up together. And frankly, I can't be arsed with that. I don't have the staff. Good staff are hard to get these days – as I'm sure you know.' I grinned at the young man and nodded towards Kylie who was doing her stare-you-down, I'm-a-hard-case routine. Only then did it occur to me – because I'm so used to it, that I don't think about it – that Kylie's large eyes and glowing black skin might unsettle a young stiff.

★ ★ ★

That afternoon Laura had a rehearsal with a new six-piece outfit put together by her pianist friend Jason Dobell, so I went to collect Danny from school – it was my turn; Juliana had collected him the day before. Standing aside from the scrum of grown-ups, little kids and buggies, beside the shed where they keep the kids' scooters, was Ruby's brother Luke. Of course – he was collecting his brother Jake. I waved and went over to him.

He seemed pleased to see me and told me that he and Ruby had visited their mother that morning. The police had taken them because Caroline had woken up.

I started to say how pleased I was. But he shook his head. 'She went out again. Into a deep sleep – sort of unconscious again.'

'Did she talk to you before she went back to sleep?'

'Not really. She looked at us, seemed really tired . . . mumbled a bit. I held her hand and she gripped mine really tight. And Ruby's too: our hands – she squeezed them. I was holding her left hand,' – he lifted his own hand and looked at it, as if checking which of his mother's hands was the left one – 'and Ruby had hold of her right.' He stared at me for a moment, and then at a door where a teacher was standing. 'I don't know what door Jake will come out of. Mum usually does this. I'm usually at school.'

'I think they come down those stairs.' I pointed to a flight of steps leading to a door on the first floor. 'Danny does, so your Jake probably will.'

Luke glanced at the door and bit his lip.

'Is Ruby all right?'

'Yeah. She's amazing. She's looking after the little ones better than Gran is. Gran's really upset. Worried . . . Well, I'm worried, everyone's worried – but Gran keeps stopping in the middle of doing something, like . . . pouring milk on

Lily's Shreddies, and staring at nothing. "Gran," I say, and it's as if I've woken her up. "Oh! Yes!" she says, and goes on pouring the milk.'

Kids and parents and teachers were milling around now. But no one had come through the door at the top of the steps.

'So the police were there – at the hospital?'

'Yeah. The nice woman, Sunita, and the one you know – with the baseball cap. Sergeant Charlie, is it?'

I asked if he knew whether his mum had said anything to the police.

He didn't know. If she had, they hadn't told him. Then Jake appeared, skipped down the stairs and rushed up to us. He pushed a sheet of paper into Luke's hands. 'I did this.'

Luke stared at it. Blue sky and bright green grass in horizontal strokes, and a stick figure lying on the ground. 'Lovely,' said Luke. 'Well done, Jake.' He took his brother's hand. 'See ya, Mr Domino. Nice to see ya.'

I turned and found Dan standing beside me. He was holding my hand.

On the way home, we dropped into the greengrocer to get some stuff for Laura.

Ron sells a vast variety of fresh fruit and vegetables, but the real appeal of his shop is Ron himself and the feel of the place; it's like it would have been in the 1960s when I was a kid. Old, brown lino, which Ron sweeps from time to time, covers the floor. Beautifully arranged fruit and veg rise in tiers against the walls. And Ron, always wearing a brown coat, picks out what you ask for, drops it in a brown paper bag and whirls the bag in the air to seal it with a twist of paper at each end. Self-service is not permitted and nothing is prepacked.

However, shopping at Ron's can take up a lot of time.

Queues build up because Ron does all the serving himself and carries on long, gossipy conversations. His wife, Di, helps by refilling empty fruit and veg trays. But, when she isn't doing that, she sits on a chair by the door staring out into the street and listening to the chat; she smiles, nods and shakes her head, but rarely speaks. Not to adults, that is. She loves children, chats to them, makes jokes and hands out sweets, lollies and, occasionally, toffee apples. This is why Dan likes going to the greengrocer.

Today Ron was nattering to a man who was staring at a long shopping list. 'So, it could be these people who don't like the posh people who have moved in; they don't like what they call gentrification. Lotta nonsense, I think – gentrification. Round here has been gentrified off and on for a hundred years – hundred and fifty years in fact. Look at some of the big houses. They weren't built for poor people, weren't built to be flats. So it's part of the history. This has always been a mixed area.'

'So what happened?' The customer was large, middle-aged, wearing a long green coat.

'Well, this woman. Nice woman who has six kids, lives up the road here. Night before last was hit on the head, knocked unconscious and left on the table-tennis table in the park.' And then Ron noticed me. 'And here, on cue, is the local bobby, Jim Domino.'

I rolled my eyes and shook my head. 'Not any more, Ron.'

'Well, he's retired now. Looks good for a retired man, doesn't he?' Ron leaned across and nudged me in the ribs. 'And I know he keeps his ear to the ground. Whaddya know about it Jim? This is Dave Shaw, Jim. He's taking over the pizza place three doors up. Dave, Jim. Jim, Dave.'

I shook hands with the large man, who was keen to tell me that he owned a well-known chain of restaurants and would be opening a new branch 'right here'. I pretended to be pleased about this and congratulated him – and then managed to escape with Laura's shopping without saying anything revealing about the attack on Caroline Swann. Well, I didn't *know* anything revealing.

But I thought about Ron's theory: that Caroline had been attacked by someone who resented posh people and gentrification. Where had Ron got that from? It was possible – not long ago there had been an outbreak of stickers on lampposts and, I remembered, on the very ping-pong table where Caroline had been found: 'Rich cunts go home.' Though, as far as I knew, no one had been attacked in London recently just because they were posh. Di had given Dan a lolly, a boiled sweet on a cardboard stick. He was still sucking it when we got back to Laura's. I let him turn on the TV and watch *Paw Patrol*. Then I rang Charlie Ritchie.

'I heard Caroline woke up for a while. Did she say anything?'

'Sunita Das was there. She asked Caroline the obvious question: who hit her? Caroline didn't answer – just looked at her, but not for long, seemed very confused – but not in pain, the medics say. Sunita asked again. Nothing. Then Sunita tried, "Who did you see in Warwick Gardens?" And that time she said something, one word; we don't know what it means – yet. And, of course, it may not mean anything. Could be from a dream.'

'So, what was it?'

'Pepper.'

'Pepper?'

'Yes. We haven't tried it on anyone yet: family, friends, colleagues. This only happened half an hour ago. Second time she's woken up today. This morning her eyes opened and sort of darted around – I was there – but the nurses

41

didn't know if she could actually see anything. And she didn't speak, even though we got Ruby and her brother in.'

'Luke.'

'Yes, Luke. Anyway, we'll be trying "pepper" on everyone – including Michel ... wosname, Ruby's dad in Canada. You never know ... He's coming over, by the way.'

'Good. He sounds all right.'

'Yes ... Thing is, Jim: Caroline drifted off again after that, muttered a bit – nothing anyone could understand – and that was it. Medics think there could be brain damage. She may have had a stroke.'

I thanked Charlie and said goodbye. Then flopped down on the sofa beside Danny and put my arm round him. He said something I didn't quite catch about Ron's shop.

Sunita Das asking, 'Who did you see in Warwick Gardens?', and the answer, 'Pepper,' were echoing in my mind.

6

I was up early. I had to meet Clayton for a coffee at the Crossroads Cafe in Bellenden Road at 7.15. Before going out, I got Danny up and gave him his Weetabix and peach-flavoured yoghurt.

I've known Clayton for years, since I was a sergeant and he was volunteering, setting up after-school clubs – self-defence, martial arts – to keep kids off the streets and away from the gangs. He started working for me soon after I set up the agency. He's an ace investigator; people trust him, like him, talk to him, tell him stuff we want to know. He's a gentle, articulate, extremely fit man in his early forties, a bodybuilder who doesn't overdo it. When he's not working with me, he's a plumber with a sideline in antique radiators – the kind that some people around here like to have in their homes instead of the modern ones. And he belongs to a small and select group of strong men who voluntarily look out for women and kids and anyone who might get hurt on the streets during demos or protest marches.

Clayton and I had a pay-up-or-get-out job on Holly Grove. I don't like that kind of work; I do it only if I'm persuaded that the tenant can easily pay and that the land-lord needs the money. I can handle the early start so we can catch people before they go out, but it often requires a little aggression and even, occasionally, muscle – which is why I take Clayton along.

Today we were acting for a friend of a friend, an elderly widow who rents out her basement. She depends on the income and is stuck with two surly young men who haven't paid for months. At our first meeting, Mrs Gray was almost in tears. 'The flat is my pension,' she said. 'I *need* the rent. I thought they were such nice boys at first – but it turns out they're not.'

The free-loading flatmates both earn good money; they gave written proof of that before being allowed to sign the lease. All right, one of them has been unwell – but that's no excuse.

It was one of those houses with steps up to the front door and a basement that is barely below ground. I left Clayton leaning on the railings across the road. He was smiling as I rang the bell on the basement door.

A tall man wearing grey trousers, a blue shirt and an expensive-looking tie appeared. He frowned.

'Good morning. Are you Mr Brown or Mr Neave?'

'My name is Brown. Why?'

'My name is Jim Domino. Mrs Gray, your landlady, is a friend of mine. It seems you haven't paid rent for four months, even though Mrs Gray has phoned and written to you many times. She's asked me to ask you to pay the rent. She relies on the money.' The man was blinking at me and biting his lip. 'You owe her £4,800. It's not fair on her. Is there any reason why you haven't paid?'

'Why do I have to talk to you? Are you a lawyer, or something?'

'It's better for you to talk to me and pay up. Otherwise, you'll find you have a court order, bailiffs evicting you, the locks being changed.'

'But who are you? Why should—'

'I'm a friend of Mrs Gray and a private investigator.' I flashed my PI licence.

He began to close the door. 'I don't deal with private investigators.' He spoke with a sneer.

I put my foot in the door and tugged at my left ear – a signal to Clayton.

'Please! Go away! I'll pay when it suits me – not when some debt collector turns up.'

'It'd be better for you if you paid something now. It would save you a lot of aggravation and an order from the county court.'

'Just go away!' He pushed the door against my calf and kicked my ankle.

Clayton was beside me now, though Mr Brown couldn't see him. He leaned a shoulder against the door and pushed. The door burst open. And Mr Brown jumped backwards.

'Mr Brown. Please meet Clayton Ginevra, another of Mrs Gray's friends.'

Brown's shoulders flopped; then he was wiping his forehead, looking at the floor, pale, shocked. 'Get out,' he whispered.

A man was standing at the end of the passage, not moving, staring, his mouth open. I brushed past the drooping Brown. 'Mr Neave?'

He frowned and nodded. 'Yes.'

I explained who I was and why I was there, handed him my card and introduced Clayton, who had followed me down the passage. Clayton raised a hand – and I went on, 'I've come to suggest that you and your flatmate pay what you owe in rent to save you the hassle of being taken to court, bailiffs, being locked out, your furniture impounded, etcetera, etcetera.'

Neave was small and slight. He was clenching and un-clenching his fingers. 'I've not been well, but—' He took a couple of steps back. 'Come in.' I followed him into a large, airy kitchen with a view of a garden. He walked around a long table and put his hands on the back of a chair. 'Yes. I'm on the mend. I'm earning again. I'm an actor, by the way.' He was wearing a white shirt; it was very white and a little too big for him. 'I think we can pay now.' He swallowed and his Adam's apple shot up and down. 'But,' – Mr Brown appeared and stood beside his friend – 'we're not happy with the way Pamela – Mrs Gray – treats us.'

'Really!'

'Yes.' He coughed. 'Won't you sit down.' He pointed – and we all sat down at the table, Clayton and I facing Mr Neave and Mr Brown. 'You see, she bangs on the floor, loudly with something' – he shrugged – 'a broom handle or a shoe—'

'Sounds like a hammer, sometimes.' Brown glanced at me and shook his head.

'This is if we make any noise – television, music, even talking and laughing – we sometimes have friends in – after ten o'clock. Sometimes she shouts at us to be quiet in the garden in the afternoon, or lunch time: in our part of the garden – just here.' He turned and waved towards the window. 'We've had some parties. But we don't any more.'

'Have you discussed this with her?'

'We've tried,' Brown said, 'but she won't listen.'

'You see,' Neave said, 'she's only been like that since she realised that we're gay. We had a party in the garden back in May. Some of the guests were a little outrageous.' He giggled, and Brown smirked.

'We thought she knew anyway,' Brown said. 'From when she first met us. We don't hide it.'

'But turns out she's a homophobe,' Neave said. 'So, we thought, OK, if she's going to be like that – bang on the ceiling and interrupt our parties – we'll respond. A bit childish, maybe. But, you know . . .'

Clayton spoke for the first time. 'Bigots.' He shook his head. 'Tell me about it!'

Sitting at the table, Bernard Neave, Paul Brown, Clayton and I became friends – of a kind. And we made a plan. I would speak later to Mrs Gray – and tell her off, tell her to stop the banging and disruption, tell her that gay people have the same rights as everyone else. And they would go to the cashpoint on their way to work and give me £1000 cash to pass on to her as a down payment. The rest to be paid later, as long as she agreed to stop banging and causing trouble in the garden. They would invite her and me and Clayton to their next party, and I would urge her to go.

★ ★ ★

'We doing social work now, are we?' Clayton smiled over his coffee. 'And that's good.'

'Yeah. Police work is social work – with aggravation thrown in. But I wasn't expecting that – any of it! I had them down as freeloaders planning to disappear before the heat was turned up. And her – well . . .'

'The old lady! Blimey! She thinks they're nice young men who want to share a flat, which they are, and then – all of a sudden – she gets it. They're what she calls *homosexuals*.' He put his mug down carefully. 'And she blames them – I'm right, aren't I? – for the horrible death of her boy all that

47

time ago. Fuck me, Jim!' He wiped his hands down his face, and peered at me over his fingers, then took his hands away and blew out a long breath. 'Good job, bruv.'

We left soon after that. Clayton said he didn't want to be paid for this gig – that all he'd done was sit around with tears in his eyes. I insisted, reminded him that we wouldn't have got through the door without him. And anyway, Mrs Gray would pay me.

★ ★ ★

I spent the rest of the morning and the early afternoon at home, did some important computer crap, worked out with Jimmy Cliff and ate a cheese sandwich. Then I pulled the curtains not quite shut, put on Miles's *In A Silent Way*, lay down on the sofa and closed my eyes. My thoughts went back to Mrs Gray. 'I know I'm wrong, but I can't help it.' Maybe Mrs Gray was jealous of her tenants because they were able to enjoy, without fear, the life that she would have liked her son to enjoy.

A sharp wind made my cheeks tingle as I walked over to Laura's at about seven. She was in the shower when I arrived, then an Uber turned up to take her to Hampstead for a gig at the jazz club in the Duke of Hamilton. I made Danny's dinner and stood dumbly against a radiator while he ate and watched *Power Rangers*.

I went to bed early for me – at about eleven. Laura wouldn't be back till half-twelve. I sucked a Rennie, read Lorca and fell asleep.

7

In the morning, before she took Danny to school, Laura told me that the creepy man had been in the audience at the Hampstead Jazz Club. The gig had been good, but he spooked her, sitting alone staring – close to her. It was a small venue. Creepy man liked small venues – Crazy Coqs, Kansas Smitty's, the 606.

I was thinking about him as I pushed a capsule of coffee into Laura's Nespresso machine. Anyone who goes to a jazz club alone, or to any kind of entertainment alone, *would* stare – wouldn't they? And many musicians – or actors, or comics, or dancers, whoever – have followers, fans, people who go to lots of their gigs. Was Laura seeing a threat where there wasn't one?

I pushed the button on the Nespresso.

But Laura would know – surely. She's been doing this for years: standing on a stage or sitting at a piano, late at night, singing love songs – mostly – to people who've had a few drinks. She's often complimented on her music – singing, the range of her voice, piano-playing, all that. Some people, mostly men, compliment her on her looks. Well ... she looks good:takes trouble with her hair, make-up – all that. It's part of the job, a small but necessary part; she's not in a punk band, she can't go on stage in a crumpled T-shirt. Some men, a few, try to go too far, almost always when it's late and they've drunk too much. She tells me about it. It doesn't bother her. She knows what to do, how to get away. And there are always people around whom she knows – musicians, managers, drivers, friends.

But a man who isn't drunk, sitting quietly, staring in a certain way does bother her. Though he always gets up and leaves after the gig.

Coffee was sputtering into the mug. My phone rang.

'Charlie Ritchie, Jim. You all right?'

'Yes, OK. You?'

'OK, but we have,' – his voice dropped – 'sad news. Caroline Swann died an hour ago.'

'Oh no!' For an instant I saw Ruby beside me in the car, lit by passing headlights, staring straight ahead, anxious – how many days ago? Three? Four? 'That's just ... the worst. Did she ... did she wake up again?'

'No. More bleeding in the brain. They couldn't stop it.' He went silent for a moment. 'I'm gutted, Jim. All those kids ... '

'Were you there?'

'No. Just Sunita Das, in case she woke up and said something. Ruby and her brother ... Luke, were there, and her mother, the granny; the medics phoned them.'

'Is anyone looking after them all?'

'Sunita is at the house now. I told her to go home with them. I know they like her. And there's a family liaison officer on the way.'

'Oh God!' Again, I saw Ruby in the headlights.

'Jim?'

Now the eldest of six motherless children.

'Jim? Are you there?'

'I'm here. It's a tragedy. Six children. Six tragedies!'

'I know.' He spoke quietly. 'And now it's a murder case – awkward, intrusive questions from us. And publicity; we'll try to protect them, but the media are on it already, of course.'

'Why, Charlie? Who? Anything since we spoke? Thursday, was it?'

'Well, we now think that she was attacked right there beside the table-tennis table where she was found. There's no sign of her being coerced or pushed around until she got close to that table.'

'OK. I guess that helps a bit.'

'Yes. Why did she go there?' He went silent. 'Anyway, there's another thing: Gary Jackson turned up at the house yesterday. By a piece of luck, Sunita and DC Haydon happened to be there. Apparently, Jackson was upset, hugged his two kids and wanted to take them away. Das and Haydon told him he couldn't, that he shouldn't be there at all. Mrs Swann, Caroline's mother, yelled at him to go – well, he beat up her daughter, so why not? Big argument; he claimed he was barred from seeing Caroline only, not his kids. And, for what it's worth, the legal eagles say that's right, but he *is* barred from the house. Which means that his kids can be with their nan and their siblings – half-siblings – but they have to stay in the house or risk being snatched by Jackson. So social services are onto it. A right mess.' He paused again. 'You there, Jim?'

'Yes. I don't know what to say.' I pulled the coffee out of the Nespresso. 'Mum is dead, and Dad is trying to kidnap you.'

'We found Tony – the shouty man. Asleep in a doorway in Brixton. Not clear why he went there. He's back at his shelter now. No reason to suspect him.' He paused again. 'I'd better go. Now that this is murder, Lightfoot is SIO, and all over it – and me – and the Super is too, of course. Just thought I'd keep you posted.'

'Thanks. Think I'll go round there. See if I can do anything ... Like tell the press, the media, to piss off.'

'OK. Just thought I'd let you know.'

'And sometimes talking and listening can help. Yes. Thanks.'

'And Jim ... '

'Yeah.'

'Let's go for a drink before it gets too long.'

'OK. Let's do that.'

I pulled the coffee from the machine and sipped at it. I added a spoonful of sugar and stared out of the kitchen window at the grey sky above the fence. A black and white cat was asleep on the roof of a neighbour's shed.

I knew all their names: Ruby; Luke; Ella, who looked like Luke; Jake, whom Danny knew and who also looked like Luke; blonde-haired Lily; and little Sammy, blond and curly-haired.

Ruby holding Sammy and looking into his eyes. *'She'll be all right.'* I gulped at the hot, sweet coffee. Would Sammy ever trust her again? I took another gulp. So Lightfoot was SIO, senior bloody investigating officer. It might have been me. I wished it were – for this case anyway.

The front door opened and clicked shut. I watched Laura hang up her coat. Then I told her the news.

'Jeez, Dad! What the ... fuck!' She sat down at the kitchen table, tears in her eyes. 'Those lovely ... kids.' She was struggling to speak. She put her head in her hands.

I squatted beside her and put an arm round her shoulder.

'How can that happen?' she said. 'Why?'

'I don't know.'

'In the park, where all the kids play.' She stood up. 'In the *bloody* park!'

We talked for a long time: me standing, leaning against the oven; Laura sitting at the table. She wanted to know if it could be a random madman. That frightened her. She was in that little park all the time, just like I was. I told her it was unlikely; only about ten per cent of murdered women are killed by strangers.

'Still quite a lot, Dad.'

'Yes. OK. I guess—'

'I love that park,' she said. 'It's not the greatest, but I love it because it's here, round the corner, and we keep going there. I don't know about it now, though.'

'It's still the same park. Full of locals, kids every afternoon, trains rumbling past . . . dogs, football.'

'Table tennis?' She shook her head and looked miserable. 'They were hardly ever used, those tables – not for table tennis. Mostly, people put their coats on them.'

We went on talking. And some of the time I was thinking about death – my own, mainly – but I didn't say so.

Laura sighed, stood up and said she must do her exercises. This meant she would breathe deeply and sing scales loudly standing up, and then sit at the piano and sing anything from 'Nature Boy' to 'Bring Me Sunshine'. Today she started with 'Summertime'. And, though I love her voice, I slipped away. I usually do.

★ ★ ★

I walked towards the Swanns', trying to imagine the misery that Ruby, Luke and the younger ones must be feeling. Should I go there now? . . . PC Das and the family liaison officer might be enough outsiders.

Suddenly, 'Jim! Jim!' Mrs Mumford – standing in front of me, blocking the pavement. 'What's happened? A policeman at that poor Caroline Swann's front door, and cameramen by her gate.'

'She's died ... Pauline.' I remembered her name, and I told her again, 'She's died.' Why not? It'd be on the news soon, if it wasn't already. 'It is horribly, terribly sad.'

Pauline had turned pale. Her face was blank. Her mouth had closed to a thin, red line. She put a hand on the nearest gatepost. 'No,' she said, shaking her head. She sat down on the garden wall and stared at the pavement without speaking. Eventually she looked up. 'What can we do, Jim? This world!' Her eyes were watering. 'I hate it sometimes.'

'So do I.' I took her hand in both of mine and squeezed it. 'So do I – and I don't know what we can do.' I held her hand and patted it – and she kept looking into my eyes.

'Does it even matter who killed her?' I said. 'She's dead.'

She looked at me blankly. We said something about supporting the children and being neighbourly. Then she stood up, shook her head and walked away, head down.

I walked a little further. And turned back – I wouldn't go to them now. Perhaps later. I walked to my flat, past the park – all of it taped off: both ends and the fenced-off playground. A police search team was poking around in the bushes along the east side, and on the west between the fence and the railway track.

Of course it mattered who'd killed her – why did I say that? – they might kill someone else.

* * *

I sat down at my table and gazed at a bunch of spreadsheets. Just looking at spreadsheets and balance sheets and profit-and-loss accounts makes me yawn, literally. But, if I shake my head and concentrate, I can wake up and understand them. Then, sometimes, I see a story – and that gives me a sense of satisfaction, excitement even.

I'm looking for fraud, money-laundering, dirty money. Stefan, who used to be Kylie's boyfriend – and perhaps is again: I don't know, I can't keep up – helps me with this stuff. He's super techie: he can write code and even hack into supposedly secure websites. He spots anomalies and patterns that I would probably miss and we work out what they mean: where the cash is coming from and going to; who's involved. The clients are a pair of journalists who write exposés of fraud and corruption. They give me the leads, the names; I give them facts, details and maybe more names.

At about 3 pm I sent a text to Ruby. 'So sorry to hear about your mum. I'm thinking of you all. If you want to talk, or if I can help, call me at any time, day or night. Jim.' I did my exercises and some more work. Managed to concentrate and tease my way towards the truth along a long trail of obfuscation: a car parts supplier ripping off a chain of garages by raising false invoices over a period of years. Who was benefiting? Who was corrupt and who was just stupid?

I stopped at 6 pm; I would look at it again tomorrow with Stefan. I put a couple of ice cubes into a large slug of Scotch, swilled the liquid around in my mouth so that I felt the burn and watched the sun drop behind the warehouses at the back. After a few minutes, I poured another and put the Barr Brothers' *Queens of the Breakers* into the sound system. Washes of red, gold and violet lingered in the sky. I turned the music off, and just sat.

I thought about death and its strangeness: the idea of not being here – of that being it. I thought of Danny growing up – I wanted to be around long enough to make sure he was OK, just as I had with Laura and Charlotte. And I imagined him and Lola and little Leo – going on living when I wasn't there. That made me sad. Yet, when it happened, I wouldn't be sad, of course, because I wouldn't be anything at all. All the pain and fun and love would have come to an end. As hard to imagine as the universe going on for ever, always expanding.

I poured another, smaller one – a drop of water, no ice – and pulled down a book I'd bought at the National Gallery three years before. I'd been to see paintings by the Spanish artist Joaquín Sorolla with Laura and Dan – and found that, like me at one time, Sorolla had a wife and two daughters. Standing surrounded by silent, slow-moving art-lovers, I had become entranced by a group of paintings that I had never seen before: Sorolla's wife, Clotilde, and his daughters walking by the sea in long white dresses. Those paintings, the sunlight, the elegant, happy women, the dazzling whiteness of their clothes and of the froth on the waves, had moved me like nothing else since Elizabeth died. Lingering in front of them, I'd imagined what might have been. What *should* have been.

Elizabeth hadn't known her daughters as adults.

I knew of Sorolla first as the lodestar of a poem by Lawrence Ferlinghetti. Then I saw a few of his paintings online. But I'd never seen them like this – bright and twinkling as if finished an hour ago. Standing in front of them, I'd cried for the first time in sixteen years.

Dan had found me: in tears, in the National Gallery. He'd stared up at me, frowning. I'd smiled through the tears, and then Laura had been there. We'd walked into another room – the three of us holding hands. 'That painting, those women by the sea. Makes me think of Mum,'

I'd started to say, as Laura put an arm round me, her hair pushed against my cheek, '– and you and Charlotte.'

We'd stood there, the three of us huddled against one another, among Sorolla's paintings of Spanish landscapes and peasants and naked children in the sea. Danny had gripped my hand and rubbed my arm.

Later, as we searched for the exit, I'd told him. 'Your mum's mum died – a long while ago now. She was my wife. She was called Elizabeth. Those pictures made me think of her – and of your mum and Aunt Charlotte.'

He'd looked up at me, biting his lip, tense and jittery. Was he too young to hear about death?

Probably, but ... 'I'm sad, but I'm also happy,' I'd said. I rubbed the tears from my cheeks with my knuckles and found that I was smiling. 'She'd have loved *you*.' I was holding him by the shoulders.

Laura had taken Dan to the café. I'd gone to the gallery's shop where beautiful books of Sorolla's paintings were piled on a table. I had taken my time and chosen the one with the best reproductions of the three women in white.

Now, I sat with it on my lap, taking tiny sips of whisky. I looked at a painting – perhaps my favourite – at the confident faces and the camaraderie, the ease and the fun. I looked away, beyond the window, imagining. And back again. I was envious of this great artist with his Clotilde. But somehow it was good to look, and wonder.

★ ★ ★

Much later, after ten o'clock, Vic rang – bubbly, cheerful, missing me. She was in France for a few days – a treat for her old mum – driving about looking at châteaux and cathedrals. She guessed something was wrong, so I told her about Caroline Swann – and then she wanted to be here, hugging me.

I went to bed, but couldn't sleep – couldn't get those kids out of my head, especially Ruby with her new responsibilities. My brain seemed to reach down into my stomach and bring on those stabs of indigestion that I'd felt a few times since I had the ulcer. I sucked a Rennie. At least it wasn't my heart. Doctor Prakash had tested that twice. 'No problem there,' he'd said. 'Just keep exercising, and don't drink too much.'

I fell asleep and was woken by a dream: Danny was being chased by a big, brown, barking dog; he was screaming and I was trying to kick the dog and shout but I couldn't make a sound. I woke up after what seemed like a physical struggle. I drank some water, then pushed the button on the CD player so that the Barr Brothers came from the speakers. I turned the volume down, sucked another Rennie and wondered about pepper.

8

A cold breeze numbed my face as I walked towards the Swanns'. I'd been woken by a text alert. From Ruby: 'Please come round today if you can. My dad is here. Come and meet him. We're going to move out for a bit.'

A small crowd of people, some with cameras, stood on the other side of the street. At the gate a uniformed constable used his lapel phone to check that I was welcome, then the door was opened by DC Haydon, the ukulele virtuoso. Pale, red-eyed children stared up at me from the gloom. Jake – Danny's friend whom I'd seen in the school playground – took hold of Haydon's hand. Haydon bent, put an arm round him and gave me a look which said, *it doesn't get worse than this*. Police would be there, he told me, until a safe house could be arranged later today or tomorrow; the family had to get away from the media and the public.

Little Sammy was looking up at me. I smiled, 'Hello, Sammy,' and squatted down, put my hands on his shoulders and hugged him.

Someone leaned in, grey hair swinging and streaked with

blonde. 'C'mon, Sammy.' She lifted the boy, turned him round, kissed and hugged him.

Bleary blue eyes stared into mine. Thin folds of skin crossed the outer corner of each eye; her face seemed noble and wise – and like the gable end on an old barn.

'Hello,' I tried to smile. 'I'm—'

'Pat. I'm their gran. Caroline's mum.'

'Jim Domino . . . I'm sorry. This must be terrible for you.'

'Yes.' She frowned and swallowed. 'Yes, it is . . . terrible.' Her face was a mass of lines – yet soft where her cheek pressed against the little boy. 'I'll make some tea.' She turned away, carrying Sammy.

Ruby appeared with Lily holding tight to her sleeve. If she'd slept, she'd slept in her clothes. She looked at me and tears welled in her eyes.

'I'm sorry,' I said.

She tried to smile and led me into the kitchen. A handsome dark-haired man stood up. 'This is my dad, Michel.'

'Mr Domino, I'm pleased to meet you. I'm Michel Leblanc.' Despite the French name, he spoke perfect English as French Canadians do. He thanked me for, as he put it, caring for the children. Like everyone else, including Pat who was now warming a teapot, he looked drained. We sat down at the table with Ruby and Lily, Luke and Ella; Michel said he would stay with them for as long as he could. 'It's a tragedy,' he said. 'There will be a lot to sort out, but we can't get into any of that yet. They need some peace.' He waved his hand.

'Yes,' I said. 'Of course.'

No one spoke. There was nothing to be said. I concentrated on the only thing on the table, a large tin of biscuits – bourbons, shortbread, custard creams, choc-chip cookies, pink wafers. None had been eaten.

Michel and I managed some small talk: his flight from

Canada, and the likely location of a safe house. 'Not far away,' I said. Luke fetched mugs and lined them up in front of the biscuits. Michel held Ruby's hand and had an arm around Ella. Smaller children came in and went out. Did Ruby mind, I wondered, that her dad was so at ease with all of them? He was hers only, in the most true sense. I couldn't help thinking that she was lucky: she had a dad, here for her now. Luke, Ella and Jake were orphans. Lily's and Sammy's dad wanted to kidnap them.

Ruby got up. 'I'll check on the littl'uns,' she said.

Again, we sat without speaking – and that was OK. Pat put the teapot on the table. And the silence continued. She came back with a blue and white jug filled with milk. 'Tea's up.'

Michel muttered something and I said, 'Thank you.'

Pat went into the hall and called out, 'Tea! Ruby! Johnny!'

Ruby returned, followed by Lily peeping out through a mat of tangled hair.

Johnny? Who was Johnny?

Tea was poured and milk and sugar passed round. I took a bourbon. DC Haydon came in and sat down opposite me.

'Here you are, Johnny.' Pat passed him a mug of tea. 'Have a biscuit. Please.'

There was more silence. What to say?

Johnny Haydon said there was no news yet about the safe house and, after a question from Ruby, that he had heard no more about the investigation.

Pat shook her head. Michel picked up his mug and walked to the window. I joined him and stared at the garden: scruffy grass, a bare fruit tree, a slide, a swing and one of those spiral tubes with a ball attached to a length of luminous yellow string.

A low moan interrupted the quiet. And then loud sob-
bing. It was Ella. She had been sitting, slight and serious,
next to Michel since I arrived. Now Pat had her arms round
her, lifting her to her feet. A huddle formed: Ruby, Jake
and Lily – and Luke carrying Sammy. 'I know. I know,' Pat
was murmuring, and rubbing Ella's back. 'We're all here
together. We'll always be here for each other.' Ella's sobs
grew deeper and longer, sustained by great gulps for air.
Smaller children began to cry too.

I looked at Michel. Michel looked at me. DC Haydon sat
and looked at his thumbs.

What could be done? Should these children be at school?
Or be taken to a zoo? Or anywhere to distract them? No.
This was painful, but right. They needed time and each
other – and that was all. No bereavement counselling or
family liaison officers. Not yet.

★ ★ ★

On my way home, I walked into Warwick Park – open
again, five days after Caroline had been found by a boy
holding a football, and just two since she died. Some thirty
bunches of flowers in cellophane wrappers were tied to the
railings outside the gate; some looked fresh; some were
wilting; some were hard to see because the cellophane had
steamed up. On the pavement beneath the railings, a line
of glasses and tins held burnt-out candles.

Two police in uniform – a middle-aged man with a
paunch and a tall guy with his hat pushed back – stood idly
near the gate trying to look friendly. I looked uphill towards
the other gate, two hundred yards away. Two more police
were talking to a woman with a dog on a lead. Four police
in a small park: a sign that someone in authority – Dave
Lightfoot or Avril Miskiewicz – wanted to reassure people

who, encouraged by the media, feared that Caroline Swann had been attacked by a deranged stranger.

I walked through the gate in the inner railings to the dog-free zone. Five bunches of fresh flowers – roses, freesias, big purple daisies, carnations, lilies – brought in since the park reopened that morning, lay on the worn rubber matting and the bare earth where the ping-pong table had stood. Had the table been taken away for forensic examination? Or did someone think it had become unseemly, or spooky? Its identical twin – there had always been two – was in place ten feet away, covered in coats and hoodies.

I read the messages fixed to the flowers. 'Sweet Caroline. Taken far too soon. RIP. With love Jenna, Tim and the boys.' 'Supermum! Why you? Why now? So sad. Anna and John xxx.' 'We will miss you and will know you are among the angels. Muriel and Joe Coster.' And, stapled to some white carnations: 'I love you. I miss you so much. Your Gary xx'.

I wandered off up the hill. The place was full of kids, couples and people with dogs, throwing balls, kicking balls, chasing around, with no signs of fear. It was Sunday, bright daylight and the police were in full view.

Three men stood together, close to the path. One of them broke away. 'Fats! How're you?' It was Ron, my favourite – everyone's favourite – greengrocer, and the only person who called me Fats; years ago he thought it was funny – Fats Domino, the great rock 'n' roller, ha ha! – but now it was just a habit. I used to retaliate by calling him Da Doo Ron Ron, but gave up on that years ago.

He didn't wait for me to tell him how I was. 'That lovely Mrs Swann!' He was shaking his head. 'What's all that about? And those kids, Ruby . . . Luke, the littler ones, Jake, Lily.'

'Ron, all I know is it's very, very sad, and devastating for those children.'

'And just down there.' He pointed down the hill. 'A bit close to home, innit?' Ron's dog was sitting, looking up at him, tongue out and panting. Ron hurled a tennis ball. The dog shot off, slithered to a halt, grabbed the ball and shot back again. By then Ron had moved on to football; he was impressed that Bentancur had scored twice for Spurs in three minutes but he still had doubts about the manager.

But I wasn't in the mood.

I went home, lay on the sofa and tried to escape into the new Sara Paretsky.

Later, as darkness came on outside, I felt like some company. Vic was still away. I thought about Laura and Dan – but I'd see them more than once next week. Charlotte and Chris? Probably a bad time – kids' bedtime – and anyway, I don't like to impose by inviting myself. Clayton? He'd always say if he's busy.

And he was. I should have remembered: Sunday evening is now family time – he's forty-three and has his first grand-child, a girl called Naomi.

I dribbled whisky over some ice and settled down to watch the fifth series of *The Crown*. Imelda Staunton as the Queen. I'm not used to the Queen being dead.

9

For a few days not a lot happened. Ruby phoned on Tuesday. They were staying in a large house in Sydenham near the woods, going for walks, playing board games and doing jigsaws. Her dad and her gran were in charge and her aunt Sarah, her mum's sister, had arrived from France.

Kylie phoned that evening to report on her first outing as a van driver delivering expensive French kitchen stuff – saucepans, casseroles, frying pans – to our friends in Oxford Street. 'Nothing happened, Jim, except two blokes unloaded the van and a boss bloke, kind of Italian called Nico, counted them and signed the docket.'

The next evening, she phoned to say that Nico had asked her out for a drink – and she'd accepted. 'Well, why not? It's part of the job, isn't it? He might try to bribe me with a few free casseroles.' She giggled. 'And he's a bit of a looker. Handsome and a bit rough – the gangster look.'

John McCormick rang on Thursday morning to tell me he'd been sacked by grey bob and the stiffs, who hadn't been impressed by the size and duration of the thefts from the cosmetics and jewellery departments.

'Sorry to hear that, John.'

'My fault.' He exhaled – an almost silent sigh. 'There were rumours, but I let it drift, took my eye off the ball . . . Anyway, my deputy is taking over. Carl Whiteman. He knows all about Kylie and goods inwards.'

I was listening to Robert Elms on Radio London, Friday lunchtime, while slicing cheese and tearing up lettuce to make a sandwich. The news came on. Something about the Duke and Duchess of Sussex, then: 'A thirty-one-year-old man has been arrested by police investigating the murder of Caroline Swann in Peckham on 8 November. Mrs Swann was found unconscious with head wounds in Warwick Gardens and died four days later in King's College Hospital.' *Who*? Who had been arrested? I wandered to the long window at the back and stared at the silhouette of the cedar behind the warehouses; the sky was washed with grey and, high up, a splash of silver hid the sun. A blackbird landed in the raggedy garden where my downstairs neighbours' kids played; it hopped about tossing dead leaves aside to see what was underneath.

Gary Jackson?

The blackbird was pulling a worm from the ground, stretching it like elastic.

Or someone new?

The bird sucked, like Dan on a strand of spaghetti, and gobbled. Then stood up straight and looked around, proud and satisfied.

I phoned Charlie Ritchie – and left a message on his voicemail. He soon phoned back. 'Can't talk now. Can you make a drink this evening?'

★ ★ ★

I had to be at Laura's by 7 to take over from Juliana, who was looking after Dan that afternoon, so I met Charlie early,

5.30, at the Gowlett Arms. We sat with pints of Adnams and he confirmed what I'd suspected: Dave Lightfoot had pulled in Gary Jackson for questioning.

'Dave makes out that he's convinced Gary did it. He thinks there's a motive: resentment at the way Caroline treated him, the exclusion order, separated from his kids – blah, blah, blah.' Charlie shook his head. 'But there's no evidence, not even circumstantial: no murder weapon, no witnesses. Forensics are examining the squat where he's been, his clothing and his bike; he doesn't have a car. But,' – he paused and raised his eyebrows – 'one thing: Gary can't or won't tell us where he was that evening, 8 November, or for the two days following.'

'Where was he picked up?'

'A squat in Newham. We got a tip-off from a snout.'

'And Gary won't say where he was?'

'No. But he's got a bloody legal rep – not a solicitor. You know, one of the ones who just has a card that says "No comment".' He smoothed his hair with both hands. 'I know that makes him look guilty. But I've been in most of the interview and I reckon he has some other reason for keeping schtum. I don't know what it is, but I don't think he hit her that night. He says he would never hit her – and I kind of believe him, even though he was violent towards her a little while ago.'

Charlie's worry was that Lightfoot wanted a quick result. Avril wasn't pushing him, but he was feeling pressure from the media and the public. 'He's hoping for a confession,' Charlie said, 'but I don't think he'll get one. There are other avenues, but he's not looking at them.'

'Such as?'

'An unidentified suspect on CCTV coming out of the park gate, a man with grey hair and a receding hairline – walking away fast, hurrying, almost running, as if trying to get away from something.'

'OK. What else?'

'Well, it's clear – from her laptop, phone, social media – especially Twitter – email, bank statements, all that – that she supported a lot of causes, cared about a lot of things, issues. Not just charities, though there's a lot of giving, but . . . well, injustices. Injustices or cruelty really got to her.'

'Such as?'

'Refugees, asylum seekers, those kids in France – some of them with relatives over here, but they're not allowed in: that drove her mad – ranting letters to the Home Office. Homelessness . . . Cruelty to animals . . . Any kind of suffering – human or animal.' He held up his hands and waggled his fingers. '"Unnecessary suffering" is one of her favourite phrases.'

'OK.'

'Then there's green stuff, green activism, Extinction Rebellion, Greenpeace – some of it very specific: like woods in the Chilterns for the chop because of HS2.' He swallowed some beer and looked at me.

'So you think she had enemies? People who wanted to kill her?'

'Enemies. Yes. She didn't mind annoying people. But I don't know that anyone wanted to kill her.' He shook his head again. 'Someone was trying to hurt her – that's certain. If they'd wanted to kill her, they'd have hit her again. Probably many times.'

I winced.

'We're still puzzled about the weapon. Heavy, curved, made of iron with some rust on it. Some idiot said it could have been the wrong end of a candlestick.' He shrugged. 'Yeah, right! It might, we think, have been a weight out of a sports bag, which could mean hitting her wasn't premeditated. Maybe someone suddenly lost it.' He raised his hands, palms upwards. 'Though people don't usually carry weights around; they keep them at home, or use them at a gym. And they don't tend to rust.' He stopped talking and lifted his hands again. 'I don't like the way Lightfoot's pressuring Jackson.' He was jerking his hands up and down for emphasis. 'He's weak, Jackson, a bit pathetic – there've been tears. Of course he could have done it – but he seems like an innocent who's covering up something else: some embarrassment.'

'Well, Lightfoot can't charge him without evidence.' I shrugged. 'So he doesn't need to say where he was that night.'

Charlie grunted. He lifted his glass, drained it and put it down. He looked at the floor, his hands between his knees. I picked up his empty glass and waved it at him. He nodded. 'Thanks.'

I went to the bar for fresh pints and carried them back. 'So, what can *I* do, Charlie?'

'I dunno. I just thought when we talked the other day . . .' He tipped down some beer and wiped his mouth with the back of his hand. 'I was reminded, seeing you there at the nick – we didn't just go for a result back then. We went for the truth, worked hard for it. Even occasionally bent the rules a bit.' He smiled and raised his eyebrows.

'Thanks, Charlie.' I smiled. 'Thanks for reminding me.'

'No. You know what I mean.'

'Yes, I do know.'

'And then, if we still didn't have enough to charge anyone, we admitted it – and the case stayed open. And people knew what was going on.' He drank some more and carried on. 'I guess . . . I wondered if you could think about it. I could show you some of what we've got.'

'That's dodgy, Charlie. I'm just a member of the public now.'

'Well, I can tell you stuff, rather than show it to you. And . . . I don't know. Perhaps the girl, Ruby, and the next eldest one, the boy.'

'Luke.'

'Yeah. Luke. Maybe they're old enough to know something – perhaps they know that their mum had a particular enemy. Sunita Das has spoken to them, but if *you* asked them they might open up more.'

I swallowed some beer and put the glass down. 'OK. I'll think about it. I'm flattered, in a way – that you think I can help. My first thought is to agree with you about Jackson; I doubt that he did it. But then, most of what I know about him I got from you. I'll talk to Ruby when I can and see how that goes. I won't press her for an opinion on Jackson – wouldn't be fair.'

'Good. Thanks. And if you don't mind, I'll send you the CCTV of the man walking away. You never know. You might know him.'

We moved on then and drank our pints chatting in that leisurely way that men, especially proud fathers, who meet after work are supposed to. I filled him in on how Laura and Charlotte were doing, and then heard about his kids: his Abbie – very impressive – was playing left back for Charlton Athletic Women's reserves.

* * *

I spent the evening with Dan – reading with him and admiring his ever-evolving Lego police station.

After he'd had his favourite dinner, gnocchi with tomato and basil sauce, I checked my emails on Laura's laptop. Charlie had sent the CCTV clip: sixteen blurred, black-and-white seconds of a man hurrying along the pavement beside the railings at the edge of Warwick Gardens. The side of his face showed for about a second, and then his retreating back: grey hair thinning on top, dark jacket and trousers, gloves, light-coloured shoes, probably trainers. I ran it three times and decided I probably didn't know him – or, if I did, I wasn't recognising him because none of it was sharp and there was no detail.

I ran it again. Dan was pressing up against me. He wanted a yoghurt. 'Hang on, Dan. Just got to look at this.'

'There's a dog,' he said.

'What?'

'A dog. There. Behind the man ... or p'rhaps that's a woman.'

The clip came to an end. I was sure that was a man. But I wanted to check for the dog. I ran it again. 'Where? Where's the dog?'

Dan prodded the screen with his finger. 'There.' He slid his finger along from left to right. 'See?'

I didn't, but I ran it again, peering where Dan had been pointing, beside and a little behind the man's feet. A grey blur, lighter than the man's trousers and the tarmac road, but darker than the pavement. I ran it again. Then paused it and zoomed in.

'There. That's a dog.' Dan was almost shouting. 'It's a dog. Not a cat. A dog, Grandpa!'

And it was: a smudge of a dog, medium-sized, with – maybe, though it was hard to be sure – a curved tail.

'Good Danny! Good! You're a clever boy.' I hugged him.

He wriggled away. 'Can I get a yoghurt?' He was walking into the kitchen.

'Of course. Strawberry or peach?'

I handed him a peach yoghurt. He had always been

observant – and imaginative. He saw the shapes of people and animals and objects in everyday things – not just in clouds and leafless trees, but in gravel paths, rumpled duvets, even piles of bin bags.

'Dan. When you've finished your yoghurt, can you draw that dog? Please. Draw it how you see it.'

He didn't answer.

'Danny. Could you draw it? Please.'

'OK.' He sounded tired.

But he drew, with an HB pencil: a longish face, a thick body, a curved tail, stick legs and a single round eye, to which he added an arrow shape at one corner.

'That's brill, Dan. Thanks.'

I emailed Charlie: 'I don't recognise this man. Did you see that there's a dog beside him? I didn't, but Danny showed it to me. Here's Dan's drawing of the dog. Looks a bit like a labrador or a spaniel.'

10

I waited up till Laura got home. I wanted to show her the CCTV clip and Danny's drawing. She came in soon after two, tired but exhilarated. She'd been singing with a band called the Random Newmans in Brighton, at a tiny venue called the Green Door Store.

She threw her bag on the floor and unzipped her jacket – the black leather one that made her look like a biker. 'It went really well, Dad. They're a cool band – good musically, *really* good. And the audience were well up for it.' She waved her hands in the air. 'They loved it. Want a quick whisky?'

'Yeah! Small one.'

'I knew they were good from the practice sessions, but it went so much better than I thought it would. Real enthusiasm – from the band *and* the audience.'

She brought the Famous Grouse and glasses from the kitchen, and I fetched a jug of water. 'Thing is – do I want to be a rock chick? Fronting a rock band? Never done that before.' She grinned as she slurped whisky into the glasses and handed me one. 'It's kind of fun, and the audience are so loud and responsive and in your face.' We clinked glasses. The

Newmans, as she called them, had been around for a few years and had made three albums. 'So, there's a great lead guitar, rhythm guitar, keyboards and synths, sax – a girl, really good, playing tenor, kind of swinging sax with a lot of oomph – bass and drums. It's funky, but not too funky ... kind of Steely Dan with a bit of Chick Corea, plus some of that thwack you get with the Amy Winehouse band – you know?'

'Yeah! I can picture that – *hear* that, maybe. Sounds great.' I couldn't help grinning; she was so excited.

'I think it's probably what's called art rock.'

'Don't ask me.' I chuckled. 'I wouldn't know.'

'Might be post-Britpop.' She laughed. 'So the songs are long, with long instrumental choruses. I went and stood in the wings – sometimes for a minute or more. If I do any more with them, I'll have to play some keyboards – so I can bloody sit down.' She smiled and shook her head. 'The leader's a man called Phil who plays rhythm guitar left-handed; he writes most of the songs and has always been the lead singer. But he's never rated his own singing.' Laura pulled the corners of her lips down. 'Isn't that sad? His singing's not bad.' Phil had seen Laura performing somewhere, checked her out on YouTube and sent her a flattering email asking if she'd like to try out with the band.

'Anyway, there's no way I'd do it full-time.' She was swilling whisky around in her glass and staring into it. 'Phil has an idea of getting me on their next album and going on a short tour to promote it.' She shrugged and sipped some whisky. 'I think that would be too much – the touring. I've got other commitments.'

'Do it if you fancy it. Try it, maybe. I can always help.'

She smiled. 'You do too much already. How've you been? How's Danny?'

'Well,' I raised my eyebrows. 'Danny has been a bit of a

blimmin' hero.' I told her about the CCTV and the dog, and showed her Danny's drawing.

She stared at it. 'Bloody good, isn't he?' She shook her head and grinned. 'Sketched that from a blur, right?'

'Yep. A grey blur that I hadn't even noticed – me, the experienced detective who's meant to notice things.'

'You know what he said to me the other day, Dad? He said, "I look between things as well as at them." Isn't that amazing? I mean, I was told to do that when I was at art school . . . painting still lifes. And here he is – six years old – and he figures that out!' She looked at me. 'You didn't tell him that, did you?'

'No,' I shook my head.

'Maybe a teacher, then? Maybe Miss Pickles. She's smart.'

'Maybe. Or maybe he just worked it out.' I took a mouthful of whisky. 'It applies to more than drawing and painting, of course. He'll probably realise that too before much longer.'

★ ★ ★

I woke before the alarm. Dan – I presumed it was Dan – was clattering about in the kitchen. He often grabbed his own breakfast; when Laura went to bed late, she'd leave stuff out in case he was up first.

I checked my phone. Charlie Ritchie had already emailed:

'Thanks Jim. And big, special thanks to your Dan. Nobody else saw the dog. We're checking out the spaniel owners of south London – via the vets, dog groomers, trainers, walkers etc.

Will keep you posted.

Charlie.

PS Perhaps Dan can keep this to himself!'

I read the message to Dan – and told him not to tell the world that he'd been helping the police. He smiled a big smile and asked me to reach down a yoghurt.

I made some coffee, ate some toast and stuck around until Laura was up.

★ ★ ★

Ruby phoned. 'I don't want to bother you, if you're busy. I hope you don't mind.'

'No. Of course, I don't—'

'It's just that I heard' – she sounded agitated, perhaps near tears – 'they've arrested Gary. I don't think he could have done it.' She went silent.

'I don't have much information, Ruby, so I don't have an opinion. But is it that you don't think he could have hit her that night in the playground? Or is it that you don't think he would have hit her at all, any time, ever?'

She hesitated. 'No. No, I can't believe he would have wanted to hurt her ... well, not that badly.' She paused again. 'Even if he was drunk or coked up, whatever. Before, he pushed and pulled her around. It was horrible, but he didn't hit her. Once she fell and hit her cheek.'

'Did you see that happen?'

'No.'

'OK ... Do you mind me asking questions?'

'No. I like talking about it all. Otherwise it just goes round in my head.' She went quiet again.

'What makes you so sure that Gary wouldn't hurt your mum in a serious way?'

'I know him. I've known him for ... more than four years. I was eleven when he came to live with us. I just know in my bones that he wouldn't hurt her ... hit her, like that.' She coughed and said, 'Mum wanted Gary away from us because of the drugs. Not because he might be violent.'

She asked me what would happen to Gary. I told her that normally the police could hold him in custody for twenty-four hours unless they charged him, so he would probably be released soon – which meant later today, Saturday. But because the crime was murder, or perhaps manslaughter, he could be held longer – maybe for four days.

'Well, whatever he's done – and I don't think he would have hit her, certainly not hard enough to ... kill her – whatever he's done, he's Lily and Sammy's dad. He was a good dad for them, until he went back to the drugs. You know, he was an addict, but he was in recovery when Mum met him. He was clean for about six years. He was all right, good fun sometimes – he used to play the piano and we'd all sing.' She gave a dry laugh. 'Well, not all. Luke and Ella didn't join in.'

'Oh, why was that? They not good at singing?'

'No. They're fine at singing.' She let out a chuckle, and it was good to hear. 'They just ... aren't totally keen on Gary. He ... he tried to be their dad, and they didn't like that.' She coughed. 'There were some rows about that. Mum was sort of on Luke and Ella's side. But then Jake – you know, Luke and Ella's little brother—'

'Yes. The one who's in Dan's year at school.'

'Yes. He's OK with Gary being a dad to him – but he's much younger than Luke and Ella, so he doesn't remember his real dad. Gary did his best with all that; he picked up that Luke didn't want a substitute dad, and nor did Ella. They were like me, really, in that way. Gary was, is, our friend. That's what Mum wanted and Gary did what Mum wanted. He just worshipped Mum – thought she was awesome.'

'I expect she *was* awesome, wasn't she?'

'Yes.' I could almost hear her gulp. 'She was ... By the way, we did Jake's birthday. He was seven on the thirteenth, the day after Mum was ... hit, so we didn't do it then. But, yeah, it was good: cake, presents ... balloons, party hats.'

'Well done. I remember you were bothered about that the night we drove to the hospital.'

'God! Yes, I was. That seems *so* long ago.'

'Ten days, I think ... We were talking about Gary. So what made him go back on the drugs – and drink too, wasn't it?'

'Yes.' She didn't speak for a moment. 'Vodka. I don't know. I'm not sure if Mum knew either.'

We talked for a while longer. She didn't want Gary to be guilty; she wanted him to be able to take up his role as a dad to her young siblings. I didn't tell her that I'd been talking to Charlie Ritchie: that he didn't think Gary was guilty either.

'Ruby, are you managing OK? This is a lot for you to deal with.'

'I'm,' – she came back quickly, but then hesitated – 'all right. Kind of. My dad's here. I'm lucky, you might say. Luke and Ella and Jake' – there was a catch, like a hiccup, in her voice – 'are orphans now. Lily and Sammy ... their dad's in trouble – the police, drugs, fucking vodka. Sorry.' She went quiet and then I heard a high-pitched sob.

'It's OK.' I couldn't think what to say. I was standing by the window. I watched the blackbird skipping about on the grass. 'Ruby, I'm truly sorry that you've lost your mum, that you have to suffer like this. And I don't want to upset you any more. Shall we say goodbye for now? But ring me whenever you want.'

'All right. Thanks.'

'OK. Let's talk whenever. I hope Gary gets out soon . . . So . . . bye now.'

'Mr Domino. Jim, I mean. Can you do anything to find out who did hit Mum . . . killed Mum? Because if you can, or the police can, then Gary will be let go – and maybe he could see Lily and Sammy. And then maybe get clean again and be a dad again.'

'Ruby, I would if I could. The police are in charge; they have to prosecute whoever killed your mum. But . . . yes, I will help if they can't find the . . . attacker. If there's any evidence they don't follow up.'

There was a silence. I could hear her breathing. Then she said, 'You see, I don't know what will happen if Gary doesn't get clean and come back. My gran can't look after everyone. Me and Luke can't. Aunt Sarah can't.' She took a deep breath. 'We might get split up. I don't want that. I *really* don't. I could live with my dad in Montreal, but I won't . . . do that. I want to stay with my brothers and sisters.'

'Yes. I understand. I'll do what I can. I promise.'

'Thanks.'

'Ruby . . . phone me if you have any ideas. Like – anyone who was angry with your mum, or held a grudge against her, for instance? Have the police asked you those kinds of questions?'

'No. Not really. Well . . . Sunita Das asked if there was anyone we thought might have wanted to hurt Mum. Asked me and Luke, that is.'

'And what did you say?'

'Well, we said no, we couldn't think of anyone. It's hard, Jim – to imagine someone who would want to hurt her.'

'Yes, of course. But maybe have a think about whether there is anyone she might have annoyed . . . And call me if you remember anyone. We can chat it over and then we, or you, might pass that on to the police. That OK?'

'Yes. OK. I will.'

'Good. Bye for now, then.'

'Bye,' she said.

I ended the call and instantly felt equivocal – and a little cross with myself; I was wishing I was still a policeman – a Chief Inspector like I used to be – and running this case. I didn't know much about what Dave Lightfoot was doing, but I felt that somehow I'd be doing more than he was – with his attempt to nick the hapless Gary.

Maybe Gary *was* guilty but, like Charlie – perhaps because of Charlie's, and Ruby's, instinctive doubts – I doubted it. And that meant, among other things, coaxing information from Caroline's kids.

11

I was warming down to Toots and the Maytals' 'Pressure Drop' at the end of my Jimmy Cliff routine when the phone rang. The screen showed a number I didn't recognise. I hesitated, then answered it. It was John McCormick apologising for bothering me – and asking for work.

I was as polite as a man who has been interrupted at an inappropriate moment can be. I told him I'd think about it and tactfully asked him to send his CV as I hadn't much idea – beyond his somnolent efforts in Oxford Street – of what he'd been doing since we last worked together. As he was thanking me and saying he'd email it straight away, I began to think that he might just be useful. I had a lot on, and there was a job that I'd been putting off, and another that I – or someone – had to do in the first week of December.

He rang off. I put 'Pressure Drop' back on and did some gentle stretches, then lay on my rug, eyes closed, through 'Sitting in Limbo'.

★ ★ ★

Later, I made a prearranged call to Kylie. It was Saturday, but she wanted to talk.

'Boss, I had a couple of drinks with Nico last night. We went to a place called the Riding House Café full of stiffs; pretty pants, in fact. Anyway, during the second drink, he came through with the scam. It's what we expected. I show up with a hundred items on board; ninety-five are unloaded; he signs for a hundred. We meet somewhere; I get one piece of French kitchenware, and he keeps the rest.'

'Right. What did you say?'

'Started off saying I wasn't interested. Then I said I didn't see why I should get only one item while he got four. After some arguing, he offered me three out of every ten – complicated, three cooking pots every two deliveries. I said it seemed risky; I didn't want to lose my job ... blah, blah. He told me it wasn't risky. He'd been at it with various van drivers for about eighteen months – and no one suspected, no one checked.'

'You were miked up?'

'Of course. To show him I'm not a fool, I asked him about barcodes. "Don't they produce computerised inventory?" I said. I thought that sounded pretty smart. Anyway, he came right back: barcodes are irrelevant to this operation because they're stuck on in store. The stuff comes from a manufacturer in France and it's up to the retailer to put a price on it.'

'Kylie, you're a wonder ... So he has no suspicions?'

'Yeah, I think he doesn't. I'm ninety plus per cent certain of that.' She chuckled. 'After that he got a bit fresh, but I calmed that down, avoided the fatal third negroni, and did the deal – I get three, he gets seven every two deliveries. We talked through the logistics – and then I left ... That OK, boss?'

'Yes. Couldn't be better. The tape will do him, but we want him on film in flagrante as well. We'll bring the cops in now so they can track him to his fence. I'll talk to the new guy, Carl.'

We got into when and where this was going to happen. She would hand over the four casseroles – Nico preferred casseroles – at 1 pm that Wednesday in a quiet mews in Marylebone suggested by him. There would be hidden cameras and probably hidden police. She should just hand over the goods and drive away.

I told Kylie to take a day off, fully paid, on Monday for R and R which, for her, meant constructing video installations for a show in a gallery in Shoreditch. On Tuesday she would do what she would have done on Monday: get her nails done – all of them, fingers and toes, separately and elaborately and as slowly as possible in a swanky West End nail bar where money-laundering was suspected. 'Just sit there, watch and listen,' I'd said.

* * *

Sometime around seven Vic arrived carrying a bottle of white Burgundy. It wasn't quite cold enough – and, besides, it would go well with the linguine *aglio e olio* that I planned to rustle up later – so I put it in the fridge and poured us each a Peroni. For us, it was a rare Saturday night together; Laura was at the Vortex and Dan was having a sleepover with his cousins Lola and Leo.

We were sprawled on the sofa, Vic's head on my shoulder, the Peronis almost drunk, Keith Jarrett tinkling away with Charlie Haden on bass, when Ruby rang – and I had to listen.

She'd been thinking. She knew that her mum had annoyed a lot of people. She and Luke had been trying to think of actual, real people. So far, they had come up with two. 'A man called Grant. I think his surname is Peterson. He's a horrible, small, shouty man with a shaved head. He knocks down old buildings and puts up horrible new ones. Mum hates . . . hated, him. We went on a demo in Brixton about a plan to build a huge new tower block, just off Water Lane, you know?'

'I know Water Lane.' I coughed. 'What happened with Grant Peterson?'

'We were standing in a small group with placards: "Homes for the homeless", "Homes for Londoners", all that. Mr Peterson came over and stuck his chin in Mum's face. He knew her from other demos. "I've had it to here with you, Caroline Swann. Why don't you mind your own business? Or I'll mind it for you."'

'Did he say those very words?'

'Yes, pretty much . . . Well, that's what Luke remembers. He's got a clearer memory of that than I have.'

'OK. When?'

'About . . . six months ago. In the spring sometime. It was blue sky but cold. She'd been annoying that horrible slug of a man. He'd had to change his plans – and then Mum and her mates objected to the new ones. There were still almost no homes for poorer people.'

Then she told me about a long-standing row Caroline had with a firm of online ticket touts called Tickety Tock. The daughter of a friend of Caroline's called Steph had bought tickets at huge expense from these touts for a McFly gig at the O2. On the night, when the four girls turned up, the tickets had been ruled invalid. They didn't see the concert, and so far – almost two years later – their money hadn't been refunded. 'That kind of thing drives Mum mad,' Ruby said. 'She's part of a group that's been threatening these people, collecting information and passing it on to an MP – not sure who. Anyway, there's a man called Ed Proddo – that's his actual name! – who Mum's always talking about – well, swearing about – who I'm sure hates her.'

'Proddo? Is that right? How do you spell that?'

'Don't know. But he's high up in Tickety Tock. I could look at her computer and find out more.'

'The police are doing that, I think. But that's useful. Now look, the police should be told about these people. They *should* chase them up. It's possible they won't, either because they don't think it likely that either of them committed the crime, or because they haven't got time or enough coppers working on the case. If that happens, as I said, I'll follow up; I'll do what I can. But the police have to come first because, ultimately, they're the ones who arrest suspects.'

'Oh.' She sounded disappointed. 'OK.'

'I'm sorry, Ruby. We have to do it like that. I can't just barge in and investigate a suspect they know nothing about. But I will, if they do know and then do nothing.'

'All right. Will you tell them about Grant Peterson and Ed Proddo then?'

'I can, but they'll want to talk to you and probably Luke about them. I can start it off if you like: tell them what you've told me and that they should talk to you. Who would you like to talk to? Sunita Das?'

'Yeah. Sure. She's nice.'

'OK. I'll get the info to her. And you might find that my friend Charlie Ritchie – you know? The one who was at the hospital that night – might talk to you as well. Would that be OK?'

'Yes – if he's your friend.'

'He is. He's a good man.'

'All right. Just one other thing. Luke and me were thinking: could it have been one of the gangs who ... who killed Mum?'

'The drug gangs? No. It's not the way they do things. Even if your mum dealt drugs – which she didn't, did she?'

'No. No way.' Ruby gave a little laugh. 'But ... but – mistaken identity?'

'Ruby, I've met your mum. She didn't look remotely like a drug-dealer.' I glanced at Vic and rolled my eyes; she smiled back. 'She didn't buy coke or whatever for Gary, did she?'

'No. She wanted him off the stuff.'

Vic was standing by the window. As I said goodbye to Ruby, she turned and smiled. I poured wine for us both. We clinked glasses and sat down again. Then I told her what Ruby had told me.

'Horrid people – the worst!' She shook her head. 'Killers?' She shrugged. 'Seems unlikely.' She sniffed the wine and took a sip. 'If I had to put money on one of them, I'd go for Peterson. I mean: all that aggression, and threats in front of children.'

★ ★ ★

We lazed around on Sunday morning, and on into the afternoon until eventually Vic had to head home. I felt sad when she'd gone. We get on so well and we have a lot of fun ... But would it be the same if she were always there? Life has highlights; they don't often endure but, if you're lucky and alert and don't push at it too hard, they – or something similar – might last, or come around again. That's what I feel, at the moment, anyway – and I think Vic does too. We both have experience in these matters. Perhaps when we're old and wearing the bottoms of our trousers rolled – because we've got shorter – we will think differently.

A loud ring on my phone broke into my mood. Ruby again. She sounded calm, in a way I hadn't seen or heard before. 'We're home,' she said. 'Came back this morning, Jim. We're all going back to school tomorrow. Seems like the best thing to do.' She sighed. 'Still got Dad and Gran and Auntie Sarah with us. And we've got Tracy, our F.L.O.'

'Tracy Upcher?'

'Yeah. How did you know?'

'I've known her for years. She's lovely. I'm really pleased you've got *her*.' I meant it. Tracy is a superb Family Liaison Officer – soft and warm with the bereaved, rock hard with anyone who bothers them, including the online trolls: those strange, sad people who deliberately offend, jeer at, people who have just lost a loved one. Tracy knows how to deal with them, as well as with everything else. 'That's good that you're home again, isn't it?'

'It's sad, Jim . . . being here without Mum. I can't believe really that she won't walk in the door – smiling and telling us to clear up the mess. But . . . I know she won't – obviously.' There was a catch in her voice. 'It's so weird.' She paused. 'But, yeah, being home is the best thing now. The littl'uns have their toys and their beds and all that.' She paused again. 'And I've got' – her voice turned to a squeak – 'my . . . room.'

'It's all right.' I heard her sniff. 'No hurry. Take your time.'

She took a long breath in. 'Sorry. I'm all right. I rang to tell you: me and Luke have been talking to Ella. And she reminded us about this puppy farm. You know puppy farming? Cruelty to little dogs, taking them away from their mums too young, keeping them in horrible conditions and all that. Mum hated that.' Ruby sounded calm again. 'Anyway, Ella – only Ella; she happened to have a day off school – went with Mum to this puppy farm, and I thought it might be good if she told you about it herself – what happened – because Mum definitely upset those people.'

Ruby wanted me to hear what Ella had to say as soon as possible. 'It could be important,' she said.

12

Fifteen minutes later I'm knocking on the Swanns' door. Ruby opens it, flashes a smile and thanks me for coming so quickly. The smile fades and she turns thoughtful as she leads me down the passage to the kitchen. Shrill shrieks and giggles come from the open door of the living room, and a deep male voice says, 'OK guys. Calm down now. Who's going to start?'

'Dad,' Ruby says. 'He's looking after the littl'uns.'

Ella and Luke are sitting at a corner of the kitchen table. They stand up.

Luke says, 'Hello'.

Ella says, 'Hi,' and she looks me in the eye and smiles. Ruby offers me tea and fills the kettle.

Ella, Luke and I sit down. Ella's elbows are on the table and she holds a mug in both hands. She has a round face and long dark hair, strands of it are plaited in braids; two silver beads sit at the end of a narrow braid that falls in front of her shoulder.

I ask how they all are.

At first none of them speaks. Ella weeps a little. Luke

puts his arm round her. Ruby says, 'Not good ... Bad ... Devastated really, now that I've time to think about it – and angry.' She looks at Luke and Ella, then up at me.

Luke says, '*Why?* Why Mum, of all people?'

'The little ones are so sad, miserable.' Ella glances towards the door to the passage. 'They cry themselves to sleep. It's ...' Her lips tremble, and she lets out a drawn-out wail. Luke pulls her towards him. 'Sorry,' she whispers and wipes her eyes.

Ruby says, 'We really want to know what happened to Mum and why.' She puts a teabag in a mug and picks up the kettle. 'Ella remembered about going to this puppy farm.'

Luke prompts Ella. 'So, Ell, was it October, Mum took you there?'

'October, yeah. Just before half term. I was off school because I had a sneezy cold – but Mum took me on this trip anyway.' She shrugs. 'I suppose because there was no one around to look after me.'

'OK,' Luke says. 'Tell Jim what happened – what you told us.'

Ella looks down at the table for a moment, and then up at me. 'Well, we drove a long way on the motorway and got to this place, Marlow – and then took a long time to find the puppies, the puppy farm. Eventually we found it. It was on a sort of island in the river – by a place ... er, by a *lock*. You know *locks*?'

'Yes,' I say. 'There's a lock at Marlow. Boats have to go through it. It slows the river down.'

'Right,' Ella nods. 'So we parked and walked over a wooden bridge and found what we'd been looking for: Riverview Kennels.'

'Did you know why your mum wanted to go there?'

90

'Oh yeah! She thought there was something wrong, that they were cruel to the puppies. People had told her that.'

Ruby turns; she's stirring my tea. 'Mum had friends in the RSPCA, and PD ... SA – is it?'

'Yes,' I say. 'PDSA is an animal charity.'

'Mum had heard from her friends,' Ruby goes on, 'about these puppies, and, being Mum, got really angry – and decided to go and have a look.'

'So, what happened, Ell?' Luke prompts again.

'OK. We went in a gate, along a path; it was kind of stony. We could hear dogs barking and we got to a ... shed – kind of a shed. A big shed which was like an office. We went in the door, and there was no one there. Then a woman came – funny-looking woman, quite tall with sticking-up hair and a hair band holding it up ... If you know what I mean.'

'OK,' I say.

'The woman asks what we want; she seems a bit surprised to see us. And Mum says we want to buy a puppy. She's seen their website and they've got spaniels. Can she see the spaniel puppies?' Ella looks across at me and shakes her head with a smile. 'Mum didn't really want to buy a puppy. She just wanted to see what was going on. Typical of Mum.' Ella sighs.

Ruby hands me the tea and sits down next to me. I can almost hear her smiling.

'So the woman went away and came back with a man – a small, dark-haired man who didn't say anything. Weird!' Ella pulls the corners of her mouth down and waves her arms. 'Anyway, they'd brought three puppies to show us. Really cute. Little black spaniels. So, Mum and me, together we chose one and Mum took a photo of him. She asked how old he was and the woman said eight weeks.

Then' – Ella paused – 'what happened?' She stared at her hands for a moment. 'Yes. Then Mum said that, before buying him, she wanted to see where the dogs were being kept. She said something like she just wanted to be sure the little dog had been looked after properly. And' – Ella took a breath – 'this horrible woman said, "Sorry! We don't allow customers into the kennels where the dogs are kept."

'So then Mum got a bit cross – said it was normal to see where puppies were kept and to meet their mothers. Could she see the puppy's mother? "No," the woman said. And Mum said, "Why not?", that usually a new owner would meet a puppy's mother. And the woman got angry and then a man, another one, came. And he said that me and Mum had better leave if we weren't going to take the puppy. But Mum went on arguing.' Ella looks at Ruby and turns to Luke. 'You know what she's like.' She shrugs.

Ruby and Luke both grin and nod – and wince.

'"We love the puppy. We just want to see his mum and your kennels," Mum says.

'The man – the second one – gets cross. He says, "There's nothing more to say. You must leave now." He opens the door and comes towards us with his arm stretched out, pointing to the door. "Come on," he says. And he comes nearer. "Don't you touch me," Mum says. "We're going. But I'm going to report you."

'And the man says something like, "Fine. See where that gets you, darling."' Ella giggles – and then frowns. 'He definitely said *darling* – but it was horrible.' She shudders. 'He was shouting and almost pushing us through the door. So ... Mum grabbed my hand and we walked away, over the bridge and got in the car.'

I'm about to speak, when Ella goes on. 'Yeah, I forgot. You know how much they wanted for the puppy?'

'I hate to think. Tell me.'

'One thousand, five hundred pounds! And they can't even be bothered to look after them properly – or leave them with their mothers till the right age.'

'Dreadful. Dreadful,' I say. 'Did anything happen after that?'

Ruby answers. 'Yes, that place was closed down. Mum told us. By the police, maybe. Or would it be the RSPCA? Who would close down a puppy farm?'

'Probably the police.'

'Anyway,' Ruby says, 'don't you think these people might have it in for Mum? Ella could show you where it is. They might still be there – even if their farm has been shut down.'

'Ruby. Like I said about those other men – Peterson and Proddo – the police should investigate these things first, or at least have the opportunity to.'

We talk some more and agree that I will get Charlie Ritchie, and Sunita Das as well, to meet with us all as soon as possible – hopefully tomorrow after school, to talk about Peterson, Proddo and the puppy farm.

I walk home, wondering whether to call Charlie now, on a Sunday evening.

13

I went to bed early and got up early. I had lots to do. Business was good. I had plenty of work for Kylie and Clayton, who were on retainers, and, on the cyber side, more than enough for Stefan, who was freelance and putting in a lot of hours. The idea of a lone gumshoe working on his own was a romantic fantasy put about by a handful of writers headed by Raymond Chandler and Dashiell Hammett. Chandler wrote an everlasting paean to this mythical man, setting him up as a totem of perfection: 'Down these mean streets a man must go who is not himself mean, who is neither tarnished nor afraid.' I liked the romance of that. Of course, I had been afraid many times, and would have been many more had I not had Clayton's company – and, on occasion, that of two, or even three, of Clayton's pals: strong men trained, as Clayton was, in martial arts.

Even Philip Marlowe would find it hard to work alone in the twenty-first century. Of course, he didn't make much of a living, was frequently beaten up, often out of work and had no dependants. How would Marlowe have dealt with money-laundering and cyber fraud when he didn't even have, as I did, an elderly bookkeeper called Alice working for him two hours a week?

By 9 am I'd arranged for Sunita and Charlie to meet me, Ruby, Luke and Ella at the Swanns' at 4.30; that would give the children time for a break after school.

Then, sipping coffee and staring out at the cedar behind the warehouses, I thought some more about the Domino Agency. I needed more help: in part so I could accept the work that was on offer and turn no one away; and in part because I liked to share ideas and have other people around – call it camaraderie. I didn't want to be a manager, but I knew I could run a small team and still do real work – what Dan would call detecting – myself.

I was building myself up to offering a job, perhaps full-time, to John McCormick, which seemed odd because, as far as I knew, he wasn't really my kind of person. But, I reminded myself, I didn't know him very well, so I could be wrong. His CV made sense and I'd done a little detecting, spoken to people who had known him when he was a cop. 'A good man, quiet but always listening, attentive, with flashes of understanding,' one said. And another: 'A safe pair of hands, brainy – I think he reads a lot – occasionally inspired, not pushy, easy to work with.'

Well, I didn't want a major-general; I wanted a lieutenant or perhaps a corporal – someone with a bit of nous who would just get on with the job.

I phoned Kylie. She'd got to know him a little. What did she think? Why had he got himself fired?

'He was bored, so he got careless. It's a boring job. Hiring and firing store detectives, security staff; arranging CCTV cameras absolutely fucking everywhere; supervising people who look at screens to watch other people fiddling about in a shop. He'd done it for more than three years. He should have got a medal, early retirement, a pension and a clock.'

Kylie liked him, which meant a lot because she had strong opinions – especially about white men, most of whom she dismissed as patronising, if not racist, gits. I called McCormick and arranged to meet him. I wanted to get on with it – so he was coming to Laura's this evening at 6.30. Laura would be there until she headed out at 7, and Danny would be there all the time, of course. Danny is a good judge of character.

★ ★ ★

Ruby let us in. This time the smaller children were in the kitchen, and Sunita, Charlie and I sat with Ruby, Luke and Ella in the living room.

Charlie said how sorry he was that their mother had died – and the children muttered their thanks. And then, led by Ruby, all three of them told Charlie and Sunita that Gary Jackson wouldn't have harmed, let alone killed, their mother.

'He *loved* her,' Ella said.

'He wouldn't hit her,' Luke said.

'He's just in for questioning,' Charlie said. 'We have to look at every possibility. He'll be released soon if he's innocent. So try not to worry.'

Michel came in with mugs of tea and a plate of biscuits. Charlie and I sucked in tea and grabbed bourbons.

The three of them spoke more than we did, telling us all about their mum. They were clearly proud of her and enjoyed telling us why. And they were happy to place guesses as to who might have been angry enough to hit her and leave her unconscious. Charlie and Sunita took notes as we heard about Grant Peterson, Ed Proddo, the puppy farm in Marlow – and a lot more. She'd been in shouting matches with the English Defence League and had stood on Waterloo Bridge dressed as a polar bear for Extinction Rebellion.

'Your mother was amazing,' Sunita Das said. 'I don't know how she found the time.'

'Where were you lot when she was doing all this?' Charlie asked.

They'd spent a lot of time with Gary Jackson who, of course, had lived there with them. Their gran had turned up every Wednesday to help out and they had friends whose homes they went to. 'But Mum was always here for us – always.' Ruby said. 'She did a lot of her activism and politics stuff when we were at school – and then sometimes she took us with her.'

We left after almost an hour and promised to look into everything they had told us.

* * *

I got to Laura's a few minutes before McCormick was due. Dan was upstairs in his room playing with his friend Felix. I opened my laptop and took another look at McCormick's CV.

'So he's single – and forty-six years old.' Laura was speaking. She'd drifted up silently and was looking over my shoulder.

'Yep.'

'Is he gay?'

'Don't know.'

'Do we care? Should we care?'

'No and no – so why did you ask?'

'Don't know. Idle curiosity, I suppose. Could have asked if he has blue eyes.'

'Do we care? Should we care?'

'No and no.'

'What about the colour of his skin? You didn't ask about that.'

'No and no.' She paused. 'What colour is it, actually – just between us and no one else?'

'Shan't tell you,' I smirked. 'Wait 'n' see.'

She flapped a hand at me and wandered off into the kitchen.

The phone rang. It was Charlie Ritchie. He'd been checking into the men we'd heard about that afternoon. 'Peterson has two convictions for commissioning GBH against people who got in the way of his property deals. We'll follow him up. Proddo is extremely unlikely: just a fat cat sitting in an office ripping people off.'

'OK.'

'Er ... Now, the dog-breeders are another thing: we found them on Caroline Swann's laptop – in her search history and emails. They were closed down, which means they are likely to have opened up somewhere else by now.' He went quiet. 'Jim, I don't know how much you want to be involved in this.'

'I want to,' – I coughed – 'be involved. I *am* involved.'

'Well, unless a new lead suddenly turns up, the investigation will be run down here soon. It's nearly two weeks since the attack. Word is Avril thinks Lightfoot is using too many resources without getting anywhere. And we've got too much else on – another fatal knifing today; you get one kid for a knifing and – you know what it's like – you end up having to round up and charge four or five. Fucking tragic. So ... anyway, the Yard are involved in the Swann case, as usual, but they've got no more clue than we have. And getting Thames Valley Police to look into these dog people in Marlow will take for ever. Also . . .' He broke off. 'Hold on, Jim. Just gotta . . .'

I could hear him talking to someone. Then a muffled, 'OK, OK. Fine. From tomorrow,' followed by the clacking of heels on a wooden floor.

Then, 'Jim? Sorry, that was Avril.' He was talking more quietly. 'She wants me off the Swann case – just what I was telling you – and Lightfoot's off it too. Wants me on the latest stabbing – along with all the other gun and knife crime I'm working on.'

'Oh! Shame. Shame for the Swann children . . .'

'Maybe. But . . . it's the way it is . . . We're all on five or six cases at a time – and any that go slow, leave them open but, essentially, forget it. So . . . where was I? I was going to tell you that Gary Jackson will be released tomorrow. We'd still like to know where he was on 8 November. Anyway, Jim, if you do want to be involved, properly, I could get you a copy of the contents of Caroline Swann's laptop – totally unorthodox and between ourselves. But do you want to be that far in? Do you want to . . .'

'Yes.' I watched Laura cross the room and sit down at the piano. 'Yes. I do. But do you? You could lose your job.'

'Well,' he sniggered. 'We've done it before and got away with it. I like crimes to be solved. If you come to me with some info, who's to know where you got the lead? You'd be working for yourself or for the family, wouldn't you.'

It wasn't a question. 'Of course,' I said – and sensed the familiar sharp tingle of adrenalin in my arms and hands.

We arranged to meet the next morning in Lucas Gardens. And I remembered that McCormick would be here soon – and now it seemed to make more sense than ever to pull him onboard.

'Charlie, didn't you work with John McCormick?'

99

'Er. Yeah. He was at Eltham. Why?'

'I'm thinking of taking him on, to join the agency. What do you think?'

'Well ... He's conscientious. Tries hard ...' He laughed. 'A bit like me, really.'

'Trustworthy?'

'Trustworthy? Yes. He's straight, Jim. Decent. Couldn't be turned ... unless ... like any of us – you know the thing – something desperate – not that I'm speaking from experience ... like a seriously sick child, say, who can only be saved by an expensive op in Florida. So, yeah, as trustworthy as anyone can be is what I'm trying to say.'

'Thanks, Charlie.' I was smiling to myself.

★ ★ ★

I had moved into the kitchen while I was speaking to Charlie. In the living room Laura was at the piano gently swaying, almost whispering, 'When the deep purple falls over sleepy garden walls' – a song she loved. I could hear Danny and Felix shouting and thumping upstairs. They were coming down. I stood at the bottom of the stairs, a finger to my lips. Dan took one look and turned round. But Felix, a boy with thick dark hair and soft features, gripped the banister and stared. Laura swayed towards him – and then away, smiling.

There was a rap on the door. McCormick? No. A man with two boxes and an electronic device. I signed with a plastic stick. And McCormick appeared at the gate.

I introduced him to Laura, who stopped playing for a few seconds – and he smiled and was gracious. Then I took him into the kitchen and we sat down. I told him more about the agency: the kind of work we do; how respected we are; the others – Clayton, Kylie, Stefan; that we work hard and often work nights and take days off in lieu. McCormick had rosy cheeks, a flat nose and neat, well-brushed hair. He maintained eye contact, always looked interested and often seemed about to interrupt – though he didn't do so once that afternoon.

Felix's father collected him, Laura left for a gig in Bexhill-on-Sea, and Dan sat at the table in the living room with the makings of a Lego police car. After a while McCormick and I joined him. I fetched cold Peronis, apple juice for Dan and a bowl of Twiglets. John passed a plastic tail-light to Dan. I wrote a number on a piece of paper and asked him if he'd like to join the Domino Agency.

'Yes,' he said.

'When can you start?'

'Tomorrow,' he said and looked me in the eye.

'Make it Thursday. It might lead into an all-nighter. Would that be OK?'

'Yes. No problem. Thanks Jim,' he smiled, then leaned backwards and put his hands on his knees. 'That's brilliant. I'm really pleased.'

'So am I. This isn't the office, by the way.' I took back the piece of paper and wrote my home address on it. 'Nor is that, really. That's my home and I sometimes meet people there. The office is whichever café or pub is closest to the job in hand. But please come there on Thursday, 9.30.'

Dan got down from his chair and walked towards the kitchen. 'Yoghurt?' he said.

'OK, Dan.'

'By the way,' – I looked at John – 'Dan works for me too, and I pay him in yoghurt.'

14

Like a Soviet spy with his handler, I sat a few feet from Charlie on a bench in a quiet corner of Lucas Gardens. We held newspapers and acted as if we didn't know each other. Charlie was filling in a simple crossword; I was reading the World Cup football news in the *Guardian* – all about the wonderful Jude Bellingham and Bukayo Saka. Soon Charlie put his pen away, stood up and walked away. I picked up the Sainsbury's bag he had left on the bench and hurried off.

I unpacked the bag at home. Just two items: a hard drive holding the contents of Caroline Swann's laptop, and a sheet of paper with a list of Caroline's usernames and passwords.

I found my old laptop – the one I'd stopped using a few years ago – deleted all my old stuff, and loaded Caroline's computer onto mine, simply by plugging in the hard drive Charlie had given me.

I'd examined the contents of dead people's computers many times, but this time I felt more than ever like an intruder – perhaps because I knew Caroline Swann a little already. I spent the day looking over her shoulder as she read and wrote numerous messages over days, weeks, months and years, trying – as if I were a method actor – to feel what she had felt. So much of our lives now sits embalmed in our computers. What – these days – is not in there? Caroline wasn't actively on Facebook or Instagram. But there was plenty without them.

Riverview Kennels and its proprietor, Martin Cranley-Smith, had taken up a lot of her time earlier in the year – an exchange of texts that grew ever more threatening on both sides. The last message from Cranley-Smith came on 6 September: a text that said simply: 'You crazy bitch! You'd better watch out! You'd better mind your back.' Caroline hadn't answered; name-calling wasn't her style.

It seemed odd that Lightfoot hadn't sent someone to question Martin Cranley-Smith. So odd that I rang Charlie to check that he hadn't and to ask, if not, why not.

Charlie seemed guarded. 'Dave didn't follow it up. He focused on Gary Jackson and interviewing people locally.'

'Don't you find that strange?'

'Er . . . Yes, Jim. I do.'

'Well. I'll follow it up – obviously.'

'Good. I thought you might.' He went silent. 'Got to go, Jim. Busy here.'

'OK. Bye.' I hung up.

I thought you might. Charlie had said those words in such a way as to give them extra charge. As if, perhaps, he knew something – and wanted me to know it too.

I took another look at the laptop. Caroline had arguments with numerous people and organisations, but Martin Cranley-Smith was the most recent – and one of the most vitriolic. Cranley-Smith seemed to blame Caroline for his kennels being closed down. Well, with a little googling I found that he deserved it. He had been importing puppies illegally from Europe, giving them false pedigrees and treating them badly.

More googling revealed that, after Riverview Kennels had closed, an outfit called Riverside Kennels had opened a couple of miles away under the proprietorship of Jennifer Stephens. Then I found a record of the marriage in Newbury, five years ago, of Jennifer Stephens and Martin Cranley-Smith who, at that time, ran a pet shop in Reading.

I went back to Jennifer Stephens's Riverside Kennels website. 'Labs, labradoodles, spaniels, Jack Russells, West Highland terriers – full certificated pedigrees. Available now. Phone if interested.' Cute photographs peeked from the page.

I checked the RSPCA website. According to them, a bona fide puppy-breeder will allow – indeed invite – potential buyers to spend time at their kennels, choose a puppy, meet the puppy's mother and siblings, go away and come back another day for a second meeting with the chosen one to make sure dog and potential owner get on. Only after that should anyone buy a puppy and take it home.

I phoned Kylie and asked her to call Riverside Kennels and say she wanted to visit them with a view to buying a labrador puppy. 'Just note what they say. Don't go there.'

'I'm not going anywhere, Jim. I'm still tied up in this nail-bar shit. Remember? I'm having a pedicure at five.'

'Good luck with that. And, if they have a puppy, tell them you want to meet its mother. That's normal procedure.'

Ten minutes later she phoned back. 'A woman answered – her name was Jennifer. She didn't want me to go there, Jim. Said it wasn't convenient because they're refurbing their facilities. But she said she could meet me in a car park on the M40 at High Wycombe almost any time, and she'd bring a couple of yellow labrador puppies for me to choose from – yellow, apparently, is what they call the colour of the ones that aren't black, or brown or whatever: the usual colour, you know? I said that I wanted to meet their mum, but she said it wasn't possible and wasn't necessary. The puppies had their pedigrees, jabs and worming records and all that. They were fit and happy and ready to go. I told her I'd think about it, and rang off.'

'Thanks. Good job. Kind of what I expected. Suggests the puppies aren't being well treated. They might not even have mothers in this country, could have been smuggled in.' I explained the background, about Caroline Swann, and – while I was talking – decided that I'd go to the kennels tomorrow and talk, if possible, to Martin Cranley-Smith and Jennifer Stephens. Marlow was little more than an hour's drive.

'Take care, Jim. Can you get Clayton to go along?'

'No. I don't want to make a big thing of it. Just want to talk to the man. I can always get away.' Then I told her that she had a new colleague, John McCormick.

'That's great. I like him. He's solid. Cheers, Jim.'

★ ★ ★

It was cold that evening. The old Victorian sash window at the back was rattling. I turned the heating up, poured myself a Scotch and wrote a list.

- Why Caroline in park? Passing through? Away from main path – why? Meeting somebody? Lured in?
- Weapon? Hit with it? Or thrown at her?
- Assailant wanted to hurt – not kill her? If so, why?
- Man with dog?

- Where Jackson that night? Next night? What he hiding?
- Pepper?

I put down the pencil, put on Kenny Barron and Charlie Haden's *Night and the City* and picked the pencil up again.

- Who was Luke, Ella, Jake's dad?
- Where Caroline's father?

I sat back and realised neither of those things was likely to matter, but ... who knows? I read a little Lorca. *That night I ran on the best of roads ...*

★ ★ ★

I must have slept, because I remember waking out of a dream, a nightmare – a new one, vivid and bleak. A rerun of what actually happened – and more. Walking across the field beside Geoffrey Stark. He was uncertain, as he had been – or had pretended to be – about where Jessica's body was. Wandering about in that boggy field, and me still hoping that she wasn't really there. In the end, Stark turning and pointing. A low, grave-like mound. Earth brushed aside by a DC wearing gloves. Staring eyes, bruised skin, clogged hair – and those ants. And somehow two dogs that hadn't been there, yellow labradors, nosing around, sniffing and licking Jessica's face.

I woke up then. Shaking it off took time; I got out of bed, went to the bathroom, splashed my face.

In the morning I felt tired. I almost didn't go to Marlow.

15

The sky was cold and grey, but it was dry. I crossed Kew Bridge a little before nine. I hadn't driven in more than a month; it was good to be out in the old Merc again and I was soon gliding along the M4. I pulled into Heston Services to pick up a cappuccino, then headed west. Twenty minutes later I took the exit onto the A404. After a few miles, I turned off at the Bisham roundabout and drove slowly through the old village towards Marlow. The cloud had thinned, and a fluid pool of silver covered the sun. I wound down the window; the day had warmed up a little.

Just before Marlow Bridge, I turned right onto a flat, straight road that heads towards the wooded hills called Quarry Woods. The river was close to my left and I guessed that the gardens behind the three or four bungalows I passed sloped down to the water where little boats would be tied up, ready for a jaunt along the Thames.

The road went under a boxy concrete bridge which carried the humming dual carriageway of the A404. Down here, beyond the bridge, there was no traffic: just a bunch of rooks and a red kite floating on an updraft. At a T-junction

I turned left along a narrow road that followed the river. Old red-tiled, brick-and-flint houses stood in spacious, wooded grounds on both sides of the road. Then, on the right, a slate sign set into a flint wall, 'Combe House' – and underneath, leaning against the wall, 'Riverside Kennels' painted on a plank.

I turned through an open five-bar gate onto a gravel drive and found I was in a corner of a large, sloping field. Five or six acres of long grass were dotted with trees, many of them old spreading oaks; it was more a park than a field: a private park. The land rose towards the woods, and up there, a quarter of a mile away, at the end of the drive, loomed a grand, stone-built house with gables and a long veranda that turned the corner of the building. In a paddock, to the side, behind a post-and-rail fence two handsome horses and a small, chestnut foal stood in front of a rustic wooden building that was clearly a stable.

A blue Jaguar XE was parked on a square of gravel not far from the gate. I stopped beside it; there were no cars outside the house up the hill. In front of me, a line of scrawny saplings. Behind them, clearly visible, two small, blue shipping containers. If the trees had been planted to hide these out-of-place boxes, they hadn't succeeded yet. Why were they there, wrecking the autumnal glory of a classical English landscape?

I climbed out of my Merc – there was no one around – and walked around the nearest container. It was clean and new-looking with nothing written on it. Could this be the office of Riverside Kennels? Unlikely: it had no windows.

A dog barked, and then another. Soon there was a ca-cophony. About twenty small dogs were fenced inside a pen, about thirty yards square, a little way off behind a pair of oaks. Spaniels, terriers, labradors – all of them puppies.

I walked closer and they grew more excited, staring at me through the wire, jumping up and down and yapping. Behind them, against a fence, were their kennels, low wooden sheds with arched entrances.

A tall woman wearing jodhpurs and a John McEnroe-style headband appeared. 'Are you looking for a puppy?' Her voice was shrill.

'No. Thank you. I was hoping to have a word with Martin Cranley-Smith. Is he here?'

She shook her head and her hair, an unruly golden mop, wobbled above her headband. 'No, he's not.' She had a long face and sharp elbows, and I guessed was in her late twenties. She looked down at my feet, then raised her head slowly, apparently taking in my trousers, belt buckle and shirt, until she was looking me in the face. 'Can I help? Or pass him a message?'

I explained that I needed to speak directly to Mr Cranley-Smith and asked when he would be back.

'He'll probably be an hour or two.'

'OK. That's fine. I'll wait. Thank you.' I turned back towards my car.

'Hang on. Who are you? What's it about?'

'Jim Domino. I'm a private investigator.' I held up my licence and handed her my card – the one that bigs me up: *Former Detective Chief Inspector, Metropolitan Police.* 'I'm sorry, I can't tell you what it's about. It has to be confidential.'

Her mouth hung open as she looked down at my card.

'Perhaps,' I said, 'you can tell me who you are.'

She looked up. 'Jennifer. Jennifer ss ... Stephens' – she made a small hissing noise, like a shy snake – 'I'm Martin's wife. Are you sure I can't help?'

I thanked her and said I was quite happy to wait in my car. 'Beautiful horses,' I said, nodding up the hill towards them.

'Yes. Aren't they?' She shielded her eyes as she looked towards them. 'So precious – and now a foal.' She turned back, smiling.

'You ride them? Are they yours?'

'Oh yes! They're mine. Bertie and Clarissa. I ride them – and some friends do too.' She was still smiling. 'Do you ride, Mr – ' She glanced at my card. 'Domino?'

'No. No, I don't. Never quite found the time.' I returned her smile. 'I love the look of horses, though, and their gentleness.' I shrugged. 'Anyway, I mustn't keep you.'

I walked over to the Merc, got in, closed the door and turned on the radio.

I reclined the seat, adjusted the mirror so that I could see the gravel drive and the road behind me, and tuned in to the Robert Elms Show. I watched as Mrs Cranley-Smith disappeared through the door of the container I'd just walked round.

I let the window down and caught the scent of cut grass overlaid with gusts of thyme. Thyme in November? Apparently, here by the Thames, sheltered by the Chilterns.

The puppies were quiet now, and I watched the horses. They were lean and graceful. I thought of horseshoes, and how Caroline Swann could have been killed with one. She was hit with something curved and made of iron. Were horseshoes made of iron? Blacksmiths made horseshoes. They worked with iron.

Robert Elms was talking to Nick Lowe about his new album. Lowe was singing a new song, accompanying himself on guitar, when I heard tyres crunching on gravel. A grey van came by – a VW with a scrape along its nearside. It stopped by the further container. A beefy man with short hair and a grizzled look got out of the driver's door. Was he Martin Cranley-Smith? As I got out of my car, a younger man, smaller, dark-haired, came from the passenger door. I walked towards them and they stared full-on, like Arsenal supporters staring at the Spurs faithful at the old White Hart Lane.

Could it be? It seemed unlikely. 'Martin Cranley-Smith?'

'No,' the older one spoke. 'You want 'im? E'll be 'ere soon, I think.' He had a European accent, but I couldn't place it.

They turned and went through the blue door that Jennifer Cranley-Smith had used twenty minutes earlier. I went back to the Merc, sat down and checked unobtrusively that the dash camera still had plenty of memory.

Apart from an occasional yap from a dog, nothing happened for fifteen minutes. Then the gravel crunched again and a shiny, black Range Rover Sport slid past and parked by the van. A man with blond hair brushed backwards, and a shirt with wide stripes got out. He glanced at me as I got out of my car, frowned, and glanced away again.

'Excuse me. Are you Martin Cranley-Smith?'

'Yes.'

'Jim Domino, private investigator.' I held up my licence and offered my card. He gazed at me for a second. He was younger than I'd expected: thirty at most.

'Private investigator?' He chuckled and pretended to look surprised. 'Is someone getting divorced? I promise I had nothing to do with it.'

'It's more serious than that—'

'Look, Mr,' – he glanced at my card and stuffed it in his pocket – 'whatever your name is. I've had enough of you people – whoever you're working for – sticking your noses into my business. You lot don't seem to understand.' He spoke loudly and with a sneer, while holding the side of his neck. 'I'm running a public service.' He let go of his neck and shook his head. 'I rescue dogs, puppies, from . . . parts of Europe and provide them to people who desperately want a dog, and they give them a good home.'

'I didn't come here to—'

'Look. That's it! Enough! You're trespassing on my land. Will you go,' – his face was reddening – 'now? Otherwise I'll have you thrown out.' He pushed past me, yelled through the blue door, 'Ernst! Max! Here please. We've got trouble.'

The two men shot out as if they'd been waiting just inside the door. The big one faced up to me with his arms out, like the front legs of a pit bull terrier. The younger one stood beside him glaring.

'It's not about dogs, Mr Cranley-Smith. It's more serious than dogs. Someone is dead. Someone you had dealings with, someone you were abusive to and, in fact, threatened.'

'Oh yes. And who might that be?'

I stepped sideways so that I could see him past Ernst and Max. 'Caroline Swann.'

His face went blank. 'Oh! . . . Oh dear!' He bit into the side of his finger. 'I'm sorry. She was a nuisance. She interfered in my business. Caused me a lot of trouble.' He lifted a hand and smoothed back his hair. 'But I wouldn't want her to be dead.'

'You didn't know that she was dead, then?'

'No. No, I didn't.'

'It's been in the papers and on the radio.'

'I don't read the papers, or listen to the radio much.'

'Since you don't know, I'll tell you what happened. On 8 November, at approximately 6 pm, she was in a small park near her home in Peckham, in south-east London. Someone hit her on the head with a curved metal object and left her unconscious. Fortunately, although it was dark, she was found and taken to hospital. Unfortunately, she died four days later. The weapon was rusty and may have been an old horseshoe.' I glanced up the hill towards the horses.

'Well, I didn't do that.' He was angry. 'I *wouldn't* do that. How dare you come in here and accuse me of . . . of murder.'

'I'm not accusing you. I just want to ask where you were that evening. And it might not be murder. It might be manslaughter. It's possible that the assailant didn't intend Ms Swann to die.'

'Well, *I* didn't do it, whatever it was.' He was shouting. 'So will you please leave. Now!'

'Listen,' I said. 'I'm not saying that you killed Caroline Swann. I'm just exploring every possibility, of which you are one. Tell me where you were on the evening of 8 November – and that's the end of it.'

'It's not your bloody business. You can't come in here asking questions. You're not even a policeman. Are you going to leave, or—'

'I'll leave as soon as you've told me where you were that evening.'

'Look! I've warned you.' Spots of spit were coming my way. 'This is trespass and harassment.' He pushed at his hair. 'Ernst! Just put Mr Domino in his car.'

Ernst came at me slowly, his arms stretched out, as if he thought he could pick me up. I hate violence. It frightens me, but I had to stand my ground. I grabbed his arm – it wasn't difficult – hooked my right leg behind his knee and pushed him over. The bigger they are, the harder they fall.

Max charged. I waited till he was almost on me – my training as a riot policeman was taking over. I stepped to the side and whacked him on the chin with my forearm as he ran past. Ernst was on his knees struggling to get up.

A sharp kick to the side of his head put him back on the ground.

I don't like to hurt people, but I know how to and I didn't want either of them to get up again – not while I was there. I kicked Max in the head and then both of them hard in the solar plexus.

I was blowing hard, taking great gulps of air. If either of them got up and came at me now, I could be in trouble. Kylie's warning, 'Take Clayton,' shot into my mind.

Martin Cranley-Smith had taken some paces backwards up the hill; his face had turned from red to pale grey. And Jennifer had come from somewhere to stand beside him; she looked angry and frightened.

I said again, 'I will leave as soon as you tell me where you were on 8 November. That was two weeks ago, yesterday, a Tuesday.'

Jennifer held up a hand and whispered in Martin's ear.

He nodded and looked as if he was going to be sick.

Jennifer glared down at me. 'I'm going to fetch my iPad. We can't remember where we were.' She went through the blue door. Ernst and Max were lying on the ground grunting.

'Are you going to call off your goons? Or shall I give them another kick?'

'They're out of it now, Mr Domino.' He shook his head. 'You've got what you want.'

Jennifer reappeared. She was staring at a small screen. '8 November is the night we went for dinner at the Trumans'.' She looked at her husband, who didn't seem interested. 'The Spicers were there, James and Sue. We were there till about 11 – six of us.'

I asked for the Trumans' phone number. 'Frank and Penny Truman,' she said, and read out the number. I put it into my phone, and then their address – on the other side of Marlow, towards Henley. And then the same for the Spicers. With that all noted, I said, 'Well, thanks and goodbye.'

Martin watched me drive off. Jennifer was speaking to him, but he didn't seem to be listening. He was standing with his hands in his pockets, knees slightly bent, gaping at me. Max was kneeling, leaning over Ernst. I stuck my hand out of the window and waved, and pressed the horn. Two sharp toots: pip pip!

★ ★ ★

I drove back towards the M4 feeling a little smug. I could still look after myself. Against a couple of clowns, at least. It had been a while.

But why all that rage, that aggro? What was going on there? What have you got to hide, Mr Cranley-Smith? What is inside those blue containers? That's too much space for storing dog food – and if those were offices they'd have windows, wouldn't they?

Did the puppy business fund the lifestyle – the big house by the river standing in its own park, the flash cars, the beautiful horses? Were Jennifer's horses funded by the suffering of little dogs? Pedigree puppies sold for a lot these days – so . . . just maybe.

Or was a slightly dodgy business a front for something more dodgy and more lucrative – something that needed a pair of thugs to protect it? Big-time villains sometimes arranged things like that. Where best to conceal a big operation? Behind a small one.

If the dinner with the people called Truman checked out, which it almost certainly would, Martin Cranley-Smith was probably no longer a suspect in the Caroline Swann case. If he didn't do it himself, would he send Ernst equipped with a rusty horseshoe to attack Caroline in her local park? Come on!

But nothing was ever certain; the Trumans, the Spicers and the Cranley-Smiths could be a ring, a Home Counties, Thames-side ring. A ring doing what?

I stopped at Heston Services and went to the gents. I washed my hands properly – not just a quick rinse – squirted frothy soap onto my palms and carried out a thorough, between-the-fingers wash. I took time over it and, as I always do, I thought of Elizabeth. She liked to watch me wash my hands with plenty of soap and water and inter-locking fingers; she even said there was something beautiful about it.

I ate a chicken sandwich, drank a coffee and thought again about those two men. They were younger than me. I had left them groaning on the grass. I detest violence. I never initiate it.

Clayton sees violence – the subduing of it, anyway – as an art, a martial art of which he is a master. In that sense he enjoys it.

But Clayton isn't happy about my gun – my dad's gun. Says he won't come with me if I bring the gun. Made me promise. An easy promise to keep.

I'm smiling. I would never use the gun – but I *do* keep it . . . just in case. Or just because it's there. Like Dad. He didn't want a gun – never used it. It was just that when he was demobbed, after working in galleys below deck on those Atlantic convoys, terrified much of the time, wanted something back – or perhaps some souvenirs – so he walked away from the navy with a duffel coat, an Enfield revolver and a box of bullets.

I drove on into London.

I wanted to see inside those blue containers. And take

Clayton with me, just in case. It was unlikely to get me closer to Caroline's killer, but something wasn't right. I wanted to know what it was.

And I wanted to watch the video recorded on the dash camera. I glanced across. It was filming the traffic on the Chiswick flyover. I switched it off.

★ ★ ★

On a flattened piece of dry grass close to the doors of the further blue container was a circular wooden tray. On it were two white cardboard plates, two knives and two forks, all of them white plastic. And I could see some strands of lettuce and the remains, the stringy skin with a tinge of red, of what must have been salami. They were there: two plates – recorded on the dash camera – when I drove in, and they were still there when I drove out, forty-one minutes later.

It seemed that two people had been eating salami salad while sitting inside a container with no windows, and that their plates had been left on a tray outside the door. Who? Why? I had seen Jennifer go into the other container, and Ernst and Max had gone in there and come out again a little later to confront me. Jennifer clearly lived in the big house up the hill. And even a pair of morons like Max and Ernst would live somewhere with a window or two.

I smiled to myself. The thugs were named after a surrealist painter? Bizarre!

Or had two people eaten salad outdoors – had a picnic – and left the tray and plates on the grass?

I looked across the room at Danny. He was sitting on the sofa eating sliced apple and dried apricots off a plastic plate. Ten minutes ago he and his friend Felix had been upstairs using Laura's bed as a trampoline – until Felix's mum showed up and took him home.

Could those plates have been there all night – been used the previous evening? If not, someone had been eating salami for breakfast.

'Dan?'

He turned towards me.

'You all right, superboy?'

'Yes.' He gave me a fake smile, the one that seems to say *there's Grandpa being weird again.*

'Why would someone have salami for breakfast?'

'Eurgh!'

'You like salami.'

'Not for breakfast. Yuk!' He made a twisty face and stuck his tongue out.

'So who would have salami for breakfast?'

'Someone who really loved it.' He bit into an apricot. 'That would be a grown-up.' He chewed and looked down at the floor, at his Lego police station. 'Maybe someone who was hungry and had nothing else to eat.'

'Good . . . yes.' I thought about it. 'Thanks, Danny.'

16

John McCormick turned up at my place on time next morning. He was dressed like a bank manager: charcoal suit, blue-striped shirt, and a dark-blue tie with little grey shapes on it – fashionistas call them lozenges, I happen to know. He sat upright on my sofa. I made coffee, sat in the chair next to him and briefed him on his first two jobs.

First, Julia Fernandez: a case which, although the protagonists live in Spain, I thought of as the Italian job. I didn't tell John that I had been going to take this on myself, and was thrilled to be able to pass it on to him. Laura would be pleased too; I knew she'd wanted me to turn it down because of the time that I would have been away.

It was a routine husband-suspects-wife-is-cheating-on-him-and-wants-to-know-for-sure-one-way-or-the-other job – except that it involved élite, cosmopolitan folk. The client was a wealthy Spanish businessman called Xavier Fernandez, whose wife, Julia, was a bright, multi-lingual Englishwoman. They had two teenaged children and lived in Madrid. Julia worked part-time as an interpreter for a Spanish politician called Pablo Mora, who attended conferences all over the world. Julia went with him, translating into and out of Spanish, English, Italian or French – whichever was needed. On Monday, Julia and Pablo were travelling to Rome for three days. They would be staying at the Hotel Hassler. John would have to book himself in, follow them about and find out whether they were shagging.

I didn't say 'shagging'. I said 'intimate'.

John smirked momentarily. Then put on a wide-eyed serious face, as if it wasn't his job to smirk. He was still sitting upright, his hands folded in his lap. 'Fine,' he said; he was used to surveillance – and I sensed that a trip to Rome and some nights in a five-star hotel appealed to him, even if he'd have to spend his time loitering in the shadows. I gave him a lapel camera and some bugging kit – and told him that I'd put three grand in his account later that day. 'You'll need a lot of it for your air ticket, expenses in Rome and your bill at the Hassler. It's a swanky joint. Hope you get a chance to enjoy it. Keep all receipts. The client is paying, but don't go mad.'

Then I told him about the other job. 'A peeping Tom, John.' He pulled his lips back in an oh-gawd grimace – and for some reason that made me smile, though such matters aren't funny. 'Here, round the corner, in Peckham.'

'OK. Er . . .' He looked at the floor and scratched the top of his head with his thumb. 'What's the story?'

'A man turns up in this woman's garden two or three times a week. The woman is married and has a small child, lives in a ground-floor flat. Her husband is away from home – also two or three times a week, sometimes four times; he's a plasterer currently working in Manchester. The strange, or not so strange, thing is that the man only appears when the husband is away.'

'OK. And what does he do ... out there in the garden?'

'Usually, he stares in the window from behind a small tree on one side of the garden until she closes the blinds.'

'And that's it?'

'So far. Yes.'

'He goes away?'

'Well ... he's not there in the morning.' I sipped some coffee and put the mug down. 'It's not nice, though.'

'No.' John grimaced again. 'Spooky. Weird.' He waved his hands. Then he seemed to relax and lean back against the sofa. 'Why doesn't she call the cops?'

'All the hassle. You know what it's like.' I sat down at the other end of the sofa, the camera and the bugs sat between us in their plastic cases. 'She wants to avoid that if she can. She's a friend of a friend – she's called Amber. I'm hoping we can sort it for her. Get him arrested if we have to – but we do the work and hand him over.' I slurped the rest of my coffee. 'Another thing is that she and her husband think it could be one of their neighbours.'

'What's he look like?'

'Tall and gangly, apparently.' I couldn't help smiling. 'And she mentioned long arms.'

'Long arms!' He smirked. Then leaned forward again. 'So what do we do? Frighten him off? Or arrest him and call the cops?'

'Shout at him. Chase him away. Frighten him. And see if that works. If he comes back, then you grab him, kneel on him and call 999, and then call me. They'll come quick if we catch a trespasser.' I stood up and took my mug over to the sink. 'Or get Amber to make the calls if you haven't got a free hand.'

He blinked. 'You think this is for real?'

'Yes.' I put the mug down and walked back. 'I can't be certain, obviously. But Amber is pretty sane, pretty hard-headed. She doesn't really seem frightened. Just bothered, disturbed, puzzled. Her husband is the same, though he's never seen this guy, never been there.'

'Should I hang out in the garden or in the flat?'

'In the flat, I would think. See if that makes him go away. But you can decide when you're there.' He was looking up at me from the sofa. I took his mug. 'The other thing would be to photograph him – from inside or outside. Might frighten him off. Amber doesn't quite dare to do that. Also, photos will be useful if we need the cops.'

'And they might see from a photo if it's the neighbour.'

'Yes. They might.' I rinsed the mugs. 'I've fixed to take you round there now and introduce you. You can sort with Amber what time to start this evening – and stay in the flat or garden till it gets light. Then, please take the rest of the day off – get some rest. You're working nights till this is sorted, which may not be till after you get back from Rome.'

He stood up and grinned. 'It's good to have some real work. You know, I managed nearly 300 people in that bloody shop – most of them stood around doing nothing – and it was all admin. I'm looking forward to being out there again, on the ground. You're doing me a big favour.'

'It works both ways. I need someone right now, someone good.' I waved my arms. 'Let's go.' He shoved the camera and the bugs into a small ruck sack. 'It's a short walk.'

★ ★ ★

122

I introduced McCormick to Amber, then went home because Stefan was coming round. Stefan, the handsome geek, the grandson of a man who had escaped to England from Poland during World War II and who had fought – heroically, I'd been told – against the Nazis. We had to make sense of a tangle of contracts, deeds of trust, accounts and tax returns connected to a high-profile MP.

More interesting was that the geek – who, Clayton said, was back with Kylie – would also look into the depths of Caroline Swann's computer, at the places that the average Joe, or Jim, couldn't reach: where deleted, or hidden, files might lie.

We worked together through the rest of the morning and into the afternoon. By 4 pm we had traced a long chain of offshore companies and trusts, set up for the benefit of the man whom we had been asked to refer to in our report as 'Mr X'. Nothing illegal but, ever since Jimmy Carr, tax avoidance shenanigans haven't been popular with the voters.

I typed a report. Stefan created diagrams covered with boxes and arrows to show connections between companies and trusts, all of which led to Mr X. I sent our work to our journalist friends. They would check it, run it by lawyers, send it to Mr X and give him right of reply.

Stefan was tapping on my old computer. After a few minutes, he turned to me. 'This is *your* computer, isn't it – with a copy of Caroline's hard drive? I can see your old files, but nothing of Caroline's that you haven't already seen.' I nodded while he sucked his teeth and tapped the table. 'Can we get Caroline's *actual* computer? I might be able to find stuff. No guarantee.'

I told him I'd try, but it might be difficult.

★ ★ ★

Mike Truman was clearly expecting me to call. He quickly confirmed, 'Yes. We had dinner with Jennifer and Martin on 8 November from about half-past seven, and James and Sue Spicer were here too.'

'Can you tell me how long you've known them? Just for the record.'

'Three ... maybe four years. Met them at the tennis club in Pound Lane. Jennifer's pretty good – truly vicious backhand. Martin less so ... But he pays for his round.' He chuckled. 'What are they supposed to have done – dare I ask?'

'I can't say, I'm afraid. But if they were with you they didn't do it.' I tried to sound light-hearted. Could he be covering for Martin? Unlikely. But, *if* he was, did he know why? Maybe.

Sue Spicer seemed to have enjoyed the dinner on the 8th. 'Such fun that night. Martin was on great form. We were together from eight till about eleven thirty.' She too said that she and her husband met the Cranley-Smiths at the tennis club about four years ago. 'But why are you asking? What are they supposed to have done? Do tell. Intriguing – and they are rather dark horses.' She giggled. 'No pun intended ... You know that Jennifer is mad about horses?'

'Yes. I've picked up on that. Why did you say they are dark horses?'

'Well. Perhaps I shouldn't say ... But the dogs, you know.'

'What about the dogs?'

'The puppies. Being closed down because of some ir-regularity. And now they've started up again. What's it all about? We're all intrigued, but they won't talk about it. Just say it was a mix-up.'

'Well, I can't say. But perhaps it was.'

I rang off, wondering whether that was a genuine alibi or a carefully planned charade: was the disloyalty to her friends designed to make the story more convincing?

17

Phil Smith is an old friend and probably the most skilful dog-handler in the Met. He was sitting at the bar with a pint of Guinness when I arrived at the East Dulwich Tavern. I ordered a Peckham Pale and we moved to a table.

I told him I was investigating a puppy-smuggler and asked if it was possible to stop a large group of puppies barking if they sensed a stranger in the night.

Phil couldn't stop himself riffing about puppies exchanging glances with Frank Sinatra. Then he calmed down and told me about Trazodone. 'Pills that make dogs super-sleepy, awake but not reacting to anything – not even to thunder and lightning. Often used for dogs on firework night. You put them in, say, liver pâté or cheese and they'll eat them. They work after about half an hour – allow an hour to be sure. It'll last for about four hours.'

Phil said he would make up a Trazodone mixture and give it to me in two or three boxes. If no one was around, I could stroll up, put the boxes in the pen and come back after one hour.

But it was likely that there would be someone around.

The Cranley-Smiths lived there, although their house was about a quarter of a mile away uphill.

'That might not be far enough,' Phil said. 'Out in the country, in the quiet of the night, depending on the wind, the bark of a dog can travel. And your problem, Jim,' he chuckled, 'is how do you feed them the stuff without them barking when they see you in the middle of the night?'

Phil talked around this problem for quite a while – I'd forgotten how much he likes to talk. He wanted to know how many puppies there were.

'About twenty – not more than twenty-five,' I told him.

And he asked how big the puppies' pen was, and could I take anyone with me. One or two helpers would make it easier to spread the Trazodone around, so that all the dogs were tranquillised together and quickly.

Yes, I said. I was going to have one person with me anyway, and I could get another if that would be better.

I bought another round, and he asked more questions, about the pen, and the Cranley-Smiths' house and land. I told him about the horses.

He sucked in his cheeks and shook his head, but, after a moment said to my relief, 'Don't worry about the horses. They'll be indoors at this time of year. They have good hearing but,' – he shrugged – 'you can't worry about that.'

Eventually he said that he would make up twelve smaller boxes of sedative and the three of us should take four each. 'Crouch down as you walk across the field, no noise at all, and then crawl the last forty or fifty yards commando-style. Put the boxes in the pen, well-spaced out, and crawl away slowly and silently. If you get away with that, you can come back after an hour – or up to three hours later. They'll see you, but they won't do anything.'

I was about to thank him when he went on, 'And, Jim, if you possibly can, do this while those people in the house are busy doing something noisy – watching television, whatever. And not after they've gone to bed.'

What might the Cranley-Smiths watch, I wondered as Phil outlined this crazy manoeuvre: *Strictly, The Crown, Succession,* World Cup Football?

And who was going to come with me? Clayton, obviously. McCormick? Or Kylie?

★ ★ ★

I went home and stared out at the cedars, the warehouse and my downstairs neighbour's scruffy patch of grass. After an hour, I had a rough plan. I rang Clayton and was invited to dinner.

Before I went out I phoned Charlie Ritchie, explained what Stefan had said and asked if we could borrow Caroline Swann's actual computer.

'Tricky. Very tricky.' I could almost hear him sucking his teeth. 'He's off the case, but Dave Lightfoot would have to OK that.' He let out a huge sigh. 'Not sure I can swing that, Jim.' Another, smaller, sigh. 'I'll let you know.'

★ ★ ★

Clayton and Marie's home is a roomy nest of a place with thick-pile carpets, soft cushions, squishy leather sofas and vast television screens. Clayton is tall and strong and muscular. Marie is strong and muscular and almost as tall – perhaps three inches off Clayton's six foot four. She's a midwife and now a grandmother. She sat in the warm kitchen with the sleeping baby Naomi, while her daughter Aymee shredded some slow-roasted pork and stirred it into rice and beans and plantain.

Clayton and I sat on the porch with cans of San Miguel and I told him about Riverside Kennels, the Cranley-Smiths, the blue containers and Max and Ernst.

'Max and Ernst! Are they called Max and Ernst?'

'Yes. Yes, they are.'

'Max Ernst!' he almost shouted. 'Do you know him? We done him in History of Art at school. Dada! Weird!' He laughed his high-pitched laugh and shook his head.

He calmed down when I told him about the fight. 'Woah! I shoulda been there, Jim.' He lifted his hands and put them carefully down again on his thighs. 'I coulda saved you some trouble.' He was smiling broadly. 'But well done. You're well fit.' He laughed.

I told him about the cardboard plates and the strings of salami skin. 'I want to look inside those containers . . .'

He interrupted. 'I'll come.'

'Will you? You don't have to. This is outside the business. Just me being curious.'

'Course I'll come. That's why you're telling me all this, isn't it?' He grinned and touched my shoulder. 'I'm with you, man.'

★ ★ ★

Later, after the women had gone to bed, and after we had polished the glasses and put away the dishes and pans, Clayton and I sat outside with another beer.

It was cold. A few stars shone brightly despite the street-lights. I zipped up my fleece and told Clayton my plan as far as it went and that I wanted to get on with it – in case whatever was in those containers was moved. I would recce the Cranley-Smiths' little estate tomorrow, Friday, day and night, and again on Monday. I'd watch from the woods above the house in daylight: to see what goes on, whether Max and Ernst were around and what they were doing. During the night I'd go in closer: to find out which rooms they used after dark, whether they watched television, listened to music, what time they went to bed. My concern was the puppies – how to keep them quiet. I told Clayton about Phil Smith, Trazodone and the need for three of us to crawl silently, commando-style, across the grass.

He laughed and patted his knees. 'OK, I can do that. I can be *very* silent! And we'd better wear black and you'd better wear a balaclava. I won't need one, of course.' He laughed even louder. 'So who else is coming?'

'Not asked anyone yet, but I was thinking about Kylie.'

'Good, good.' He smiled.

'OK, I'll ask her. I'm thinking that we'll break in on Tuesday night or – more likely – at 1 or 2 on Wednesday morning.' I looked at him. 'Are you free?'

He was still smiling. 'Sure.'

'We – just you and me – when the dogs are sedated, we'll go in from the road and break into the containers. I'll have a close look and see what we'll need – bolt cutters, crowbar, whatever.'

'What does Kylie do?'

'She sits in the driver's seat ready to go. Possible we'll have to get out fast. She's a good driver – she's driven the Merc before.'

A taxi stopped a little way down the road, and people got out, laughing. The taxi drove away, passing us, and the yellow light came on above its windscreen.

'What do you think is in there, Jim? In the containers.'

Above the glow of the city, I watched a satellite moving slowly among the stars. I raised my hands in a shrug. 'Don't know . . . there will be something.'

'Something?' Clayton had turned towards me, his big hands clasped between his knees. 'Or someone?'

I looked down at the road – at a tangle of shadows thrown by the streetlights among the trees. 'Yes, perhaps someone.'

18

I phone Kylie at 8 am from Heston Services on the M4. I tell her what I told Clayton: why I went there; my confrontation with Martin, Jennifer, Ernst and Max; the alibis from the Trumans and the Spicers; the puppies; the new blue containers; the plates on a tray on the grass. I manage to condense the story into about two minutes. And I stress something that Clayton knew but hadn't waited to hear: that joining me next Tuesday might make her an accessory to a crime – trespassing or even breaking and entering.

'But we won't get caught,' she says.

'I hope not, but there's no guarantee.'

'Well anyway, I'm with you, Jim. It sounds like it might be important.'

'Thanks. I appreciate that. You're a star, as ever.'

★ ★ ★

I drive on. I'm thinking about Kylie. She'd said nothing about Max Ernst – and she's an arty person; she met Laura at art school. I'd said, 'Ernst and Max' instead of 'Max and Ernst'. That's probably why.

I arrive a few minutes after nine and settle in a line of low rhododendrons about eight yards outside the post-and-rail fence that marks the boundary of the Cranley-Smiths' land. I am uphill from, and to one side of, the house – away from the horses so as not to disturb them. I have brought binoculars, a spare fleece, water, sandwiches, Kit Kats and Rennies, and plan to stay for the rest of the day and into the night. I've left the Merc a mile away at the top of Winter Hill in a place where people park to stare across the Thames Valley to the Chilterns. From there I scrambled downhill through the spongy leaf-mould under the beeches of Quarry Wood.

It's cold; the sky is clear and deep blue, the sun high over the woods, lighting the river but leaving me in the shade, sitting, engulfed in the scent of damp earth, the trilling of songbirds and a faint thrum of traffic from the A404. Below me and to my right, the puppies sniff and snort in their pen and a couple of kayakers drift downstream towards Cookham. The house, the outbuildings, the paddock, the park and those out-of-place blue containers are still and silent; there is no smoke, not even vapour from a boiler. A light is on upstairs, in what I guess – from the positioning of drainpipes – is a bathroom. The blue Jaguar and the Range Rover Sport that Martin had driven are lined up outside the house.

Shortly before ten, without standing up, I shift a yard to my right, just to move my limbs. I kneel, sit back on my heels and peer between shiny green leaves. A door opens in the side of the house and Jennifer appears, dressed as she was when I last saw her: jodhpurs, striped sweater and that wide royal-blue headband.

She walks across the paddock and into the stable – and comes out heaving a bale of hay by the string that wraps it and drops it on the grass. Then she leads out her stallion, a tall, haughty horse with a dark brown coat and white feet and nose. She cuddles him and strokes his cheeks. Next, she fetches the mare, who is creamy brown with a dark mane and tail; she is followed by her foal. Jennifer hugs and pats them both. Is the stallion the foal's father? The pretty little thing has long legs and seems to be a mix of the two – reddish brown with white feet. Jennifer cuts the string on the bale, strews hay around and stuffs some of it into the string bags hanging on the fence.

Martin appears and walks down the drive, wearing a black, quilted coat and red – perhaps maroon – trousers. He must have come from the front of the house. I watch through my bins as he goes to one of the blue containers – the one closer to the road, which Jennifer and Max and Ernst were in on Wednesday. He pulls handles and lifts them to undo long vertical bolts which secure the double doors at the end of the container. He opens only the door on the right; it opens outwards. There is no lock – only the levers. He goes in, leaving the door open.

Jennifer is going back to the house, and the three horses are munching grass and ignoring the hay.

Martin reappears holding a bag of what is clearly dry dog food. He leaves the door half-open and goes over to the puppies' pen. The dogs yelp and jump up as he fiddles with a latch and opens the gate – and go quiet once their bowls are filled.

Could Clayton, Kylie and I open that gate in the dark and put the Trazodone down without causing those puppies to kick off?

No. No chance. But the fence – the flimsy chicken wire that keeps the puppies in the pen – is four feet high at most; we can reach over and put the boxes down. We'll go in through the gate from the road, cover fifty yards at a running crouch, and crawl the last fifty silently on our bellies. When we're close to the wire, we'll space ourselves out along it, slowly stand up and lower the boxes over the fence to the ground.

Martin fills the dogs' water bowls from a hose, takes the bag of dog food back to the container, closes it and trudges back up the hill. And I find I'm wondering if I've got this wrong: are those containers just containers – for storing nothing unusual?

At about 10.30 Jennifer drives downhill in the Range Rover. She picks out three spaniel pups, sticks them in the back of the SUV, opens the five-bar gate to the road and drives off leaving the gate open. A few minutes later Martin puts a sports bag in the Jag and roars off towards Marlow. Jennifer comes back soon after 11.30 with just one spaniel; she holds it by the scruff of its neck and dumps it back in the pen with the others. Martin returns at 12.20 and, for a long time, nothing happens except an occasional squeal from the puppies. I munch a chicken and avocado sandwich and retreat into the wood to piss silently into the gnarled crevices of an ancient beech.

At close to three o'clock I crack open a Kit Kat. I'm biting into the second stick when the grey van with the scrape along its side – the one that Max and Ernst arrived in two days ago – crunches across the gravel and stops by the other container – the one further from the road and nearer to me now, the one outside which two plates with salami skin were left on a tray two days ago. I drop the Kit Kat and pick up my bins. No one gets out of the van.

Then I see Martin walking down the drive from the house. As he reaches the bottom of the slope, Max, the smaller of the thugs, climbs out of the van. It seems he is on his own. Martin opens the door of the container – by pulling handles, just as he opened the other container – and stands idly watching as Max struggles to carry a large, flat cardboard box into the container. Max is sweating and his dark hair looks a little greasy. This box – whatever it is: a trestle table? – is followed by two packs of bottled water and a large green Marks & Spencer bag containing groceries. I can see a loaf of sliced bread, the top of a cereal packet and a jar of what might be sauerkraut. Max and Martin exchange a few words, and I see Max smiling. He goes to the van, pulls out something and turns to walk back. He's carrying a bunch of chrysanthemums! I can see them clearly – red, yellow and orange, with their stalks wrapped in brown paper.

What's happening in there? *Who* is in there? Whoever they are, they need food and water. But flowers!

Are they hiding? Or are they being hidden – against their will? That container isn't just for storage. How many of them are there? What, who, is in the other container? It can't just be for dog food.

Then I have doubts again: *could* they be storing groceries, flowers and flat-pack furniture?

No. There's someone in there. Must be.

Max drives off through the gate. Martin closes the container and walks, arms swinging, uphill to his mansion.

I pick up my Kit Kat and blow earth off it. What to do? *Someone* is in there.

Jennifer comes out and spends many minutes brushing, then saddling and bridling, the two adult horses. While she does this, a woman drives up in a black VW Golf GT and parks in line with the Jag and the Range Rover. She gets out, shakes her head and scoops her hair back and over her shoulders. She's wearing jodhpurs, riding boots, a white shirt and a natty little black jacket. She jogs over to

Jennifer and stretches out her arms. After a quick two-sided cheek-to-cheek, both women put on riding hats and swing themselves into the saddle: Jennifer on the stallion, her friend – perhaps she is Penny Truman or Sue Spicer – on the mare. They trot for a moment, then break into a canter and zigzag downhill to the open gate. They slow their horses to a walk and follow the road to the right along the river. I guess they will turn onto a bridleway through Quarry Wood and perhaps reach the flood plain that, on my map, is called Cock Marsh.

Only Martin is here. I think about creeping onto his land behind the blue containers and breaking in right now. I want to know who's in there and why. Someone to whom Martin gives flowers.

But that would be daft. Better go in at night with Clayton and Kylie – and tranquillise the puppies first. But it can't wait till Tuesday – four days, four nights, from now. Whoever is in there might move on, or *be* moved. Two plates, two people. Friends of Martin and Jennifer – villains they're hiding? Or – who?

19

It's growing dark. A clear sky, a bright star in the west above Bisham, and others, more muted, across the river.

A light comes on in an upstairs room and I see Martin in the window, just for a second.

The women come back, unsaddle the horses, brush them, wrap them in blankets and shut them up for the night. Both go into the house and three deep windows to the left of the front door light up – the living room perhaps. Soon smoke swirls from a chimney.

I text Clayton. 'Can you come out tomorrow night – Saturday instead of Tuesday? Understand if not. Sorry about short notice. Looks urgent. Jim.'

The light upstairs goes out. Perhaps Martin is joining the women. My phone vibrates. Clayton: 'OK. Can do. Be careful! Clayton'. A few minutes later, light comes from somewhere on the far side of the house and lights up the trees.

I text Kylie.

After almost an hour inside, the horse-riding friend comes out and drives away, her headlights raking the grass.

Martin appears and walks downhill, swinging a torch from side to side. He closes the gate to the road; it doesn't have a lock. He lets himself into the container – the one where he stores dog food. He feeds the puppies, puts the food away and comes back to the house.

I put on my spare fleece, eat another sandwich and wait. I think about Dan and Laura. A memory surfaces: Laura talking about Saturday. Am I babysitting? I check my phone. Yes. Shit! Laura has a gig with the Random Newmans.

I text Laura: 'Really sorry, love. Any chance Juliana can do tomorrow night? Routine job has suddenly turned urgent – but of course will postpone if necessary.'

Laura replies instantly. 'Will try Juliana. If not, he can probably go to Charlotte. Otherwise I'll pull out. A little awkward. They've put me on the bill and sold tickets.'

I wait some more and get colder and feel bad about letting Dan down as well as Laura. I retreat into the wood, stretch my biceps behind my back and push against a beech to flex my calves. I decide to leave this job till Sunday or later, rather than make Laura miss her gig.

The lights go out at the front of the house and stay on at the side. I edge round keeping under the trees and well back from the fence. Light from French windows shines on a veranda which looks west towards a bend in the river. I crawl under the lowest rail of the fence. I want to see in. A green oil tank – plastic with grooves along its sides – stands on a square of concrete. I climb onto it and peep over the top into a large kitchen: an Aga and one of those posh islands with high stools beside it, a palm tree in a pot and a large print of that painting of a butler and a maid on a beach holding umbrellas while a couple dance. Jennifer appears from the right. I duck down and peek round the raised lid of the tank. She looks down at something on the island – perhaps a recipe – then pulls a small copper saucepan from a ring of pans that hangs from the ceiling. I duck down again and move sideways along the groove in the tank to get a better view. I find that I'm looking down at the back of Martin's head as he sits on a sofa watching England play the USA in the World Cup on a huge flat screen. It's as if I'm in the row behind him as Harry Maguire heads the ball away from a corner. Martin is holding what looks like a gin and tonic and has his knees crossed; he's still wearing the red trousers.

It's half-past eight. Jennifer puts a bowl of salad, two plates and some shiny cutlery on the kitchen island. Martin sits down on one of the stools and sips his drink. Then he stands up and pulls a cork from a bottle of red wine. He walks away and comes back with two wine glasses. Jennifer brings a bowl of potatoes and a steaming casserole, and the two of them sit down.

I cling to the oil tank, cold and uncomfortable – and wonder if I want to watch these people eating. My phone vibrates in my pocket. I drop back to the ground. Kylie: 'Tomorrow night OK. Don't stay out there too late Jim. It's cold. Frost forecast. And we could be up late tomorrow.' She's right, but I want to see what time the Cranley-Smiths go to bed and in which room. I slip back through the fence and up into the trees.

Ten minutes later, Laura again: 'It's OK. He's going to Charlotte. He likes that.'

Tomorrow night, then, with Clayton and Kylie.

A little before midnight the kitchen lights go out and lights go on upstairs. The Cranley-Smiths' bedroom is above the kitchen, around the side of the house, away from the front door and not looking downhill towards the puppies or the blue containers; it must have a view of the river, upstream from the stretch that can be seen from the front of the house. As I watch, someone closes the curtains – but not quite; a beam of light shines out from a gap in thin, pink curtains.

I'd like to know if the bedroom light can be seen from anywhere on the road, but I can't walk across the Cranley-Smiths' land to get there in case I rouse the dogs. Instead, I move downhill again to the fence and follow it westwards for about thirty yards to the edge of the wood. From there the fence continues west along the line of a field. I climb over it and head north towards the road.

I'm still high up – and in the neighbours' garden, it seems. A large house with tall, square chimneys looms in front of me, but there are no lights showing. Stars twinkle in a deep-black sky and I can see the glow above Marlow to the north and west. The dim, parallel lines of the A404 cross the valley, and a solitary set of tail-lights speeds through the darkness towards High Wycombe.

Shall I walk across the garden to the road? It's big – a large field like the Cranley-Smiths'.

Perhaps there are no lights here because the neighbours have gone to bed. But they may have a guard dog – or an alarm system. Or both.

I walk fast, eyes and ears on full alert. Even so, I almost walk into the back – the stern – of an old clinker-built boat that seems to be suspended in the air, perhaps on a trailer. I touch it. It's sticky – and there's a smell of varnish. Could this be a boatyard? I saw no sign when I drove past on Wednesday. I keep walking over rough grass following the line of a tarmac drive – and come to a high wrought-iron gate. It's padlocked with a chain. Beyond it is the road. If I climb the gate, it might rattle. To either side, trees and shrubs and a ten-foot wall. I move along slowly, touching the wall in the dark. It feels old. Maybe find some uneven bricks that would help me climb it. I come to a big tree with low branches – an oak from the feel of the bark. Higher up, a fat branch against the dim light in the sky. Climb. Feel your way.

I lower myself onto the wall, then jump and roll, a parachute landing. And find myself on a grassy verge. Lucky.

I cross the road and look back, uphill towards the Cranley-Smiths' house, more than a quarter of a mile away. I can see the bright ray of yellow light and even the faint pink glow of those curtains. It's 12.15. I stand under a weeping willow on the river side of the road and wait, silently stamping my feet and swinging my arms to keep warm. After ten minutes the light goes out.

So we'll dope the puppies at 11 pm. And break in sometime after 1 am.

I go back to the junction and walk slowly uphill under a glittering sky: Orion, the Plough, the silver smudge of the Milky Way. Weird, I think, that I'm out here in the middle of a cold night because a woman was murdered in a park in Peckham – a woman who was concerned for the welfare of puppies. At last I see the Merc, and walk more quickly.

I drive back down the hill and past Combe House. I'm looking for somewhere to turn the car tomorrow in the dark, without headlights, and for somewhere unobtrusive to leave it while we drug the puppies.

That done, I drive back uphill and through sleeping Cookham and Maidenhead to the M4. A bacon sandwich and strong tea at Heston Services, and home about 2.30.

20

Perhaps the tea was a mistake – or the bacon. But I'd be awake anyway – wouldn't I? There's so much to think about. Why am I doing this? It's trespassing. Therefore illegal. Why am I dragging my friends into it?

There's someone in there – I'm almost certain – so I have to find out. But I could just get the local police. But how quickly?

Get up, suck a Rennie, put on Miles, *In A Silent Way*.

I'm not doing this because it's exciting. I've not taken risks for fun for years. It's *not* exciting ... It's making me tense. Something is wrong. If I don't act quickly – like as soon as possible – something bad will happen. *Might* happen.

Why is Cranley-Smith so aggressive? Why does he employ those hopeless goons? Because he's got more than puppies to hide.

The local cops wouldn't act quickly. They wouldn't handle this as well as I would – whatever *this* is.

Really? Are you sure? ...

Yes. Almost sure.

And what are you going to do with whoever is inside there?

Stop thinking. Lie down. Pull up the duvet. Pull it right up. Listen to Miles.

★ ★ ★

A horrible dream. Jessica. Looking down at her: staring eyes, bruises, orange ants on her face.

Turn on the light, get up, fetch water – and remember the field in the dream, a strange field in a green valley, no trees. Not the field Stark took us to, where we found her.

Why? Why dream about Jessica now? It happened almost four years ago. And why is Jessica in a new field – a field I don't recognise?

Lie back down. Relax. Sleep.

★ ★ ★

The alarm wakes me – at eight. I text Kylie and Clayton and fix to meet them at the Crossroads Cafe at nine. I'm very grateful to them both. I'll buy them late breakfast or anything they want.

I shower, drink a coffee and dress in black; I stuff my balaclava in the pocket of my bomber jacket. Before I leave I go to my toolbox and look at its contents. The containers weren't locked. But they could be – those handles have holes for padlocks. I pick up bolt cutters, the medium-sized crowbar, the big standard screwdriver and the old felt bag with pockets that stop tools rattling against each other. I notice my favourite adjustable spanner – the small one – and grab it. I squeeze in a length of rope and cut and roll three short lengths of gaffer tape just in case we need to gag anyone noisy. Will I need a torch? I pick up my Maglite, flick it on: enough beam to blind a herd of elephants. I put the bag and the torch in the boot of the Merc, beside the twelve boxes of Trazodone mixture prepared by Phil, and drive to the café.

Kylie is already there, bright-eyed, dressed all in black, sipping at a cup of milkless tea, and eager to hear more about what we are going to do. 'I've cleared the day and,' – she pauses and grins – 'the night.'

'Oh! Well, I don't want to interfere with—'

'It's fine, Jim.' She's still smiling. 'Absolutely fine.'

Clayton arrives. He and I order eggs, bacon, toast, marmalade and coffee; Kylie asks for a croissant. Andy, the waiter, brings our food as I sketch the layout of the place in my notebook: the road, the river, the house, the woods on the hill behind, the horses, stable, paddock, the puppies, pen, kennel, the blue containers, the black Range Rover Sport, the blue Jaguar, the grey van. I try to eat as I explain.

Then I tell them what I saw yesterday. When I get to Max carrying food, water and flowers into the container, Clayton's eyes widen and Kylie says, 'Jeez, boss!' She taps the table with a fingernail. 'So there is someone in there. Locked in by those bolts.'

'Well, it seems likely. And that's why I want to act tonight rather than next week.'

'Flowers!' Clayton's mouth is full. He gulps and swallows. 'So there's a woman in there. Fuckin' hell, Jim.'

'Why a woman?' Kylie glares at Clayton and then grins. 'Oh. OK. A *person* in there.'

'But why,' – Kylie taps the table again – 'is anyone in there? Kidnapped for ransom, do you think?'

'I don't know.' I raise my hands, palms up. 'There might well be more than one person. There was plenty of food and water along with the flowers.'

I fill them in on what happened after dark: when the

lights went on and off, and where the rooms in the house are. And I outline my plan for the day and night.

I stop talking and look across at Kylie. She's sitting back with her palms on her temples pushing back her braids. 'So, boss, if there are people in there, what do we do?'

'It depends who they are. How they are. What they want. We might lock them back in and fetch Thames Valley Police.'

'Would they come quick enough?' Clayton is frowning.

'If these people are crims, I hope I can persuade them to. Yes.'

'If they're criminals hiding from the law, you mean?' Kylie says.

'Yes.'

'Then why are they locked in?' Kylie shakes her head. 'If they're mates of the Cranbourne-Smiths?'

'Cranley-Smiths. I don't know. They may not be crims.'

'I don't think they're crims.' She swallows some tea. 'But what are they then?' She stares across at me. 'They, or she or he, must be people who are being held against their will, been kidnapped.'

'Maybe.'

She pulls at her croissant. 'But if they are victims, imprisoned there, what do we do? Release them?'

'Yes. Probably. Get them into the car, if there aren't too many of them, and take them . . . somewhere. Probably the cop shop in High Wycombe. Or lock them back in, as if we haven't been there, and fetch the cops.'

Both of them grunt as if they don't like that last suggestion. Clayton is frowning again.

'Look,' I say. 'We'll have to decide quickly. And get them in the car and away fast, if they want that and we think it's right.'

146

'You decide, Jim.' Clayton gives a little sigh. 'There won't be time for a discussion.'

* * *

A little before noon we leave the Merc on Winter Hill and walk down through the woods. We sit in a row among the rhododendrons, peering through the leaves at Jennifer, who is grooming her stallion while the mare and her foal mooch about in the paddock. The Jag is outside the house but not the Range Rover, which suggests that Martin is out somewhere – and the gate to the road is open. No grey van and no Max or Ernst. A couple of puppies yelping.

On the river, a white fibreglass cruiser – pointed prow and slanty, assertive windows – cruises upstream towards Marlow Lock carrying a family, a dog and a dad in a nautical cap. As it glides out of sight behind trees, another similar boat comes into view. And then another. It's the end of November. The sky is grey and the air is cold. But fun on the river goes on.

I hand the binoculars to Kylie; she studies the house and then turns downhill to the puppies and the blue containers. I whisper and point to the stretch of rough grass between the gate and the dog pen that we must cross in the dark, with four little boxes of sedative each.

Jennifer puts her combs and brushes away in the stable. The stallion wanders over to the mare, lines himself up alongside her and bends his neck, as she does, to nibble grass. Jennifer goes back to the house and in at the side door, about twenty yards from where we are sitting. Kylie hands back the binoculars and I pass them to Clayton. The three of us sit in the rhododendrons for a few more minutes. Then I lead them back into the wood and around to the other side of the house.

147

We stay under the trees where the shade is so thick that we can't be seen. I point to the kitchen window and then to the windows above it. The pink curtains are drawn to the sides and cinched in their middles like a pair of belted dresses. 'Bedroom,' I mouth the word to Kylie, and again to Clayton.

I look downhill. The blue containers are at least 400 yards away. I'm thinking about the break-in. As long as we're quiet and these people are asleep, we should be all right.

My mind moves on to the commando squirm with the boxes of sedative. Then, I hope they'll be in the kitchen – also on the further side of the house – absorbed in World Cup football, with the sound turned up; or maybe they will watch Stormzy and Joan Armatrading, who will be on *Jonathan Ross* – I checked.

We walk up through the woods to the car park on Winter Hill and drive – Kylie drives – back down, past the junction at the bottom of the hill and into the lane that runs along the river. As we pass Combe House, I duck down in the back in case the Cranley-Smiths or their thugs are standing around. I peer from behind Clayton and show Kylie the place I spotted late last night: a broad, shared entrance to two houses where it is easy to turn.

As Kylie makes a quick three-point turn, I tell her, 'Tonight, after you drop us off, turn here, drive back and wait just past the gate where the car can't be seen from the house. Lights off all the time.'

'OK. I guess I'll be able to see enough.' She begins to mumble. 'Bend left, big tree on right, bend right, straight, gate to Cranleys on left, stop.' She drives on. 'Got it.'

At the junction at the bottom of the hill, I ask her to turn right towards Marlow. We soon come to a locked and unused entrance to a place where kids go to camp and have fun on the river. This is where we will leave the Merc during our first visit to Combe House tonight.

We drive up the hill now. Kylie drops me off at the start of the path that leads down into the woods – and the two of them set off to spend the afternoon and evening in London.

21

M y face is brushing the leaves – leaves that are now so familiar, I'm recognising them individually: their spear-like shapes, their shades of green and their harsh, spicy smell. The earth, too, is familiar – soft and smelling of beech mast and leaf mould.

The Range Rover is there, but not the Jag, nor the grey van. They both drive both cars, so either one of them is here alone, or they have gone out together and no one is here. And nothing is happening, unless you count horses snuffling and dogs yapping.

The blue container? Something *is* happening in there. You just can't see it. See them. Someone. Or more than one.

A boat on the river. People – a couple – walking slowly on the towpath on the other side. Young couple, no dog, just them, holding hands. They stop. She points. A swan glides into view.

Eight hours of cold and damp – until I see Clayton and Kylie again. And then we go for it.

You're breaking rules again. Breaking the law this time. You broke the rules to save Jessica. And to catch a serial killer. You caught him but didn't save her. And you were suspended. Now you're doing it again. Why – when you could be on the riverbank walking with Vic ... or Danny?

To find something, someone.

And your friends will break the law with you. For you.

And time passes. And nothing happens.

Hello! The van. Stopping by the containers. Max gets out – just Max again, no Ernst. He pulls and lifts those handles – that's all we need to do! – and goes in. He leaves the door ajar – and no one comes running out.

Five minutes ... six minutes ... and he comes out carrying a grey plastic box. He closes and bolts the door. I grab my binoculars. The box has a plastic pipe coming from the top of it. Max is carrying it up the hill towards the house. He's walking slowly, holding the box carefully in both hands. The pipe has a lid. Max keeps walking. It's a long way. What's in the box? He seems to be terrified of dropping it.

Maybe ... *It could* be a tank from some kind of camping toilet, a tank full of piss and shit.

My God! I'd been thinking: if there's someone stuck in the container – not going out – there has to be a toilet. Kylie said that too, this morning. I *think* that's what it is. Why's he taking it to the house? To empty it. The pipe is for pouring.

He's not that far from me now; he's reached the side door. He's pressing a bell. The door opens. Jennifer. She stands back, holds the door. In he goes.

Six minutes. And out he comes. Little bloke. Dark hair. He's holding it upright now, with one hand. It's much lighter. It would be, wouldn't it. Walking back downhill. Couldn't he get a better job than this? Into the container.

And out again. Closes bolts – no padlocks. Wipes his

hands on his jacket. And gets back in the van. Drives off through the open gate.

And time passes. Lights on in living room, 4.35.

★ ★ ★

Dark now, 5 pm.

5.45, car. The Jag. Stops by blue containers. Person with torch gets out. Martin. Dog food from other container. No padlock on either container. No need for wire cutters. Martin feeds dogs – some yelping, not much. Back in car, drives up towards house. Headlights. Keep down.

Parks by Range Rover. In front door. Hall light on.

Gate still open. Good. With luck it'll stay like that.

Hall light goes out. They're both in the living room at the front. Are they going out tonight – Saturday – or staying in? I'd almost rather they stayed in, because then I'll know where they are – and that they're not going to drive in, headlights blazing, when we're doping the dogs.

Stars to the west, cloud directly above, no moon, glow from Marlow. Outlines of buildings, trees, the river. Cold. Eat sandwich. Drink a little water.

★ ★ ★

Nothing. Quiet and boring. Wondering whether to change plan and have Kylie with me when I go into the container. In case there's a woman in there. Kylie might reassure her. Anyone who is in there must keep quiet. But ... take Clayton as well, in case there are several huge men! Armed men? No! If you shut someone in a container, you take away their weapons.

Beams of light on the road outside the gate. Swerving in. The grass lit up. Dazzle. Close eyes. Duck! It's the van. Stops beside the Jag. Porch lights come on. Max – just Max, no Ernst. Someone opens the front door. He goes in; he's carrying a small bag. Door shuts.

Light on in a gabled window, two floors up. Drop back into the woods and move round. Small window. Yellow light. Someone – Max, I think – standing by window beside open curtain. He lowers a blind. Then closes curtains. Little light coming through now. But enough. It goes out. It's just eight o'clock; he can't be going to bed now.

But: carrying a bag, and a room upstairs. Is he staying the night? Why? He didn't stay last night.

Does Max showing up affect us? No. Maybe something is going to happen in the morning? Or very late tonight? So . . . we'd better get on with it.

* * *

Lights on in kitchen – nearly half-eight. Light on road again, and something comes through the gate. Busy here tonight. One light. Motorbike. Coming this way. Get down. Scooter. Futting. Up to front door. Two white bags. Takeaway.

Jennifer at the door. Puts something in his hand. A tip. Scooter away, through gate. Futting into the distance back to Marlow.

So they're eating in. Probably Indian: papadums, naan, rice, tandoori something, vindaloo for Martin.

Creep back into wood and round. Under fence, onto oil tank. They're all there. Jennifer and Max in front of the butler on the beach. Martin sitting on a stool, with a glass of red wine and a bottle. Silver foil containers of food on the Aga. Max wearing a clean blue sweater and he's brushed his hair.

* * *

153

Go now. Find Kylie and Clayton. Can't go up through the wood in the dark. Across field behind neighbour's house, over gate, into road.

Trudge up the hill – long hill with hairpins. Stars above. Some light away from trees. It's cold. Breath comes out like steam and drifts upwards.

Why? Why do this?

Have to do things, *do* something – useful.

Pathetic ... No, not really. Millions subsist on doing something useful. Same as wanting Chief Inspector. Wanting more ... usefulness. Since Elizabeth went ...

Just say it: since Elizabeth died. When she was here, regular work – and overtime for the money – was enough. No extras. Sixteen years now – and still ...

What else to do? Look after Dan, Laura ... Charlotte, Lola, Leo ...

Vic ... Give more to Vic. She wants more. She doesn't say, but she does. I know ... Well, I *think* I know.

Top of the hill. Flat from here. Thank the Lord!

Funny: Vic looks like Clotilde Sorolla, dark-haired and slim. Yet Clotilde with her daughters is Elizabeth to me.

★ ★ ★

The car's there. No lights. They're there – sitting in the front. Open the door and get in the back.

'Hello, guys.' I'm whispering. 'What've you been doing?'

Kylie has had a sleep at home. Clayton's been play-ing with Naomi and watching Argentina play Mexico. 'Amazing goal by Messi, Jim. You have to see that.'

We drink tea – Clayton has brought a big flask. I eat a sandwich and tell them about Max emptying the toilet.

'Eurrgh,' says Kylie.

'So there's definitely someone there,' I say. 'And it looks

as if Max is staying the night. His van's parked outside the house and he seems to have a bedroom upstairs. Last I saw of them, they were eating a takeaway in the kitchen.'

Clayton has turned in the passenger seat to look back at me. 'Maybe they're planning something for early tomorrow,' he says.

'Yes. Maybe.'

At half-ten we drive down the hill and park outside the locked and unused gates of the kids' campsite. Then we walk. And with our little rucksacks and walking boots, we look like hikers returning late from a day out in the hills above the river – except that all three of us are dressed in black and I'm carrying a balaclava. The only sound is the intermittent hum of traffic on the A404. We turn left towards Combe House and pass the willow where I waited for the bedroom light to go out last night. There's no light there now. I want them to be watching telly with the sound turned up.

I hold up my hands. We've been over this a few times. Get into formation. Gloves for all of us; balaclava for me. Clayton ten feet to my right. Kylie to my left. Crouch. Walk quickly. Don't run.

We cover about fifty yards fast. I lower myself to the ground and they copy me. I think of what my friend Phil Smith the dog handler said, and work my way forward commando-style on elbows and knees. It's slow going, and the ground is cold though not damp. There are no sounds bar a distant rumble from the road. I can make out Clayton and Kylie: dark shapes sliding slowly forward.

We get there. It seemed to take an age, probably about ten minutes. The wire fence is in front of us. A dog yelps – not loud, from surprise rather than anger. And then another. I move to a crouch, tug off my rucksack and grab the four boxes. Lids off two, lean over the wire, lower them to the ground. Scrabbling, yapping, a growl. Move to my right and position the other two. More whining. More scrabbling. Rucksack back on, turn, lie down on my front.

Look to my left, beyond Clayton, uphill. No one charging towards us yelling. Three windows at the front of the house lit up – the living room – and a beam from the side, the kitchen. Still, nothing has changed. Look to my right. Kylie moving on elbows. She sticks up a thumb and I see, or imagine, a grin.

Again, ten minutes. Again, a running crouch. And we're away, through the gate. Into the lane. Silent high fives. And fast walking. When we reach the Merc I grab them both by their shoulders, pull them towards me: 'Bloody good! What a team! Thanks, comrades.'

22

Kylie drives us back up to the dark and empty parking place on Winter Hill. She kills the engine and turns out the lights. Clayton is in the passenger seat. I sit in the back. We congratulate ourselves, and Clayton and I each swallow a thimbleful of whisky from my flask. 'Later, maybe,' Kylie says.

I lean forward between the front seats and tell them I've decided that I'd like Kylie to be there when we go into the container, because there might be a woman, or women, inside. I turn towards her. 'Would you be up for that? We can't afford whoever is in there to make any noise. You might reassure them.'

Kylie is peering at me over her shoulder.

'Men as well as women,' I add quickly.

'Of course.' She grins. 'Actually, I was a little disappointed that I had to sit in the car while you guys had all the fun.'

'Well that's OK, then.' I turn to Clayton. 'But I want you there as well. Who knows what horrors are inside that door. I've brought rope and gaffer tape, in case we run into bother.'

'OK,' he mutters. 'OK.'

'So all three of us bust in: me, then Kylie, then you, Clayton.'

'And what about the car?' Kylie asks.

'We leave it in the same place, by the hedge, just beyond the gate – where we went this morning.'

'And who drives?'

'So we have a clear plan, let's say I drive. You in the passenger seat,' – I nod at Clayton – 'Kylie in the back. If we have anyone else with us, we might change that, depending who it is. OK?'

They both mumble agreement.

'Key stays in the ignition, ready to go.'

Headlights loom out of the darkness and a car moves past. It's 11.40 on a Saturday night. I'm feeling the cold, and I don't want us to sit here for almost two hours with the engine running to keep us warm. 'We don't need to stay here. We've nothing to do till half-past one. Let's go somewhere and warm ourselves up.'

* * *

We drive through Bisham to the A404, on up to the M40 and along to the all-night services at Beaconsfield. We eat a little, drink hot drinks and play pinball. We're not talking much, and certainly not about the job we're on. But that doesn't worry me. We all know what we have to do, and that what will happen can't be predicted. We're good at winging it.

At one o'clock we go out to the car and get ready. Balaclava and gloves; I hang the rope from my belt and push the gaffer tape into my pocket.

I drive. As we get close to the lane I turn off the lights. Faint starlight shows the edges of the road ahead. I slow by the willow, stop the car, get out and stare up at the house. No light from the bedroom. I slow again by the open gate and look up the drive. No lights anywhere. I drive on to the turning place, make a three-point turn and drive slowly back past the gate. I stop far enough from the hedge for Kylie to get out while leaving space for a late-night driver to get past.

We walk towards the gate. I nod to my companions and run towards the thin line of trees that shields the containers. I steady myself in front of the door, check that Kylie and Clayton are behind me, then lift and pull the two handles. The door opens with an almost silent pop.

I step in – and sniff something floral. Air freshener. A dim light comes from the ceiling. The container is deep and narrow. In front of me is a table, a vase of flowers, two chairs, long bare metal walls.

'Jim!' Kylie is pointing to the furthest corner.

A pair of eyes. Staring. Perhaps scared. Hair. Lots of dark hair.

'Hello.' Kylie steps forward and whispers. 'Who are you? Do you want to be in here?'

An arm moves. A thin arm. A woman, surely. The hand reaches further into the corner and pokes at something soft, which moves. A head appears. A man sits up. A man with dark hair and a beard.

'We are friends,' Kylie says. 'Do you want to stay in here? You can come with us, if you like. We have a car outside. But we must be quiet and go quickly.'

The man and the woman are staring at us.

'If you want to, let's go now. We can talk later. It would be safer.'

They go on staring. They don't look as if they are hiding there voluntarily. Nor do they look like criminals.

They just look astonished. The man stands up. He is tall and slim. 'We don't want to be here.' He looks down at the woman and whispers something. She mutters a few indistinct words. He turns back to us. 'Yes ... please. We would like to go.'

The woman wraps a sheet around herself and stands up. I turn away. And find that Clayton is standing behind me. 'Get dressed as quickly as you can,' I say. 'Bring anything important. But be quick.'

'We have a baby,' the man says.

'Where?' I look around. 'Where's the baby? Bring it, of course.'

'Here.' He points to the ground at the end of the bed. 'In there. She is sleeping.'

The baby is in a cardboard box. Her parents are pulling on clothes. 'They took our passports,' the man says.

'Something can be done about that – but not now. Now you must just come with us.'

The woman is throwing things – clothes, toothbrushes, combs, cotton wool – into a bin liner. Kylie is holding the bag open.

'The passports and our phones could be in that other ... house,' the man says. 'We were put there when they first brought us.'

'The other house there?' I point through the wall – and glance at Clayton.

'Yes. We were there. Our passports were in here. Then we were changed.'

'I'll go look,' Clayton says.

'What colour are your passports?'

'Green. Dark green. South Sudan. We are from there.' He has pulled on trousers and a T-shirt and is putting on a beaten-up pair of trainers.

I give Clayton a thumbs-up. 'Go in. Have a look. We're off in a minute.'

Kylie is whispering to the woman, who is putting baby clothes in a small airline bag. We're ready. We walk out. The man carries the cardboard box. The woman brings her bag and Kylie carries the bin liner.

Out of nowhere a bright light surges towards us. And a deafening roar. A motorbike. It stops. Clayton is there. The bike rider sounds his horn – loudly on and off. Lights go on in the house. Clayton grabs the man, pulls off his helmet. Ernst! And others are coming now.

'Go!' I shout at Kylie. 'Take them. Drive anywhere. We'll see you later.'

'Go with her.' I tell the South Sudanese man. 'She'll look after you.'

The bike is on the ground, its rear wheel spinning. Kylie runs round it. The South Sudanese people run after her, the man holding the box out in front of him.

Clayton picks Ernst up, lifts him above his head and drops him to the ground. He falls on his back with a thud, and lies winded, gasping.

Full headlights are coming at us. High. In our faces. The Range Rover. It stops a few feet away. Doors open. Max and Martin and Jennifer.

'What are you *doing*?' Martin shouts. 'You fucking idiot! You ... bloody detective!' Jennifer scowls. Max looks puzzled. But they keep away from us. They will have seen Clayton dealing with Ernst – and they know what I can do.

I move sideways, away from the headlight beam. 'Who are those people? Why were they here?' Clayton lines up beside me.

'They are no business of yours. But they are friends – friends who we're looking after.' Martin looks across at the container and sees that the door is open. 'Where are they? What have you done?'

The sound of Ernst panting is suddenly drowned by the Merc's engine revving and a squeal of tyres. Kylie is driving away. 'Hear that?' I say. 'They've gone – to a better place.'

'You fucking,' – Martin leaps towards me – 'bastard.'

Jennifer catches his arm. 'No, leave it,' she says. 'No point. You'll only get hurt.'

Martin turns away. His shoulders slump. Max shakes his head and looks as if he might be sick.

'So what were you doing with those people?'

'That's *not* your business.' Martin is shouting again. 'I *told* you.'

'Maybe you should leave now,' Jennifer says. 'You seem to have done what you wanted to do.'

'We'll go soon. But we'd just like to have a little look around.' I'm thinking about the other container and the passports. 'Why don't you get in your car and go home?'

I move towards them, and Clayton steps up beside me.

They look at each other and, after some shrugging and head-shaking, get back in the Range Rover. The engine starts. The car turns. The lights swivel away. And we watch the tail-lights move slowly up the hill.

I let my shoulders drop and breathe out. 'Good old Kylie!'

'Yeah! Well done, Kylie.' Clayton chuckles. 'Do you want to look in there? I'd just opened it when the bloke on the bike turned up.' He gestures to the second container.

The bike is lying on its side, its headlight throwing a beam across the grass. Ernst is on his back, grunting. Clayton leans over him. 'They forgot you, sonny. Are you all right?'

Ernst groans and burbles something that sounds like, 'Can't breathe.'

162

'Sorry about that.' Clayton lifts Ernst's arms, pulls him to the wall of the first container and props him up. 'Rest up for a bit and you'll be all right.'

I go into the second container and am struck by a sharp, salty smell that seems familiar. I feel around for a light switch, find it and a dim light comes from behind frosted glass in the ceiling. As in the first container, there's a low bed, a table and upright chairs. Clayton comes in and looks around.

Dog leads and warm coats for dogs hang on hooks. Plastic tubs of dog food sit on the floor. On a set of steel shelves against a wall sit a pile of collars and some cardboard folders. I look inside one and find certificates of pedigree. And beside the folders, two passports, dark green with REPUBLIC OF SOUTH SUDAN in gold capitals on the front.

I pick one up and flick it open. 'Ruth Hoth.' Born 16 August 1992. A striking face, wavy hair and large dark eyes. Clayton picks up a phone and presses the on button. Nothing happens. I look at the other passport and see dark eyes and a strong nose in a narrow, bearded face. 'Kamal Nyang'. Born 21 December . . .

Behind me the door clangs shut. I turn – the door shudders and I hear a set of bolts click into place. And then another set. And the door is still. And someone kicks it.

23

'Fuck!' I shout.

Clayton charges at the door, launches his full weight, shoulder first. It doesn't move.

'Fuck, fuck, fuck!' I shout again.

Clayton has his ear to the door. 'My fault, Jim. Should have hit him or tied him up – the bloke with the bike.'

'Ernst. Bloody Ernst!' I look around. 'We gotta get out of here.'

We hear the roar of the motorbike, muffled by the walls of the container. 'Shame,' I say. 'We could have used that.'

★ ★ ★

I take a good look at the walls and the doors and Clayton thumps every surface including the wood veneer floor which lies on top of steel. There are no weak points. Six ventilation slots – three on each side wall – sit high up, part of the original structure and no help to us – except that they might save us from suffocating. A cable carrying electricity comes through one of these openings and leads to a junction box high on the wall; from there a narrower cable runs to the ceiling light, and another to a four-socket gang on the floor. Thick grey gaffer tape holds it all in place.

The double doors at one end of this long metal box seem to be the only way out.

'We *have* to get out!' I shout, as I walk up and down looking again at the ceiling – solid steel, no way through. 'What the hell is Kylie going to do? She needs us.'

'Hey! Hey! Calm down, man.'

I sit down on a hard, upright chair. Clayton is right. I must calm down. There is no way out. We will get out only when – *if* – someone opens the door.

We can't get signals on our phones. We're inside a steel box!

This is my fault. I'm in charge. I could have knocked Ernst unconscious. Or I could have tied him up; I had rope – it's still dangling from my belt – and I had gaffer tape to close his mouth.

I worry about Kylie. It's nearly 3 am. Is she with the police in High Wycombe? Is she parked somewhere quiet while she waits for us to get in touch? Is she on her way to London – taking the South Sudanese couple and their baby to where? Her flat? By now, she will know a bit about – I pull their passports out of my pocket – Kamal Nyang and Ruth Hoth.

How had they come to be in that box – ten feet away, and identical to this one?

Clayton is sitting on a chair close to the door. When he found the portable toilet behind the plastic curtain, he told me with a smile that, if we could get hold of some water, we could live here for months; we had chairs, a bed, a toilet and a huge supply of dog biscuits.

Now, he's looking serious – nervous, even. Which is un-usual; Clayton never looks nervous. 'Jim, this bunch,' – he flicks his thumb to his left, towards the big house up the hill – 'might be hopeless amateurs, but it looks like they're into people trafficking, which makes them dangerous. Puppy smuggling isn't good, but people smuggling, people trafficking, is evil. And who knows who they're working for?'

'Organised crime, I'm thinking.' I move my chair so that I'm sitting opposite him. 'These idiots could be a way station – paid to conceal people till they're required. It's not just trafficking; it's kidnap and false imprisonment.' I look at the doors – between them they form the end of the container. 'We must be ready for when the door opens.'

'Yes. We have to keep listening.' He dropped his voice. 'We may hear whoever shows up before they grab the handles out there.'

'Clobber whoever it is, and run,' I say.

'I should be here, I think,' – Clayton moves his chair into the corner beside the door to the right – 'because doors open outwards and that one opens first.' He points to the door on the left.

'So I should be over here to distract them, while you grab them from behind. Right?'

'Yes. Good. That's good.'

'And this might be useful.' I hold up the gaffer tape. 'In case we want to shut someone up.'

'OK.' Clayton nods as I stick the three foot-long strips to the wall by the door.

'And we should turn off the light so whoever comes in can't see us.'

'Yes. Good.'

I stand up, flick the switch – and am shocked at how dark it is. I flick the switch again, look to see where my chair is and flick it off again. I walk over, feel the back of the chair and sit down. 'You know, they might want to hold on to us until we return the South Sudanese.' My mind moves on. 'Although Kylie may have taken them to the police.'

'Even if they got the people back, they wouldn't want to let us go. Because we know that they're people traffickers. We rat on them and they're in deep shit, Jim.'

Suddenly I feel tired, very tired. I look at the luminous hands on my watch: 3.13. 'We *have* to get away as soon as we can ... Otherwise ...'

'Otherwise ...' Clayton laughs, a deep, drawn-out chuckle.

We sit in silence, in total darkness. I imagine how this might end: Martin Cranley-Smith contacts his bosses. Professional crims, hitmen, are despatched. Clayton and I end up at the bottom of a reservoir a hundred miles away, with stones in our pockets.

* * *

I smell salt again – mingled with some kind of spice. Dog biscuits. Bloody dog biscuits.

'I think I should turn the light on.' I am whispering. It's half-past three. 'If someone were to come through that door with a weapon, it would be good if we could see it.'

'I was thinking that too. Yeah, and I could kick the gun out of their hand, up in the air and catch it,' – he chuckles – 'with my left hand, while I punch them with my right ... Turn it on. You're right. I've had enough dark.'

I walk across, hands flat in front of me, until I feel the wall and then the switch. For a second I'm dazzled. I look at Clayton. He gives a closed-lip smile and shakes his head. 'Fuckin' hell, Jim. A fine mess or what?'

I laugh then – quietly. References to Laurel and Hardy always make me laugh. 'Don't forget. You take the first intruder and I take the second, knock them out cold, run to the gate and turn left.' I laugh again. 'Simple.'

★ ★ ★

There is nothing to read except the South Sudanese passports, which takes less than a minute. Ruth Hoth was born in Juba; Kamal Nyang in Bor. I look at the floor and the walls and glance occasionally at Clayton. His head, arms, hands and feet move from time to time, while his eyes stay fixed on the dark, vertical shadow between the doors – as if he is willing the one on the left to open. Every few minutes he stands up, clasps his hands high above his head and leans to both sides three or four times; then he pulls his feet back and up to his bottom, stretching his quads.

I too go through a shortened version of my exercise routine. I watch the door. And I think about Caroline Swann. Did she know or suspect that the Cranley-Smiths went in for people trafficking and false imprisonment? Did they find out that she knew something? If so, did they, or someone from the world of organised crime, order a hit? It was a strange hit for a professional – with a rusty object and not hard enough.

★ ★ ★

At ten past four, a scraping sound. We both stare at the door. And it moves perhaps a quarter of an inch.

Clayton raises a hand and stands up noiselessly. I do the same. If the door opens, I'll be in the intruder's line of sight. Clayton steps forward a little and raises his arms with elbows bent, ready to grab whoever might come in.

I keep staring at the door. There are no more sounds. But is it moving? Or am I imagining that?

It *is* moving. I raise my hand and glance at Clayton. He's

168

seen it too. I can see a gap, less than an inch. I'm staring at it, a narrow strip of darkness.

I keep on staring. Is the strip getting wider?

No. Clayton is frowning at me. I frown back.

I wait a full minute. The door doesn't move. And there are no more sounds.

The door is open. We can walk out.

What then? A trap. If the Cranley-Smiths work for organised crime, then this could be professionals. While we've been in here they've had time to get thugs, hitmen, from London.

I look at Clayton. He's staring at the door. He can see it's open, but not the line of darkness that I can see. His hands hang as fists at his sides, but he seems calm.

Are they on the other side of the door? I don't think so. But they could be. Clayton looks across at me and gestures with his hands and then his thumb. I walk towards him. Cool air hits my hands and face. 'Go? Yes. We have to. They probably don't want to kill us in here or on Cranley-Smith's land. But they will, if they have to. We've got to get outside, where we can move.'

'Which way?' he whispers. 'Stick together or not? Have you got your balaclava?'

'Yes.' I pull it from my pocket and over my head. 'Together, but a little apart – a few feet – so we can help each other if we need to.'

'OK. Good.'

'Too far to run to the woods. So … we go to the road and right towards the fields by the river. OK?' I turn out the light so they can't see us leave.

'OK, and we can jump in the river and swim if we have to.' He chuckles.

I can't see him, but I sense his confidence. *We can do this.*

If we can get beyond the gate and away up the road into the dark and the trees.

'If we get separated, meet where?'

'In the churchyard. You know it? Beside the river, by the bridge.'

'Yes.' He pushes my shoulder. 'Jump out fast in case they're right here. I'll be right behind you. Then you set the pace. I'll keep a few feet away.'

I push on the door – it shakes and rattles – and I burst out. No one there. Nothing. I jog along the side of the container and cross the space to the other one. I walk beside it, letting my eyes adjust to the faint light that comes from the stars. No lights in the house on the hill. Are they up there looking and waiting for something to happen? Maybe they've gone – gone to find an alibi.

Clayton is ten feet behind me. I run. Fast, across to the bushes beside the wall. Then, not far – forty yards – along the wall to the gate. Clayton a shadow off to my left. We reach the gate, the road, and lurch right. A popping noise. Fuck! A gunshot. A voice shouts, 'Get down!' – a woman's voice, loud, commanding. I drop flat onto the road. Clayton lands beside me. His hand is on my head. My face on cold tarmac. Another shot and another.

'Stay down!' That voice: I know it.

'Kylie,' Clayton says in my ear.

An engine starts. High revs, wheels spitting gravel. Headlights, high up, coming straight at us, fast. Jump sideways and run. Then, another bright light comes from somewhere else. Its beam is on the car. 'Jeep' – I can read the logo. I can see the driver, a man in a baseball cap. And the passenger holding a gun with a long barrel, a silencer. But they can't see. And we can. They're dazzled by the light. The driver's eyes are scrunched shut. He turns the wheel. Crunch, and a tinkle of breaking glass. He's hit something: a tree. A crescendo of revving, whirring wheels. He's backing – and driving away. Fast. The beam follows him – bright, like my Maglite, in the thug's mirror. The Jeep disappears round the bend. Seconds pass. We see their headlights climbing Quarry Hill.

'We're OK, Jim.' Clayton is kneeling. Someone is running towards us. The light that saved us is swinging up and down – as if it's painting the road.

'Follow me. I've got your Merc.' She – it *is* Kylie – jogs down the road and turns off the torch. 'Must get away in case they come back.'

I pull off my balaclava. We run back to the junction without speaking and take the right turn. 'I left your car by that locked gate,' Kylie says. 'Where we left it earlier. Then I walked. Saw those guys. A Jeep and a man with a gun.'

'You saved us,' I gasp. 'What made you come back?'

'Didn't know what else to do. Neither of your phones was connecting. What happened?'

I can see the Merc up ahead. A dim shape under the stars. 'We went into that container to look for their passports.' I pat my pocket to check I have them. 'Someone, Ernst probably, the man on the motorbike, locked us in. Nightmare! If it wasn't for you – God knows!'

Clayton is beside me. 'Shining that light at them was bloody genius,' he says.

'I grabbed it out of your boot. Thought it might be useful. Fabulous beam, mega dazzle.'

'My Maglite! Lucky I brought it.'

We reach the car – and there's no one in it. 'Where are the . . . Sudanese people?'

'Beaconsfield Services. Left them eating burgers and feeding their gorgeous baby.'

'Jeez, Kylie!' Clayton bends and looks down at her with a huge smile.

'Respect!' He looks as if he's about to kiss her – but then straightens up. 'You think of everything.'

'They're refugees. They've been in this country for ten days. Never been here before. Those burgers were their first meal out in Britain. Will you drive, Jim?'

'Could you?'

'Sure.'

'Brill Kylie!' We're in the car – me in the front, Clayton in the back. I'm smacking my knees. 'Fucking brill! You get a pair of refugees set up with burgers and you save us from professional killers.' I spread my arms. 'We'd soon be at the bottom of a reservoir with bricks in our pockets, but for you.'

Kylie is driving fast towards Marlow, headlights dipped and tracking the short grass in the field to our left. She says nothing, but looks at me and smiles with a shake of her head.

'*I* want a burger. Are they still serving?' I look at my watch: 4.20 am.

'Should be. McDonald's is open. And KFC. Nothing else, except the toilets.'

'You want a burger, Clayton?'

'Sure. Cheeseburger, fries and a Coke. I'm hungry.'

'I'll have a coffee with mine.' I turn sideways in the passenger seat and look at Kylie. 'Did you have anything to eat?'

'A veggie burger. Ate it while I was trying to phone you. Was OK – tasted mostly of mayo.' She turns left and drives towards Bisham.

'Did the Sudanese have veggie burgers?'

'No. He had a quarter-pounder. She had a McChicken.'

She glances across at me. 'They're Christians – from *South* Sudan.'

'Yes. *South* Sudan. We've got their passports – and a phone.' I'm smiling, almost laughing ... like the happy stage of being drunk. Relief – and release, from captivity ... and a few seconds of terror ... But ... I can't just sit in this car grinning.

No one speaks for a minute. Kylie turns on to the A404 and accelerates.

'There's a policeman there, Jim.' She says it matter-of-factly, as if it doesn't matter. 'And two security blokes. Just the sight of them bothered Ruth and Kamal. I thought of bringing them with me to look for you guys, but,' – she sighed and took her hands off the wheel – 'I think they'll be OK. There's other customers, and the cop and the other guys are more interested in chatting to the women who run the KFC.'

'What we going to do with them, Jim?' Clayton is speaking quietly close to my ear.

'Well,' – I sit up straighter – 'if we take them to the police, they'll end up with Border Force. I guess they want asylum?'

'I can tell you what they want.' Kylie takes a hand off the wheel and waves it towards me and Clayton. 'They want to go to Birmingham to stay with her brother. He and his wife and kids live in Handsworth. They're expecting them – been waiting for them for ten days.' She stares at the road – no traffic. The car seems to move faster. 'Ruth and Kamal are terrified of the police or any authority. They think they'll be sent back or get stuck in prison.'

'Have they told you how they got here?'

'Yes.' Kylie looks across, catches my eye for a moment. 'You two should hear it from them. It's a hell of a story. We'll be there soon.'

'OK. What do *you* think we should do with them?'

'You should decide when you've spoken to them. But, for what it's worth, I would take them to the brother in Handsworth.'

'Blimey!' I'm rubbing my eyes. 'Right. Let me think.'

'Don't decide till you've spoken to them. Hear their story.'

'We have to do something about the bloody Cranley-Smiths.'

'Fuckers!' The sound of Clayton punching his palm comes from the back. 'And what about those hitmen?'

'They'll melt away. That light didn't just blind them; it'll have scared them. They'll think someone knew they were coming. Hallo! How did that happen, they'll think. Who was that?'

Clayton chuckles. Kylie looks across and smiles.

'But we've got to put the cops on to the Cranley-Smiths,' I say. 'Which won't be so easy if we spirit the South Sudanese out of existence.'

'I told them about you, Jim. They think you're wonderful: their saviour. And you, Clayton. They were worried about you, where you'd got to. Just like I was.' We're shooting round the roundabout at the top of the hill above High Wycombe. 'You'll listen to them, won't you? You've gotta give them time. *I* haven't heard the half of it. I've still got questions.'

'Of course. Of course. There's lots I want to know. How they ended up in that container. And why . . . Maybe they don't know why. How they got into this country. How they got out of their country. I want to know.'

We whoosh down the ramp on to the M40 – five minutes from here to Beaconsfield Services. A black BMW 4×4 shoots past, followed by a grey Mercedes – early birds heading for the city. Kylie keeps to the 70 mph limit – no way we want to be stopped by police now. We pass a pair of massive trucks, one following the other – 18-wheelers with Polish plates. The sky is turning crimson and, as we glide into the services, a golden disc rises behind a bunch of trees.

24

A long, low building, glass and steel, with a lopsided roof like a broken wing. Clayton and I stroll in behind Kylie and follow her, past acres of chairs piled on tables, to a pool of light filled with blond wood and red plastic – McDonald's.

There are our people, our South Sudanese: Kamal standing with the baby on his shoulder; Ruth sitting, looking up at him – and at us.

She smiles. Kamal turns to Kylie, 'You found them.' He smiles. 'We worried you wouldn't come back.'

'I wouldn't have done that to you.' Kylie touches his arm.

I look at the sleeping baby: full cheeks, dark lashes, a white hat. Tiny fingers rest on her father's shoulder. A girl, I seem to remember – though I'm not certain. I gamble. 'Beautiful girl! What's her name?'

'Emilie.' He spelled it. 'She was born in ... France. Was ... erm ...' – he frowns – 'thirteen weeks ago. 31 August. Early in morning. Was a Saturday. Ruth was helped by a woman called Emilie. That's why she called Emilie. A French woman. She stayed with us all night – was very kind ... gentle.' He is beaming at the memory of this.

As he speaks, I see desks, form-filling, aggressive people asking questions, crowded rooms – weeks, months, of hellish bureaucracy and living in a tiny room. I won't – can't – take them to the police. We will take them to Handsworth.

I look around. No police. A man who might be security sitting at a table with a magazine at the KFC, which is now closed. A few tables away, two men eating burgers. A man and a woman behind the McDonald's counter. Otherwise, just us – the five of us. Six including Emilie.

I look at Kamal and Ruth. 'I'm Jim. This is Clayton. We're going to have something to eat. Then we'll take you to Birmingham, to Handsworth, where your brother is.' I look at Ruth. 'Is that right?'

'Yes.' She whispers. Then stands up and speaks more loudly. 'Yes.' She moves towards me. 'Thank you.' And holds out her hand.

I take it and squeeze it. 'It's a pleasure. But I do want to know the whole story of how you came to be here.'

She grins – and takes a little skip. 'Yes. We will tell you.'

'Nice one.'

'Good call, Jim.' Kylie and Clayton speak at the same time. Kylie nods at me and smiles. Clayton claps my shoulder and waves a fist in the air.

I eat a quarter-pounder. I'm hungry and it tastes like the best burger I've ever eaten – and I watch Clayton happily munching. I smother chips with ketchup and drink coffee. Kamal sits. Emilie sleeps on. Kylie and Ruth suck up something called a Maltesers McFlurry.

★ ★ ★

Like Kylie, I keep to a steady 70 mph, and the old Merc purrs over the smooth surface of the motorway. We're lucky that Ruth's brother lives in Birmingham rather than, say, Newcastle or Penzance; we'll be there in less than two hours.

I see the sun in the mirror as it climbs in the sky, and I warm to Ruth and Kamal as they tell us their story. They are sitting in the back with Kylie.

Kamal is on the left, leaning forward behind Clayton. He does most of the talking – often quickly with hand gestures and waving fingers. They left their village, about 100 miles from the capital, Juba, forty-seven weeks ago.

'Jeez! You been travelling that long?' Kylie says.

'No. It wasn't all travelling, but we been to a lot of places, a lot of countries. First we hitchhiked and took buses through Sudan and Egypt. That was OK. People are nice, mostly. Then, in the north, beside Alexandria we went into Libya, and that was,' – he pauses – 'horrible. We were in Libya for four months . . . and was horrible – and again later. Again horrible.' There's a catch in his throat. 'I'm sorry. I don't want to talk about Libya. After weeks, months – we got a boat . . .'

He has stopped talking. Glancing over my shoulder, I see him leaning forward, his head pressed against the back of the passenger seat.

Somewhere behind me, Kylie – or is it Ruth? – clears her throat. Then a voice: Ruth's. 'I was raped in Libya . . . many times, perhaps twenty times.' Her voice is faint; she clears her throat again. 'Kamal hates to talk about that – or think about that. It happened to me – not him – and that's why I can tell you, perhaps, and he can't.'

'I'm so sorry.' Kylie whispers. 'My God!'

Clayton's fists lift from his knees, clench and unclench.

'There was a good thing,' Ruth says. 'I was already pregnant.' She is speaking more loudly, without emotion or anger, just passing on facts. 'So this one protected me.' I can't turn to look, but I sense that she is staring at, perhaps stroking, her sleeping baby.

I feel miserable, angry – and a kind of empty, what's-the-point feeling. I've confronted rapists – and listened to their victims. It's always the same feeling. Rape – an inversion of goodness, of what is best in us all. This innocent woman treated as if she were ... nothing. Not a person. Not a person who mattered. 'I'm sorry,' I say.

I think about Kamal: how he must feel.

The car shudders. An artic – 18-wheeler – is slowly hauling itself past us. I see that my speed has dropped to 55 mph.

'In Libya,' Ruth is saying, 'we were kidnapped by a gang of men with guns, and kept in two rooms with other people, lots of people. We had to get money from our families to pay ransom. Then we were kidnapped again, by another gang.' She seems to laugh as she says this. 'A nicer gang. No rape, no beating, better food. And we pay again and they put us on a boat.'

The truck has pulled past and is returning to the inside lane.

'A long, narrow, blow-up boat with sixty people on it.' Kamal is speaking again – quietly. 'We went on the sea in the afternoon and we moved on through the night sitting up, one leg in the water. In the morning, the boat was filling up with water. Too many people, I think. We were rescued by sailors on a big boat and taken back to Libya. To a detention centre. Horrible. Not enough food, or water. Locked up with eight people in a tiny room.' He sounds angry, louder, now. 'Not let out. No one cared.' He stops speaking and drinks some water from a bottle.

179

I speed past the truck – and wink my hazard lights.

'This is a beautiful place,' Kamal says. We're driving past the exit to Stokenchurch – a field of sheep beside us and a pair of red kites floating above. Kamal sounds calmer and I sense that he is smiling. 'So green – green like France. We were in France later. I'll tell you about that. But we were at Gharyan, the detention centre, for three weeks. Then the United Nations – three people, very *nice* people – came and took us, and a lot of other people, away in a bus – to Tripoli, to a place where we could wash and shower and eat nice food and sleep on a mattress. Then they took us, after a few days, to the airport. We were so happy, but not sure we would really be leaving Libya. We *hated* Libya. We had been there so long. But the plane took off and we flew to Niamey in Niger,' – he says it the French way – 'and we had a little hut of our own in a camp. Two huts in one … building, you know? So there was people close to us. And we had friends. Was good. Very clean. Toilets, showers. We were there for—'

'Was six weeks,' Ruth interrupts. 'I remember because I was counting the weeks till baby would come. We left there August 22. And she was born August 31 in Dijon.'

'We asked to go on to the UK because James, her brother, is here,' Kamal says, 'and maybe we could but maybe we couldn't. If we could, would take a long time, United Nations people said. And they said we could go to France very soon. Was easy to go to France from Niger, they said. So we thought, France would be good place for baby to be born. And it was. We stayed in a house, like a hotel, all clean and people cared and a doctor to see Ruth – and, when it was time, they took us to the hospital where Emilie looked after Ruth. And new Emilie was born, easy—'

'No. Not easy! Not easy for me,' Ruth is laughing. 'Pain,

180

horrible pain, for a whole day. But OK after she was born. Sleep then, with Emilie, and then tea with lemon and sugar.'

'You had lots of pain, I know – and I was sorry.' Kamal sounds sad. 'I was there.' He is talking to us three Brits now. 'French nurses told me to be there. In Juba I wouldn't be there.'

25

The Merc hums on the tarmac. We pass the Watlington exit and sweep on towards Oxford. I'm happy for them – happy that they have their Emilie. After everything. After rape. Why do men do that? I look at Clayton. He wouldn't do that. What would I have done if I'd been Kamal? Jumped on them, kicking, punching, screaming . . .? And made it worse.

Kylie coughs and says, 'When did you leave Dijon?'

'The United Nations woman, Patrice, said we could maybe get asylum in France. And we thought about that.' Kamal pauses. 'But James is here and we don't speak French. We speak English. Most people in South Sudan speak English. So, when Emilie was one month, we went to Calais to try to go to England. We didn't know how hard that would be.' Again, he pauses. I keep my eyes on the road and wait. 'Actually, from then till now, was all bad. Patrice told us it would be horrible, and that we should stay in Dijon. I wished we'd stayed in Dijon – when we were in Calais and then in that horrible box. But now: you found us, got us out of that box, driving us across England

which we can see through the windows. Is incredible. I'm
so happy.'

'So am I.'

I feel a hand on my arm. Ruth's hand. And I see Kamal's
hand on Clayton's shoulder.

'What happened in Calais?' Kylie says.

★ ★ ★

We cruise past a line of trucks on a long hill and pass the
exit to Banbury. Ruth has been telling us about their time
in the refugee camp: four weeks of squalor, privation, hassle
and hustle softened by small kindnesses from strangers from,
it seemed to them, all over the world. Ruth and Kamal
were often without food and often had to move home – a
tiny tent – at the whim of brutish gendarmes. Meanwhile,
Emilie thrived on breast milk and gathered presents and
cuddles from children and adults.

Kamal is explaining how they got out of Calais. A people
smuggler tried to befriend them. Ruth interrupts to tell us
that he was creepy and had a droopy moustache. 'It was the
only way out,' Kamal says.

The man wanted £5,000, but they had only €1,200.
When he offered to let them pay the rest by working for his
friend in England, who would meet them when they arrived, they were pleased at first. 'But we didn't know where
we were going, only that we would get in a truck one night.
He said something about Buckingham, like Buckingham
Palace, but we knew we weren't going there.' He laughs.
'And his friend? He just said he was a businessman who
would have work for us. So we gave him our euros and
hoped it would be OK.'

'You are so brave,' Kylie says.

'We *had* to get away from there. It was wet, smelly . . .

dangerous. At any moment the camp might be destroyed by police. So, two days later, the man took us to this big truck and we were pushed in at a side door. There were four boys, young men, already in there – from Afghanistan – frightened like we were. They shut the door and it was dark. Our phones gave some light, but we wanted to save our batteries. We sat on boxes and waited and waited. And, after a long time, the engine started, the truck moved and we bounced around in the dark as it drove onto a boat. And—' He stops talking and I hear him swigging water from a bottle.

I'm pleased – pleased they got into a truck, got onto a boat. But I've known all along that they got here, to England, somehow. And I feel low, sad – a kind of brain ache that I know well: a doc might call it depression. The cruelty of rape, gangs, people smugglers, traffickers. I feel disgust at the behaviour – the uncaring, psychotic behaviour – of so many men. Mostly men. Some women – consider Jennifer Cranley-Smith. And not all men, thankfully. I look across at Clayton's hands resting on his knees. Long strong fingers, pink nails.

'We sat there, lay down on those boxes – and felt the boat moving.' Ruth is talking. 'Emilie didn't like it. She cried. We moved away from the boys so as not to upset them. But they were OK. Two hours, the boat stopped, no engine. Crashing noises – and after more time – our truck drove – we felt it bumping up and down – off the boat. We shouted. The boys whistled. We did high fives with those boys. "We are in UK." We were happy, even though we didn't know what would happen next.

'The truck stopped there in the port. Was it your Dover? We don't know. We thought the door might be opened by police. But no. Nothing. And then it drove for about two hours. And stopped. And the door opened. We were at the side of a road with many cars, trucks. A man waved us to get out, but not the Afghanistan boys. He shut the door on them. And then these two men were there: Ernst and Max.'

'That was Ernst,' Kamal says, 'the man on the motorbike tonight – you know, after you got us out.'

'They put us in the back of a van,' Ruth says. 'Emilie cried. Max, the other man, was nice. He tried to make us comfortable with pillows. And we drove again, sitting in the dark until they got us to Martin's place. Then we had to go into the metal container. And we been there five days – and then you came.' I can almost feel her smiling. 'How you know we were there?'

'I didn't know it was you. But I thought perhaps someone was in there. I came a few days ago to talk to Martin, and I saw plates on a tray on the ground outside your container – your blue box. Did you eat salami one—'

'Yes. Yes. We did,' Kamal answers. 'Max brought it on plates, paper plates. With cabbage, cut thin, with mayonnaise. Was nice. That was third day we were there, I think.' He drinks more water. 'You're not a policeman, are you? Why did you come back to see if anyone was inside?'

'I'm not a policeman. Don't worry. I'm a private investigator, a private detective. And Kylie and Clayton work with me. I went there to ask Martin something about his dogs – it's just a job I'm doing.'

Clayton turns sideways and speaks over his shoulder. 'Jim thought someone might be shut in there – and once he thought that, he had to find out. Jim's like that.'

'Jim's a good guy,' Kylie says. 'He likes to help people.'

'We thank you,' Ruth says. 'We are very lucky.'

'Yes,' Kamal says, 'we are.'

We talk about Max and Ernst. Ruth actually likes

them – especially Max. 'He brought me flowers.' She thinks they are refugees from somewhere, but she's not sure.

'They're not British?' I ask.

'No. They speak English very badly,' Kamal says. 'Worse than us.' He chuckles. 'And they speak to each other in some language – I don't know.'

I glance at Clayton and raise my eyebrows. He smiles and shrugs his thumbs.

We're closing in on Birmingham – and, not for the first time, our passengers are wondering whether to phone James, Ruth's brother, to warn him of their arrival and to make sure he's at home. He works in a hospital and could be at work on a nightshift. It's 6.30; we should be there within an hour. If he's at work, his wife and his three kids should be there. Ruth and Kamal decide to just turn up. 'It's so amazing, so exciting!' Ruth is almost squealing.

I ask about James's wife.

She's called Maggie, and is Irish. Ruth hasn't met her; nor has Kamal. Ruth hasn't seen her brother since he left South Sudan eight years ago. She's seen photos and films of Maggie on the internet. 'She looks nice. You'll see.'

'You want *us* to meet your brother?'

'Yes. Yes. That would be so nice.'

Clayton is grinning and nodding.

'Kylie, you OK with that?'

'She is asleep,' Ruth says.

'Oh! Good. Don't wake her.'

'She'll want to meet your brother and his wife and kids,' Clayton says. 'Just like we do.'

26

They hugged and shouted and kissed. They jumped up and down and tossed Emilie high in the air so she squealed. If they'd had any champagne, they would have squirted it all over each other.

We looked on for what seemed like several minutes. Eventually, they shook our hands. Then, when Ruth explained that we weren't taxi drivers but had freed them from imprisonment in a container, we got the hugs and the kisses.

As we left I gave Ruth and Kamal my card and told them to contact me if they needed help.

★ ★ ★

The three of us were tired and pleased with ourselves. Clayton drove; Kylie stretched out on the back seat; I did a little thinking. Should I go to Thames Valley Police?

But how to convince them that the Cranley-Smiths were involved in people trafficking and false imprisonment when I couldn't produce Ruth and Kamal as evidence?

I had another idea: follow Max, try to talk to him, find

out more. He bought food in Marks & Spencer, I knew that. Was there a branch in Marlow? It was a small town, but maybe.

I took over the driving at Heston Services, dropped Kylie and Clayton near their homes, and got home around 2 pm. By then, all I wanted was sleep.

I kicked off my shoes, drank a little water, turned off my phone, put the Barr Brothers on low and lay down.

★ ★ ★

I woke around 8.30 pm with a dry mouth. A couple of regular stars – nothing to get excited about – winked in the sky above the warehouse.

I rang Vic. I wanted to hear her voice – and it was there for me: clear, bell-like, loving. By comparison, I must have sounded flat; I didn't want to tell her that I had been locked in a container and shot at, and had uncovered a pair of people traffickers. Not now, not on the phone. We arranged to meet on Tuesday evening. Monday, I was looking after Danny. She sounded disappointed. She would have liked to meet sooner. That's how it seemed. I told her I'd had a hard and busy weekend and would tell her all about it. She'd come here on Tuesday and we'd eat in Bazaar in Consort Road; we both loved that place.

I called Laura. Her phone was switched off. Maybe she was at a gig. Perhaps Juliana was at home with Danny; Laura had said that she was happy to babysit again.

Then I saw that John McCormick had called while I was asleep. I called him back; it was almost 9 pm.

A woman's voice answered. 'John's tied up right now . . .' She sounded embarrassed. And I realised that, except that he lived in the Maze Hill part of Greenwich, I knew nothing about McCormick outside of work. The woman muttered,

'It's Jim Domino,' and then, after a pause, 'But ...' And then, to me, 'Here he is.'

'Jim. Good news. I caught our man with the long arms last night. Round about midnight. Small struggle, some tears, and then he came with me to the cop shop, willingly. One of those ... you know ... types who can't understand why they're doing what they're doing.'

I told him I knew many people like that, and congratulated him. 'Quick work. Amber pleased?'

'Yes. She's good ... The man wanted to be caught. Fed up with himself – you know ... Weird: he's married, works in the City trading foreign currency.'

'Weirdos – tell me about them.' And I almost told him about the night I had had while he was sorting out our peeping Tom. But I was tired – and, besides, I don't like to steal people's thunder. 'Well done, John. Great work.'

'Thanks Jim. And I'm off to Rome tomorrow – 1.30 flight from Heathrow. You're keeping me busy. I'm grateful.'

I commiserated with him, and admitted it wasn't my idea of fun: hanging around a hotel to see if adultery was being committed.

'It's work and it's a change of scene,' he said, and told me again that he was grateful.

★ ★ ★

I slept from about midnight and got up early. After a shower I did my knee-bending and arm-waving in time with Jimmy Cliff. As I warmed down, I decided to take the day off – 'Fuck it! Why not?' – and go fishing.

With a thermos of tea, a cheese sandwich, my rod and my fishing bag – the one that unfolds into a chair – I drove to the tackle shop on Lee High Road, bought half a pint of maggots, and went on to Keston Ponds.

The air was cold, the sky a faded blue behind bare trees, the sun a glimmer low in the sky. I switched off my phone and walked away from the parked cars; rust-coloured leaves crunched under my feet. I reached a spot on the bank of the lower pond that I'd first found about thirty years ago: in the lea of a pair of oaks. I'd passed just one fisherman; we'd nodded, smiled and shrugged. Otherwise, no one.

I was going only for small stuff. Sometimes I'd caught pike at the ponds, but it's complicated; it needs planning and close attention. I just wanted to sit with an eye on the float – and maybe hoick something out of the water. I thought about Danny, imagining him in the playground at school and then at home where I would see him this evening.

A jogger came past, breathing heavily in a high-vis vest. I reeled in the float and hurled two handfuls of maggots into a stretch of dark water beyond a patch of reeds. Concentric circles spread, elbowed each other and spread some more. I sat down and waited . . . and thought about Spurs, Antonio Conte and the enigma of Tanguy Ndombele, who had been loaned to Napoli: why did this man fail to use his great talent? Which reminded me of Artie Shaw: bandleader and virtuoso clarinettist, who gave up his career in music when he was forty-four and spent the next fifty years writing and painting. And then I remembered Jim Domino, who was once a DCI.

Small splashes and dimples appeared in the water where the maggots wriggled and sank. I watched and waited. And fixed up my bait.

Two maggots on a single hook. Cast – and in less than a minute, out it came: a small perch.

And another, and another, and a small roach, a skimmer, another roach. I had fun for almost an hour, pulling them in and throwing them back. Where small fish feed, larger ones follow. I rested the rod against an oak, sat down, drank tea and ate a sandwich.

I gazed unfocused at the rushes, the lilies, the light on the water – and remembered Rupert Brooke:

> *Fish say, they have their Stream and Pond;*
> *But is there anything Beyond?*

Is there?

Unlikely. Then where is Elizabeth?

She's here in me, and Laura and Lotte; and Danny, Lola and Leo.

And that's good for her and us.

In the afternoon I picked up my gear, walked to the south side of the lake, and set up in a small cove with the sun low to my left. Three or four ducks turned up, wanting food. I ignored them and cast about twenty feet into deep water. Nothing, but I persisted, casting further. A sharp bite, the line shot out and a struggle turned into a fight. Landed it eventually: a green, greasy tench – not big, about two pounds. It lay still on my landing net, handsome and exhausted. I took a photo and put it back fast.

★ ★ ★

I drove home feeling lethargic and in need of a Rennie. I scrabbled in the glove compartment, found what I wanted and pushed the little square pill into my mouth. It didn't help much. I drove straight to Laura's – and sucked another when I got there. I try not to bother my daughters with my stomach troubles, but Laura noticed and commiserated. She had a gig at the Vortex with the Jason Dobell sextet that night. She'd try not to be too late, but I shouldn't wait up, she said.

I showed Dan my photo of the tench and asked if he'd like to come fishing sometime.

He yawned. 'P'rhaps. If Mum can come.' He found a pad of paper and a soft pencil and started to draw the tench. He began with its head and back and dorsal fin – and stopped. Too tired to draw, he was soon in bed, asleep.

I heated up and ate a Pieminister pie Laura had laid in for me – she knew I liked them – with a load of peas, and googled Marks & Spencer; there's one in Marlow, in Spittal Street, the road that goes east out of town. I went to bed early, around 11 pm, sucked in some Lorca and another Rennie – and woke early, a little before Dan.

Laura came downstairs and wanted my opinion of 'My Blue Heaven'; she wanted to add it to her repertoire, but felt she couldn't compete with the Norah Jones version which she called sublime. She stood at the piano, played, cleared her throat and sang.

It came out as a soulful ballad – no rhythm, just some blocked chords on the piano and the ring of her voice which, of course, I love.

'*That* was sublime. You should sing it whenever you want.'

Dan was standing in the kitchen doorway holding a spoon and staring at his mother.

'You like that, Dan?' I said.

'Yeh.' He nodded and went on smiling.

'It's a fabulous song, and you make it sound great.' I meant it, but she pulled a face as if she didn't believe me. 'Doesn't matter if Norah Jones does it too. You're not better or worse than her. You're different. She has a kind of twang in her voice. You might say it's a bit contrived. You're more natural.'

'Yeah?' She looked sceptical. 'I agree in principle, but in this instance I'm not so sure.'

'Well, I think you should do it.'

'Yeah!' She played a few notes. 'I'd like to add it to the stuff I do solo. The band left the stage last night and I did "Nature Boy". It went really well.' She turned, smiled and raised her eyebrows.

'Great ... Well, you know who also sang "My Blue Heaven?"'

'Millions of people.'

'Uncle Fats. He did it rock 'n' roll style.'

She grinned. 'So he did.'

Laura used to kid people that Fats Domino was her uncle – only when they asked. In fact, my Dominos came from France back in the 1800s, and before that – my dad reckoned – Italy. Fats's Dominos were French Creole.

'Do you still tell people Fats was your uncle?'

'No, Dad.' She smiled. 'Don't think that joke would work these days.'

★ ★ ★

Laura took Danny to school. I walked with them to the end of the street. Then went home to get the Merc and a few supplies.

27

I'm back in the wood, watching. I half-expected that the blue containers would be gone. If not both of them, then the one where Ruth and Kamal had been kept, at least. But nothing has changed. Were the Cranleys not worried that police could show up looking for evidence of people smuggling? They couldn't know that the cops hadn't been told.

Could they?

No. Only Clayton and Kylie, Ruth and Kamal knew what had happened.

Perhaps the Cranleys had got rid of every trace of the South Sudanese, and steam-cleaned the container.

Horses in the paddock wearing blankets. Cold, flat grey sky, no sun. Just the Jag outside the house – so at least one of the Cranley-Smiths is out in the Range Rover. And at least one of Max or Ernst is out in the grey van.

A little over two days ago, I was locked in that box with Clayton. Me tense. Clayton cool, calm – like I'm supposed to be.

11.05 am on Tuesday and nothing happening.

I remember Laura singing 'My Blue Heaven'. She wants *my* opinion. Magic.

★ ★ ★

Ernst is coming out of the house by the side door. He jogs downhill to the gate, unlocks a hefty padlock – that's new – and opens the gate. A black VW Golf drives in, the Golf that was driven by Jennifer's horse-riding friend – who might or might not be Penny Truman or Sue Spicer. Ernst fastens the lock with a key and walks up the hill towards the house.

So Max is out in the van.

Max was nice, Ruth said. *He* brought her flowers – not Martin or Jennifer. 'Nice' was the word she used. She even liked the thuggish Ernst. They might be refugees too, she and Kamal thought. And perhaps not in control of their own lives.

Horse-riding woman is let in the front door by Jennifer. So Martin is out in the Range Rover.

Maybe Max has gone to Marks & Spencer . . . Drive over? Take a look?

No. Too long a shot.

But . . . nothing happening here. So . . .

★ ★ ★

Liston Road Car Park – all along the back of the shops in Spittal Street. M&S off to the left. Two women, both with kids and bags of groceries, coming from the rear entrance. He'd park here.

But no grey vans. Park in back row, halfway down, back to the wall. Walk around. Check. Could be hidden by a white van. Or could be on the street, round the corner.

No. Back to Merc. Radio on. Robert Elms . . . Talking

to a man about beer. Is it better canned or bottled? 'Bottled,' the man says.

Wait. Give it half an hour. Long shot, but he might have gone somewhere first.

★ ★ ★

My God! That's him . . . Isn't it? Just drove past and round to the front row. VW. Grey with scratch on nearside. Parking to the left, towards M&S. He's getting out. Standing by the van, tapping his phone, listening to his phone, tapping . . . He's paying for parking.

Now he's walking. Quick. Follow.

Walking round the corner – not to M&S. Keep back.

He's carrying an envelope. Turning off pavement – down alley, brick walls . . . and into a pedestrian square: trees; a florist; a jeweller, a bridal boutique. Left onto High Street. Past Sainsbury's Local . . . And he goes into an estate agent.

Walk past, twenty yards. Stop by tree.

★ ★ ★

He's coming out already, heading back towards the car park, not carrying envelope.

Estate agent's window. Four-bed detached, Pinkneys Green, £1.9 million – looks nice.

Go in. Woman at desk facing the door. She looks up. She has glasses hanging round her neck on a multi-coloured chain. Two or three empty desks. An agent in a tight suit, shirt, tie, behind desk at far end talking to middle-aged couple.

'Er . . . I saw the house at Pinkneys Green in the window. Is it still available?'

'Yes. Only went on sale yesterday.' She smiles and puts

196

on her glasses; they have black rims. The envelope is on her desk.

'Could I see the details?'

'Of course. I can show you now on screen. You can sit over there,' – she points to a desk – 'and have a good look. Or did you want them on paper?'

'Paper would be good. I can show my wife this afternoon. Then, if she's interested, could we ring you for a viewing?'

She wants my details. I give my usual alias: John Brander – name and email. She taps her keyboard for a minute, then gets up and crosses the room to a big printer. She has her back to me. The printer whirs and begins to pump sheets of A4. The agent with the couple is talking and pointing to a screen. I pick up the envelope and push it inside my jacket.

'All right, Mr Brander.' She hands me a bunch of stapled sheets with her personal card on top.

I put the details on the desk where the envelope had been, hold her card up and read it: 'Heather Greaves – Sales Associate.'

'Any relation of the great Jimmy?' I smile.

'I wish.' She smiles back. 'He was a laugh.'

I pick up the details and leave, saying that I'll phone later if we want to see the house. I walk back to the car park. The grey van with the scraped side is there, but there's no sign of Max. Perhaps he's shopping in Marks & Spencer. I go over to the Merc and stand by it so that I can see if Max returns.

I look at the envelope. It's addressed to the firm of estate agents: Timothy Mann and Co. It's made of stiff brown paper, long and narrow, sealed at one end. I squeeze the sides. The seal is loose – someone has licked it in a hurry. I poke at it with my little finger; there's space for me to blow into it. I blow, inflate it and clap it between my hands as if it were a balloon. It pops open.

Inside is a three-year lease on a house in Claremont Road, Marlow, granted to Martin Charles Cranley-Smith of Combe House, Quarry Wood Road, Marlow, at a rent of £1500 a month, starting on November 27, 2022 – two days ago. A letter from Cranley-Smith to the agent says that he is enclosing the signed lease and a letter guaranteeing the rent from his guarantor. The lease is signed with a hasty scrawl by Martin and witnessed by a name I recognise: Susanna Spicer, who describes herself as a 'Public Relations Executive'. I study the guarantor's letter; a signature that looks like a bird's nest sits above the typed words: *Sidney Alexander Stockton, Company Director, 74 Dorset Street, W1U 3MT*. One at a time, I flatten both letters and the key pages of the lease on the bonnet of the Merc and photograph them with my phone. Then I put the lot back in the envelope and seal it by licking my finger and wetting the dry gum.

★ ★ ★

I hang around by the pay and display machine, as if I am waiting for someone. Which I am. It's just that he doesn't know it.

Can't be much longer.

I'm humming. 'My Blue Heaven.'

Here he is. Here he is. Carrying two dark green bags. Wait.

OK.

'Max. Max, I just want to talk.'

He's opened the van door. Slinging his bags in. 'No. No. I don't want to talk. Leave me—'

'Max. I'm not a policeman. I might be able to help you.'

'No. I don't want. Don't bother me.' He's in the seat, pulling the door shut.

'Max. Here's my card. Call me if you want help. I helped,' – he takes the card and slams the door – 'Ruth and Kamal and the baby.' He's started the engine. Reversing now. I cup my hands. 'I won't harm you.' He stares at me for a second – curiosity in his dark eyes – looks away, and drives off. Into Liston Street and away.

★ ★ ★

'I'm so sorry. I picked this up with the house details.'

She takes the envelope, puts on her glasses and stares at it. She smiles – 'No problem,' – and puts the envelope back where it was ten minutes ago. 'I hope your wife likes the house.'

'So do I. We'll soon find out.'

★ ★ ★

I walk to Claremont Road – not far – and stroll past number 48. A big house set apart from its neighbours and hidden from the road by a wall and a tangle of tall trees. I pass an open gate and glimpse a lawn strewn with leaves and, beside it, space for parking – but no cars. I walk on and come back for another look. There seems to be no one around. I walk purposefully along a concrete path to the front door. I glance in at the ground-floor windows; there are no curtains and no furniture – just beige carpet. The doorbell gives a clear, hollow ring. I wait and ring again. No one comes. I peer through the letter box: a slew of junk mail, topped by a flyer for takeaway pizza, lies on more beige carpet. The hall is large and empty.

I walk away. Why do the Cranley-Smiths want this place? Who is Sidney Alexander Stockton?

★ ★ ★

I drive home – and do a little admin, bill paying.

Charlie Ritchie phones. 'Can you make a drink this evening: Gowlett Arms?'

'Not this evening. I've got a date.'

'Oh!' He sounds surprised and disappointed. 'Tomorrow any good? I've got something for you.'

We agree to meet at the Gowlett tomorrow at half past six.

I do my exercises. Then sit at the table, under the light – gets dark so early now – and turn slowly through Sorolla's paintings. Beautiful. Whiteness. Long white dresses.

Dinner tonight with Vic. Victoria. She looks like Clotilde Sorolla. A lovely woman. And not Elizabeth. Elizabeth was ... not just lovely. She was everything. But now she is not ...

'Nobody knows you. No. But I sing of you.' Lorca.

Wipe your eyes. Close the book.

★ ★ ★

The restaurant is warm and dark. We eat chicken with hummus and drink wine from the Bekaa Valley. I tell Vic about Ruth, Kamal and Emilie. How we rescued them and drove them to Birmingham.

Vic takes my hand across the table. 'You're breaking the law again – you terrible man.' She puts on a doe-eyed expression and shakes her head. Then she smiles and laughs, raises her glass and says quietly, 'Here's to you and the South Sudanese – and freedom.'

She rests her hand on mine as I tell her that I served my sentence, that Clayton and I were locked in a container for two and a half hours until we were released by the sainted Kylie.

'Oh! I love Kylie.'

I tell her how freaked I was, while Clayton was calm – ready to bust out as soon as the door was opened. She grins. 'I *love* Clayton too.' But her smile fades. 'You got to take care, Jim. This thing' – she taps the table – 'is getting ... dangerous.'

★ ★ ★

We leave soon after ten. Outside it's cold and clear.

Vic is lovelier than ever tonight. Tall, dark, warm, close. I take her hand and tell her that I love being with her. 'I love your company.'

'You love my *company*.' She's smiling and pouting at the same time.

'Yes.'

Then, a moment. The moment before something happens, something that you *want* to happen, that you *know will* happen. After this instant of suspense. Heads tip. Then hands, arms, grab.

Kissing. Pulling, pressing. On the pavement outside Bazaar. And we hurry home chuckling, tripping over each other.

28

Vic has to leave early. I walk with her through the cold and dark of Warwick Gardens to the station.

I look across at the lone ping-pong table, and at the patch of earth beside it where its companion had stood.

'So sad.' Vic takes my arm. She is looking too.

I put my hand on hers. 'I'd like them to bring the table back, or produce a new one. That empty space is a symbol of evil. No one needs to be reminded of what happened.'

We leave the park and stroll towards the station. 'When the table returns,' – Vic pulls me closer – 'let's bring bats and balls and play on it.'

'Yes,' I say. 'Good idea. I'm not bad at ping pong.'

'Well, *I* was table-tennis captain at school. So you watch out.' In the bright light of the ticket hall, she strokes my forehead. 'You must be careful, Domino,' she says, and slides her hand down to my cheek. We kiss quickly, deeply, her hands around my neck. '*My* Domino. Can I say that?'

'Yes,' I mutter, my face buried in the softness of her hair. 'Of course.'

She skips away and taps with her Oyster card. The gates jolt open with a crash and she hurries up the steps.

★ ★ ★

I go home, drink some coffee and type 'Sidney Alexander Stockton' into Google.

Nothing.

I delete 'Alexander' and find links to the deputy manager of a pub and to the obituaries of two Canadian soldiers. No company directors. I put in the address, '74 Dorset Street, W1U 3MT'. I should have done that before. Sidney Stockton is a chartered accountant. His website says that his clients are family-run businesses and 'high-net-worth individuals'. And, for a bit of clarity, I google the Financial Conduct Authority where I find a definition of high-net-worth individuals: 'people who either earn more than £300,000 annually or have assets of more than £3million'. OK ... I already knew that Martin Cranley-Smith didn't make his living by selling dodgy dogs.

I spend several minutes staring from the window watching the blackbird hopping about, lifting leaves and peering underneath them. Is he always the same one? He looks the same – and sometimes he has a girlfriend, but not today.

My mind moves on to Gary Jackson. Where is he? Where *was* he on 8 November?

I think about phoning Ruby. But it's 3.15 pm; she's probably at school. I text instead: 'Hallo Ruby. How are you and your brothers and sisters? Would you like to meet for a coffee or something? It would be good to see you and catch up on your news. I'm free most of the time. Jim.'

Ten minutes later she replies: 'Hey Jim I'd like to meet you. Are you free today. Could be at Crossroads cafe at 4.30. Ruby'

I turn up early and sit at a small table near the door. She arrives on time and comes towards me. I stand up. She is smiling in a strained, perhaps shy, way. We greet each other a little awkwardly and end up shaking hands. Her hand is cold and small. I want to hug her, but I can't of course.

'How are you? How is it all?'

We're sitting down now. 'It's OK.' She pushes her hair behind her ears. Andy, the waiter, comes. She asks for a Coke and I order a cappuccino. She seems slighter than before, a little pinched in the face – and paler. My God, I feel for her – it's just been a couple of weeks since her mum died.

'Is your gran still with you?'

'Yes. And Gary's come. Social services – a court,' – she shakes her head – 'a magistrate – said that was OK. And so did Tracy – she comes in most evenings for a chat.'

'So that's good: having Gary? Is it?'

'Yeah, yeah.' She's nodding and looking at the table. 'He's good. Particularly for the littl'uns, Lily and Sammy.' She looks up and gives a thin smile. 'He's clean. He goes to meetings – you know: where they talk about being addicts?'

I nod. 'Yes, I know about that.'

'Every day, I think. And he's all smart now.' She shrugs. 'Shaved off his beard, had a haircut.'

'And it's good for you and Luke?'

'Yeah, yeah. Luke's pleased.'

'So you can get a bit back to being a little more normal. You're going to school. Is that OK?'

'It'll . . .' She looks down and then up again towards me, 'never be . . .' she breaks off; her eyes are filling with tears, '. . . normal.'

'I'm sorry.' I reach across the table instinctively and

touch her arm. 'I shouldn't have said normal. Of course, it's not . . .'

'It's OK.' She blinks. 'Not your fault.' She picks up the paper napkin that Andy has put on the table under her glass, unfolds it, crumples it and dabs at her eyes. 'Are you still trying to find out what happened? You must have lots of other work.'

'I am still on it. There's nothing I'd like more than to find out who attacked your mum.'

She looks suddenly happier. 'Thanks.'

I tell her a little about our adventures with the Cranley-Smiths and mention people trafficking.

Her eyes widen. 'So they aren't just into selling dogs?' She's shocked and almost whispering. 'Do you think Mum knew about that?'

'I don't know. I'd like to find out.' I suck the froth off my coffee. 'I'd like to talk to Gary. Do you think he'd talk to me?'

'Yes, but . . . why? You don't think he . . .'

'No. I don't. But I'd like to know where he was that night – the night when your mum was attacked. You know he wouldn't tell the police?'

'No. No. I didn't.' She frowns and looks at the floor.

Perhaps I'd said too much. 'Please don't be worried. I don't think he is in any way guilty. It's just curious, and there might just be something that he doesn't realise might connect to what happened.' She's still looking upset. 'Don't ask him anything about it. I will. Maybe I can take him out for a drink and have a chat?'

'He doesn't drink now.' She grins. 'Not vodka, not any alcohol, he says.'

'Of course. Silly me! Coffee then . . . or something. The point is to talk.'

We chat: about school, the other kids, her dad – he's gone back to Canada, but is coming back; he will be here for Christmas.

On the pavement outside I say that I'll come round soon in the hope of finding Gary. And we shake hands again as we say goodbye.

* * *

My phone rings. I'm on Fenwick Road, heading for the Gowlett. Charlie. He's there already. Do I want a pint of Adnams? Of course.

He's sitting at the same table – the one we sat at two weeks ago. He greets me loudly with shoulder claps, and hands me my pint.

He picks up his beer and lowers his voice. 'I've brought Caroline Swann's laptop for you. You can borrow it – probably for as long as you like.'

'Oh! Thanks.' I take a long drink. 'How come? What about Lightfoot?' I lick froth from my upper lip.

'It's all right.' Charlie says. 'Lightfoot isn't involved.'

'So ... what's happened?' He's looking away from me, towards the bar. 'Did Avril authorise this?'

He turns to me and widens his eyes without smiling – a don't-ask-questions look, which I find irritating.

'Come on, Charlie. We can talk, surely. What's going on?'

'Look. Let's just say that there are people who would like you to have it.' He nods sideways towards a Tesco bag on the bench beside him.

I swallow some Adnams and sit back. 'OK.' I raise my eyebrows and stare at the ceiling – at Victorian mouldings, thick with paint the colour of nicotine.

I take another sip and put the glass down.

'And ... Lightfoot ... doesn't know I've got it?'

'No. I don't think he does.'

So Avril wants *me* on the case and *not* Dave Lightfoot. Again, I stare up at the ceiling. Fuck! What *is* this? Lightfoot ... Lightfoot failed to investigate the Cranley-Smiths and their smuggled puppies. So ... is Avril wanting me to investigate Lightfoot? What does she think he might have done? Or not done? And why not? Avril and Charlie don't know about the people smuggling – because I haven't told Charlie.

'It's not on, Charlie. I can't work for the police.'

Charlie shakes his head, looks at me and puts his finger to his lips.

'For free. Or at all. Why should I?'

He leans back, puts his hands on his bald head and pulls a sad face.

And then I remember Ruby: *her* sad face – a genuinely sad face; not a face put on for effect like Charlie's. And hear myself saying, *There's nothing I'd like better than to find out who killed your mother.* Or something like that. I raise my hands. 'OK. OK. I'll take it ... Thanks.'

He drops his hands and smiles. 'Well, you did ask for it. "The laptop itself," I remember you saying.'

'I did,' I sigh, then gulp my beer. 'But I didn't know ...'

'No. Nor did I. And I don't really know much now, either.' He looks weary – and raises his glass.

I raise mine. And I carry on thinking. Was it just laziness that stopped Dave Lightfoot examining Caroline's dealings with the Cranley-Smiths? Was Dave so convinced that Gary Jackson was guilty that he didn't think it worth investigating anyone else? But no, he checked out the others Caroline had confronted: the ticket tout, the property developer.

Charlie knows Lightfoot better than I do. I ask his opinion of him.

'Very bright. Efficient. Thinks fast. Sometimes gets ahead of people – like me, for instance.' He laughs. 'You know what I mean? You don't quite know where he's coming from sometimes, but you might get it later.'

'Sounds like hard work.'

Charlie swallows some beer and puts his glass down. 'To be honest,' – he turns to me – 'I don't like him.' He pulls a face – lips forward, nose wrinkled. Then he shrugs. 'He can be kind and thoughtful to the lower ranks, but he's often a bully. Expects people to do what he says without discussing it. Ignores other opinions.' He shakes his head. 'He upsets the younger blokes and the female officers. I'm old enough to ignore it. Put up or shut up? I shut up when he's around.'

'Do you know anything about his background?'

'Grew up on a council estate in Harlow, went to Cambridge and studied criminology. He fast-tracked to DI – and seems to have stopped there.' He looks at me with a glum, deadpan expression. 'Dunno why.' He shrugs. 'The likes of Avril – good, plain coppers without degrees – have leapfrogged over him now.'

'That could be why: what you just said – unpopular, seen as a bully. Sometimes they don't promote people because they're hoping they'll leave.'

'Yep. Maybe.' Charlie is nodding. 'I think he might resent it. He's been a DI for a while now.'

'He's married, isn't he?'

'Yep. Think she's a teacher – a deputy head, something like that. Two kids. The usual.' He laughs. 'Nothing odd as far as I know.' He gives me a look. 'But then, I wouldn't know, would I?'

So Dave is off the case and, secretly, I've been given a prime source of evidence. Secretly? We're in a pub ... But a long way from the nick – not a police pub. Maybe

Charlie thinks the old sitting-on-a-bench handover is less secure – besides, it's December now, too cold for sitting around outdoors.

Charlie is turning towards me. 'You've got someone, you said, who can find the old stuff, the deleted stuff?'

'If we're lucky.'

'Let's hope we're lucky.' He nods. 'How did your date go?' He laughs. 'Glad you're dating.' He doesn't know about Vic ... He would have met Elizabeth years ago, but he didn't know her well.

'It went fine. Thanks for asking.' My turn to laugh. 'How's your girl getting on at Charlton?'

'Played for the first team on Saturday – somebody was injured. They beat the Daggers – Dagenham and Redbridge, that is.'

'I know who the Daggers are.'

'3–1. Good game. She was good. Got well into their half. Put in some good crosses.' He drinks some more. He's getting to the end of his pint. 'How are those children: Ruby and her brothers and sisters? Have you seen them?'

'I saw Ruby just now, before I came up here. She's ... as OK as someone could be whose mother was murdered three weeks ago. She was sad, tearful, but holding it together – helped by various people: her gran, her Canadian dad who has gone home for a bit but is coming back for Christmas, her brother Luke ... and Tracy Upcher—'

'Tracy! She's so good! Genuine. Compassionate. Salt of the earth!'

'And Gary Jackson. He's living there. Magistrates lifted the restraining order.'

'Didn't know that.' He's raising his eyebrows.

'Well ... Ruby is really pleased he's there; he's the father of the two youngest kids. Tracy helped make it happen. She asked the kids and Gran what they felt, and they all – even Gran – were in favour. So Tracy went to court and spoke to the magistrates. And apparently he's cleaned up his drug habit and stopped drinking.'

Charlie's glass is empty. I pick it up and wave it at him. He nods. 'Thanks.'

I wait at the bar – lots of people trying to get served. I think about Dave Lightfoot: what the hell has he done? I know what he's not done – interview the Cranley-Smiths. Why not?

Back at the table, I tell Charlie about Martin Cranley-Smith renting a large, empty house in a back street of Marlow. And that the rent is guaranteed by an accountant called Sidney Alexander Stockton who works for high-net-worth people. Can Charlie run a police check to see if he's ever been in trouble?

He will – tomorrow.

We sit in silence for a while. We seem to know each other well enough to do that.

Then Charlie plonks his empty glass on the table and says he needs to get home to watch something new on telly called *The Traitors*. Would I like a lift? We go out into the cold and climb into his Ford Focus.

29

Stefan came round at about 3 pm. He sat down, hitched on his mad-scientist spectacles, shook his splendid hair and opened Caroline's laptop. Soon he was folded over the keyboard like an anxious jazz pianist – prodding at the keys, peering at the screen, up, down and back again – and again, and again.

I made coffee for us and sat in my armchair under the window reading, glancing at, Lorca. I couldn't concentrate. So I didn't mind when my phone warbled. John McCormick in Rome, about to get a plane home. 'There's nothing, Jim. Julia works for Pablo, and that's all she does for him. I've written most of my report. I'll email it later.'

'Good. So often the way: the paranoid husband and the innocent wife. How was it for you?'

'Not bad. Saw some sights, some restaurants, the inside of a theatre – even there they didn't touch. Hotel corridors, dining rooms. That's about it.' He paused and coughed. 'Except ... Pablo *is* playing away, but not with her. But I don't mention that, do I?'

'No! No, you don't. Our client does not need to know that.'

'OK. Call you tomorrow?'

'John, there's another job. Could you come by here, my place, in the morning – say ten o'clock? And can you bring your car? Just a short day-trip out of London.'

I put the phone down and sat staring at Stefan's broad back and his mane of hair. I picked up Lorca – my twin-language edition – and realised that I was in *un remanso de silencio*, a backwater of silence. Stefan wasn't tapping the keys. He seemed to be thinking.

Eventually, he said: 'There's stuff here.' He turned to check I was there. 'Stuff here, Jim – but I can't get straight at it. Gonna have to download something. Not sure what yet. It'll take time.'

'OK. Something there. That's good. Well done.'

He twisted his watch around his wrist and stared at it. 'Can I take it home? I could work on it later.' He waved his thumb at the laptop. 'And give it some time tomorrow. Could take a while though.'

'Take it, but for Christ's sake don't lose it. And bring it back as soon as you can.'

'I don't usually lose things.' He looked me in the eye, and then looked away.

'Do you know what's there? What type of thing?'

'It has to be emails or word files – perhaps both. Stuff she erased . . . unless someone else had access.'

'No one had access after she died. The police took it that night.'

'OK.' He nodded.

I stuck a piece of card into my Lorca to mark my place, and put it down. 'Unless . . . Unless a copper took it on himself, or herself . . .'

Stefan looked up, raised his eyebrows … and slid Caroline's laptop into his bag beside his own.

I stood up and stretched. 'We'll just keep that in mind … And … If … when you find something, look out for these names.' I scribbled on a notepad: *Gary Jackson; Martin Cranley-Smith.* 'Remember them, and then eat this.' I handed him the note.

He stuffed it in an inside pocket. 'OK Jim. I'll eat it later – with chips and mayo.'

★ ★ ★

On the way over to Laura's I bumped into Mrs Mumford under a lamppost in Lyndhurst Grove.

'Jim!' She grabbed my hand. 'How *are* you?' She stared and spoke as if she'd heard that I had a serious illness.

'I'm fine, fine. How are you?'

'OK. OK. I'm well really.' She wandered into the road, pushed up the tailgate of a black SUV and began to pull out a Christmas tree. 'Only twenty days till Christmas, you know. I'm trying to get ahead this year.'

I hadn't known that she lived in this street – in a tall, narrow, early Victorian house. 'Here, let me help you.'

'So kind. Thank you, Jim.' It was a big tree wrapped in plastic netting. I helped her slide it off the tailgate and lifted the stump end, which had been chopped to a point and rammed into a slice of pine log. We struggled up the steps to her front door. 'So lucky, meeting you. A strapping man to help!' She smiled. 'So kind.' We lugged it into her living room and stood it in the bay window overlooking the street. 'That'll do. Thank you so much, Jim.'

'Pleased to help, Pauline.' I rubbed my hands.

She was peering at me. 'Any news about poor Caroline Swann?'

'Not that I've heard. But they might be making progress behind the scenes.'

She came closer and stared at me even harder. 'Do you think it's to do with these county lines?'

'Well . . . I don't know. It's possible.'

'Well, I think it is, Jim. Possible. From what I hear.'

She offered me a drink, but it wasn't even 5.30 – far too early for me.

I left soon afterwards amid a shower of thanks, and walked on under the dim street-lighting. I'd thought about county lines – specifically the moving of drugs to, and around, a small town like Marlow – before. After all, drugs and people trafficking: a gruesome twosome.

★ ★ ★

I spent the evening with Danny. He was unusually quiet. And later he got cross because there were no chocolate digestives, or chocolate biscuits of any kind, in the cupboard. I guessed it was more than that. I sat on the sofa, put my arm round him and asked if everything was OK at school.

He was watching *Andy's Dinosaur Adventures*. 'Yes,' he sighed, and kept staring at the screen. 'Everything's OK.'

'Is Felix all right?'

'Felix! Why Felix?' His eyes stayed on the screen.

'He's your friend, isn't he?'

'Yes.' Another sigh. 'He's OK.'

I gripped his shoulder more tightly. 'What's up, Dan? I can tell something's up.'

'Nothing's up.' He moved away from me a little – but not completely. He pretended to be intrigued by the fast-rolling credits of a programme he's seen many times before.

He went to bed at about eight. I read to him from a book by David Walliams. A few days ago, it made him giggle.

Tonight: nothing. I stopped reading and sat on his bed with my arm round him. 'Do you miss Mum, Dan?'

I felt him squirm. A long pause. Then his face puckered. 'Yes.' Tears trickled ... and then rolled. He drew a long breath and howled: 'I want Mum!' Another deep breath. And a drawn-out shriek. 'I'm sorry ... I miss Mum.' Words broken by shudders. 'I want her ... to be safe.' Then convulsive sobs as he drew in air. 'I can't help ... help it ... I'm ... sorry.'

I picked him up and sat him on my knee. 'You don't need to be sorry. You haven't done anything wrong. You're missing Mum. That's OK. You know, your mum used to miss me sometimes when I was out at work at night.'

'What? Being a detective?'

'Yes. That was it. Being a detective.' I pulled him towards me, hugging him tighter. 'It's OK to miss people – and to feel sad. Everyone does that sometimes.'

'Do you?'

'Yes. I miss ... your grandmother, your mum's mum.'

He leaned away from me. He was looking into my eyes and seemed to be thinking.

'She was my wife – and she was mum to your mum and to Aunt Charlotte.'

He leaned into me – rubbed his cheek against mine. 'I love you ... Grand ... pa.'

'I love you too.' I pull him closer. 'You know that. It's OK.' He was still breathing in short gasps. 'Come downstairs.' I picked him up the only way I can now. In a fireman's lift, his head over my shoulder, my arms around his legs.

By the time we got downstairs, he was giggling through his sniffles.

He lay flat on the sofa with his head on my lap. We talked

about his mum and her work. And then his dad, which was difficult. Then he went quiet, and I tried some word association – an idea I'd had a few days ago.

'Green.'

'Bananas.'

'Football.'

'Goal.'

'Peaches.'

'Er ... peaches ... er ... skin.'

'Car.'

'BMW.'

'Pepper.'

'Pig.'

'Sausage.'

'Jumbo.'

'Jumbo! Why jumbo?'

'Jumbo sausage! From the fish 'n' chip shop.' He looked up at me. 'Duh!'

'Tree.'

'Leaves ... Leaf. Dead brown leaf.' He yawned.

'Park.'

He didn't answer.

'Park.'

'Football.'

'You had enough of that?'

'Yeh.'

'Are you sleepy? Do you want to go back to bed?'

'No. Stay here with you.' He yawned again.

I fetched a soft rug that Laura sometimes draped over herself when she sat in her favourite armchair. I laid it over him and sat down beside him. He wriggled so that his head rested against my thigh. Soon he was asleep, breathing easily.

Peppa Pig? Weird creature with eyes on the side of her snout, Picasso-style. That didn't help.

I sat beside Danny for ten minutes – and my thoughts meandered: Gary Jackson, Martin Cranley-Smith, Max, Ernst, DI Lightfoot, Avril Miskiewicz, County Lines. Then I picked him up – fireman's lift again – and took him up to bed.

★ ★ ★

'Jeez Dad! Thanks so much for staying up. Everything all right?' Laura leaned down and kissed my cheek. Then she stood up straight and blew out her lips. 'I'm knackered. But it was great! Huge venue – for me, anyway – thirteen hundred people sitting down and another hundred, hundred and fifty maybe, standing at the back and down the sides. Amazing! Three encores! Exhausting! But wow!'

It was after 1 am. She'd been at Watford Colosseum with the Random Newmans. 'Fantastic! Well done.' I stood up and clapped her shoulders. 'These people. The audience – hundreds of them. They're there for *you*, aren't they?'

'Well . . .' She shrugged. 'And the band. It's a good band. I wouldn't do this otherwise. Fancy a whisky?'

'Er . . . maybe.'

'I know it's late.'

'Yeah. If you do.'

She moved towards the kitchen. 'Phil is a good singer; we've got the harmonies going – and some call and response. It's fun. And Esther, the sax player, is great: Joshua Redman with extra oomph.' She came back with two glasses and a bottle of Grouse.

I fetched a jug of water. I'd waited up to hear about the gig. But also to tell her about Danny's freak-out; it would be wrong to hide it – unfair on them both. 'I've got to tell

217

you. Danny wasn't altogether happy tonight. After you left, he went quiet – just staring at the telly and answering me in monosyllables.'

'Oh no! Poor boy.' She splashed whisky into the glasses.

'I got it out of him when I took him up to bed. He was missing you, I'm afraid. He said so. And then he threw a bit of a wobbler. Was in tears and finding it hard to speak – you know. Then he said he hoped you were safe. Seemed like he was worrying about you being out at night.'

'Dad. That's awful. I'm so sorry. What then?'

'Well, I brought him downstairs.' I poured water into both glasses and took a sip. 'We talked – about you. He worships you, you know that. So proud that his mum is a singer. He cheered up. He did say he wished he saw his dad more.'

Laura nodded and rolled her eyes.

'He was sleepy. Tired. He fell asleep here and, after a while, I carried him back up.'

'Oh God! He's only six. I sometimes forget that.' She took a slug of whisky, rinsed it around her mouth and swallowed. 'I'd better stop this Random Newmans stuff. I was thinking about it. I've either got to stop or get in deeper. They want me on all their gigs – and on an album. So ...' She swallowed some more whisky. 'I think I'd better get out and let them find another singer.' She shook her head. 'If that's what they want ... Well, it *is* what they want. I do add a lot. I can see that. But ... I'm a jazz singer, Dad. They're an indie band, post punk whatever – you know? – but they're good musicians, all of them.' She dropped her shoulders and looked across at me.

'You don't have to decide about your career now, at half past one in the morning. It's the first time in ages that Dan's been upset. He was really tired.'

We talked some more. Phil wanted her to go on tour

with them – Europe as well as the UK. He'd suggested that she might get a nanny who could travel with her and Dan – the band would pay. She'd told him that Danny had to go to school. And they'd left it at that.

'Maybe I can just be an occasional guest with the Newmans – when it fits, when maybe I can take Danny . . . No, that won't work . . . Er . . . I don't know . . .'

'Leave it for now,' I said. 'It's really late. One of us has to take him to school tomorrow.'

'I'll take him. And do his breakfast. I want to.' She tipped her glass up, taking a final sip. 'Oh God! I want to get him up now and hug him.' She put on a sad face.

'I'll get up anyway. McCormick's coming to mine at ten.'

★ ★ ★

I woke in the dark. Danny was crying.

But it was all right: Laura was talking to him – and soon all went quiet. He would be in her bed now – cosy with his mum.

Heartburn. I shouldn't drink whisky so late. I turned on the light, sucked a Rennie, read a little Lorca: 'Ode to Walt Whitman'. I don't understand it all, but it's beautiful – and angry – translated by Stephen Spender and someone called J.L. Gili. Light off. Heartburn defeated.

30

McCormick arrives in a white Toyota Prius, three-years-old, clean and neat like its owner. I nudge the Merc closer to the house so that John can squeeze into my off-road parking space.

Upstairs, he takes off a black quilted jacket and tells me about the Hassler Hotel in Rome. He's wearing a blue suit over an open-necked shirt and a V-necked sweater: plenty of layers – it's cold out there. He takes a blue folder from his rucksack and hands it to me. 'I emailed this to you. Thought you might like a hard copy.'

It's labelled 'The Italian Job, 2–5 December, John McCormick'.

'I read your email. Nice and detailed. You did a great job. And good news for our paranoid client.' I tap the folder. 'Thanks. Big thanks.'

I make coffee for him and tell him about the Caroline Swann murder. Pretty much everything – except the curiosity that I've been given her computer without the knowledge of the SIO. John sits on the sofa and listens almost motionless until I get to the Cranley-Smiths and their imprisonment of Ruth, Kamal and Emilie in a shipping container. Then his mouth opens – 'Oh no!' – and he punches the sofa beside him. The news that Kylie, Clayton and I released these people and took them to their relatives delights him. 'Brilliant!' he shouts with a big smile. And, for a moment, I wonder if I've told him too much.

Did he really need a job? Could he be spying on me? No. Spying for whom? He asked for a job days ago. Days before Lightfoot came to light as dodgy . . . maybe. Everyone rates this quiet, efficient man. He got bored when he was the boss of 300 people. So what? Good for him.

I show him the google map of Marlow, point to the Cranley-Smiths' house by the river and then zoom in on 48 Claremont Road. 'I need you to watch this place.' I switch to street view and manage to swivel the picture towards the house, most of which is hidden behind a mass of trees and shrubs, and invisible from the road. Only the left side of the building and the gravel drive can be seen through the gate.

'Look out for these people.' I show John photos, grabbed from my dash camera film, of Martin and Jennifer Cranley-Smith, Max and Ernst and I send them to his phone. 'The Cranley-Smiths have just taken a lease on this house. We want to know why. The place was empty – no furniture, nothing – on Tuesday, my last visit. There may be someone there now. If so, photos of them would be good, if you can manage that. If no one seems to be around, make an excuse, ring the bell, take a look through the windows. See if there's any furniture yet, or anything happening. Can you stay till about half five? Then knock off and give me a call. And relax over the weekend.

He's been nodding as I speak. Now he says, 'OK. I'll get going.' He stands up and I show him out, to the top of the stairs. As I turn to go back into the flat, he says, 'About

Christmas. I don't suppose you know what will be happening. It's just our boy's coming back from uni. I'd like to spend some time with him.'

'That's fine. We're very flexible. Anything like that is fine. Anything to do with kids; I know what it's like. Anyway, we try to take a break, Christmas to New Year, but ... if there's a job that can't wait, well, that's bad luck for someone – maybe me. Just tell me whenever you need time off for family stuff.'

'Thanks, Jim. That's brilliant.' He turns away.

'Didn't know you had kids, John.'

'Just the one. But I'm not married.' He says this as if it's a matter of pride. 'Been with Jo for twenty-one years, and never got round to it.' He gives a big grin. 'Sometime though, maybe – who knows?'

★ ★ ★

The front garden of Caroline Swann's house has been tidied. Someone has pulled weeds out of the gravel; the kids' bikes are lined up and chained to the railings; even the scooters are standing upright in a row.

The door is opened by a tall, pale man, with blond hair and sharp features. I recognise him. I've stood beside him at the swings in Warwick Gardens; we've exchanged smiles and mutters, as adult strangers do in children's playgrounds. He looks different: smarter, clean-shaven, clean clothes, short hair. I recognise him, but, till now, I didn't know his name.

'Gary. I'm Jim Domino.'

'OK.' He looks surprised. 'OK.' He nods and smiles. 'Ruby's at school. Pat's here, Caro's mum? Or did you want to see me?'

'You, actually. Have you a few minutes?'

'Yes. I've plenty of time.' He smiles again and holds the door open. 'Come in.'

I follow him along the passage to the kitchen. 'Did Ruby tell you that I'm unofficially looking into Caroline's ... er ... death?'

'Yes. Yes. She did. Thank you for that. I'm – we're – grateful. The police seem to have given up on it.'

The kitchen is warm and smells of damp washing. Two blue plastic baskets are full of it. An ironing board is set up and piles of neatly folded clothes sit on every surface. 'Is this you, or Pat, doing the ironing?'

'It's me. I love ironing.' He laughs. 'Very calming.' He goes to the ironing board and picks up a huge iron; it looks streamlined, like a speedboat. 'And I'm fast. I learned from Caro. "Don't waste time. Doesn't have to be perfect," she used to say.' He puts the iron down. 'Bless her.'

'I'm sorry. You must miss her.'

He gives me a long look, then blinks and wrinkles his nose, which raises his upper lip at one end. 'Oh God! Yes.' He looks through the window to the garden at the back and lets out a long, almost silent, sigh. 'I screwed up.' He turns to me. 'You probably know that.'

I nod, and sit down on a stool by the table.

'I should have been around – protecting her – not that she needed protecting. She could protect herself.' He looks at me again. 'She could usually. But something happened. And they accused me.' He shrugs, wide-eyed, and looks out of the window again. '*I* don't know what happened. Have you got any ideas?'

'No. Not yet.' I shake my head. 'It's a puzzle. I don't think they actually accused you. It's called questioning.'

'It felt like being accused.'

'It must've been hard. I'm sorry.'

'Not your fault.' He sighs again. 'Mine. I let her down.'

'How? In what way?'

'My drug habit – cocaine.' He stares at the floor, then up at me again. 'I'm an addict, a recovering addict. I'm clean now.' He raises a fist high in the air. 'Fourteen days clean! Hurray!' He drops his arm. 'It might not sound long, but it is.' He raises his voice. 'It is! It's since I was arrested. I spent a night in a cell. It was horrible.' He's speaking more quietly. 'I was cold *and* sweating. But I was thinking. Caroline is dead. I thought about the children – *all* of them.' He looks at me and raises his hands, palms up. 'I wanted to look after them. And now that's what I'm doing. Thank God! With Pat. The authorities let me. Despite what I did before. My stupidity.'

He sits down at the table opposite me. With his sharp features and blue eyes, he looks like a tortured rock star. 'Are you all right? Listening to all this?' he says – and doesn't wait for an answer. 'I was recovering when I met Caroline five . . . almost six . . . years ago. We met on New Year's Eve. I was clean, going to meetings. I had work – I'm a cabinet-maker; I can make you anything as long it's made of wood. I was in a band. Rehearsal – more of a jam session – once a week. A gig now and then. I got together with Caro and,' – he raises his hands – 'everything was great.' He stops talking; his elbow is on the table, his wrist to his mouth.

'And what happened?'

'OK.' He drops his arm and turns to me. 'I moved in with Caro – a while, a few months, before Lily was born. And . . . you *could* say . . . I took on four kids. And I was grateful that Caroline let me do that, wanted me to do that, be a dad, step-dad, to Luke and Ella and Jake – they had no dad. You probably know that.'

'Yes.'

'Ruby had, *has*, a dad. Michel. God, he's cool – in his way! Huge in Canada. Women love him. Tom Jones for Canada, except he sings in French – and writes a lot of songs.' He glanced out of the window – and back at me. 'Anyway, I moved in – and it was good. Caro was happy. I was happy. Gradually the children accepted me. We had fun as a family.'

He goes on talking and I go on listening. He makes coffee for us both, and takes a cup to Pat, who is upstairs – he seems to be checking that she won't interrupt us or overhear him talking about himself and Caroline. All was good, very good, according to Gary, for about four years. Lily was born and then Sam. It was difficult with so many children, but it worked.

'We *made* it work,' he says. But then small things began to go wrong. He had less work. He blamed austerity: people had less money; they moved house less often; developers were building fewer houses and flats. He spent more time with his band; they were getting gigs and they were paying him money that he needed. He became partly dependent on Caroline – and he hated that, though she told him she didn't mind.

At the same time, she got involved in more and more campaigning. 'She was obsessed, I have to say, with climate change. Fair enough, but I was responsible more and more for looking after the kids. We began to argue. *I* wanted to be with my band; *she* wanted to be on a demo. One night we were playing a gig in Soho, a swanky cocktail place – not our usual kind of venue. Someone ordered a load of shots, put one in front of me: sambuca, with the coffee beans. It was late. I was tired. Anyway, I picked it up and chucked it back. No one said anything. No one noticed, even though I hadn't had a drink for ten years. It felt good and ten minutes later, I had another one. I went to the gents. This bloke – not anyone in the band; most of them did coke but they knew I was clean; they respected that. This bloke, young bloke, offered me a line. There it was – on the china, rolled-up tenner. And—' He looks up at me. 'And that was it! Two days later I scored some myself.' He shakes his head. 'What a fucking . . . *That's* how I let her down.'

He stands up, walks about, stares out of the window. 'And, almost worse, I let the children down – six of them by then. From there, in a few weeks, we were rowing. I was spending what money I had, and some of hers, on drugs and vodka. She got angry, rightly, many times. I retaliated.' He sits down across from me again. He's biting his lower lip. 'I kept promising to stop. But somehow I couldn't – always one more hit. I needed money – for my habit. When she wouldn't give it to me, I got angry. There were times when I was so desperate, I grabbed her purse. And we fought.' He puts his elbows on the table and his head in his hands. 'I didn't hurt her. I wouldn't . . . but there was shouting, screaming, frightened children. Neighbours butted in. Called the police. I was taken to the police station and charged; got six months suspended for battery, and she was granted a restraining order.' He's still holding his head. 'Which meant I had to move out.' Now he's close to tears. 'I screwed up big time. All for the sake of . . .'

'It's an illness. You know that.'

'But I have to fight it, don't I?'

'And you are.'

'Yes.' He lets out a sob. 'But she's dead.'

'That isn't your fault.' I stand up and come round the table, put an arm on his shoulder and my face down close to his. 'That isn't your fault.' I say it again. 'Don't blame yourself. *You* didn't kill her. You're already doing the best thing – the thing that matters. Looking after all those lovely kids. I respect you for that.'

I stand upright. He leans back. 'Yes. Thank you for saying that. I'm sorry.'

'Don't be.'

'I don't know why I told you all that.'

'I'm glad you did. Helps me to understand. Caroline, the children, you.'

'OK.'

'There's just one thing I'd like to know. Where were you on 8 November?'

He looks at me, bleary-eyed, and shakes his head. 'I can't tell you. I said "no comment" to the police.' He's silent, still looking at me. 'You think I did it, I killed her? Is that why you're asking?' He says it quietly, as if he wouldn't blame me for thinking that.

'No. I don't. It's just . . . Look. You were dealing, weren't you – to pay for your habit.'

He doesn't answer. He just looks at me.

'I can guess where you're at. Someone has threatened you. If you blab – consequences.' He's still looking at me. And he's sliding an empty coffee mug around on the table. 'All right. I understand. It's only that you might think there is no connection with Caroline's death – and there probably isn't – but there just might be. Neither of us can be sure of that. Not yet. So can you tell me where you were? I won't tell anyone. I swear.'

'No . . . I can't.'

'You could be in danger. It might be better if I knew.'

'I'm not. It's all right as it is.'

'The children could be in danger. Have you thought of that?'

'Yes, I have. And they're not.' He takes a long breath in

227

and breathes out. 'I know what you're saying, but it's best as it is.'

I sit back. 'OK. I appreciate that you've told me so much. Is there anything else you want to say? Anything that would help me work out what happened?'

'I don't think so. No.' He stands up. 'Except thank you for listening. I'm glad I told you all that.' He comes around the table. 'It's good – in a funny way – to talk. Thank you.'

I stand up. He holds out his hand. I shake it.

I give him my card and ask him to ring me if he wants to tell me anything else.

31

I walk out into the cold, and head for home. Lunchtime, but I'm not hungry. I'm thinking about Gary and the children – and his refusal to say where he was. I'm certain, almost, that to fund his drug habit he'd been working for an organised crime gang for a while – perhaps as much as two years. Long enough to have got too far in, to know too much.

When Caroline died, he stopped dealing and gave up the drugs. Coming off drugs would have been – would still be – torture; leaving a gang might be even harder. They don't like to have ex-members ... unless they're dead. His bosses had put the frighteners on him. Which is why he won't say where he was. Will they forget that he was once one of them? Or will it nag away at them – that there's a man out there who knows who they are, and where and how they operate? If so, what might they do? A beating? A knifing? A drive-by shooting?

Is Gary living on hope, trusting to luck? What else can he do? Disappear? But he cares about those kids; two of them are his; they are the reason he cleaned up and left the gang. He could tell the authorities all he knows. But if he did, he'd need witness protection – a change of identity and a move to somewhere new. That way, he'd lose the children. That whole family couldn't be put in a witness protection programme. Too many of them; there'd be too many broken connections. Ruby . . . Ruby has a father. She can't be separated from him, or from the others. They're a unit.

Gary *is* living on hope.

★ ★ ★

Soon after I get home Charlie Ritchie calls. He's found out more about Sidney Stockton. 'A bagman for villains. No police record. Never been charged. My pal at the FCA – the Financial Conduct Authority, that is . . .'

'I know what the FCA is, Charlie.'

'. . . all right. Sorry. He says, my contact – you'll like this, Jim – quote, "Stockton is the type who dances on the edge of the toilet bowl but never slips into the shit."' Charlie laughs.

I laugh – and wince at the same time.

'Anyway, according to my pal, Stockton earns plenty by advising fat cats on tax avoidance and what my pal calls legal laundering. If there's a loophole, he'll find it – but he stays inside the law. Doesn't mean he hasn't worked for criminals. He has. If a client is charged, Stockton will say: "I told him not to do that, but he did it anyway."'

'Good source you've got there, Charlie.'

'And . . . one more thing. Stockton comes up in the Panama Papers. You know the Panama Papers?'

'I do.'

'He's there – advising all sorts. Even a couple of politicians – Tories, of course.'

I thank Charlie, ring off and make myself a chicken sandwich.

★ ★ ★

I mess about through the afternoon: a little admin, exercises, and half an hour lying on the sofa thinking – about many things ... including Dave Lightfoot and Avril Miskiewicz.

McCormick phones at half past five. Max, Ernst and the grey van with the scrape on its nearside have been at Claremont Road. John recognised them from the photos. 'Two deliveries came in. First, a big vanload of what I'd call metal furniture. You know what I mean, Jim? Warehouse-type equipment: loads of grey metal strips and flat surfaces. Looks like it has to be bolted together to make shelves, tables, etcetera. Two blokes who came with the van plus Max and Ernst spent almost two hours unloading it all – tons of it; chairs as well, folding metal chairs. Then, in the afternoon, another van, smaller, brought two beds. Single beds – sort of tubular design, painted white, with mattresses. Just practical narrow beds. Nothing luxury. Like you might have in a barracks.'

'So they're going to store stuff there, and two people are going to sleep there?'

'Yep. Looks like it.'

'Any bedding, duvets, whatever?'

'No.'

'So no one there tonight then?'

'Probably not. Max and Ernst left at about five. No one there now.'

'OK. Good work ... I'm going to stake it out on Monday. Now, you have a proper weekend.'

I'm about to say goodbye when John says he'll fill me in on a couple of discreet surveillance points he's found. He'll drop in on his way home and draw me a map.

I check in with Kylie. She's minding a young singer who is over here from the states for three gigs in six days. I'd never heard of her, of course, but she likes to have a female minder and Kylie has a good reputation.

'Jim. All good. No trouble – yet. Though we've got Glasgow: Sunday and Monday. It's fun, but not such fun as Gwen Stefani. There's the usual: limos, parties, hanging around backstage, fans, flowers – all that.'

'So why don't *I* get these gigs?'

'Oh, poor you – stuck with murders and people trafficking.' She laughs. 'But this . . . It's so easy, it's almost boring. She doesn't want to do anything except rehearse, perform, talk to her boyfriend in New York, eat – a little – and sleep – a lot.'

'I did bodyguard duty for Brian Wilson a couple of years ago. I thought it went all right, but since then nothing in that line.'

'Brian who?'

'Naff off! Have fun in Glasgow.'

★ ★ ★

I sit on the sofa and gaze at the cover of my book of Joaquín Sorolla's paintings, which lies unopened on the table beside me. Tomasz Stanko's *Lontano* wafts – and occasionally shrieks – from the sound system. I think about opening the book; I know that a receipt from Lidl marks a particular painting that moves me: *My Wife and Daughters in the Garden*. I remember the scene: three women close together and happy on a bench, with a sleeping dog at their feet. I leave the book unopened, lie back and stare at the ceiling.

By the time John arrives, I'm ready for a drink: a

Scotch – perhaps a single malt; a bottle of Highland Park is unopened in the cupboard.

John is wearing a clean, black, cable-stitched sweater, and neat blue jeans. He thanks me for the offer of a drink, but, no thanks, he's driving. He'll have a glass of water now, and a beer when he gets home. I give him the water, pour myself a slug of Highland Park and splash a little water into it.

He sits down at my table and asks for pencil and paper. 'I just want to show you a couple of things,' he says. I give him sheets of A4 and a pencil, and he sketches a simple diagram of 48 Claremont Road. I look over his shoulder, and he speaks and annotates the diagram in small capital letters as he goes. 'House ... lawn ... parking ... wall ... trees ... number 50 ... hedge ... gravel drive ... Claremont Gardens ... number 46 ... builders' yard.'

He leans back, holds up the paper and stares at it. 'The scale isn't right, but it's good enough.' He puts the paper back on the table. I sit down beside him and he pushes it towards me.

'I walked past a few times. Then I sat in the car, way up the street, to see what comings and goings there were. None at all – until, at about 10.30, a woman came out of number 50 with a kid and walked off towards the High Street. I took a chance, ran into her driveway and bundled into this hedge.' He points with the pencil. 'It's high, higher than this wall, and it's thick, dense, so you can hide yourself in there, look over the wall and have a view of number 48: the house, the grassy bit and the parking area.'

'Nice one,' I say, and sip a little Highland Park.

'Yeah. Not bad.' He smiles. 'I was in there from ten-thirty till three o'clock because the woman soon came back without the kid, and she didn't go out again till three. When she'd gone, I scarpered. But, it's from there' – he points with the pencil – 'that I saw Max and Ernst and all that metal furniture being unloaded.'

'Did you take a break after that?' I want him to have taken a break. I think he works too hard.

'Yes.' He shrugs and grins. 'Nipped to the High Street. Used the facilities in a pub called The Chequers, bought a sandwich in Sainsbury's and ate it sitting on a bench.' He swallows some water and wipes his mouth with the back of his hand. 'Then,' – he picks up the pencil and draws a small square between the house and the wall that he'd been looking over from next door – 'I hid in here.' He doodles, thickening the lines, as if to show the importance of the square. 'It's a little brick building: probably an outdoor toilet back in the day. I saw it in the morning; no one went anywhere near it. It's towards the back of the house, but from there I could see plenty – the side of the house, lots of windows, the parking area, all the comings and goings.'

'How did you get in there without being seen? You didn't just walk through the gate and—'

'No. I walked up here.' He points to the side road, Claremont Gardens. 'And through here.' He points with the pencil. 'That's a builders' merchants – a yard full of stuff, diggers, concrete mixers, pallets of bricks, breeze blocks, cement, all that – and a shop. Easy to dodge through – and round behind the shop. I climbed over the wall here – and into the back garden of 48. I walked round. If anyone saw me, I was going to say I was a surveyor from the council looking for my assistant – had they seen him?' He glances at me, grins and shakes his head. 'That's an old one, isn't it? Anyway, no one saw me, and I went in.' He taps the square. 'No lock on the outside; there isn't usually on the outside of a toilet, but this wasn't a toilet any more, just flowerpots and a bike with flat tyres. There's a gap at the top of the door, so I could see over.'

'Is there a gap at the bottom as well? Often is with toilets.'

'Yes.' He laughs. 'So I stood well back, leaned on the door with my arms.'

He drinks some water and pushes his chair back. 'Anyway, that's it. Just wanted you to see: two places to hide.' He flips the pencil from the hedge to the toilet.

'Excellent.'

We both stand up, and I find that I'm patting him on the shoulder.

32

Stefan phones to check that I'm home. It's 9 am on Saturday. At a quarter past, he arrives with Caroline's laptop under his arm and a grim look on his face. He says hello and accepts my offer of coffee. Then he sighs and says, 'Jim. This is pretty weird.' He knocks on the steel case of the laptop with his knuckle and sits down at my work table. 'I've spent a lot of time with this. Spoke to some digital forensics people. Tried different programs, different tactics, different apps.' He flips the lid open and Caroline's screensaver comes up: her six children standing around granny Pat in the garden. A photo I know well; it's on my old laptop, along with the rest of Caroline's files.

'I found deleted emails that had been permanently erased – not just put in the trash folder.' He pauses, looking at me with his finger between his lips – and I sit down facing him. 'I don't know about you, but lots of folk erase stuff they no longer want so as to clear space on their computers.'

'Yeah, I do that. Erase deleted emails, junk mail – now and again.'

'Do you also erase stuff because you don't want anyone to see it?'

'Er . . .' I have to think. 'No, but . . . I guess some people would.'

'Right. Well, I'm guessing . . . but I think that Caroline, or,' – he gives me a long stare – 'someone, did erase some of this for that reason. I'm talking about emails from and to those people you told me to look out for: Gary Jackson and Martin Cranley-Smith. There are emails from those two in the regular inbox and in the sent box and in the trash – not erased; we've seen those before. But there are also *erased* emails to and from those two – emails that no one was meant to read again.'

'OK. When can I read them?'

'Now.' He shrugs. 'No problem.' He picks up his coffee mug for the first time and looks across at me. 'Do you know of someone called David Lightfoot?'

'Yes. Why?'

'There are emails to and from him.'

'Are there?' I stare back at him. 'I didn't know that Caroline knew Lightfoot.'

'Really? Who is he?'

'Good question.' I'm smiling – perhaps I shouldn't be. 'He's a policeman, here at Peckham, a DI.'

Stefan smiles back at me and nods – and his hair falls forward over his face. 'I thought he was police. I've read some of those emails. The thing is there are no emails to or from him in the regular inbox or sent box or trash box. *All the emails* to and from him have been erased. That's not the case with Cranley-Smith or Gary Jackson. It's as if Caroline – or someone – wanted to erase him altogether, wipe out any connection with him.'

'OK.'

'I mean, no other recipient has been completely erased – except a few incidentals from maybe a year or more ago: a plumber, a charity she sent money to – that kind of thing.'

'Pretty damn interesting, Stefan. Thanks.'

'Right. I've made four folders of *erased* emails. Four sources: Martin Cranley-Smith; Gary Jackson; David Lightfoot; the rest. Each folder contains three folders: inbox; sent – sent by Caroline, obviously; and deleted or trash – whatever you want to call it. I stress: all the emails in these folders were erased by someone; that someone didn't expect them ever to be read again. I sent the folders to myself, so that we have a back-up on cloud. I'll send them to you now so you can look on your own computer. OK?'

'Yes. Fantastic.' Emails between Caroline and Dave Lightfoot; Caroline and Martin Cranley-Smith. Progress! At last!

Stefan puts his laptop on the table, opens it and starts clicking. I sit opposite him and open mine. Three aluminium laptops on the table – identical, save for an 'I'm In' sticker, a relic of the Brexit referendum, on Caroline's. 'OK. They've gone,' he says.

Bing. Four folders plip into my inbox in quick succession.

Stefan comes round the table and looks over my shoulder. 'OK. Each of those has three folders inside it.'

I click on Lightfoot. 'Three folders: inbox, sent, trash.' I click on inbox and find the Apple Mail grid with seventeen emails waiting to be opened.

'Like I said, I've read some of those. They look pretty interesting to me, but I don't know what you're expecting.'

'Not expecting anything.' I look at him over my shoulder. 'But I'm *hoping* for answers. Thanks Stefan.'

'All right, Jim. If it's all clear to you, I'll head off. OK?'

'Of course. Thanks again – and invoice for all your hours.'

'OK, man.' He smiles and clicks the door slowly shut as he leaves.

Today Stefan is like someone from the 1960s: all hair and softness.

★ ★ ★

At 2.15 I stand up, walk across the room, put the kettle on and wander over to the window. Two blackbirds pottering about, male and female. Late in the year for them to be together.

I pour water onto a teabag and go back to the window.

David Lightfoot: did he kill her? Or arrange the attack on her? Clumsy, if it was him. But he had plenty of motive. Bastard! She knew about him. Knew he was bent. He was telling her to lay off the Cranley-Smiths – *or* he would pinch her man, Gary Jackson, for dealing.

He pinched her man later anyway. For murder. Why? To show the world he was doing something. And ... to frighten Gary, make sure he kept quiet.

Gary would be frightened anyway – long-term frightened. Because this is how it works. Grass on us, and we'll kill you.

The male blackbird has found a worm. He doesn't share it. The female is still searching.

Lightfoot the bully. Charlie said that. Well, Caroline stood up to him. Bullies hate that. They retaliate. And – if caught out – pretend nothing happened. Erase the emails – to and from: every email.

What else? A loving relationship wrecked by drugs.

And a couple who think they deserve a stately home and will do anything to get one: trafficking people, false imprisonment, dealing in drugs, distributing them, importing them perhaps.

I spoon the teabag out of the tea and into the bin.

But she went to the park of her own volition.

Didn't she? Did Lightfoot somehow persuade her to go there in the dark? Or arrange to meet her there? Under what pretext?

Pour in milk.

But *he* wouldn't kill her. Someone higher up. Lightfoot, Cranley-Smith: they're small players. Links in the chain. Look at the emails – they reek with aggression and fear: neither of them is bossing this. Lightfoot, a well-rewarded, co-operative, corrupt policeman; Cranley-Smith, edgy, nervous, a middle manager on a percentage. Neither of them would kill anyone. Someone more important would arrange a hit man. And a hit man wouldn't use a rusty, unidentified object as a murder weapon. He would do the job properly.

The sun's low behind the cedar. A pretty sky. I should eat something: a few almonds while I make a cheese sandwich.

If it wasn't Lightfoot, or Cranley-Smith, or a hit man . . . what the hell happened that evening in Warwick Gardens?

33

I finish the sandwich and pop a few grapes. The phone rings. Laura. Tonight's gig is cancelled. Someone – a guitarist – is unwell and can't be replaced at short notice. I'm lined up to look after Danny, but there's no need now. I offer to go over anyway, but she says she'll be fine. She'd like to have a Saturday night and Sunday morning with him; it doesn't happen often.

I understand. Some weeks he spends more time with Juliana and me than with his mum. But I'm disappointed.

I mooch around eating almonds. Then I walk to the Rye. I've had enough emails – read them all, except for the boring ones in the folder marked 'Others'. It's cold out, grey sky and a bitter wind. I stop for a coffee at the café by the playground and sit outside warming my hands on the cardboard cup and catching the sweet scent of passing marijuana. I watch the kids on the big slide, and the mums and dads who fuss, and the grandmums and granddads who sit beside piles of children's coats. I walk to the lake where a pair of ducks land feet first, like seaplanes – and then I head for home.

I pass the Gowlett Arms and remember Charlie Ritchie's daughter who plays left back for Charlton Women. And I think some more about Avril: how to contact her. I don't want to be seen with her at the nick – and she wouldn't want that either. With Stefan's help, I've done what she wanted. She suspected that Lightfoot is bent. But how could she prove it?

Perhaps by getting someone independent of the force to delve into Caroline Swann's computer. Avril is smart. Smart enough to see that there could be a connection. A connection that might explain Lightfoot's reluctance to pursue the case wholeheartedly.

Charlie Ritchie turns up in Avril's office – 'Jim Domino would like to borrow this laptop. Jim's interested in the Swann case; he's a friend of the family.'

'OK Charlie, let him borrow it – and don't tell anyone.'

I walk on to Bellenden Road, then up through Warwick Gardens and down Bushey Hill Road.

Soon I will report to Avril, but first I want to see more of the house in Claremont Road ... No. Why wait? Send her the emails between Caroline Swann and Dave Lightfoot now. Put them on a memory stick and get them to Charlie to pass on to Avril.

I get home at six. I phone Charlie and arrange a handover on Monday morning.

A little later I ring Vic. 'It's me. What you doing?'

'Nothing. What about you?'

'Me too. Nothing.'

'Come over.'

'You sure?'

'Yeah! That'd be nice.'

'Great. See you in about an hour.'

'I'll rustle up something.'

'Sure?'

'Yeah! It'd be nice.'

'OK. See you.'

'Hey! You got any veg?'

'Er. Yeah.'

'What?'

'Leeks.'

'Wonderful! Bring 'em.'

'Will do. See you.'

I don't have any leeks, but I like leeks and I know Ron will be open. He always has leeks and he doesn't close till seven on Saturdays.

★ ★ ★

I wait while Ron serves a man whose small son stares at me; he seems to recognise me. He's about Danny's age and might be in his class at school. I smile at him and he looks away. I gaze at the display of vegetables and fruit. Even though it's the end of the day, it looks splendid – a mass of shapes and colours. But I can't see any leeks.

Ron turns to me. 'Fats, what can I do you for?'

'Leeks. Have you got any?'

Ron looks at an empty tray next to a pile of shallots. 'Hang on.' He goes to the open door at the back. 'Di!'

'Yes.' Her voice sounds as if it's coming from a cave, a long way below ground.

'Any leeks out there?'

There's a short pause. Then: 'Yes.'

'Bring 'em in, please.'

Ron is keen to talk. Even now, four weeks after the crime, he wants to know if there's any news about 'Caroline Swann's killer'. He likes the word 'killer' – he's used it before – and he says it with an unsettling relish.

I pretend that I know nothing new, that the police don't talk to me. Why would they? I turn the conversation to England's chances against Senegal in the World Cup.

'We'll beat them, no trouble. But then,' – his eyes narrow – 'it'll be France: Mbappé and Co.' He shrugs.

Di arrives carrying a box of fresh-looking leeks. I choose three large ones and leave with a sense of triumph.

★ ★ ★

Vic cooks the leeks slowly in butter, sautés some potatoes, roasts strips of pepper and serves with rare rump steaks and English mustard. This, with a warm bottle of Malbec, a cluster of candles and Vic's Saturday-evening calm, nudges me into a peaceful haze.

On Sunday, still peaceful, we drive out of town and fetch up in Cookham where we loaf about in the Stanley Spencer Gallery, then eat thick-cut sandwiches off lumps of wood at the Crown.

I ask about a case Vic is working on: a young man who is charged with breaching a stalking protection order. Vic has advised him to plead guilty and, if he does, with luck, he'll get a suspended sentence. This man, Matthew – I'm not supposed to know his name – has harassed and frightened a young woman by following her all over the place, hanging around outside her work and her home, and sending her hundreds of text messages over a period of more than two years. Yet Vic, bless her, feels sorry for him. She doesn't want him to go to prison.

And nor do I, having heard what a lonely, miserable life he has. 'Aren't we wonderful, magnanimous people,' I say.

'Don't be facetious,' she says. 'We have consciences. Empathy. That's all.'

'But is *anyone* actually evil? Or do they all have excuses?'

'This lad we're talking about isn't evil.'

'Is *anyone*?'

We natter on with mentions of Hitler, Stalin, Jimmy Savile and Andrew Tate; we reach no conclusion and order apple pie with ice-cream to share.

We walk down to the Thames and follow it west along the towpath. Ripples rush on the water, and a weak sun sits low behind trees. I draw my scarf up against the wind.

Vic likes walking, whatever the weather – she's wearing her hiking boots and a quilted jacket. The path leaves the river to follow a fence that protects a group of riverside houses and their private road. We're at the foot of Winter Hill, on the flood plain called Cock Marsh where Jennifer Cranley-Smith goes riding.

Did I mean to come here? I don't think so. I haven't given a thought to Winter Hill or the Cranley-Smiths. I was relishing a day of idleness with this woman who – whose company I love: a day for looking at paintings by an artist who intrigues me, lunching in a pub and walking by the river.

Have I been drawn here by some tick in my subconscious?

No. This is coincidence. 'Shall we walk up the hill?'

'Yes.' Vic takes my arm. 'I love the big sky up there.'

★ ★ ★

I'm following Vic on a zigzag path that cuts deep into thick, tufty grass. I'm lagging about twenty yards behind her – and I've lost that peaceful, easy feeling. I'm thinking about Martin and Jennifer Cranley-Smith and wondering whether, when we get to the top, I might stroll to the other end of the ridge and slip down through Quarry Wood to take a look at their house, their horses, their dogs and their blue containers.

Why? Why do I want to do that? What purpose will it serve?

Vic is at the top looking down at the Thames. I sidle up to her. Would she mind waiting on a bench for a few minutes – well, actually, about twenty minutes – while I go off to check on the home of the people-traffickers I've told her about: the couple called Cranley-Smith?

She looks across to the Chilterns and up at the sky, stretches her arms wide, drops them to her sides and turns to me. Yes, she *would* mind. Twenty minutes sitting on a bench on top of a hill on a cold day! No bloody way! *But* she'd be very happy to come with me; she'd enjoy walking through woods and snooping on villains.

'Really?'

'Really.'

'You'd enjoy doing that?'

'Yes. Of course!' She laughs and grabs my arm again.

We take the path down between the beeches – mostly beeches, some sycamore, conifers, holly.

Half a mile on we veer right, away from the path, downhill, sliding through the beech mast – almost tumbling in the steepest places – until the ground begins to level off and we see openings, dim light, between the trees.

We stop, peer ahead and listen. No sound except the rumble of traffic on the A404. We walk on until we are hidden only by the last line of trees.

'Beautiful place,' Vic whispers.

She's right to whisper. The house is just thirty yards away. 'Yes,' I nod.

Crouching, I move forward into the rhododendrons, the ones I hid in for all those hours, and kneel – bum on heels. Vic follows and kneels to my left. The blue Jag is outside the house and the horses are in the paddock with the foal. But the blue containers aren't there. Instead, behind that thin line of trees, the wooden frame of a new building: a small house, or a large shed, or an office.

That was quick: the containers were there on Tuesday. Four days later: concrete foundations; a skeleton of 4 x 2 waiting for walls, floor and roof; a small digger; and a pile of something, probably timber, under a tarpaulin.

I tell Vic that the container in which Clayton and I had been imprisoned has gone, along with its companion. A patch of bare earth beside the fresh concrete shows where it was.

'Horrible!' She grabs my wrist and squeezes. 'I hate thinking about it . . . But for Kylie, anything could have happened.'

'Yes. Good old Kylie.'

There's no one around. No Range Rover. No grey van. Perhaps they're all out.

'Would cost a fortune, this place,' Vic says. 'All this land – with oak trees, on a bend in the river – and that house. Did one of them inherit it?'

'Don't think so. They're smugglers, traffickers, kidnappers, fraudsters.' I shrug. 'Might be killers.'

'Jim! You *must* be careful.'

'I know . . . I don't think they're killers. Let's go. Just wanted a quick look.'

'Do you have to do this? Shouldn't the police be dealing with these people?' She sounds concerned for me, rather than cross or argumentative – and I'm grateful for that. Because I've been thinking the same thing.

'I'm going to tell Avril about Lightfoot soon, and then she'll find out all about this lot. But I can't give her proof of trafficking or false imprisonment unfortunately, because I let the victims go.'

What I want to do is solve the murder that Lightfoot

gave up on – erased the emails because he thought he might be exposed. Solve it so those kids know what happened to their mother.

We creep away and, when we are under cover of the trees, Vic sighs and puts her arm through mine.

★ ★ ★

Vic drives us back to London; she likes driving – especially, she says, the Merc – though she doesn't have a car. I sit low in the passenger seat and wonder about Martin Cranley-Smith and the house in Claremont Road with its rent guaranteed by a dodgy accountant.

I think back to the Cranley-Smith house, to looking out through the rhododendrons. There was something missing – something that had been there before.

I'm meeting Clayton for breakfast tomorrow. He phoned to ask if I could give him more work. His antique-radiator business isn't doing so well – and his martial-arts classes for kids and teenagers are non-profit. Is non-profit different from charity? I asked. Charities raise money and give it – or something – away, Clayton said. Whereas the kids, some of them – those who can afford to – pay to go to Clayton's Martial Arts, but that only covers the costs. 'I don't make anything out of it; I don't want to,' Clayton said. 'Non-profit. See?'

'Yes I see,' I told him. 'And I can give you more work. That's great – suits me very well. The business is growing. We're getting a reputation; more people, new people, are contacting me.'

★ ★ ★

Dogs. No dogs. That was it. 'Did you hear any dogs barking when we were there looking at that house and garden, and the river?'

'No. No dogs. Just saw the horses.' She glances across at me. 'Should there have been dogs?'

'No. Not necessarily. But there were – not long ago.'

'Well. Well. And what do you think that means, Lewis?'

★ ★ ★

Vic presses a button on the CD changer: 'Well, I'm running down the road trying to loosen my load.' She smiles across at me and taps the steering wheel – and the Eagles stay with us as we drive under the M25 and tuck into the Sunday-evening traffic as it edges towards the Chiswick flyover.

I lower the window a little; we're moving slowly now. A vision and an idea arrive from somewhere. Gary Jackson and his troubled-rock-star looks: had he been working for a rival gang – a rival to whoever had Dave Lightfoot on their payroll? It might not matter. On the other hand, it might help to explain Lightfoot's efforts to pin the murder on Gary.

34

The Crossroads Cafe is packed; people are standing around looking for tables. But Clayton has got here early; there he is at a table near the back, waving a hand and grinning with a coffee and an empty chair in front of him.

He stands up and comes towards me, high-fiving, hugging and back-patting; I haven't seen him for a few days, but it's as if it's been a few months. 'Good to see you, Jim.' He leads me to his table. 'I'm pleased to be getting more work – really pleased. Thank you.'

'Like I said, it suits me just fine. If you weren't coming further onboard, I'd be looking for someone else – and I'd rather have you.'

He grins. 'Jim, you say the nicest things!'

Andy the waiter comes over and we both order a full English. Why not? We seem to be celebrating. I suggest how we might work together from now on: more time, responsibility and money for him; help with management and pulling in clients, as well as his usual work, for me.

His grin comes back, wider than before. 'It's something for me to be seen as more than a pile of muscle.' He clenches his fists on the table. He'll wind up his radiator business, while keeping his martial-arts classes going. 'I love doing that, Jim. It's not a job; it's a hobby: seeing those kids growing in confidence, keeping themselves safe, staying away from the gangs.'

Which reminds me of Gary Jackson and Dave Lightfoot. I lean closer to Clayton and speak quietly. 'What do you know about the local gangs? I'm out of touch.'

'I hear what the boys in my classes say – some of them, anyway. Round here – Lambeth, Southwark, Lewisham – there's loads of gangs and bits of gangs, broken down by age, you know that. But there's two gangs that count and cause trouble: the Peckham Boys, as ever, and the Mileys. And they're warring for territory.'

'Mileys?' I know the Peckham Boys, obviously. But the Mileys are new to me. 'Miley . . . Cyrus?'

Clayton laughs. 'Mile Enders. From across the river, trying to grab bits of south London.'

'Who's winning?'

'I dunno.' He waves his hands in the air and shakes his head. 'I hate them both. And their fucking drugs! Did I tell you I'm getting kids sent to me by social services now? Got one who's eleven years old. A little boy! But tough, hard. Me and the others have had instruction in safeguarding and prevention. I don't really want to do that – it's just talking; I want to make them physically strong, confident, skilful, proud of themselves. But I *do* do it – the chatting, the questioning. Anything to stop them joining gangs, carrying knives, drugs.'

'Do you have *time* for more work with me?'

He smiles. 'Yeah, yeah!' He looks down at the table. 'It's not just me at Clayton's Martial Arts. There's four of us now. My mate Buzz – you know him? You met him more than once; he came with us when we had to repossess that Roller – or was it a Bentley?'

'It was a Roller. Course, I remember. Nice bloke.'

'Yeah. He is, and he's part of Clayton's now. *He* was a gang member not that long ago. He tells them what it's like. Terrifies the little bleeders. But it works. "You'll get money if you're lucky – eventually," he says, "and one day you might get a flash car, but you'll be controlled twenty-four-seven. And if you don't do what they want, you'll end up dead. And if you *do* do what they want, you'll probably end up in prison."' Clayton chuckles. 'Terrifies them.'

We eat our huge breakfasts and discuss the boring, important stuff: the nitty gritty of how we will work together. Then we talk about a job he's working on with Kylie: exposing an insurance fraud – one of those where all the client wants is their money back – no prosecutions, no publicity, but all their money and their costs: *big* money.

'Good. *Very* good. Two new sources – inside sources – almost ready to sign affidavits. They'll cough. I'm confident. Kylie's so good, Jim.' He raises his hands, palms up. 'So fucking direct – and she keeps smiling at them.'

'I know. I know.' I put my elbows on the table and raise my thumbs. 'We're lucky to have her.'

I update him – quietly – on the Caroline Swann investigation and tell him about the mysterious secluded house in a backstreet of Marlow rented by Martin Cranley-Smith. I don't mention Dave Lightfoot or Avril Miskiewicz – in case I'm overheard. I tell him what John McCormick saw on Friday, and that I'm going there this morning to see if there's anything new.

He's holding a knife and a fork, and listening with raised eyebrows and a small grin. He puts his knife and fork down and leans across the table. 'You said just now you didn't think Cranley-Smith was capable of . . .' He mouths the word 'murder'.

'No, I don't. But I think he's evil – and I want to find out what he's doing in that house.'

'You do too much, Jim.' Clayton shakes his head, smiling.

'So do you.' I point a finger at him.

'Well, if there's any trouble, just call me, man.' He chuckles, picks up his fork and prongs a chunk of sausage.

'I will. I quite possibly will.'

★ ★ ★

Charlie is sitting on a green bench in that narrow park that faces the houses in Holly Grove – we haven't time to visit our favourite rendezvous in Lucas Gardens. He's deliberately plonked himself in the middle of the bench and spread himself out so that, wherever I sit, I'm close to him. He's studying his phone and doesn't look up when I sit down at the end of the bench to his left. I take out a paperback of Lorca's poems and open it randomly.

> *Although I know the roads*
> *I'll never reach Córdoba.*

I turn the page and let the book fall to the ground. As I pick it up, I push the smooth plastic memory stick into the side of Charlie's shoe.

I carry on reading. Charlie crosses his legs, scratches his ankle and palms the memory stick. Three minutes later he puts away his phone, stands up and walks towards Rye Lane.

I sit for a couple of minutes. Women with toddlers and buggies pass in both directions. I read and reread the Córdoba poem.

And then a familiar voice. 'Why are *you* here, Grandpa?'

'*Danny*! Why are *you* here?' He's standing in front of me, wearing his navy-blue school trousers and his quilted coat. Juliana stands behind him, smiling with her hair spread around her shoulders.

'I went to the dentist. Had toothache.'

'No! What happened?'

'Had a pain yesterday. Now I got a filling, and it'll be better.'

'His first filling.' Juliana sighs and raises her hands.

Danny holds his mouth wide with his thumb and pushes his face into mine. I feel his breath and can see only perfect teeth. He points with his other hand. The filling is at the back at the top: a small silvery dot. I tell him that it's small and neat; the dentist has done a good job.

'Why *are* you here, Grandpa?' His eyes widen. 'Are you really reading or are you pretending?' He stares at me, a hard stare. 'Are you detecting something?' He turns and looks at the houses across the road. Then leans close to me. 'Has there been a murder? In that creepy house – the one with the wonky roof?'

Juliana and I laugh. 'Well, I hope not, Dan.' Unlike its tidy neighbours, the nearest house has slates missing, a sagging ridge and a plant growing out of its chimney stack. Of course, Dan would notice it. He has an eye for things that are unusual, or out of order.

Juliana tugs on his arm. 'Come on, Danny. Time for school.'

I walk with them to the park gate and give Dan a hug. 'Bye. See you soon. Have fun at school.'

He runs to catch up with Juliana. 'Bye. Have fun detecting.'

35

I park in the Liston Road car park and walk to Cromwell Gardens, a quiet backwater that leads into the almost as quiet Claremont Road. I stroll towards the veil of trees that shrouds number 48 and see, through the gate, the black Range Rover Sport and, beside it, the grey van.

So: Martin Cranley-Smith and Max or Ernst or both have called in – and perhaps Jennifer Cranley-Smith too. The whole gang ... Except they aren't the whole gang; they're part of a bigger gang which, curiously, includes Dave Lightfoot.

I slow a little to take in the gravel drive next door at number 50, and there it is: the tall hedge that grows over a chest-high brick wall. The house is big and Victorian, like its neighbour. Dare I walk in and hide in that hedge as John did on Friday? A good vantage point – McCormick's Lookout – as long as I can get in without being seen. I walk on around the corner and down Glade Road. I stop outside a Baptist Chapel and pretend to read a painted sign that gives the times of church services and Sunday school.

I walk back, quickly cross the gravel at number 50, and

push my way into the hedge. It has stiff branches and shiny leaves: hornbeam, I think.

'Hey! Stop that!' A middle-aged woman is standing on the gravel holding a black plastic bucket. 'You can't urinate here,' she shouts and points towards the road. 'Go on. Get out!'

I speak quietly and hold up my PI card. 'I'm a private investigator. I wasn't going to urinate. I'm sorry. Would you mind if I watched next door from here for a few minutes?'

She stares at the card – in a folding wallet, with my photo, like a police warrant card. 'Why? What's going on?'

I hold my finger to my lips and step out of the hedge. 'Can we go somewhere to talk?'

She stares a little longer and I stare back; she's wearing subtle, carefully applied make-up and her hair is well cut. She narrows her eyes and nods. Then she turns and beckons me to follow. She walks around the front of the house, to the other side, away from number 48, and stops by a bench. 'Why do you want to look at them?'

'It's probably nothing. We had a tip-off. But I'm sorry, I shouldn't be in your garden.' I begin to turn away.

'What kind of tip-off?'

'I'm sorry. I have to keep that confidential.'

She sits down on the bench and waves her hand suggesting I sit beside her. She waits while I sit down. 'My daughter and my son-in-law – this is their house; I just visit now and again. Anyway, they're surprised ... upset that it doesn't seem that number forty-eight will be a family home any more. It belonged to a lovely old man who was once high-up in the RAF. He'd been there for forty years – more, probably – raised his family there; his wife died a year or two ago so he sold up and went to live with his daughter. Developers bought it, did it up and put it up for rent. And it looks as if it's now,' – her voice has turned shrill and she's waving her hands – 'going to be some kind of business.' She pauses and turns to look at me. 'Anyway, what do *you* think? Why are you interested?'

'I can't go into detail. I'm working for a client and their business is private. Let's just say that the new owner is,' – I pause – 'someone in whom we have an interest.'

'Oh!' she says. 'Oh, well, that doesn't tell me much.' She shrugs and looks away.

'I'm sorry. I can't say a lot more. But I don't think your daughter and her husband should be concerned. What happens over there,' – I wave my arm towards the hornbeam hedge – 'shouldn't affect them.'

'No? Well, they'd prefer to have a family next door, you know. They were wondering if it's allowed to have a business there. You know some places have to be residences – change of use is a legal term I think.'

I look up at the side of her daughter's house and hold a hand over my eyes because the sun is reflecting off a window. 'Can you see any of next door from upstairs?'

'Yes – quite a bit. From the attic on the top floor.' She stands up and looks at me closely. 'Come and have a look if you like.' She smiles. 'You seem all right.'

'Well ...' What can I say? 'Thank you.'

We enter the house through a French window, and cross a room with a deep carpet, four sofas and a piano. 'I'd love to know what you think they might be doing over there.'

'Well ...'

'No. I know you can't say. I understand.'

'It may be nothing. Or, if it's something, it shouldn't be any bother to you or your family.'

'So reassuring!' She turns and smiles. I follow her up the stairs. She's wearing sheer black tights and brown leather trainers.

We cross a landing and pass a pastel portrait of a blond-haired boy with big eyes. 'Your grandson?' I ask.

'Yes. He's older now. Six – nearly seven – but just as sweet.'

'Have you lots of grandchildren, or ...?'

'No. He's the only one. Bless him! I've two daughters: the one who lives here, who is his mum. The other has no children; but she lives here in Marlow, so she sees a lot of this fella.'

We've climbed a second flight of stairs. She opens a door into a wide room with a low ceiling and a double bed, and walks to one of the two windows. She pushes a curtain to one side. 'There you are.' She spreads her hands. 'What do you think they're doing?'

The Range Rover and the grey van are still there. I can see one side of the house, from the roof to the ground. I look at my watch; it's 12.10. 'Funny that all those ground-floor windows have drawn blinds.'

'Yes.' She looks at me. 'I don't think they were like that yesterday.' She's still staring at me. 'But then I didn't come up here yesterday, so ...' She doesn't finish the sentence. She turns away, picks a cushion off the bed, plumps it and throws it back. 'Is it exciting being a private detective?'

'Occasionally. It's mostly hard work.' It occurs to me that I'm in a bedroom with a woman of about my own age, whom I've only just met.

She's looking at me again. 'It sounds exciting – and a bit dangerous.' She's widening her eyes. Is that a pout? 'I'm sorry I accused you of urinating. It's just that men do urinate in that hedge sometimes – usually at night, on their way back from the pub down there – the Donkey, it's called.' She waves towards the road and looks out of the window.

'Well, I'm sorry I just barged into your hedge.'

'It's a nice pub, the Donkey. Oh! Look! There's someone.' She steps behind the curtain and points. I get behind the opposite curtain and peer out. It's Max – walking towards the grey van. He gets in and slams the door. Ernst appears from the side of the house and climbs into the passenger seat. The engine starts and tyres crunch on gravel as Max drives to the gate and turns left into Claremont Road.

'Did you recognise them?' the woman says.

'No. Have you seen them before?'

'No. But I haven't been looking. They look like workmen, with that van.' She's backing away towards the door. 'I must get on with my gardening. Do you want to stay here, or have you seen enough?'

I look at my watch again; it's nearly 12.15. 'Can I stay for a few minutes? Would that be OK? Maybe half an hour – unless something interesting starts to happen.'

'Yes. Yes. Debbie won't mind. She's out till this afternoon, anyway.' She walks to the door and calls over her shoulder, 'Come and say goodbye before you go.'

'OK. Thank you ... What's your name, by the way?'

'I'm Mary. My daughter is Debbie and her husband is Don. What about you?'

'I'm Jim.' I hand her my card. 'Jim Domino.'

'Oh yes. Nice name. I saw it on your ID.'

★ ★ ★

She leaves the door open and I listen to her walk downstairs. I look at the room; it's tidy, not lived in, a spare room. A lamp on a bedside table, a small armchair, a chest of drawers and a shelf of books: Elena Ferrante, Stephen King, *The Quiet American* by Graham Greene. A framed print, *The Thames at Marlow* on one wall; a Matisse poster, *Blue Nude II*, facing it. I peep into a cupboard – I have no need to and I know I shouldn't, but ... I'm a detective – and I find women's clothes on hangers; I look into the drawers, two empty and a tartan rug in the bottom one.

A weak sun comes through the windows, while the side of the house next door is in shade. I stand by a window and look out for a few minutes, and then – just for a change – move to the other window. Both windows give me the same view: the whole east-facing side-wall of number 48; an oblique view of the front of the house, though the front door is out of sight on the further side; the front garden; the tarmac parking area; and the open gate to the road. I examine every window opposite several times. Blinds are still closed on the ground floor. The first and second floors have curtains: most of them are closed; some are beige and some are blue; all are lined with calico.

I think I see movement through a first-floor window and focus on it for a minute, but see nothing more – perhaps my imagination, or the reflection of a passing cloud.

Just when I'm ready to leave, Martin Cranley-Smith appears. He crosses the tarmac towards the Range Rover. He has a bald patch which sits on the top of his head like a small pink saucer. He's carrying an orange plastic bag, probably from Sainsbury's. He starts his engine, spins the wheel and zooms off in a spray of gravel, turning right into Claremont Road.

I walk downstairs and out into the garden through the French windows. I find Mary up a ladder pruning an apple tree. She climbs down to the bottom step. 'Did anything happen?'

'A man came out – blond-haired man with a bald patch. Drove off in the Range Rover. Have you seen him? Might be the new tenant.'

'No,' she steps onto the grass. 'I haven't seen anyone. Don

has – but I don't know who.' She smiles. 'I'd love to know what you find out about him, or them. Come back and tell us when you can.'

'Yes, I will if I can. You've been very helpful. Thanks.' I turn away.

'And come back again if you need another look.'

'OK.' I wave, as she climbs back up the ladder. 'Thanks.'

36

I walk towards Glade Road. What next? I could try getting into number 48 now. No one there ... maybe. No
cars. Break in somehow, see what's happening, take photos.

Or find that pub, the Donkey. And have a think.

Funny: neighbours are often ready to help with spying
on next door. But I've never been helped so readily. What
a nice woman.

I pass the Baptist Chapel. And there's the Donkey at
the bottom of the road ... by the station ... Of course:
The Marlow Donkey is a train ... goes to Cookham, then
Maidenhead and back.

★ ★ ★

Friendly barman. OJ and soda water, and sit by the window
and look at the fire. Not crowded. Only 12.30; it'll fill up.

What to do?

Hand all info and computer files to Avril now: emails
nail Cranley-Smith and Lightfoot working with organised crime to distribute drugs. People trafficking – not
quite proven and can't mention Ruth and Kamal. False

imprisonment, no proof. *And* something illegal, suspected, not proven, at Number 48 ... No. Not good enough. I want to see what's going on in there, photograph it. Give that – proof – to Avril ... Without that, the job's only half done.

So – get in there. This afternoon? Tonight? Tomorrow? Tomorrow night – yes. And bring Clayton, just in case?

Go back this afternoon. Recce around the back and find the easiest way in.

Here's the man with the sandwich.

'Chicken ciabatta?'

'Please.'

He puts the plate down, along with a wooden carry-all filled with the usual stuff. 'Anything else I can get you?'

'No. That's it. Thank you.' Knife and fork wrapped in a paper napkin. *Just let me carry on thinking.*

This is big. It's organised crime *and* at least one corrupt policeman – almost certainly more. Avril will have fun. *But* this lot: drug dealers, people traffickers, Mr Bigs, Mr Littles – they didn't kill Ruby's mum. Why would they?

Revenge for something Gary Jackson did? No. That doesn't make sense. And the weapon: a professional wouldn't touch it – or botch the job, for that matter.

★ ★ ★

Walk back the way I came. Past Number 50. Number 48 – nothing has changed; still no cars. Turn into Claremont Gardens and then the builders' merchant's yard at the top. Two men talking, pointing, looking at pallets loaded with bricks, old bricks – with the black marks that come from sitting in someone's chimney for a hundred years. Go to the right, as John said, past piles of sand, gravel, stone until you're behind the shop. A digger parked beside the wall.

Stand on one of the caterpillars, lever myself up and drop down the other side.

I'm beside a fat tree trunk and behind some kind of shrub. I walk a few feet to my left so I can see the back of the house; it's at least twenty yards away. In between: a large wooden building with windows, big enough to be a bungalow where someone lives. To my right: a red-brick double garage. To my left, a greenhouse, a small shed and, to the side of the house, the old outdoor toilet.

Every window on the ground floor of the house is covered by blinds, as they are at the front. The windows above have lined curtains like those at the side that I saw from next door. An extension – probably the kitchen – sticks out from the back of the house to my right. Next to it is a yard with an old stone floor, outdoor armchairs and a table; creepers climb the wall: a cosy sitting area – though the back of the house faces north. A French window in the middle of that wall, and another door comes from the kitchen. I look at both doors; they're locked with mortise locks. I could crowbar my way in. It wouldn't be easy, there could be bolts – perhaps padlocked bolts – on the inside. No sign of cameras or an alarm.

I walk around to my left. Almost all the windows are sash windows – the building is Victorian – but they look like new replacements which will be locked with tight, modern locks. I tiptoe towards a bathroom window on the ground floor – the window glass is frosted; a soil pipe reaches up into the sky and it's in line with the old loo, McCormick's hide-out. The window is hinged and opens outwards; it's made of wood and is older than the sash windows. I could open it with a pallet knife and a screwdriver – or, if necessary, my small crowbar – and, with Clayton to help, I could scramble through, and he could haul himself in behind me.

I scan the wall above. Another bathroom with a similar window two floors up. I go into the outdoor toilet and peer out over the door. McCormick is right; it's a good surveillance point. I focus on the first-floor window where something seemed to move this morning. Nothing. I stay for ten minutes. A couple of cars pass in the street. Otherwise, nothing happens, nothing moves – even the trees and the leaves that litter the ground are still: no wind and the sun already low down.

I come out of the toilet and walk around the front to the further side, the west side. It's the same, with a hinged, frosted, bathroom window on the first floor. Halfway along, the front door is set back under a gabled porch, its old tiled roof supported by glossy white columns. Two brass mortise locks and a Yale glint in the fading light; they look new. I slide in a credit card in case the door is held by the Yale only. No movement: the Yale has been double locked – presumably by Martin Cranley-Smith when he left this morning. So there's probably no one inside – though dear Martin is known for locking people up. I walk on, along the side of the kitchen, past two windows, far apart, both with closed blinds.

The garage is locked electronically; I peer through a dirty window: no cars – just piles of paint tins and a ladder. I look at the bungalow. It's plumbed and has electricity. Perhaps someone *does* live there. If so, they're away or asleep or sitting in the dark; all the windows are covered by shutters and no light is coming through the cracks. The front door has a brass handle and a shiny mortise lock. I move over to the small shed. It has a small, rusty padlock on its door, and a dusty, plastic window. It feels abandoned.

The door of the greenhouse slides open when I push on it. Inside I gaze at towers of plastic flowerpots and a dozen unopened bags of compost. I step back, haul out my phone, switch off the flash and take a photo.

I've seen all I can. I brace my shoulders and walk quickly round, past the front door and out into Claremont Road. After turning the corner into Glade Road, I slow to my usual stroll. As I walk towards the Liston Road car park, I check tonight's movies at Cineworld in High Wycombe on my phone; it's a fifteen-minute drive, close to the junction of the A404 and the M40.

★ ★ ★

I take off my coat and sit down in a plush seat near the back. There are nine people in front of me. Well, it's Monday. I recline the seat, throw a palmful of popcorn into my mouth and gape at a trailer for *Frozen 2*. I don't care about Princess whatever-her-name-is − or is she a queen? I think about tomorrow. I want to do it because I want to do a proper job − the whole job − which is to find criminals *and* produce evidence of their crimes. Who am I working for? I'm going to hand the evidence to Avril. But I'm working for me. I wrench the lid off the Coke bottle, sip and gulp. And for Ruby and her brothers and sisters. *Not* finding their mother's murderer − *yet* − but carrying on her work, completing it as far as I can.

Explain to Clayton. Give him a choice ... although I know, I *think* I know, what he'll say ... Still ...

The sound is too loud. It's always like that for trailers. *Cats* − looks awful, Judi Dench dressed up as a cat, and Taylor Swift − apparently. *Playing with Fire* − big-jawed American firefighter annoyed by kids: corny. Meryl Streep in *Little Women* − nice girls, Saoirse Ronan, how do you pronounce that? Saw her in something else. *Star Wars* − again! − *The Rise of Skywalker* − gimme strength!

'Time to put away your phone.' OK.

* * *

Christ! They're good actors: Lesley Manville and Liam Neeson.

I knew it was about this. Rave review in the *Observer*.

Eat the popcorn. Cry if you want. No need to hold back.

* * *

OK. Drive. Out of here. What a movie! Great title: *Ordinary Love*. It was different from us. Joan had breast cancer, mastectomy, but she didn't die. Their daughter died. Earlier. Ours didn't ... So I have daughters, grandkids, but not Elizabeth. Tom and Joan have each other. And that's it. To them: everything.

Stop crying – you jerk!

* * *

You gotta do something – concentrate – now.

Park. By the Baptist church. 8.30: dark, as dark as it will get. No one around. Zip up coat. No, here's someone – three people, chatting; off to the Donkey – I bet – after-dinner drinks.

I turn into Claremont Road and pad along like a burglar – long, springy strides in my Nike Air Maxes. No one in the street. Curtains open at number 50 and the flickering of a television screen. Number 48 dark, no cars. I walk close to the left wall – the one that runs beside Claremont Gardens; the gravel is thinner and I step on it gently to reduce crunching noise.

I walk slowly – heels down first – across to the front of the house. No lights. Nothing. All seems to be as it was.

A car passes in the street. I go to the right, past McCormick's outdoor toilet, and look up at the top-floor windows of Number 50, where I stood this morning. No light there. I go over to the bathroom window – the one I will crawl through tomorrow – and think through what I'll need. And I imagine Clayton here too.

This is it, I whisper to him. I don't know that there will be no one inside. McCormick saw two beds carried in. I feel that tingle in my arms which means a thrill and danger: both. *We'll see. We'll deal with it.* Me and Clayton.

I walk on. Greenhouse, bungalow, garage, all as they were. No lights. No sounds.

'Hey!' A woman's voice. I freeze. 'Where you going?'

'I gotta have a walk,' a man says. 'Gotta sort my head out.' His voice comes from my right, from Claremont Gardens.

'OK . . . But don't go to the pub.'

'I won't. I promise.'

'You can sort it out with me, you know.'

'I know. You're a darling. I just need a bit of air. Back soon.'

''Kay. See ya. Keep warm. Love you.'

'Love you too.'

A lock clicks, and I hear soft footsteps on the other side of the wall. I wait until they fade away and walk to the Merc.

37

I turn off the M4 into Heston Services to call Clayton.
He's free tomorrow and chuckles, 'Breaking and entering? Of course. With you, Jim, it's always a pleasure.' He
sounds as if he can't wait and, of course, he gets the point.
'Fucking drug dealers: the lowest of the low. Stick 'em in
prison and maybe they'll come out and get a proper job.'
He chuckles again. 'Fat chance, I know.'

'And I want those kids to know that their mum had an
effect, that she made things happen – you know?'

'Yes. Good one. And ... er,' – he laughs – 'should we
take Kylie as a getaway driver?'

'Nice idea, but I think we'll manage. She's probably busy.'

'It's all right. Was a joke. Just remembering how she got
us out of a hole not long ago.'

'OK. I'll collect you from your gym at 4 pm tomorrow.'

'See ya then. But it's not a gym, Jim.' He giggles. 'Not a
gym, Jim. See what I did there?' The giggle develops into a
racking laugh which becomes more and more high-pitched
until it disappears. 'It's Clayton's Martial Arts – and it's a
space, a space for kids ... or anyone.'

We say goodbye. And all I want to do now is get home, pour a whisky and listen to Miles's *In A Silent Way*. I start the Merc and back out of the parking space. And then I have another idea. I stop the car and ring Laura.

'You at home?'

'Yes, Dad. You all right?'

'Yes. Good. Can I drop by – have a quick drink? Is that convenient?'

'Of course. That'd be lovely. Dan's asleep. I'm just messing on the piano. You sure you're all right?'

'Yes. Just thought it'd be nice to see you. Haven't seen you for a bit.'

'Aww! That's nice.'

'I'm at Heston Services. I'll get to you as soon as I can. About ... three-quarters of an hour. That OK?'

'Great. Have you eaten?'

'No, but don't go to any trouble. I had some popcorn.'

'Popcorn?'

'Yeah. I'll explain later.'

'I can heat you up a pizza? Or a Pieminister – chicken and mushroom?'

'Well. A Pieminister'd be lovely. Great, in fact. See you soon.'

★ ★ ★

I could hear her through the front door. I didn't want to interrupt – she was playing the piano – but I had to. She was always being interrupted and she put up with it.

We hugged. She poured me a whisky and I splashed some water into it. The pie was in the oven; it'd be about fifteen minutes. Would I like peas with it?

Yes, peas would be nice.

She went back to the piano. 'Do you mind Dad? I've

270

been working on something. Like to know what you think.' She had some music in front of her – music she'd written herself. I could tell. I know what her crotchets and quavers and minims look like – fast, confident flicks of a soft pencil. She started writing music way back, when she lived with me and her sister; it began some time in her teens. A pencil lay at the end of the piano beside the bottom A.

It was slow and rolling with plenty of what I think are called blue notes – notes that sound wrong but, when you think about it, not wrong, just unexpected. That's what I like about jazz. The what-the-hell of it – let's do something radical. It was melodic and dreamlike – echoes of Debussy and Bill Evans. She didn't need the music after a while and I could hear that it was going somewhere – not just back to where it started. She hated pianists – any musicians – who just noodle, get nowhere and end abruptly with a treble diddle-diddle and a bass note. It was good, really good. And I knew that she knew that.

She ended on a high note after six or seven minutes, turned and smiled. 'What do you think?'

'Fantastic! One of your best … Quite possibly your very best.' I took a big sip of Famous Grouse and swilled it around my mouth. 'How long you been working on that?'

'Not long.' She stood up and stretched. 'About two, maybe three, weeks – when I've had a few moments. You know – when I'm here and Danny's at school or asleep.'

She talked about where it came from – and played little bits. In her mind it was about Danny and her and how she wanted things to be – 'what I want for him and how that might play out for me'.

'Kind of calm with some exciting bits?'

'Yeah … things are better, calmer, now. I'm shot of that

idiot, Pete. That's it. He's gone.' She waved both hands above her head, palms up towards the ceiling. 'Thinking about him – he doesn't bother me. Seeing him doesn't bother me. It's just flat, practical – no emotions. Hurt, anger . . . affection: all gone. Which is the best – bliss. I'm about me now, and Danny, and my work, my music.'

I was nodding as she spoke. 'Good. Bloody good.'

'Yes. It is.' She looked down at me. 'And why *were* you eating popcorn – may I ask?'

I told her I'd been to a movie to take a break from a surveillance job. And then about *Ordinary Love*: what it was about, how well it was acted.

'I know you, Dad. You were in bits, right?'

'Yeah!' I nodded – and my eyes moistened, just a little.

'Oh God!' She stood over me and put her arm round my shoulder. I sensed her shaking. 'And I haven't even seen it.' Her voice was shrill. 'What am I like?'

'What are both of us like?'

We stayed like that – me sitting down, she with her arm on my shoulder – in silence.

Until she walked away and said, 'Well, what else is new?' She took the pie out of the oven and shook some peas onto the plate beside it.

I ate at the small kitchen table and told her about Clayton becoming part of the Domino Agency management, and she was pleased. She likes him; I knew that. I didn't mention that tomorrow we two managers would break in to what I hope is an empty house.

We talked again about her song. She ha an idea of putting words to it and singing it with the Newmans. I told her she could play it as it is, as a piece of jazz piano, anywhere – 606 Club, Café Oto, the Bull's Head, Ronnie Scott's.

When I'd finished eating, Laura went back to the piano.

I settled into the armchair, as she picked out the melody of her new piece. She stopped and began again with both hands – and played on without music, head up, eyes half-closed, with an occasional glance down at her fingers. She seemed to be taking it further than she had earlier.

Suddenly she was bending forward, looking to her left. She smiled. 'Hallo. Who's this?'

Danny was standing on the stairs in his Minions pyjamas.

'Are you all right?' She smiled, played a couple of chords, plinked a high note and stood up. 'I'm sorry. Did I wake you? Are you all right, Dan? Did something happen?'

'I had a dream and then I heard Grandpa talking, and then I heard you playing the piano.' He was frowning and poking at an eye with his knuckle.

'Come on. Come down here.' She reached for his hand and led him to the sofa. She sat down and lifted him on to her lap. 'Tell us about your dream.'

'Grandpa was in my dream.' He looked at me and half-smiled. 'He was talking to Mr . . . Ron, the man in the veg shop. And then Mrs Ron . . .'

'Yes. She's called Di.' Laura lifted him onto her lap. 'So you were in the veg shop with Grandpa.'

'Yes. Di was going to give me a lolly. She held it out . . . and then I woke up . . . and Grandpa was *here* . . . and I had to come and look.'

'Yes.' Laura stroked his cheek. 'To make sure you'd stopped dreaming?'

'Yes. Because I thought Grandpa and me were in the veg shop. But we're here.' He looked round at me. I stood up, flopped down beside them both and patted his arm.

The three of us sat, bunched together, watching the lines of light that squeezed between the louvres and on to the ceiling as cars drove past.

. Danny said, 'It's funny. Di gives me lollies and sweets and says stuff to me, but she never says anything to grown-ups.'

'No, she doesn't,' I said. 'She's quiet as well as kind.'

Soon he fell asleep and Laura carried him up to bed.

I left then. Just the one whisky. I had to drive the half mile to mine. Laura was tired, and I had stuff to do the next day.

★ ★ ★

I spend the morning with Alice, the Domino Agency's bookkeeper and impromptu business adviser. A grey-haired, financial Jeeves who turns up roughly once a week, she happens also to be Vic's aunt. A week ago she was a little shocked to find a new employee on the staff, but she calmed down when I told her how much income John McCormick had already brought in. This week she's surprised by the sudden rise of Clayton.

'So he's not just muscle?' She stares at me through large, black-rimmed glasses.

'Oh no! Brain. Lots of brain. *And* muscle.' I grin and raise my eyebrows. 'A bit like me, in fact.' I bend my arm and squeeze my bicep.

She gives me her best stare. 'Steady on, Jim. We've got work to do.' She opens her case, takes out a spreadsheet and smooths it lovingly on the table between us. And we work. We study spreadsheets and talk about gross profit and net profit, above the line and below the line, deferred income and cash accruals. I produce a piece of paper on which I've worked out, in pencil, how increasing Clayton's involvement would add to profit and turnover. Alice studies it for a few minutes while tapping away on her giant laptop.

Then she shows me a series of profit and loss, and cash-flow, projections: worst-case scenario, best-case scenario and in-between scenario. 'This is good, Jim, as long as' – she points a finger and glares at me – 'the work keeps coming in.'

'It will,' I tell her. 'And Clayton will bring in more. He's widely respected around here ... and further afield. A bit like me.' I'm repeating myself.

Alice gives me a look – the kind of look you might give to a precocious child: benign but sceptical ... and perhaps a little patronising.

She leaves. I put on Jimmy Cliff and work through my exercise routine. As usual, I warm down to 'Pressure Drop', and then lie on the rug, eyes closed, listening to 'Sitting in Limbo'. But, instead of falling into an easy, exhausted calm, I'm climbing through that bathroom window into an uncertain darkness, with a small torch in my hand.

★ ★ ★

At 11 pm I'm driving along the M4 with Clayton. We're both dressed in black, and my tools are in the boot. Now that we're on our way, I feel confident. Clayton is like he always is: cool and unflustered while giving off, to me at least, a sense of high alert.

I talk about the business and my discussions with Alice. He listens and comments – and then we fall into silence.

At a quarter to midnight I park in Glade Road opposite the Baptist chapel. The moon, a few days from full, sits bright above the chapel behind fast-drifting clouds. The few streetlights are far apart and cast a yellow gloom.

I put my tools and torch in my thigh pockets. Clayton has a torch, as well as his phone. We walk together up Glade Road, turn left into Claremont Road and stroll slowly towards number 48, which is on the opposite side. Three people cycle past talking loudly; only one of them, a young woman, has lights. I look beyond them at number 50, where a light shows in the front window on the first floor. At number 48 there are no lights and no cars or vans.

We cross the road and walk up Claremont Gardens to the builders' yard. No lights are showing. A pair of metal gates, ten-feet high and topped with vicious spikes, are held together with a padlock and chain. While Clayton holds the gate to stop it rattling I scramble up, avoiding the spikes, and drop down. I hold the gate firm for him, and he follows. We walk quickly through the yard, finding our way by the light of the single streetlight in Claremont Gardens. The digger is by the wall, as it was yesterday. This wall is easier than the gate; we fetch up beside the fat tree in the garden of number 48. The house appears to be in complete darkness. If a light were on behind one of those ground-floor blinds, I'd see at least a chink somewhere, wouldn't I?

We walk left around the outside of the building. The only light here comes from the moon – a cold, blue light which comes and goes as the clouds move. I point to the ground-floor bathroom window and Clayton gives me a thumbs-up. We keep walking, right around. No cars, no lights. Just the streetlight from over the wall on the far side.

We don't speak. We return to the bathroom window. I slide my palette knife into the hairline gap between window and frame and jerk it upwards. Nothing gives. Clayton taps my arm. He wants the knife. He pushes it in higher up and presses downwards. No movement. He grips the knife with his left hand and thumps it with his right fist. The lock gives and the window pops open less than an inch. I work my screwdriver through the gap and flip the stay off its peg. I'm startled by a sudden clatter as the stay falls onto the sill inside. I grab the frame and swing the window open.

I put my foot on Clayton's clasped hands and kneel on

the sill. I reach in and feel a rectangular china basin and two taps. The basin feels solid, supported from below. I put my left foot in it and swing my body through the window; I find the floor with my right leg. I'm in. There's a sweet smell – some kind of disinfectant. I tiptoe forward. Clayton is now beside me. I put my hand on his arm and we wait for our eyes to adjust to the dark.

We're in a large room – an Edwardian free-standing bath with legs, a lavatory with cistern high on the wall and a chain. A modern shower in a glass box stands in one corner. I go to the door, open it and switch on my torch.

I'm in a high-ceilinged passage. Clayton is here with me. The torch beam falls on an oil painting in a gilded frame: a pretty woman, bright-eyed with her hair in ringlets; in a high- and narrow-waisted dress . . . Something behind me, a footstep, a thud.

Clayton grunting, Clayton falling forward. Another thud, piercing pain. Torch falling from my hand . . .

38

Falling. And Elizabeth falling. I try to catch her, but I can't. She's still falling. I try again ... The book, the Sorolla book, is in my hands. I drop it. How can I catch her with this book in my hands? I keep falling – and so does she. On and on and on – and my head hurts. Inside, bad headache. And my jaw.

Can't open my mouth. Can't move my hands – they're behind me. Or my feet.

Someone has tied me and gagged me. Hands behind me, tied tight. Feet, ankles tied. Move knees – a bit. Mouth held shut with tape – can't move it, tongue moves but dry – gaffer tape.

Eyes open. Can't see anything. Dark. Blackness. Lying on floor. Carpet. Feel it. Smell of carpet – new carpet.

No sounds. Nothing. Bang feet on carpet. Thump, thump. Jeez, my head hurts!

Thump, thump. Not me. But here, beside me.

Thump, thump. Me.

Thump, thump. Not me.

Something – someone – commotion, rolling. Rolling into me. On top of me. Kick on my forehead – not hard.

Lie still. Think ... Came through window. Basin, taps, through door to passage. Painting of Jane Austen woman. Not Jane Austen – blonde, pretty ...

Clayton! Clayton was there! He fell.

And torch fell. I fell. Hit on head from behind ... Now tied up. Both of us. That's him. He rolled into me. Just here now. Try rolling. Yes. Can rock, but not roll. He's moving. Feet, knees. His head, his face here by mine.

He's moving again ... Fingers feeling my face, my cheek. Pulling my lips out. His back is by my face. Hands tied like mine, fingers pulling, pulling the tape. Jeez, that hurts. But can breathe through corner of my mouth. He's holding it, rolling, tugging. Rolling and tugging, over and over. It's coming off. Can breathe. Can talk. 'Clayton.'

He can't answer. He's thumping the carpet with his feet. It's him. Obviously.

'Clayton,' I whisper. 'Lie still. I'll take the tape off your mouth, like you did.'

He's here. I swivel and squirm. My back against his head. Squirm up more. Fingers by mouth. Pull and pull and ...

Clicking sound. A lock. Door noise. Torch shining in my face, and another. Man in front of me, shines torch on himself. Max! Another man with a torch: Ernst! Max puts finger to his lips. He whispers. 'We free you.' He holds up a knife. 'Will you help us? We've had enough, want to escape from those people, Cranley-Smith.'

'Yes,' I say. 'Cut us free. Now. Quickly.'

He's cutting the rope between my wrists. Ernst is with Clayton. I can hear him: Clayton. Low whisper. 'Thanks. Quick. Let's get out of here.'

They keep cutting.

'What's the time?'

'Five. Five in morning.'

279

We came into the house at midnight ... Five hours ago!

Free now, standing up. Clayton too. But stiff, stiff as hell, legs and arms. Head throbbing. Dry, so dry. Want water. Cold water. *Any* water.

'Have you got car?' Max is talking. 'Can we go in it?'

'Yes. We have a car.' Can see him dimly. Torches pointing at floor. 'Round the corner.'

They lead us, our saviours. I'm leaning on Max. Clayton's arm is around Ernst's neck – his feet dragging. We move along a passage, through a big space, the hall. Out the door! Into the air – dark, the moon is there, it's crossed the sky. Max puts his finger to his lips. We walk to Glade Road. I'm still holding on to him. And I can feel: he has a small bag on his back. My head hurts like hell. 'I can't drive. Can you, Clayton?'

'I drive,' Max says.

'OK. Good.' Walk, so stiff, along the pavement. Pat pockets – both wrists still have rope, or some kind of plastic, round them; ankles too. I don't have my phone; I have my tools and I find the car key.

Clayton and I lean on the car as Max unlocks it. Ernst shrugs a small rucksack off his back, takes Max's bag, opens the boot and slings them both in. 'We left the van in the High Street.' He smiles. 'We locked it and dropped the key down a drain. Martin's van! Ha ha!'

I smile. And my mouth hurts; it is so dry.

They help me and Clayton into the back seat. They sit in front. Max in the driver's seat.

'Where shall we go? We can't go back now. We must go somewhere. Foreign office. We are refugees.'

'Away from here. Fast. We need water.' I feel the top of my head. Gently. A bump at the back.

'Water. Yes.' Clayton nods. 'Please.' He is slouching against the corner of the seat, his eyes half shut.

'Beaconsfield Services on the M40,' I say. 'Open all night. You know where that is?'

'Er . . . yes.' Max starts the engine, turns in the car park of the Donkey pub and drives back up Glade Road.

As we pass the end of Claremont Road, I tense up and the throbbing inside my head gets worse. I manage to speak slowly. 'You are refugees. How come you rescued us?'

'Because we think you are a good man,' Max says. 'And because we want to escape from Cranley-Smith people . . . and other people.'

'We have hope that you can help us.' Ernst turns in his seat and speaks for the first time. 'Please.'

'We'll help you. You're helping us.'

'Yes. You might have been killed . . . tomorrow.' Ernst is staring at me; he has thick, bushy eyebrows. 'I don't know what else they were going to do.' He shrugs.

I feel a flutter in my arms and a pain in my jaw. I haven't had time to think. What *would* have happened if they hadn't rescued us? I look across at Clayton. He blows out his lips and widens his eyes.

'Who are they? The people who did this to us.'

'Bosses. Bosses of Martin. Drug business people. They sent gang men, tough guys, to catch you and keep you.'

'How did they know we were there?'

There's a silence. Ernst has turned away. Max is accelerating. I can see the A404 – empty, no traffic. Max is looking at me in the mirror. 'You know there's people live next door to that house. Did you talk to them?'

'Yes. To a woman . . . called Mary.'

'OK. I thought that. I heard them talking. She is the mother of Jennifer . . . Jennifer Cranley-Smith. Gang men were waiting for you.'

'Fuck!' I close my eyes. Open them. And look at Clayton.

His eyes are closed and he's shaking his head. 'You're joking ... What a *fucking* idiot! She *was* very friendly. I should have thought. But ... she fooled me. *Me!* DCI Jim Domino! I had no idea ... Sorry Clayton.' I touch his knee. He opens his eyes, smiles and shakes his head again.

Max is there in the mirror: eyes with dark lashes, glancing at me and away, back to the road. 'They are all involved – Jennifer's family. Jennifer's father is the big man, big boss. Lives in Spain, on a big boat, I think; never comes to England. He tells them what to do. Stop with the dogs. Sell drugs, smuggle people, traffic people to work for you. Cannabis – skunk – is their thing. That house will be cannabis farm.'

'I guessed it might. I wanted proof. That's why we broke in.'

We're on the big roundabout above the M40.

'They took my phone,' I say.

'Took mine too, Jim.' Clayton frowns.

'They'll smash them so they can't be found,' Ernst says.

'Two people will work there,' Max says. 'Frightened people, immigrants, trafficked. There are already plants there, growing in pots with special lights.

'There's another cannabis farm in Marlow, in Portland Crescent. We have a room there – not any more. But we didn't look after the plants. Another man does that; he comes from Vietnam. We just work for Martin, moving stuff, drugs, people, around.'

'We did everything: gardening, shopping, fixing things.' Ernst paused, then turned and smiled. 'We fed animals, looked after them. Waited at table sometimes. We were servants, you could say.'

We're on the M40 – in the middle lane, passing two trucks. Max is a good driver.

Ernst carries on. 'We stayed there, six months now, because we were safe. Martin took us from the truck we came in. We owed him money for smuggling us. He'd give us jobs, he said; took our passports, said he'd give them back when we had paid him the money. We are from Belarus. We are what you call dissidents. They want to take us back – the FSB, the President's men – put us in prison, torture us. That is what they do to people like us.'

Max glances at me in the mirror. 'Lukashenko. Alexander Lukashenko is President of Belarus. He is a dictator. An evil bastard. We oppose him for many years. And about a year ago, *more than* a year ago, we had to leave our country.'

'I know who Lukashenko is. I understand.'

Max turns the Merc onto the slip road that leads to the services. 'That's good,' he says. 'Now we will stop hiding – at least from the British – and apply for asylum.'

'We have no passports.' Ernst is looking ahead. He slaps his thighs. 'But we are well-known in Belarus.' He turns back to me. 'Less than a year ago we were podcasting from Poland. There are Belarussians here who know us, and people in your foreign office.'

Just three cars in the car park. Max drives past them and parks by a clump of bare trees. He gets out of the car, leans in and says, 'If you can stand up out here, we can cut those straps off your arms and legs.'

The air is cold. A line of streetlights throws a bluish light on the tarmac. Beyond them the sky is black. There's no one around. I lean against the Merc. Clayton stands beside me. Max and Ernst both have large knives with serrated blades. 'Did you know that you'd find us tied up?'

'Yes,' Max says. 'We heard them talking. They forget we're there sometimes.'

The ties are thick, black plastic, pulled tight. Max cuts

through mine, wrists first, then ankles. There are deep creases in my forearms. I try to shake my wrists. So stiff. Ernst cuts the ties from Clayton. Both of us hobble around, holding on to the car, shaking our ankles and wrists. Slowly the pain eases.

'You wanted water. We will buy it for you – a litre each, I think. You should stay here and rest. Do you want something to eat?'

'Thank you.' I feel my pockets. I have my wallet, and my palette knife, screwdriver and crowbar – and my watch. Almost 5.30. They took only my phone.

'We will pay. It's OK. I have Martin's credit card,' he chuckles.

'You shouldn't use that for much longer. It could be traced.'

'No. I will cut it up soon and throw it away – but we can have one last treat. What would you like? Some chocolate? I don't know what they have.'

I look at Clayton. He's leaning forward, hands on the bonnet of the Merc. I don't feel hungry. In fact, I feel a bit sick; it goes with the thudding headache.

Clayton lifts a hand and tries to smile. 'Last time we were here in the middle of the night, there was just McDonald's … If there's a ham sandwich, I'll have it. Otherwise a plain McDonald's burger – no cheese. And a big bottle of water, cold. Please.'

I ask for the same – and some paracetamol. The two of them walk off. I see that Max has left the key in the ignition.

'Jesus Christ, old friend! I'm sorry I led you into this.'

'It's OK, OK.' He raises his eyebrows. 'Bad stuff happens sometimes – often when you're trying to do the right thing. Who would think that a respectable-seeming woman living in a street like that, next to an empty building, belongs to some crime dynasty?' He grins. 'Fuck it: the Sopranos belong in New Jersey for Christ's sake!' He shakes his head. 'We're alive, Jim – thanks to these guys.' He sticks his thumb over his shoulder. 'We're bloody lucky.'

'I'll say it one more time: I'm sorry.' I'm facing him across the bonnet. 'And then we have to think. We can't dump them outside the foreign office. For their sakes and ours, we must put them up somewhere – and I'll find Avril. We didn't get any pictures of cannabis growing, but these blokes are witnesses – not just to drug offences: people trafficking; false imprisonment – who knows.'

'They've been trafficked themselves for fuck's sake!'

'Of course. Yes.'

'And we're witnesses. We've suffered GBH and imprisonment.'

'Yes.' Of course he's right. *We* are victims of a crime.

'So weird! You beat these guys up not long ago.'

'Yeah – and you picked Ernst up and dropped him on the ground.'

'And then he locked us in that container ... Fuck!' Clayton is smiling; it's good to see.

'Yep!'

There's a silence. I look at the ground and try to think. 'They'll be shitting themselves when they find we're gone and that those two released us and are gone too. These guys know so much – and *we* know quite a lot.' The implications are only now occurring to me. 'It's a big operation: south London, out to the west and who knows where else? Big villain in Spain. Mrs villain here, for now ... Bent cops. It won't just be Lightfoot.' I feel a sudden shaft of pain. 'My head!' I put my hands on the bonnet and take deep breaths.

'Come on, man. You need water. You'll get some in a minute.'

I feel Clayton's hand on my shoulder, and I carry on thinking aloud. 'I *was* thinking I could take them to my place and get Avril to come over, but that's silly, not re-motely safe. And not for Avril either. They might know where I live. Or Lightfoot can find my address.'

'So ... what do we do?'

'I want *you* to be safe.'

'I'll be OK. They don't know where *I* live.' He sighed. 'Can Avril protect *them*? It won't just be the gang after them. What about immigration? No way they should just walk into the Foreign Office.'

'If this goes right—' My head is still throbbing. I push down on the Merc. 'If they'll appear as witnesses, make full statements of what they know – I'm thinking the Commissioner can fix things for them. Or maybe Counter Terrorism or SIS, MI6. This is big. Much bigger than Martin Cranley-Smith or Dave Lightfoot.'

'So, where do you suggest we take them – or *they* take *us* in *your* car?' He's speaking softly and he's leaning on the Merc, rotating his neck and flexing his fingers.

'Well ... OK ... I think the Hilton at Heathrow Terminal Four. Good place to hide witnesses who need protection ... They're coming back. Looks like burgers ...'

Max holds out a bottle of cold Evian water. I take it and swallow the lot – a litre. Magic! Clayton does the same and holds the almost-empty bottle above his head, letting the dregs run down his face.

I need more water to swallow the paracetamol. Max runs off and returns with two more bottles. We munch burgers and drink more slowly.

* * *

As we drive east towards the M25, I ask Max and Ernst what they think of the Cranley-Smiths.

Unusually, Ernst answers first. 'They are horrid, evil people – who don't care about anyone else: psychopaths, I think. They make lots of money from dealing in drugs and smuggling people. Also,' – he turns right round in the passenger seat so that he can see both of us – 'they are igno-rant pigs. They know nothing about us. They don't bother to ask. They think, because they have our passports, we will never leave. They don't know *why* we left Belarus!' He raises his hands in a gesture of despair. 'We are journalists and dissidents. We work in television, radio, newspapers and then online from Poland. They don't know. First we went to Lithuania, and then Estonia, Tallinn where our families now live, then Poland, and now here. They think we're going to stay working for them for ever! Bloody fools!' He laughs. 'I'd like to be there when they find out what's happened. We've gone – and you've gone.' He laughs again – and Max joins in.

When he calms down, Max says that he hated working for them. 'What persuaded me that we must leave there was when they started locking people in those metal boxes. Till then, it just seemed to be dogs – though there were drugs also. I hated locking people up – and *we* had to look after them. There were those two with the baby – the others had all been young men. You freed them. That was wonderful, glorious.'

'Yes. And I'm sorry, very sorry,' Ernst says. 'I was angry that night. You,' – he looked at Clayton – 'hurt me a lot. But I know why,' – he shrugs – 'and I'm sorry I locked you into that box.'

'You gave me your card, which shows you were a police-man once, and you offered to help us.' Max is speaking over his shoulder and glancing at me in the mirror. 'We thought about that. And we knew that you helped those people from South Sudan and their baby. And then, last night, we heard what was happening to you. So we decided. No more! Let's get out of here – and get you out of there.'

I ask them if they will give evidence to the police. I tell them that we are investigating a policeman who is suspected of corruption, and that we found a connection between that policeman and the Cranley-Smiths. I would like them to tell our friend, who is a very senior policewoman, all they know about the Cranley-Smiths: the drug dealing, people trafficking, imprisoning people – everything.

Ernst looks across at Max, who is staring ahead at the road.

'If you will tell the police what you know,' I say, 'I will do my best to make sure you are helped with asylum claims and immigration. I can offer you as witnesses, in return for your being treated well and looked after. Kept safe, I mean.'

Max glances at Ernst. Ernst nods.

'Yes. We'll do that.' Max speaks first.

'OK. Yes.' Ernst turns in his seat. 'That is good, as long as we have promises of asylum in this country, and of being safe.'

'We would want somewhere safe to live.' Max is looking at me in the mirror.

'Yes. I understand. I will do my best to get you that.'

'OK. A deal, then.' Ernst pushes his hand between the seats.

I take his hand and shake it. Without lifting his head from the headrest, Clayton takes Ernst's hand. 'Deal,' he says.

Max sticks his right hand over his shoulder, and we repeat the ritual.

I explain about the Hilton Hotel. That I will get them a

room there and come back with the senior policewoman as soon as I can. Today, I hope. My headache is lifting: a good sign – no concussion so far. I feel the back of my head and ask Clayton how his head feels.

'Better. Not completely better. Reckon they used leather saps. With luck we'll be OK.'

39

Three receptionists are on duty and six or seven people are checking out – bright, well-rested people with small suitcases, about to board planes.

It's 7.15 am. I wait with Clayton. It has to be us who check in. Max and Ernst have no passports, no ID of any kind. They could be anyone . . . and I don't care. They are just these great guys who rescued us, saved our lives – and I'm sure they are who they say they are.

A young man in a suit and open-necked shirt appears from somewhere and brushes a plastic card, which swings from a lanyard attached to his belt, against a computer. The computer lights up and so does he. I ask for a room from now until tomorrow.

'Of course.' He smiles and looks at his screen. We can have a room for two now and we can keep it until check-out time tomorrow, 12 noon.

I pull out my credit card, and have a vision of a crowd of police, including Avril, and some grim people from Border Force, arriving in Max's and Ernst's bedroom.

'Could we make that a suite? We'll be meeting one or two business associates.'

Smiley man taps for several seconds; the keyboard rattles like muted castanets. He nods. 'Yes. Suite 409 on the fourth floor. Just £230 until noon tomorrow.'

Inside the suite, Clayton grabs a bottle of water, swigs some and picks up a telephone from a long desk with a TV screen on it. He is soon speaking to Marie, telling her where he is and that he is OK.

I fetch Max and Ernst from the Merc. Max leans against the wall of the lift and hums; they both seem tired, but excited. I show them their bedroom. 'OK!' Ernst says. 'Very nice.' He strokes the sparkling white sheet and duvet. They both want to take showers and then sleep.

'Before you do that, there's something I need to know. I'm going into London to talk to the police and I have to tell them who you are.' I pick up a Hilton-Hotel pad and a pen. 'So what are your names? First names and second names.'

'Of course,' says Max. 'Now, we want people to know that we are here in this country,' – he wags a finger – 'but not where.' He points the finger at his chest. 'I'm Maxim Posnyak, but call me Max.'

'Ernst Zhdanov. Call me Ernst.' He chuckles and looks at his hands. 'Zhdanov is a Russian name. My father was Russian, but I was born in Minsk.'

I hand the pad and pen to Max. 'Please, can you write it down?'

Max writes slowly and passes the pad to Ernst, who writes even more slowly.

I read both names aloud. 'Is that right?'

'Yes.'

'Are you known by those names in Belarus? To Belarussians?'

'Yes.' They both speak at once.

'We are famous,' Ernst says with a smile.

'Belarussians who are in exile here will know our names,' Max says. 'We are both writers, and we were on radio and TV. And we had a podcast for many years. An illegal podcast.'

'Illegal, but ten, twelve thousand people followed us, subscribed. A lot more listened to us. We know that. But they didn't risk subscribing.' Ernst scratches his cheek. 'People who subscribed were sometimes arrested, beaten up.'

'And so were we – beaten up.' Max is looking at the floor and shaking his head.

It's time for them to wash and rest; they've been up all night. Before I leave and shut the door of their bedroom, I thank them again for rescuing us.

They flap their hands and smile. Then Max kicks off his trainers.

Clayton is stretched out on a long grey sofa with a white cushion on his stomach. I want to phone Charlie Ritchie but, without my phone, I don't have his number. I put the 'Do not disturb' notice on the door and go downstairs to find a computer. Smiley man sends me to the business centre where another polite young man points me to a computer and tells me to log in with my room number.

I hate iCloud; it's always popping up on my screen demanding that I log in – which I never do. Now, though, it can't be more helpful. Everything from my stolen phone is there. I write down Charlie's number – and then Avril's, just in case.

Before I go back upstairs, I google Maxim Posnyak and Ernst Zhdanov. There they are, with their photographs, separately and together. Both have entries on Wikipedia, written in English. Ernst trained and worked as a physicist;

Maxim as a teacher. Both became active dissidents in the 1990s. Their podcast is called '*Smiena z Maksam i Ernstam*'. I find a translation; it means 'Change with Max and Ernst'.

I walk back through the cavernous reception area. It's almost eight o'clock and it's crowded: people checking out, checking in, drinking coffee, poking at phones, milling about: a cosmopolitan ragbag – journalists, spies, asylum seekers, football managers – where no one stands out.

Back in the suite I phone Charlie. 'I need to see you – pronto. It's important.'

'OK, Jim.' He sounds surprised. 'Where? When?' And intrigued.

'Ten o'clock. On the Rye, the benches across from the Clock House. Bring A if you can.'

I can hear him breathing, almost thinking. 'OK. I'll try. See you.' He rings off.

★ ★ ★

Cold and damp. Uphill, in the distance, pines and cedars coated in mist. Here, where I sit, a line of bare trees above a line of grey benches, nothing green except the grass. Children are at school. Grown-ups trudge about with dogs. I turn up my collar. I see Charlie, from a hundred yards, walking quickly up the path towards me. He's wearing the usual baseball cap. I stand up.

He grips my hand. 'What's happening, Jim?' He looks anxious.

'Thanks for coming so quickly. Is Avril—'

'Yes. Soon, I think. She's driving ... or being driven.' We sit down. 'What's it all about?'

'I'll do the detail when Avril gets here but, in brief, it's about drugs, people trafficking, kidnap, false imprisonment. Lightfoot is involved – and, you can be sure, more coppers.

The urgency is that there are two crucial witnesses who are at risk and need to be looked after – soon as.'

I feel a hand on my shoulder and jump up. Avril, in a long overcoat, woolly scarf and floppy velvet hat. 'You should check behind you, Jim, before you talk about crucial witnesses.' She laughs, walks around and sits down. She pats the bench. 'Tell us all.'

They sit either side of me, leaning forward, listening – and I speak for what feels like several minutes and at first they barely interrupt – just an occasional grunt or sigh. I tell them about the blue containers, the house in Claremont Road and the other house in Portland Crescent, and that they will find marijuana farms and trafficked people, so long as they act quickly – like today, before both places are cleared of people and drugs. I tell them about the links to Dave Lightfoot found in the depths of Caroline Swann's computer.

Avril interrupts. She thanks me for finding the emails and sending them to her. 'You'll realise, Jim, that they give me proof of what I suspected. Not good news.' She shakes her head. 'But thanks for that.'

Then I tell them about last night's break-in. Avril smacks my knee and says, 'Naughty!' And I move on to what happened to me and Clayton – and how we were rescued by Max and Ernst. I find myself saying, 'Their names are surreal and so is their role in this investigation.' I explain who they are, where they come from and why they are important. 'We have two witnesses to the doings of the Cranley-Smiths and their fellow villains over a period of six months, up until yesterday.'

I tell them about the family who live next door to the Claremont Road cannabis farm, and Mr Big, who lives on a yacht off the coast of Spain.

I seem to have been talking for a long time, and at last I'm getting to the end of the story. 'Max and Ernst are in danger: from their own government – think of the Skripals – *and* from our Border Force. If we want them to co-operate in exposing organised crime and a bunch of corrupt coppers – if we want them to tell us all they know, put it on record and appear in court – we have to protect them and hide them for a while. And to do that we must make sure they are given asylum, a safe and decent place to live and some money; they have nothing – not even a passport – at the moment.'

'Good.' Avril claps her hands together, then claps my shoulder. 'Do they want new identities?'

'We must ask them, but I would guess they don't. Their dream is freedom for their people. I suspect they will want to come out in the open – when, *if*, they have given their evidence and the threat of deportation has receded. They want to campaign against the Lukashenko regime, as they used to. But we must ask them. And, by the way, they both have families, exiled I think in Estonia at the moment.'

Avril nods. 'Smart work. Congratulations. Smart of me too, come to think of it – to send you Swann's computer.' She looks me in the eye and smiles. 'You should be a police-man!' She asks for the room number at the Hilton. 'I'll see you there,' – she looks at her watch – 'around 2 pm. OK?'

'Of course,' I say. 'Sooner the better.'

She looks past me at Charlie. 'Charlie, you come too. Get a trusty to drive. Bring recording equipment. We'll talk in the car back to the station. Time to move.' She stands up. 'There's a lot to do.' She turns to me. 'Jim. Do you need some protection?'

I don't answer straightaway because I do and I don't.

'Don't be shy!'

'I don't need it. My job is to protect people.'

'This is organised crime, Jim, and you ain't a policeman. And certainly not a firearms officer.'

I think about it. 'OK. Maybe tonight – at my flat?'

'Good. Would hate for anything to happen to you. We'll assign people.' She waves goodbye and walks off with Charlie. An unmarked car is waiting by the nearest kerb.

★ ★ ★

I park in Lyndhurst Grove, close to Mrs Mumford's, and walk from there. I pass my home on the other side of the road. No one is sitting in cars or standing around. I walk around the block and come down the other side. Still no one. I go in. Inside, all is well. No break-in.

I dump the tools that have been in my pockets since last night and find my old phone and its charger in a drawer full of electrical left-overs. It has a sim card and my old phone number. I put it on charge. Then make coffee, take a shower without touching the back of my head, put on clean clothes and eat toast. The phone is still charging, but I manage to download my contacts, apps and all from iCloud. I send the number to a few important contacts: Laura, Charlotte, Kylie, Vic, Charlie Ritchie. After that, I want to lie down, though my head is clear. But I have to keep moving. I put my computer in my bag – if there's a break-in, I don't want it stolen – and head for the door. I have a hand on the handle – and turn back. The gun – Dad's gun. Take it. Just this once. I push it into my belt, on my left side, under my jacket.

★ ★ ★

I'm back at the Hilton a little after one o'clock. A tray with the two plates and the remains of what might have been club sandwiches is on the carpet outside the door of our suite.

Inside, Clayton and Max are watching television together: *Bargain Hunt* – people are studying what looks like a brass heron.

'All right? How did it go?' Clayton mutes the television.

'Good. They're coming at two o'clock. Avril and Charlie Ritchie. She's on to it. All go. Where's Ernst?'

'Still asleep, as far as we know.' He points to the closed bedroom door. 'Before they come Max has something to tell you.' Max has been slumped on the sofa. Now he sits up straight. 'This is pretty damn interesting, Jim.'

'Yes,' says Max. 'When you first came to Riverside Kennels, you asked where Martin Cranley-Smith was on 8 November in the evening.' He clasps his hands in front of him. 'You said that a woman called Caroline was hit on the head at about 6 pm and she died later. This was in a park in Peckham, you said. Martin and Jennifer said that they went to a friend's house for dinner that night. That could be true, though Jennifer would have arrived very late for dinner, because at about 6 pm, she was in a park in Peckham meeting a woman to give her a dog.'

'What!' I've been standing up, listening. 'Are you sure? How do you know?' I sit down on the desk chair.

'Yes. It's true. I know because I drove her there – in the van. Not from Marlow, but from the station at Clapham Junction. My job that afternoon, evening, was to drive with the dog from Marlow to Clapham Junction, meet Mrs Cranley-Smith there and drive her on to the park in Peckham. I remember it very well because I had never been to Clapham or Peckham before and I had to find the way with satnav.'

'What was the park called?'

'Warwick Gardens. Clayton says that's the one where Caroline was found.'

'It is.' I can't believe this. Clayton is nodding wisely; he's heard it before, had time to take it in. 'And what happened when you got there?'

'Well, it was ... you know ... weird. Jennifer picked up the dog – and a bag with a box of its food – clipped on the dog's lead and led it into the park. It was dark in there, except for a path lit by streetlights. I waited in the van – beside the park, but away from the entrance because there's a zebra crossing there. Very soon she came back and she still had the dog; she took off its lead and put it back in the box where it had been all the way. Then she sat down next to me. "Let's go," she said. '"Don't you want to wait?" I said. I thought maybe the woman hadn't arrived yet.

'"Just drive," she said. She seemed ... not angry ... more worried, upset.

'So I drove. I did a U-turn. I set the satnav for the M4. A bit later I asked whether the woman – I knew the dog was to be given to a woman – wasn't there, or had she changed her mind. And Jennifer said, "She was there but she doesn't want the dog now." And that was all. She didn't say anything else all the way to Marlow.'

'How long was she in the park?'

'Not long.' He pauses and looks up at the ceiling. 'It seemed like two minutes, but was probably more: three or four minutes.'

'Do you know if anything was in the bag with the dog food? Anything else?'

'I don't know. It's possible.'

'You don't know why she was planning to give a dog to Caroline?'

'No.' He shrugs. 'Caroline could have bought it, or it

might have been a present. They gave
few, around then and since then. They ~~~ away, a
dogs – but they are still selling them. They ~~~ with
any more from Europe. It's like drugs are ~~~ing
now – and people smuggling.'

I ask if he thinks that Jennifer could have hit
with something.

He doesn't know. But he has wondered about tha~
since I came asking where Martin had been that nigh~
when I said that Caroline had been hit and had died late~

I'm trying to sort this out in my head. I feel assaulted by
questions. What was Jennifer doing? She arranged to give
Caroline a dog in Warwick Gardens. Was that a trick? Why
there, in the park – if not to get her alone, away from other
people? And why did Caroline agree to meet her there?
What did Caroline want with a dog? She already had six
children and a cat.

'What kind of dog was it?'

'Little black spaniel. Very nice. A puppy.'

40

Ernst appears. He smiles and shakes my hand. He looks sharper and cleaner than the rest of us.

Clayton wants to leave but says he'll stay until Avril arrives. 'Avril. There's a woman my size!' He laughs. 'Wow!' He slaps Max on the shoulder. 'You're gonna love Avril.'

'Shhh! You can't talk like that,' I say.

'She's a friend of mine, Jim – you know that. A very good woman. She's head of the police in Peckham.' He's talking to Max and Ernst now. 'And she's come to talk to my martial-arts boys three, four, times – teenagers I teach how to defend themselves and keep safe. They love her and respect her.'

My phone rings. The old one that had sat in a drawer for three years. It works! 'Jim? Charlie. We're outside in the car park. Can you come down for a few minutes? Avril wants to talk before we come in. All right? We're in a black Audi A6, second row in car park, right hand end as you look at it.'

A plain-clothes driver is behind the wheel; Charlie is in the passenger seat, Avril in the back. I get in beside her, and she introduces me to the driver. 'DC Steadman. Meet a legend, former DCI Jim Domino.' The DC turns and smiles. 'Good to meet you, Mr Domino,' she says.

'OK, Jim.' Avril is sitting sideways, facing me. 'How are our Belarussians?'

'Well, I think. They've both had a sleep and at least one of them has eaten a club sandwich.'

'Oh! Is one of them off his food?'

'Not as far as I know.' She's looking at me as if I'm hiding something. 'How much detail do you want?'

'All of it. You know me. I'm a details person.'

'Well, my business partner, Clayton Ginevra, is there too. I told you he was on the jaunt last night.'

'Yes. Good man, Clayton Ginevra.'

'He says you two are friends.'

'Yes.' She seems to be thinking about it. 'Well, that might be overstating it. I certainly know him and like him. Anyway, go on. Why might someone be off their food?'

'All right. There were three people in the suite and, when I got back, there were two plates on the floor outside showing evidence of triple-decker sandwiches. That suggests one of the three didn't have a sandwich.'

Charlie is sniggering in the front seat. 'No shit Sherlock,' he says.

'OK. Business.' Avril leans back against the door and looks across at me. 'We've done a lot in three hours. They check out. As long as they are Max Posnyak and Ernst Zhdanov – and you've seen photos of them. And they look right. Right?'

'Yes. And they act right too.' I nod – and remember how I was fooled by Jennifer's mother, Mary. 'I'd give it 95 per cent.'

'Counter Terrorism and SIS know a lot about them. They disappeared six months ago. And their story makes sense: they wanted to hide, so accepted being the slaves of those creepy people with the double-barrelled name. But they're educated men with a mission and could only live that way for so long. Fair enough. I'll buy that.' She's looking at me and nodding. 'SIS want to talk to them. I hope they'll accept that – I would think they'll be pleased. The spooks are on their side; regime change in Belarus would be a blithe outcome.'

I can't help a small grin. English is Avril's second language – and she likes to show off her vocabulary.

She laughs. 'OK. I know you don't say 'blithe', Jim. But I like it. It means what I mean. Blithe. I don't know why you don't use it.'

'I like it too. But it doesn't come naturally.'

'Because you're a stuffy Englishman. Charlie too. All of you English.' She's shaking her head and laughing. 'Anyway, there's more news and I know you'll like it: Thames Valley Police shot up off their arses, so we have your Cranley-Smiths in custody in High Wycombe, and Mrs Cranley-Smith's mum, sister and brother-in-law in for questioning. And from the other address you gave us, they liberated a Vietnamese man who has almost certainly been trafficked. He will, we hope, be another witness. We've taken possession of the two houses in Claremont Road and the palatial house and grounds down by the river, and we are wreaking havoc on their contents. The mum, sister etcetera will probably be released later – unless we find something to charge them with – because there are children, horses and dogs to be looked after. But,' – she looks at her notebook – 'Martin and Jennifer Cranley-Smith will remain in custody and will be charged, probably tomorrow. Exactly when, and what they are charged with, will depend to an extent on the evidence we get from your Belarussian pals.'

She stops speaking and looks across at me. The back of her head – no hat now, just thick, tousled brown hair – is against the window, and she's holding the handle above the door with her left hand.

'Perfect,' I say. 'And we have something else, something startling. Max spoke to Clayton while I was out.' I begin to give her and Charlie a run-down of Max's latest bombshell.

I'm some way into it when Avril lets go of the handle above the door and waves both hands. 'Hang on,' she says. 'Are you going to say that this woman murdered Caroline Swann?'

'No. I don't know that. Max doesn't know that.' I look away from her towards Charlie who has turned round in his seat. 'But she might have.' I speak slowly. I'm thinking. 'I heard this a few minutes ago. I've hardly had time to think about it.'

'Let's go in. I, we, had best hear this from the man himself: Max, right?'

'Yes, Max. But first, can you tell them anything about their future? These guys have nothing. No ID. Nothing.'

She sits back and takes hold of the handle above the door again. 'Yes. We will move them somewhere tomorrow: to a safe house or flat. I've got people working on it and the spooks say they'll help. They can cut through to the Home Office – and the Foreign Office.

She leans forward. 'This is a big deal. I know you know that – and I congratulate you. If they're what you say they are – and I trust you, Jim, so I'm sure they are – we, and not just us, will help them. Asylum, ID, the rest – money; they'll need money. But we'd better talk to them now.' She twists in her seat, opens the door – and turns back. 'And we have to talk about murder as well.' She smiles. 'Good work, Jim.'

As we walk towards the hotel Avril says she'll reimburse all expenses. Then she stops walking, turns and looks into my eyes. 'Come back. Pick up where you were: DCI. I need one and you're the best.' We're standing on the path beside the revolving entrance door. She takes my arm and tugs me away from the door onto some grass beside a flower bed. 'You caught a serial killer. It was a little unorthodox, but ...' As she speaks I see Stark, staring at me, and then Jessica, dead with earth in her hair. '... sometimes needs must. Jim, you should never have been let go. Come back.'

I look down at the grass and shake my head. 'I'm flattered. In some ways, I'd like to ... to work with you. But I like my new life. I've got a business, good, loyal colleagues and my time's my own.'

'OK, I understand, but maybe don't rule it out. Take time and think about it.'

I tell her I will think about it, but I don't expect to change my mind.

She sucks in her lips and raises her eyebrows. '*And* I'm losing a DI.'

'Lightfoot?'

'He's gone. Well, not quite yet.' She drops her voice. 'He's under surveillance. A sprat to catch a shark, perhaps – or at least a herd of sprats.' She looks at the ground and shrugs. 'Gambling seems to be his problem, or it may be his dad's problem. We're finding out. We'll see what he does. There will be others – and I want them out too.'

★ ★ ★

Clayton and Avril have a swift reunion: smiles, hugs and pats on shoulders. Charlie sets up a digital recorder. Max and Ernst sit on the sofa facing Avril, who takes the only armchair. Charlie sits on a desk chair, and Clayton and I sit on a hard window seat.

Avril tells them what she told me: that in return for them co-operating and providing information, she will find them a safe place to live, give them money until they can earn and, together with SIS, who usually get their way in such cases, she will help them gain asylum and identity documents. She explains that SIS is the UK's foreign intelligence unit, commonly known as MI6, and that senior people would like to talk to them about the politics of Belarus.

They nod and say they understand, and they seem happy.

It's their turn to talk. Max fetches glasses of water for himself and Ernst, and Charlie presses 'record'. Ernst tells their story, starting with their hiding in a truck in Belgium. Max interrupts to add detail.

Clayton soon leaves; he's heard much of this and he deserves to get home. I would like to leave too; I'm tired and would just like to go to sleep. But I want to make sure that the Belarussians – the surrealists – don't leave anything out.

When they begin describing the work they did for the Cranley-Smiths moving drugs and people around, Avril interrupts. 'You were doing that work for six months. Over much of south London and along the Thames Valley. Is that right?'

'Yes,' says Ernst.

'Did you meet any policemen? While working for the Cranley-Smiths, I mean?'

'I, we, met many people,' Ernst says. 'Some – the clever ones – had no names, no identity. Some we knew, or were told, were policemen. Yes.'

'And taxi drivers – lots of them,' Max says. 'And people who work on the railways – and truck drivers.'

'Did you come across anyone called David, or Dave, Lightfoot?'

They look at each other. Max shakes his head. Ernst says, 'No. I don't know that name.'

Avril looks at Charlie. 'Charlie, have you ...'

He picks up his bag and pulls out a photograph. He hands it to them. 'Did you ever meet this man?'

I stand up to look, and see Lightfoot frowning and sucking in his cheeks – a blown-up mug shot, probably from his warrant card.

Max holds the picture and they both stare at it. Ernst mutters something and looks at Max. Max holds the photo at arm's length and squints at it. They look at each other and speak in their own language. Finally, Ernst looks up and says, 'Yes. We didn't meet him, to talk to. But he came twice to Combe House, Cranley-Smith's place. Both times he came with another man, and both times they stayed maybe half an hour.' He looks at Max.

'Yes.' Max is nodding. 'I saw him only once. Ernst saw him twice.'

'Can you say when?'

'Sometime in the summer,' Ernst answers. 'And then, I saw them again – maybe two weeks ago. Max was there then.'

'OK, I would like you to take time – not now,' Avril says, 'to remember as much as you can about this man.' She takes the photo and holds it up. 'Every detail helps: what he was wearing, anything you saw him do or heard him say, what the other man looked like, were they in a car, what kind of car – anything you can remember.'

'OK. I'll try,' Ernst says.

Avril goes on to ask them to think about other people they came across during the months they worked for the

Cranley-Smiths – and to give her names and details. The sooner we have names, the better. We want to stop them getting away, going into hiding, leaving the country. 'Write them down, please.' Again, she says, 'not now, but after we've gone'. She will be coming back – she looks at her watch – at about 9 pm. 'Are you happy to do that?'

Max and Ernst look at each other, shrug and mutter. Max says, 'Yes. I will tell you names.' He coughs. 'But I would like to keep the names of children secret. Adult drug dealers, people traffickers, kidnappers – I will tell you. But not the children or teenagers – kids who are innocent; they are not evil, they are trapped into carrying and selling drugs.'

'We don't want to know about kids right now – not if they are just couriers. Although we can help them, you know. We can direct them to people like Clayton, who just left; he runs a martial-arts centre for kids – to keep them away, get them away, from gangs. But, OK, let's have a deal. Give me the adults, the criminals. Leave the kids out of it.'

'OK,' Max says.

'Sure, we can do that,' Ernst agrees.

'Good. And when I come back I should have news of a safe place for you.'

They smile.

'Deal?' Avril says.

'Deal.'

'Deal.'

Avril tells them that over the next few days, when they are somewhere safe, she will send someone to go over their last six months in as much detail as they can remember. They can take as much time as they want then – days if necessary. For now, today, there is a rush to get names and, if possible, locations.

There is a pause. Max fetches some water and begins the

strange story of Jennifer Cranley-Smith failing to deliver a dog to Caroline Swann, in a park in Peckham on the night of 8 November. Avril pays total attention, staring into Max's eyes. Charlie glances at the little recording machine, as if daring it to miss any of this.

I find myself thinking about Vic, and that I'd like to see her.

Max is getting to the end. He describes Jennifer coming back to the van with the puppy, and the silent drive back to Marlow. He looks around at the four of us. 'And that's it,' he says and leans back into the sofa.

Avril stands up and goes to the window. A plane flies low overhead. Avril turns and faces us. 'Do you think Jennifer hit Caroline with a metal object while she was in the park?'

Max looks up. His dark hair is hanging forward over his forehead. He pushes it back. 'I don't know,' he says. 'If I had to bet, I'd say she didn't. And ... and maybe someone else had already done that.'

Ernst has been sitting beside Max through all this. 'I knew Jennifer quite well. I think she didn't hit her, but only because she would be too scared to do something like that. I hate her – and Martin. They're psychopaths. Their consciences wouldn't stop them hitting people or killing them, but they haven't the guts to actually do it.' He sighs and looks at Max. 'We stayed with them for six months.' He leans forward, his hands dangling between his knees. He seems to be wondering why and how they endured the Cranley-Smiths for so long.

'Yes. We stayed that long because no one would find us there,' Max says. 'Not Lukashenko's clowns, or you British police, or your border guards.' He smiles at Avril and then Charlie.

It's 4.15. The three of us stand up ready to leave. Avril

makes sure that the Belarussians have paper and pens to make notes of people and places, and tells them to take a walk outside at some point; it will help their memories.

I hug both of them – men whom I knocked to the ground and who have now saved my life – and I tell them to order room service; I will return in the morning.

★ ★ ★

When we get outside Avril grabs my sleeve. 'We'll question Jennifer about the assault on Caroline tomorrow. I'll have her moved to Peckham. Please come. I'd like your opinion. You could watch on a screen.'

I hesitate. Right now, it's the last thing I want to do. But tomorrow is tomorrow. And, even if Jennifer isn't guilty, she knows more about what happened to Caroline than I do. 'Yes. I'll come. Thanks.'

'Good. We'll let you know a time. See you then. Bye, Jim.' She turns towards her car. 'And send me an invoice for your time: consultant's fee.'

'I will,' I say – and on a whim add, 'just for the question-ing tomorrow, presumably?'

'Yes.' She walks back towards me. Her lips are a little drawn in – and I know that that was a foolish thing to say; in fact, I knew before I said it. 'I'm very grateful for your work on the Swann murder and on … shall we call it the Cranley-Smith/Lightfoot/organised-crime gang? You've committed break-ins and unearthed the emails that con-demn Dave Lightfoot.' She takes a step back and smiles. 'But all that was voluntary on your part.'

'Yes. Yes. I know. That was meant to be a joke, Avril.'

'I know, Jim. I'm asking you to come and help tomor-row – to give me your opinion, based on your experience which is far greater than mine, on this Jennifer: has she committed murder or manslaughter, or is she innocent? That would be blithe and I'll pay plenty for it.'

'Fine. Fine. Thanks. I'll see you tomorrow. Must go.'

'OK. Go! Go! See you tomorrow.' She walks away.

I wander towards the Merc and look across the car park. DC Steadman is leaning on the Audi chatting to Charlie and drinking coffee from a cardboard cup.

41

I get into the Merc. My head is bursting – not just with pain but with information and questions, theories and ideas. I woke up this morning at five o'clock, bound and gagged – and it's now only half past four in the afternoon. So much hammered into my head in less than twelve hours.

I think about the dog that Danny spotted on the CCTV clip. A man was walking with a dog south from the park gate. Max had parked the van to the north, beyond the zebra crossing. Danny had said that the man could be a woman. Man or woman, that person was walking the wrong way and therefore wasn't Jennifer Cranley-Smith. But why hadn't Jennifer shown up on CCTV? Because the camera was looking south at the zebra crossing. The park gate wasn't in the frame – only the pavement leading south. Jennifer had approached from the north.

I'd like to see Vic, to sprawl on a sofa with her. At the same time I'm preoccupied with Caroline, Jennifer and the dog. I drive along the M4 slowly – more slowly than usual – thinking. There had to be an arrangement between

Caroline and Jennifer about the dog. Had to be some communication about meeting . . .

A hunch forms. The erased files from Caroline's computer, the ones that Stefan put into four folders: Cranley-Smith, Lightfoot, Gary Jackson and Others. Others – I barely looked at Others. Just a hunch, but worth checking.

I turn off the M4 on the Chiswick flyover and cross Kew Bridge. Dark now and a drizzle has set in. I turn into Kew Retail Park, stop in a space away from other cars, not far from Marks & Spencer, and sit in the passenger seat with my laptop. I find the Others folder and open the inbox: thirty-seven emails that someone wanted no one to see. Who erased them? It has to be Caroline or Lightfoot.

Or both? Quite likely both. For different reasons – obviously.

The first three are from Ed Proddo – the ticket tout who Ruby told me about. They were written more than a year ago and are pure abuse: *Butt out, bitch!*; *Fuck off out of my business*; *You piece of shit*. Further down, someone calls her 'a green tart'. And another email contains ten lines of ranting abuse, repeating every four-letter word over and over; I give up on it without learning what the writer was complaining about. These would have been erased by Caroline. Who would want stuff like that on their computer?

The emails are in date order. Anything about the dog would be recent. I scroll to the bottom of the list. And . . . Jennifer Stephens! In other words, Jennifer Cranley-Smith. Five emails from her. The first on 27 October, less than two weeks before Caroline was attacked in the park.

Dear Caroline
    I know we've had our differences. Martin
and I were angry when, because of your

campaign, our business was closed down in
April. We managed to start a new kennels,
to up our standards and to supply well-bred,
healthy puppies to the public. However, we've
decided to change direction and therefore
we are winding down our puppy business.

I am offering free puppies to family, friends and
business associates. I know you came to us looking
for a puppy, and perhaps you found one. But if
not, perhaps you would like one of ours. We have
Jack Russells, spaniels and yellow labradors.

Let me know if you would like one. All our
dogs have had the appropriate jabs and are
microchipped. We have done everything above
board since you got our knuckles rapped.
I've always cared about animal welfare, so it's
good to have got it right. Thank you for that.

Kind regards
Jennifer

I scroll to the bottom of the list, to an email dated
7 November, the day before Caroline was attacked.

Caroline
Confirming 6 pm tomorrow, near the
entrance to Warwick Gardens. I will bring the
spaniel with a lead, her vaccination certificate,
microchip details and some food for her.

Regards
Jennifer

Below this is a thread. I scroll quickly down – and find a
photo of a cute black spaniel puppy sitting on grass in front

of some chicken wire – the pen that three of us invaded not many nights ago and that has since been emptied.

At the beginning of the thread I find Jennifer's email of 27 October that I have just read. Above it is Caroline's reply of 2 November. She took some time to think about Jennifer's offer.

> Jennifer
>   Yes. Thank you. I would like a puppy. Do you still have any spaniels? If you do, would it be possible to take him or her on the 8th, Tuesday? It is my son's birthday soon – on 9 November. I could store the puppy overnight with a neighbour and give him to my son on his birthday before he goes to school.
>   Thanks and regards
>   Caroline

There follow five emails – to and from – discussing practical arrangements. Caroline offers to go to collect from Marlow, but Jennifer insists that she will deliver personally. Where? Not to Caroline's house because this is a surprise for her son. They settle on Warwick Gardens, and date and time are confirmed.

I climb out of the Merc, stretch and walk towards Marks & Spencer. I feel some clarity now. The question that remains is whether Jennifer set this up in order to get an opportunity to assault, or kill, Caroline. Or did she have a genuine attack of altruism: had she sought to combine finding a home for an unwanted dog with an apology for maltreating animals to the woman who had successfully accused her of just that?

I go into M&S and head for the food section. I want a bottle of water. Why had Jennifer wanted to deliver the puppy personally? She could have sent Max to hand it over. Again, did she want a chance to attack Caroline? Or did she want to play Lady Bountiful, to add the personal touch to her largesse, rather than send a man who she saw as a servant or a slave?

I take water back to the car and swallow two paracetamol.

I phone Ruby. She seems pleased to hear from me. I tell her I have some news and want to ask her something. Is she at home? I can drop by in about an hour. 'I'll be here,' she says. 'Come and have a cup of tea.'

Before I leave Kew Retail Park, I phone Vic. She's at her office – which is surprising. It's dark and seems late. 'What time is it?'

'Quarter past five.'

'Oh. Thought it was later.'

'Are you OK? You sound a little . . . strange.'

'Oh. No. I'm OK. I had a busy night . . . working. Wondered whether you were free later? Would love to see you. Say about eight.'

'Er . . . Yes. It'd be lovely to see you too.' She sounds concerned and upbeat at the same time. 'Shall I come to you? If you're tired after your busy night?' Her voice has that bell-like quality that I love. 'I can work here till after seven and get to you around eight.'

'Great! Great!' I really want to see her. 'Perfect. I'll cook – No, hang on.' How could I have forgotten? 'Just re-membered. I'm in a . . . slight degree of danger. There'll be police minders lurking about outside. Might be better to—'

'Jim! What's happened? What have you done?'

'Well, I gave police some help with their enquiries. And certain people might not be too pleased about that.'

'Is this to do with that set up by the river in Marlow?'

'Yes. Arrests have been made. Several charges coming

tomorrow. Organised crime is part of it. You might feel safer somewhere else.'

There's a silence. Then she says in a quiet voice. 'Would you like to be there, at yours?'

'Er ... I would really. It'll be fine. But I don't want to impose it on you.'

'I'll come. I'm not scared, if you aren't. For God's sake!'

'Are you sure? Really sure?'

'Yes. Of course. If you are. You've got locks on the doors and windows haven't you? And police outside.'

'Yes. All that. And I've always got my gun.'

'Don't make jokes about guns. It's not as if I'm Mae West.'

'I dunno about that.'

'Jim. I'll see you later. About eight.'

'OK. Pasta and red wine all right?'

'Lovely. Bye now.' She rings off.

I'm smiling. I swallow some more water and drive away from Marks & Spencer.

It's good that Vic now leaves a few clothes at mine. I resisted that – defending my territory ... But it's fine. And now I have a drawer at hers: socks, underpants, toothbrush, Rennies. Makes sense.

★ ★ ★

Lights on all over the Swanns' house. Ruby opens the door wide. 'Come on in.' She smiles and puts a hand up to her mouth. Jake and the two smallest ones come to see who it is.

Granny Pat appears. 'Jim, hello.' She looks a little tired. 'Didn't know you were coming. Who've you come to see?'

'Ruby, first of all. But,' – I shrug – 'anyone who'll see me.' I drop my voice. 'I have some news and a question to ask. Won't take long. Gather round if you want to, but better not the younger children, I think.'

'Come in the kitchen.' Ruby says. 'Gary's there.'

Pat insists on making me a cup of tea – and unusually I accept her offer of sugar, two spoons; I feel I need it. Gary, Ruby and Ella sit at the table and Luke stands in the kitchen doorway. The little ones are watching telly in the front room. 'OK. I thought you'd like to know ... I've found out something new: your mum,' – I'm looking at Ruby and Ella – 'arranged to meet a woman in Warwick Gardens that night, 8 November, at six o'clock. The woman was going to give her a puppy.' Pat's eyes widen and her mouth drops open. Ruby and Ella frown at each other. 'We have a reliable witness who saw some of this happen, but not what happened inside the park. He drove the woman and the dog there in a van. The woman took the dog into the park – and when she came back a few minutes later, she still had the dog with her. The woman is under arrest for other offences and is going to be questioned tomorrow in connection with your mother's death.'

Gary has been staring at me. He seems to be both fascinated and horrified. 'Who's the woman?' he says.

'She's someone who emailed Caroline offering her a dog for free, no payment. Your mum seemed to think about it for a few days, and then she said yes, because she wanted to give the dog to Jake for his birthday. The dog was a spaniel puppy – your mum saw a photo.' Ella is resting her head on Ruby's shoulder; this seems to be upsetting her. But I have to go on. 'Your mum arranged that the woman would bring the puppy the night before Jake's birthday, and she would hand it over in Warwick Gardens. Then your mum would leave the puppy with a neighbour for the night and give it to Jake on the morning of his birthday.'

Luke is now standing behind Ella with his arms on her shoulders. Ella is looking up at me. They're all looking at me.

'None of you knew about this?'

'No,' Ruby says, and looks around. They all shake their heads. 'But it doesn't surprise me now that I *do* know about it. Jake's always liked dogs and puppies. He's got books about them and toy dogs. It's very like Mum, though. To have a secret surprise for all of us.'

Pat looks up. 'She always loved surprises.' She shakes her head.

'I'm telling you this because the police will want to talk to you about it, and I wanted to tell you first. They might tell the media that they are questioning someone about your mother's death. It may be that this woman *didn't* attack your mother, that she genuinely wanted to give her a dog, that your mum was attacked by someone else. That's a possibility.'

I pause. Most of them – Gary especially – are looking puzzled. 'I'm sorry we don't know more yet. We should find out more tomorrow. The woman will be questioned by a superintendent from Peckham and someone from Scotland Yard – and I'll be there too.'

'Can we come?' Ella asks. 'Is it like a court?'

'Afraid not. They're questioning her at the police station.'

Gary speaks up. 'Just for clarity, Jim. This woman might have killed Caroline. Or she might have just been delivering a dog, which would mean someone else killed Caroline before she got there. Which would explain why the woman was seen leaving with the dog.'

'Yes,' I say. 'But either way she would have left with the dog. If she'd attacked Caroline, she would have taken the dog away with her.'

'OK.' Gary nods. 'The dog is either a genuine gift, or it's part of a plot to get Caroline into the park in the dark.'

'Yes. That's right.'

318

'OK. Got it.' Gary sits back and runs his fingers through his hair. 'My god!' he says.

Pat is shaking her head with her hand over her mouth. 'Why,' she says, 'would this woman want to kill Caroline?'

'There's a possible motive, but,' – I look Pat in the eye – 'I'm sorry. I can't say more than that.'

Gary says, 'And you can't tell us this woman's name?'

'I can't. I really can't. She may be innocent. It'd be wrong for me to tell anyone her name.' I look around the table and up at Luke. 'Now, I want to ask you a question. One thing is certain: Caroline was expecting a dog. That's why she went to the park that night. And we can check that. She was going to leave the dog with a neighbour.' I look across at them all. 'Any ideas who that might have been?'

'Muriel and Joe,' Ruby says straightaway.

'Yes, Muriel and Joe,' Pat says. 'They would do anything for Caroline – and they're right next door.' Everyone nods, agrees.

'Will they be at home now?'

'Muriel for sure with the kids.' Ruby says. 'Maybe Joe too.'

After some discussion, we decide that Ruby, Ella and I will go next door in search of Muriel.

It turns out that Joe is there too. Their children are watching television. We sit at a table to one side, and I ask them: 'Did Caroline ask you to look after a dog on the night before Jake's birthday – the night she was attacked?'

'Yes.' They both speak at once.

'She did,' Muriel says. 'We were going to have the dog for the night, but of course she never brought her. Little black dog. She showed me a picture on her phone.' She looks with big eyes at Ruby and then Ella. 'So sad. I'm sorry.'

Joe has left the room. Now he comes back. 'This is her

bed and these are her bowls for food and water.' He holds them up. 'Caroline . . . your mum . . . had everything ready.' He smiles and shakes his head.

'Why you asking, though?' Muriel says. 'We told the police all this.'

'OK . . . I didn't know that. Do you remember who you told?'

'Don't know any names, but first there was a man and woman,' Joe says. 'Young, in uniform. Then the man came back with an older man who was plainclothes – and we went over it all again. I remember he had jeans and a short suede jacket, like a bomber jacket.'

'Did he tell you his name?'

'He might have, but I don't remember it,' Muriel says. 'He was an inspector. I remember that. But his name? No.'

Joe shakes his head.

'What did he look like?'

'Short hair. Probably about forty years old. Fit. About your height.'

'Could his name have been Lightfoot? Detective Inspector Lightfoot?'

'Yes,' Muriel says.

'That's right. That's right,' Joe says. 'I remember. Funny name.'

'Why are you asking? Why does it matter now?'

'I'm sorry. I can't really say. Not now. But you've been really helpful. Thanks and sorry to disturb you.'

★ ★ ★

I go home with the girls. Luke is with the small children. He follows us into the kitchen. I tell him, and Gary and Pat, that Muriel and Joe were indeed ready for the puppy to be left with them that night.

320

'They've got a dog bed and food bowls that Mum had bought for the puppy,' Ella says. 'So sad.' She sniffs and her eyes fill with tears.

Pat hugs her and kisses the top of her head. 'Maybe we'll get a puppy for Jake, then – and he, or she, can have the bed and the bowls.'

Ruby suddenly jerks upright. 'You know what?' She puts her hands flat on the table and looks round at us all. 'Jake had a name he wanted to call a dog if he ever got one.'

'Oh – My – God!' Luke shouts. 'I know what you're going to say.'

'Yes. So weird.' Ruby is talking to Luke. 'He hardly watches it any more, but Lily and Sammy do. And he still likes the name and wanted to name his dog after it – if, when, he got one.'

'Name the dog after what?' I ask.

'Yes, what? After what?' says Gary.

'Pepper,' Ruby says. 'After Peppa Pig.'

42

It's dark, raining and twenty-five minutes to eight. As I get into the Merc, my phone rings.

Charlie Ritchie calling to say my protection is now in place. 'Unmarked blue VW Passat.' He gives me the registration number. 'Across the road from yours until 7 am. Two officers. There'll always be one in the car. The other might be on patrol round the back – perhaps in your garden.' He laughs.

'Better not in the garden, Charlie. There's a family downstairs. Might freak them out.'

'Right. I'll pass that on.'

'Are you with Avril?'

'Yes. We're with your friends at Heathrow.'

'Good. Can I have a quick word with her? Away from Max and Ernst.'

There's about half a minute of silence. Then, 'Jim, it's Avril. You all right?'

'Yes. Just wanted to tell you I managed to check Max's story about Jennifer Cranley-Smith and Warwick Gardens. I found more emails on Caroline's laptop. An exchange between her and Jennifer.'

'OK. Go on.'

'Five emails confirm that they were going to meet in that park at that time so that Jennifer could hand over a spaniel puppy. It was to be a birthday present for Caroline's son Jake. It would have been left with neighbours overnight and given to the boy on his birthday the next day. I spoke to the neighbours, and it checks out. Caroline even gave the neighbour a bed for the dog. I've seen it.'

'Good. Good. Thanks Jim.'

'Also, it came out that the neighbours told all this to DI Lightfoot, after first speaking to door-knocking uniforms. So Lightfoot knew Caroline went to the park to meet Jennifer to collect the dog. And he didn't act on that info.'

'No. He bloody didn't. Would have moved the case along, wouldn't it. We would probably have located Jennifer much sooner. Thanks for that too, Jim.'

'And don't forget: Lightfoot tried to erase the emails that would have revealed the Caroline-Jennifer connection.'

'Yes. Yes. It's stacking up against DI Dave.'

'One more thing. Ruby, Caroline's eldest, remembered that her little brother – the birthday boy – was going to call the dog Pepper, after Peppa Pig.'

'So ... Oh ... I know: Caroline's last word in hospital? OK!'

'Yes. If I remember correctly, PC Das asked Caroline who she saw in Warwick Gardens, and got the answer Pepper. Which *might* suggest that she saw the dog *before* – perhaps just before – she was attacked and rendered unconscious. And you can see the implications of that.'

'If she saw the dog, she saw Jennifer. Which makes it likely that it was Jennifer who hit her. Is that where you're going?'

'Yes. But it's not conclusive. She could have been

dreaming about her boy's birthday and giving him his Pepper.'

'Umm ... It still adds something, I think, to the case against her. Blithe, Jim.' She gives out a little chuckle. 'Sounds like you're working overtime.'

'Yes, and I'm working for my client: Caroline's family. Remember! Not you. But I'm happy to pass information on for free.'

She laughs. 'Touché. Nice one – and much appreciated ... Charlie will call you tomorrow early with a time for the Jennifer interview. Gotta go. Bye, former DCI Domino.'

★ ★ ★

The Passat is there, parked opposite and a little down the hill, away from streetlights. A shadowy figure sits in the driver's seat. I park the Merc and stroll to my front door, alert but pretending not to be. Upstairs, I turn on lights. I leave the bedroom dark and stand at the side of the window looking down at the street. Nothing happening except for a light, slanting rain. I hang up my coat, put the gun in its drawer, wash my hands and go back to the window. After a minute a Toyota Prius pulls up. Vic gets out, shouts thank you to the driver, slams the door and runs through the rain.

I let her in and we hug silently for a few moments. She pushes me away, pulls me back, kisses me, pushes me away again and stares into my eyes. 'What happened? What's all this about organised crime and those people, the kidnappers who live by the river?'

'Well.' I take a deep breath. 'I broke into a house with Clayton and we both got hit on the head and laid out cold. We woke up hours later and were rescued by a couple of asylum seekers from Belarus.'

'Are you trying to be funny?'

'No. It's true.' I laugh and shake my head. 'I know it sounds mad.'

'For God's sake! Asylum seekers from Belarus! Sit down. Let me see your head.'

'All right. But just look. Don't touch it. It's tender.' I sit on the sofa and lean forward.

She peers at my head. 'Fucking hell! There's a big swelling.'

'I know. But it's OK. It's stopped hurting and I got shot of the headache with paracetamol.'

'Oh God, Jim!' She sits down and puts an arm round me. 'I hate even the idea of you getting hurt ... Silly thing to say, I suppose, but couldn't you be more careful?'

'I could try.' I squeeze her and kiss her twice, and stand up. 'How about some wine?'

'Yes. Please. Were you assaulted by the people who you're being protected from now?'

'Er ... yes.' I begin to uncork a bottle. 'It's brave of you to come. And wonderful that you're here.' I feel like adding, 'in my hour of need', but I hold back.

We slump on the sofa with glasses of rioja and the Barr Brothers on low. I tell her it all in detail, beginning with my deception of an estate agent that took me to the house in Claremont Road. She knows the story that leads to there; she's even seen the empty space left by the container that Clayton and I were locked inside.

She's an easy, attentive listener. She interrupts only to say, 'My God!' and 'Fucking hell!' many times, and 'Oh no!' now and again. When I reveal that this time Clayton and I were liberated by Max and Ernst, she says, 'Oh, I love Max and Ernst.' And she giggles. 'Sorry. Still find it funny: Max and Ernst! What about Stanley and Spencer?'

I fill our glasses and cook spaghetti *aglio e olio* with a few slices of chilli. We listen to Chopin's Nocturnes as we eat, and Vic tells me that tomorrow she will be in court helping to defend a woman accused of neglecting her children. She looks up from a fork full of spaghetti. 'Child breaks his arm falling off a bike and social services go apeshit because mum wasn't there! She'd left him in the care of a neighbour. Single mum who works all the time to feed her kids.' She smiles. 'Luckily I left one of my dark suits in your wardrobe.'

We finish eating, go back to the sofa and I turn on the TV news. We turn it off after the headlines; there's enough going on in our own small lives. I put on the other Barr Brothers album, *Queens of the Breakers*. Vic takes my hand, strokes my arm and rests her head on my shoulder – and there's no need to talk.

My phone rings. Kylie wanting to know if I'm OK. She spoke to Clayton and he told her what happened. 'My God!' she says. 'You could have been terminated, but then you were saved by these two weird guys.'

'Weird but wonderful.'

'I should have been there, Jim. Waiting in your car, at least. Then I would have rescued you like I did before.'

'Well . . . next time. We'll take you along next time.' Vic is looking at me and shaking her head. I grin back at her. 'But there won't be a next time – not on this job, anyway. We've pretty much stitched it up.'

'You got your murderer? Is that right?'

'Maybe. Maybe. Not certain. We'll see. Kylie, it's great of you to ring. How's it going with you?'

'Fine. Fine. I'll let you go. Just wanted to check you were OK. Bye, Jim.'

I come off the phone. Vic is staring at me – with wide

eyes and a kind of half-smile. 'I guess it's pointless for me to say, "Could you stop taking risks like breaking into empty buildings?"' Her smile broadens.

'It is, yes, pointless.' I put my arm round her shoulder and bury my head in her hair. 'I don't intend to make a habit of it, but sometimes it's a great way to find out what some bastard will never tell you.'

'Of course, if you survive, it's a great way. Funny though, I've never done that and I'm always wanting to know what some bastard won't tell me. I get by though. Make a living and keep the odd innocent person out of prison.'

Her head rests on my shoulder. The Barr Brothers fill the silence. She yawns. 'Time for bed,' she says. 'You must need some rest.'

I leave the bedroom door open and the Brothers play on.

★ ★ ★

Vic slurps down a coffee, kisses me, asks me not to break into any empty buildings – 'because they might not be empty' – and leaves.

I look out at the empty garden behind. Nothing moving. No wind. I go to the sink and wash two plates, two mugs, two knives. After Kylie phoned last night, I thought how lucky I am with women – women who care about me: Vic, Laura, Charlotte, Kylie . . . And Elizabeth. So lucky to have met her, lived with her, loved and been loved. But it finished too soon – or, rather, it didn't finish, hasn't finished.

My phone rings. Charlie. 'You all right, Jim? How's the head?'

I tell him my head is fine, and he tells me that my protection has just left; they had nothing to report.

'Those boys, Jim. Max and Ernst. We had a hell of a time last night. They told us so much. This is Jack Stephens' mob,

327

you know. He'll be furious that his daughter and her hubbie let those two loose inside his organisation.'

'*The* Jack Stephens! Fuck, I remember him. Horrible villain. Hoo bloody ray!'

'So you're even deeper into Avril's good books than you were already.'

He tells me about the morning's arrangements. Can I get there at 10.45? Questioning of Jennifer Cranley-Smith is set to begin at eleven. DCI Matthew Bowman from the Met's Homicide Command will be interrogating alongside Avril.

★ ★ ★

I have plenty of time, so I call John McCormick. He's on a new job – counter-industrial espionage – pretending to be an employee of a City bank – not easy – but he says it's going OK.

I do my full exercise routine with Jimmy Cliff right through to 'Sitting in Limbo' – and feel no pain from my head. The lump at the back hurts only if I touch it. So I don't.

43

As Charlie ushers me into her office, Avril stands up, comes towards me and says, 'You're a bloody genius – you are.' She stretches her arms wide, bends forward and back to upright, arms still wide. 'What've you done? You've only blown Jack Stephens' empire up in the air so it's already falling to earth in little pieces.' She's almost shouting – and is reminding me a little of Catherine Tate. 'Your Max and your Ernst are like twin encyclopaedias of villainy.'

I should be embarrassed. But somehow I'm not. Praise from people I respect is a tonic. Praise from people who know nothing is just air. 'Thrilled to hear that,' I say. I can't help grinning. 'You're looking after them, I hope.'

'This afternoon, they'll be on their way to a safe place, north-east of London. Better you don't know exactly where, for now. Days of debriefing ahead of them, and they're up for it. There's even talk of getting their families over here – free visas and all that.'

'Fantastic! That's great.' I'm still grinning and find that Avril and Charlie are grinning back.

'Sit down.' Avril waves me towards a chair facing her

desk. 'There's something I want to ask you. Our friends told us about the couple you liberated from a blue container – not to mention their baby. What happened to them?' She's frowning theatrically. 'Max and Ernst don't seem to know.'

'Oh. Well, we were taking them to the cop shop in High Wycombe – the nearest to where we liberated them from, you know. And ... er ... we stopped off at Beaconsfield Services on the M40 because they were hungry and so were we. They went off to change the baby's nappy and ... disappeared. We looked all over. Couldn't find them. We never saw them again. They must have ... hitched a ride.'

'Not like you. Rather clumsy. I expect you reported them though, didn't you?' She's still frowning. As is Charlie. At the same time both of them are trying to hide indulgent smiles.

'No. I didn't think that was my responsibility. I mean ... I'm not a policeman. I thought to myself: we found these people who got themselves stuck inside a container – and we let them out. And that was it. If they didn't want help from the police, that was up to them.'

'I see,' she squealed. She rocked in her chair and laughed, long and squeaky and high-pitched with some arm-waving. Charlie joined in. And even I was smiling. 'You haven't changed, Jim. Oh, and I love you for that – and your big heart.' Again, I felt embarrassed. She looked at me and seemed to calm down a little. 'Anyway, maybe it's better for you – and some others – that you're not a policeman these days.'

'Maybe it is.' I sit, nodding and grinning.

'But you will help us now with this interview?'

'I think so. Yes.'

★ ★ ★

I sit in a small room with Charlie watching two screens: one shows Jennifer Cranley-Smith and a lawyer called Stuart Linford; the other Avril and, to her left, DCI Bowman, the man from Homicide Command. There's a timer showing minutes and seconds in the top corners of both screens, so we can note clips we might want to watch again.

Jennifer seems tired and irritable. Her hair is dishevelled – no young-McEnroe-style headband – and her skin seems lined; perhaps she doesn't have her usual make-up. She spent a large part of yesterday, Charlie told me, answering questions at the nick in High Wycombe; then she was driven in handcuffs to Peckham where she spent the night locked in a cell.

DCI Bowman has a strong chin and a shaved head. He speaks softly and sensitively. He cautions Jennifer and then asks why she wanted to give a dog to a woman who had, not long before, exposed her husband's business and caused it to shut down.

She says that she decided to close her business and wanted to find homes for the remaining dogs. She felt guilty about Caroline. Caroline had been right: at their previous kennels they hadn't treated the dogs as well as they should have. She offered Caroline a dog by way of an apology.

'You regret your treatment of dogs.' Bowman is still speaking softly. 'Do you also regret your treatment of humans?'

Linford, the lawyer – a fleshy young man in a rumpled suit – points out that nothing is proven regarding Jennifer's treatment of humans. He asks if the questions can focus on the central issue: the events of the evening of 8 November.

Avril, speaking in a calm, measured way, asks Jennifer

about her actions that evening. Jennifer's story matches what Max told us, up to his parking the van outside Warwick Gardens.

'I walked through the gate. I had the puppy, a lovely black spaniel, on her lead. I was a couple of minutes late. I hoped Caroline would already be there. But I couldn't see her. I expected her to be on the path, which was lit by streetlights. I waited there for a minute – I remember a couple of cyclists came past. But Caroline didn't come. I stood around waiting.' She hesitates and pushes her hair behind her right ear. 'There was an open gate in the fence which divides the park. It was dark over there. Something – perhaps the puppy was pulling on her lead – made me walk through the gate. There was a children's football pitch and a small goal. Beside the pitch were two table tennis tables. Something – it turned out to be a woman – was lying on the nearest table.' She pauses, and swallows some water before carrying on. 'I didn't realise it was Caroline at first. I went up close. I couldn't see her very well, it was even darker there. And I'd only met her that once. Her eyes were half open and her mouth was open. Then I recognised her. She didn't move. I said her name. She didn't answer.' Jennifer looks down at the table and rubs her nose with the back of her hand. 'I just panicked. I didn't want to get involved in whatever had happened. I rushed back to the van and asked Max to drive away.'

'You didn't think to get help?' Avril says.

'No.' Jennifer shakes her head.

'Or ring 999? You could have done that anonymously.'

'No. No. I just wanted to get away. I'm sorry. Very sorry.' She looks down and her voice drops to a whisper. 'I should have got help.'

'That seems curious to me, Jennifer.' Bowman is still

speaking slowly and quietly. 'You were on a mission to, let's say, clear your conscience. Is that a fair way to describe it?'

'Yes.' Jennifer nods while looking down.

'Yet you find Caroline in some kind of physical distress and you walk away.'

'Yes. I did. And I'm sorry now. As I said, I panicked. I ... thought they – someone – might think I had attacked her. I thought it better to act as if I had never been there. No one would know.'

'And they didn't until Max spoke up.' Bowman was at the end of the table, close to Jennifer. He drew his chair still closer to her. 'There's something else we should think about. Caroline lay unconscious in hospital for three days and four nights. She woke up once during that time. A policewoman was there. She asked Caroline: "Who did you see in Warwick Gardens?" Caroline managed to say just one word: "Pepper".' Bowman lifts his index finger from the table and lets it fall. 'Do you know what that meant, Jennifer?'

Jennifer shakes her head, and mouths, 'No.'

'Pepper is the name that Caroline's little boy Jake was going to give to the dog you wanted to give to Caroline. The next day was Jake's birthday. Pepper, named after Peppa Pig, was to have been his special present. Caroline told the policewoman that she saw Pepper in Warwick Gardens that night.' Bowman lifts his finger again. 'But, if what you have told us is true, she couldn't have.'

Jennifer sniffs and looks up with watery eyes. She pushes the back of her hand across her nose.

'Caroline couldn't have seen Pepper if she'd been lying unconscious on the table tennis table when you arrived with Pepper. Could she?'

Jennifer swallows – more than once. And sniffs. She takes the glass and gulps some water. 'No,' she says, and looks as if she might cry. 'No, she couldn't.'

'So what *did* happen?'

'It's best to tell the truth, Jennifer,' Avril says. 'What *really* happened?'

'I found her. She was on her knees holding on to a tree – inside that open gate. It was dark; I could just see that it was her. She didn't speak. She made noises – like moaning, mewling – like a puppy; it was horrid. I helped her stand and led her – she leaned all over me; I almost carried, dragged her – to the table. Laid her on the table. She was still making noises.' Jennifer is holding the glass; she swallows more water. 'Then I left. I didn't know what was wrong with her ... I didn't think that she might die.' She is looking at Avril. 'I didn't even think of that.' She glances at DCI Bowman, and back to Avril.

'What happened to the puppy,' Bowman says, 'while you were helping Caroline to the table?'

'There are railings. The gate is in the railings. The railings have spikes on top. I dropped her lead over a spike, so she wouldn't run away.' She puts the glass back on the table and looks up at Bowman. 'I remember now. She barked. She didn't like being tied there.'

'Would that be when Caroline saw her, perhaps?'

'Yes. Yes. Perhaps then. She might not have noticed her before. She was in some pain.'

There's a pause. And then Avril speaks. 'And then you went back to the van with the puppy? Did you see anyone – in the park, or in the street?'

'No. Only Max.'

'And what did he say? Didn't he think it odd that you'd come back with the puppy?'

'Yes. I think he did. I didn't tell him anything about Caroline. I told him to drive home.'

'Did you tell anyone about Caroline?'

'Yes. My husband.' She looks at Avril, as if expecting another question. But Avril doesn't say anything. Jennifer blinks twice and carries on. 'He could see that I was shaken up. He was kind, sympathetic. And he understood why I hadn't done more to help Caroline. She had been hit on the head by someone. That was obvious.' She stares at Avril, who again doesn't respond. 'But we, Martin and I, we didn't know she would die.' She looks down at the table. 'We thought she'd come to of her own accord, or else someone would come along and help her. It was when that man Domino – you must know him?'

'Yes. I know him,' Avril mumbles.

'Mr Domino came. It was two weeks later; I'd begun to forget about what had happened. But then Mr Domino said she was dead. We freaked. And I was glad then that I hadn't drawn attention to myself.' Avril and Bowman stay quiet, waiting for her to go on. 'Of course, we were upset. It was sad. I know she had a lot of children.'

'You were glad you hadn't drawn attention to yourself? You mean that night, do you?'

'Yes. That night.'

'Drawn attention by calling for help?'

'Yes.'

'But if you had, she might still be alive.'

Jennifer's mouth drooped; her face went blank. 'I didn't think of that.'

'And you say you – *and* your husband – were upset when you heard that Caroline had died. Were you really upset?' Bowman asks. 'She'd caused you both a lot of trouble. Your husband had sent her some very aggressive emails.'

'I, we, didn't want her to die.'

'Do you sometimes want people to die?'

'No.' She's angry now. 'Absolutely not.'

'All right.' DCI Bowman looks across at Avril. 'Shall we?'

'Yes. We'll take a break now, Jennifer. Just for a few minutes.' Avril turns and points towards the door, where a uniformed PC sits during an interview. 'Tell him if you'd like a cup of tea.'

★ ★ ★

I turn to Charlie. 'What do you think?'

'I don't think she did it, Jim. If she did, she's putting on a good act. What do *you* think?'

'I agree. The untruth at the beginning isn't very different from the corrected version. They're almost the same story. She had to tweak the untruth to allow for Caroline being sufficiently conscious to notice the dog. I don't think she could have faked all that.' Charlie is nodding.

The door opens. Avril comes in, followed by Bowman. 'Hello, Jim. Long time.' Bowman shakes my hand. 'Thanks for your work on this. Not just this.' He waves his thumb in the direction of the interview room. 'I mean the drug ring, the people trafficking, the dodgy cops.' He rolls his eyes.

'It fell into my lap, Matthew.' I sigh. 'You know how that happens sometimes?' Blimey, I can't help thinking: this little squirt has grown up. The shaved head helps.

'What do you think, Jim?' Avril sits down. And the rest of us join her.

'I think she didn't do it. Probably. Almost certainly. OK, she had to change the story to allow for Caroline seeing the dog. But she did that straightaway, without thinking about it. I believed her then. I certainly don't think you can charge her. Not enough even circumstantial evidence, let alone no murder weapon, no prints. But, what do you think?'

Avril agrees with me. And Charlie says his bit.

Bowman nods. 'Yes. Looks like we all have the same impressions of that performance. But I'm going to take the other line: she's lying and she's guilty.'

Avril says, 'Yes. Better do it.'

'To see what happens. And we might learn something.' He coughs. 'Though I don't think it will get us closer to who killed Caroline.' He looks round at the three of us. 'Don't you think it's strange that this is Jack Stephens' daughter? She doesn't have that front, the in-your-face, fuck-you arrogance.'

'I think it's there underneath to an extent,' I say. 'But she and her husband aren't capable of killing anyone – they're squeamish, namby-pamby. Unlike her dad.'

'Yes. There's a hardness. She's thrown by this, though. If we're right, she's accidentally walked in on someone else's crime. A crime for which she has a motive.' He rubs his eyes. 'A weak motive. They wouldn't have gained anything by killing Caroline.'

★ ★ ★

'Jennifer.' Avril speaks softly, as she did in the first session. 'It's time to tell the truth. We can't mess about any longer. What really happened? You planned to kill Caroline – didn't you? You and Martin together.'

'No. No. I didn't. We didn't. I told you what happened. I found her and helped her.'

'Come on now.' Bowman is speaking now. 'You and Martin wanted to get revenge on Caroline Swann and get her out of the way. She'd caused you a lot of trouble. You resented her superior behaviour, the way she treated you as

337

if you were idiots and pathetic criminals. You didn't like that, did you?'

'No. I didn't think—'

'Martin sent her some abusive emails.' Bowman has raised his voice. 'We've all seen them. You both hated her, and you came up with the idea of luring her in with the offer of a free dog. You sent her a photo of a pretty little puppy. At first, you thought you'd entice her down to your place by the river. But then, when she said she would like a dog as a birthday present for her little boy and that she wanted to keep it a secret until the actual day of his birthday, you came up with the idea of meeting her in Warwick Gardens at six pm, when it's dark, on the day before the boy's birthday. And Caroline grabbed at that idea. It worked for her.'

'No. That's not what happened at all.'

Bowman doesn't respond to this and goes on staring into Jennifer's eyes. 'You had a bag with dog food in it. You had a heavy iron item in there too. Was it a horseshoe? You distracted Caroline Swann with the dog. Did she bend down to stroke it? Is that when you raised your arm and brought the horseshoe down on the back of her head?'

'No. That isn't true. No.'

The lawyer, Linford, butts in. 'With respect, this line of questioning is inappropriate. There are no facts to back it up.'

'Aren't there? Have you read the emails from Martin Cranley-Smith to Mrs Swann? And have you seen the email exchange between your client and Mrs Swann? It's all there.' '

Linford puts his hands on the table and leans towards DCI Bowman. ' I have to remind my client' – he turns to her – 'that she is not obliged to answer your questions.'

'May I continue?' Bowman doesn't wait for an answer. Instead, he turns to Jennifer. 'You said, "That isn't true". So what is true? Did you hit her earlier when you first arrived? Or did she arrive after you? Were you waiting for her? Did you call out to her from the shadows, to lure her away from the path and the streetlights? Which was it, Jennifer?'

The lawyer comes in again. 'You don't have to answer. You can simply say "No comment" if you want to.'

'I will answer.' She glares at Bowman. 'That – what you've been saying – is all nonsense. You've made it up in your sick little head. I never hit Caroline with anything. I found her crying and hardly able to move and I helped her to the table, as I said. That's all that happened.' She looks away from Bowman towards her lawyer. 'I've no more to say.'

Bowman glances at Avril with raised eyebrows. Avril shakes her head, a sign that she has no more questions.

'Thank you,' Bowman says. 'We just need a minute or two.' He's speaking quietly again. He and Avril stand up.

★ ★ ★

'She did well,' Charlie says.

'Yes, they can't charge her after that.'

Avril arrives with Bowman. 'No charge,' she says.

Bowman agrees. 'Domino, what do you think?'

'Like I said before. Almost certainly didn't do it. You can't charge her.'

'Sergeant Ritchie?'

Charlie agrees and Bowman says, 'Right. I'll tell them: "No charge at this time."' He thanks Charlie and me for our help, tells Avril he'll be back, and leaves the room.

Charlie turns to Avril. 'Back to square one then, guv.'

'Yes,' she says. 'So who *did* do it?' She puts her lips

together and shakes her head. 'We're back to the random stranger.'

'In which case, we'll probably never know,' I say. I try to relax my shoulders. I don't want to give up on this case. I want to know who killed Caroline. I want to know for Ruby and her siblings – so that their mother's story comes to an intelligible end.

44

I wait in the playground among a crowd of parents and small children. Felix's mum, Lucy, strolls up. 'Jim. You all right? Haven't seen you for a bit.'

I smile and shrug, and explain I've been busy.

It's Monday, four days since the interview with Jennifer Cranley-Smith – and I'm still going over it in my mind. *Could* she have done it? And fooled us all – we four, who have so much experience of judging whether a suspect is telling the truth? She began by lying – telling us that she found Caroline slumped unconscious on the table – but it was an excusable lie; it made her story simpler and therefore more believable; she wasn't to know that Caroline woke up and said 'pepper'.

Lucy and I stand side by side and watch as lines of children stream from the building, led by their teachers. The youngest kids come first; we must wait a little longer for Dan and Felix. 'Wish my dad would collect Felix. Felix would love that. But – no chance! He lives in Nottingham.' She laughs.

I hear this kind of thing from time to time. 'It's a matter

of geography,' I sometimes say. 'It's a shame more grand-parents don't live near their grandkids.'

But after one lie, could she have so quickly made up a new one? Possible, but I have to stop thinking like that. And think about random strangers, instead.

Lucy is talking to another mum, or perhaps a childmin-der. I see Luke several yards away, leaning against a post. I think of going over, but decide to stay where I am, by the low brick wall where I usually wait, where Dan will look to see if I am here.

And here he comes. He sees me. He doesn't smile. He just lifts his hand in a desultory way. He's probably tired. I signal to his teacher. She nods and points him towards me.

We walk past the shops with Felix and Lucy. They go into the supermarket. I grab Dan's hand and take him into the greengrocer's where we bump into Mrs Mumford, who is leaving with a full wheelie bag.

'Jim. How nice to see you. How are you?'

'Well, thanks. You?'

'Very well, thank you. Are you keeping busy? I expect you are.'

'Oh yes. Always busy.'

'Well, I'm not surprised,' she says. She puts a hand on my sleeve and drops her voice. 'So much divorce and gen-eral naughtiness these days.' She smiles, and I notice that her lipstick has overshot her lips and wonder whether it's a mistake or deliberate – perhaps an attempt to make her lips seem fuller.

She tells me about her daughter. 'Antonia will soon be home from Durham for Christmas. She's at uni there now.' Can the mention of general naughtiness have reminded her of Antonia? 'Started in September. A little bit wobbly at first. But she's made friends now – and seems to be OK.'

I manage to get away. Ron is waiting to serve me. Dan is by the door chatting to Di and sucking a lolly she has given him.

I read from Laura's list – and Ron natters as he fetches things, puts them in brown paper bags and weighs them. He likes the new pizza place up the street. He and Di have been ordering takeaways. 'I love the truffle pizza. Deelish! Di likes the artichoke ...' He whirls a paper bag full of onions by its corners and hands it to me. 'What about that Harry Kane missing a penalty? I knew France would win, but not like that.' He's picking out apples and turns to give me a look.

Eventually we leave. Di strokes Dan's hand and says, 'Goodbye Danny.'

★ ★ ★

Later, after he's eaten, Dan lies on the sofa, his head resting on a cushion, drawing with several colours – a map-like picture of a town with houses, cars, roads, trees. I'm sitting in Laura's only armchair peering at my laptop.

'Grandpa.'

'Yes.'

'You know that thing with weights – on that old table.'

'Er ... No.' I look around. 'Which old table?'

'The old table in Ron's shop.'

'Yes ... Yes. I know it. The table ... The weighing machine. I know. It's always been there. That's what they weighed the vegetables and fruit with years ago.'

'That weight – it's still not there.'

'Which weight?'

'You know. I told you. The one which should be one from the bottom of the pile, the second-biggest one.'

'OK ... Well, maybe Ron's using it for something.'

'S'pose he must be.' He puts his head back on the cushion and carries on drawing – a tree in two greens.

'Could be a useful door stop, or paper weight.'

'S'pose it could.'

★ ★ ★

Danny falls asleep before I've read him a page. He took a lot of trouble with his picture, finished it and propped it on the piano for Laura to see.

I watch a Bill Bailey show – wonderful. It ends well after midnight, just before Laura comes home. She's not been far away – the Orange Tree, Wimbledon with her pal Jason Dobell and his trio: 'great music, small crowd'.

She loves Danny's picture. And I remember the weight missing from Ron's shop. If Dan says it's missing, then it almost certainly is.

But so what?

A weight like that might have killed Caroline. Forensics say she was hit with something circular or curved, made of iron, sixty to seventy years old. But there must be a lot of weights like that in the world. Mustn't there?

Could someone have taken it from Ron's shop and . . .? Crazy! Crazy!

But way back I thought she could have been killed by a horseshoe, so . . .

Laura was talking about an encore of 'Begin the Beguine'; how she had had to sing it three times: during the set, as an encore, and as an encore of the encore. 'Had to change it the third time. Couldn't just go on repeating myself. Improvised – what I'm supposed to do, in fact.' She grinned. "And the boys stayed with me – they're smart, no problem. So now we have two versions of "Begin the Beguine".'

'Amazing! But how do you do "Begin the Beguine" without trumpets and clarinets and saxes?'

'You should come and hear us sometime. It's subtle. It doesn't need a lot of decibels. Have you heard Ella's take?' She looks at her phone and taps it a few times.

The warmth of Ella Fitzgerald fills the house – and my head. 'Dance with me,' she's saying. 'This dance. It's called the Beguine.'

'Dad, I have to tell myself, "*I* can do it. I *do* do it. Not better. Not worse. *Certainly* not better. No one does it better than Ella. But differently – and well."'

And we sit and listen – and nod and tap – to Ella singing the *Cole Porter Songbook*. All of it. And we drink whisky . . .

Well, not all of it, as it turns out. Half of it. Half the *Songbook*. When Laura suggests we listen to Volume 2, I somehow remember that one of us has to take Dan to school in the morning.

★ ★ ★

I get up at eight. Danny is already up and I can hear Laura moving about. I shower and shave, and remember the weight that is missing from Ron's shop.

I toast a bagel for Danny's breakfast – he's decided recently that he likes bagels – and we sit together in the kitchen while he has his morning yoghurt. I ask him, 'Dan, about that weight in Ron's shop: why did you say "it's still not there"? Why still?'

'Because it's *still*' – he leans into my face and shouts 'still' as though I'm a total idiot – 'not there.'

'All right – no need to shout! So, when did you first notice that the weight was missing?'

'That day when there was a man called Dave there; the

man who owns the pizza café. I told you about it that day. You've forgotten.'

I was a fool – he'd told me the weight was missing that day: weeks ago now! It must have been one of those times when I'm thinking about something else and don't hear him – *me* who believes in listening to children. I tried to remember when that was, when Ron had introduced me to Dave, the pizza tycoon. 'So was that *after* that night we went to the hospital with Ruby?'

'No. Not the day after, but one after that I think. I was waiting for you to finish talking and I saw that one weight wasn't there.' He spoons in some yoghurt. 'Mrs Duberry gave me a lolly. It was yellow, sort of lemony.'

Christ! He told me two days after Caroline Swann was hit with something heavy and iron, like a weight – and I wasn't listening!

'And when was the next time you went to Duberry's and didn't see the weight?'

'Yesterday.' He puts his spoon into the yoghurt.

'That's brilliant, Dan! Your memory is just ... fantastic.' I clap him on the shoulders.

'Why?'

'Because ...' – I begin to spread butter on his bagel – 'it just might affect a case I'm trying to solve. You know, someone might have stolen it from Ron's shop.'

'To hit Jake's mum with?'

'Well ...' – I slap jam on top of the butter and put the bagel in front of him – 'it's possible. Unlikely, but possible.' I pick up my mug and swallow some coffee. 'What made you think of that?'

'You did.' He laughs. 'You wanting to know when I was in that shop.' He bites into the bagel, chews and swallows. 'She was hit with some heavy thing, wasn't she?'

'Yes.'

Blimey! I think about going along and asking Ron about the weight. Suppose it *is* the murder weapon. If someone stole it, they might have left prints on the other weights that were sitting on top of it.

★ ★ ★

After dropping Danny off at school, I go back to Laura's and call Charlie. 'Are you busy?'

'Of course. Why?'

I fill him in. And he gets it. We arrange to meet at ten up the street, outside the Crossroads Cafe.

45

I wait outside until Duberry's is clear of customers.

Ron is holding an empty plastic crate. He greets me in the usual way, 'Hallo Fats Domino. Nice to see you again. You all right? Busy?'

'Yes, busy as ever.'

'Just a minute.' He calls through the open door at the back of the shop.

'Di.'

'Yes?'

'We need a refill of cos.'

'Comin'.'

I study the old weighing machine. Danny is right. The one-pound weight is missing from near the bottom of the pyramid. It should be sitting neatly between the two-pound and the half-pound. Gazing at the two-pound, I imagine the shape and size of the one-pound: a small jam tart cast in iron, two inches across and an inch deep. If you hit someone on the head with it, you would cause serious damage ... that's if you didn't kill them.

I tap my phone as Di comes in carrying a box of cos

lettuces. She puts the box in place beside round lettuces, icebergs and cucumbers, and hurries back out to the back. A few seconds later Charlie walks in – baseball cap, bomber jacket, jeans, as usual.

'Ron,' I say. 'This is Sergeant Ritchie from Peckham CID. I'm working with him and we're checking every possible lead in the search for information regarding the death of Caroline Swann.'

'Oh!' Ron's eyes open wide. 'Don't know how I can help, but very happy to if I can.' He looks from me to Charlie.

'Do you mind if I shut the door, Mr Duberry?' Charlie says. 'Just for a minute or two? It's better that we don't get interrupted.'

'Of course.' Ron blinks at Charlie. 'I'll do it.' He closes the door, locks it, turns the sign round to show 'closed', and pulls the blind down over the window.

I turn to face him. 'It's a small thing, Ron. And it may well have no connection to the case. Someone – it doesn't matter who – drew my attention to these weights.' I walk to the table and point at them. 'In particular, that one of the set, the one-pound weight, is missing. Do you know where it is?'

Ron glances at the old weighing scales and frowns. 'No, I don't. Why is it important?'

Charlie answers. 'It could have been used to strike Mrs Swann. It could be the murder weapon, Mr Duberry. She was attacked with something circular, made of old iron.'

'My God!' Ron looks at the floor and puts a hand to his chin.

'When did you last see it?'

'I don't know. I don't look at it. It's just there. Always.' He looks up and squares his shoulders.

'Could it have been stolen?'

'I suppose so, but why would anyone . . . Di takes that one with her, sometimes.'

'Takes it where, Mr Duberry?'

'When she walks the dog after we've shut for the day, and I'm doing the till. Puts it in her bag – "just in case," she says. This time of year, when it's dark, she's a bit scared of some of the people round here.'

'Can we talk to her, Ron?'

Ron calls through the open door at the back. 'Di. The police are here. They want to know where the old one-pound weight is. Any idea where it is?'

I can hear Di humming – not much of a tune – and then she comes in from the back. 'The old one-pound weight?' She's looking at her husband, ignoring Charlie and me. 'I lost it.'

'Lost that one-pound weight?'

'Yes . . . no.'

'What then?'

'I lost *it*.' She sits down on her usual chair by the door and puts her hands over her ears and stares at the floor. 'I lost *control*.' She's shouting. 'I hated her, that Caroline . . .' She goes quiet. And then speaks more quietly, almost as if speaking to herself. 'No . . . I didn't *hate* her . . . But I didn't like her much. I was angry. Stupidly – stupidly angry. I've always been angry with her. *Her* having all those lovely, adorable children. But . . . I didn't want her to die.'

I glance at Charlie. Is he recording this? He seems trans-fixed. But he turns to Di and gives her the usual caution. She doesn't have to say anything, but what she does say may be used in evidence . . . and so on.

Di doesn't seem to be listening. She's looking up at Ron. 'It never seemed right, her having so many children when you and me . . .' She begins to cry silently.

350

Ron crosses the room, squats down and puts his arm round her shoulder.

'I'm sorry.' She takes his hand – and looks at me. 'I went for my walk with Jules, my dog, like I do every evening. Took my bag and put that weight in it, for safety. I sometimes do that, but I always put it back when I come in. The two-pound is too heavy, but the one-pound is just right; you could throw it at someone if they came at you.' She pulls a tissue from her sleeve, wipes her eyes and blows her nose. 'I let Jules off his lead as soon as I got into the park. He rushed off into that bit where there's benches and a basketball net. He likes to cock his leg against that post which holds up the net. Then I saw there was someone standing in that dark bit . . . under the trees just inside the park.'

She sniffs and looks from me to Charlie and back at me. 'It was this strange person looking at me. I was pretty sure she was a woman, though it was dark. She was on her own. She didn't seem to have a dog. People don't usually stand still in the dark – unless they have a dog. I was a bit fearful – just a bit. I walked away up the hill and called Jules to come to me. I wanted this person to know I had a dog for protection – not that Jules would do anything if I was attacked.' She looked at Ron and smiled. Ron just went on holding her hand and staring. 'Anyway, *she* walked towards the gate in the railings – the ones that separate off where kids play football and all that, where dogs aren't meant to go. That gate was open. It's not meant to be, but it often is. I saw her face in the light over there, and I saw who it was. Caroline Swann. That was a surprise. What was *she* doing there?

'She saw me, looked at me. Didn't say anything. In fact, she looked a bit annoyed and then she turned away.' Di lets go of Ron's hand and looks down at the floor. 'Perhaps she

351

was fearful of me. I hadn't thought of that. She had her back to me. I walked across the grass towards her. She looked at her watch and stood in the dark by the railings, staring up towards the little football pitch. I thought about her kids: why wasn't she with them? I felt angry with her. What was she doing just standing there? The weight was in my hand. I lifted my arm and threw it ... It spun in the air and ...' Di sobs suddenly and loudly, head bent. She wipes her cheeks with the tissue. 'A kind of crack. A horrible noise!' She is gasping between words, but seems determined to tell us what happened. 'She grabbed her head and sort of fell through the gate and held on to the tree that's there.'

Ron is kneeling on the floor stroking Di's back. She takes a deep breath and shudders. 'I threw it, like –when I was a kid – I would throw a stone at a kid I didn't like.' She lets out a sob and her voice becomes a childlike whine. 'I thought she'd be all right – like a kid hit by a stone is after a bit. I didn't want it to kill her. I really didn't, not at all ... I'm sorry, so sorry!' Her sobs grow louder. 'I only wanted to hurt her a little bit – to show her I was there. That I ... I didn't mean ... I'm sorry.'

Ron lifts her to her feet and hugs her – his cheek against hers.

'We're all sorry, Mrs Duberry.' Charlie tells her he's arresting her on suspicion of manslaughter. 'What did you do with the weight, Mrs Duberry?'

'I picked it up. I called Jules and put him on his lead. I walked out of the park, along the pavement, under the railway bridge. There's a bit of wasteland after the bridge – behind blue railings. I chucked that weight over the railings into the brambles and whatnot.' She shook her head and blinked. 'I didn't want to bring it home.'

'All right. We'll look for it.' Charlie rocks back on his

feet. 'Now I'm going to phone for a squad car to take you and your husband to the station.' Charlie looks at Ron, who has an arm tight round Di's shoulder.

Ron shakes his head as if trying to wake himself from a dream. Then he nods. 'OK ... OK.'

★ ★ ★

I go out into the street and phone Vic. 'Can you help a friend of mine? She'll soon be charged with manslaughter or murder at Peckham nick. She confessed, but ... Vic, she needs help.'

'Right now? For a friend of yours, of course.'

★ ★ ★

I lean on the wall beside Ron's shop and remember watching CCTV with Danny. He pointed to a dog – and, for the second time, I remember him saying that the dog-walker, whom I had called a man, might be a woman.

Avril comes out of the shop. She takes me aside. 'Excellent work, Jim. You must come and tell me how you did that.' She smiles a thin smile and makes a little shrug. 'Come now if you can. Afraid you'll have to walk though. We're taking Ron with us – as a witness.'

The squad car roars away – Di in the back between Avril and Charlie, Ron in the front beside the driver. And I start walking.

★ ★ ★

I go round to the Swanns' at about 9 pm. Ruby, Luke, Ella and Granny Pat are watching television – Jake and the little ones are in bed. Gary comes down from upstairs. I ask them to turn the television off because I have something to say. Gary sits down. I sit on an upright chair next to him and tell them that Di Duberry, the greengrocer's wife, has confessed to killing Caroline. She didn't mean to kill her. And I tell them why she did it.

There's a long silence. Then Pat stands up and sighs. She walks across and sits on the arm of the sofa where the three children are sitting with Ella in the middle. She reaches over and puts an arm around Ella and rests her forehead against Luke's temple. He takes her hand. Gary is staring into space with his head in his hands.

'So Mum was murdered because she had so many children,' Ruby says.

I stand up and take a few steps, and sit down again. 'I don't think you should think of it like that,' I say. 'She died because another woman loved children so much that it drove her mad.'

Luke raises his eyebrows. Tears form in Ella's eyes and she stares at me with her mouth half open. Pat sits up and shakes her head.

Ruby looks at me. 'OK,' she says – and smiles with sad, tired eyes.

I look back at her, and the others: five of them – and three more upstairs.

What else can I say? What else?

Acknowledgements

I am lucky and grateful to be published by Muswell Press, a publishing company that exudes fun and looks after its authors. So thank you to its founders, Sarah and Kate Beal, and to Fiona Brownlee and Laura McFarlane. I have also received inspirational advice from my agent, Sally Holloway, to whom many thanks.

Some authors have apparently received help from everyone they have ever met, and even some they haven't. I would like to thank the following, from whom I really have received help: Mark Ram, David Pirie, Philippa Campbell, Mike Davies, Martyn Forrester, David Hunt, Jessie Hagedorn and John Lloyd.

My grandchildren – Fred and Rocco, Flo and Archie, and Albert and Margot – helped me simply by being grandchildren, and by leading me into Warwick Gardens at all times of day and, even more importantly, at night. Special thanks to them – and to Martha, Grace and Rose. And, as ever, to Penny.